LIFE ON THE 64 BUS

BRAD C. HODSON

JOURNALSTONE
YOUR LINK TO ARTIST TALENT

ISBN: 978-1-950305-99-5 (sc)
ISBN: 978-1-68510-000-1 (ebook)
Library of Congress Catalog Number: 2021943644

First printing edition: August 6, 2021
Published by JournalStone Publishing in the United States of America.
Cover Design: Don Noble | Cover Layout: Scarlett R. Algee
Edited by Sean Leonard
Proofreading and Interior Layout by Scarlett R. Algee

JournalStone Publishing
3205 Sassafras Trail
Carbondale, Illinois 62901

JournalStone books may be ordered through booksellers or by contacting:
JournalStone | www.journalstone.com

To Shannon
Our 7 is an upside-down 2

LIFE ON THE 64 BUS

PROLOGUE

I AM NOT A good man.

Though this is the first part of my story, it's the last I've written. Finding how to start seemed easy until it ended. When it was over, I sat back and read through what I'd written about all of them, all the Misfits, scratching out words with a red pen and scribbling apt replacements in the margin to be sure I described each just right, that I captured their peculiar essence in every syllable. If they ever read this, they will no doubt have criticisms about how they're portrayed, but every word is true. Maybe not true as it happened to them, but true as it happened to me. Perception, as the Carny was fond of saying, is reality.

Yet, in reading what I'd written about them, it made me wonder what could be said about myself. There are positive traits that could bleed out onto these pages, but finding those in yourself is easy. The difficult part comes in delving deep, squinting so hard your third eye aches, and seeing yourself as you are, stripped of ego, bias, and juvenile fantasy, covered in your own tears and someone else's blood and embarrassed by erectile dysfunction.

That kind of squinting is not easy. Most of us would like to think we're the good guys, the William Wallaces or Peter Parkers, fighting to do what's right. But if you look at your story objectively, if you sit back and ask, "How will others remember me?" you may find a different answer. Especially if you already know the ending to your story.

Here's mine:

We were on the Wallet Eater when the gun fired.

That's the ending. Sure, there were things that happened after, things happening still, but that gunshot on a cramped Roman bus was the period that concluded our glorious sentence together.

So I know how I'll be remembered, and it's not as a good man.

I used to be. I'd like to be again. But as I write this, I must be truthful. The time has come after so many lies for complete and brutal honesty.

And being honest, what can I say about myself?

I am not a good man.

But perhaps I could be a great one.

PRIMO

Remember tonight… for it is the beginning of always.
-Dante Alighieri

CHAPTER ONE

IT COULD BE SAID my story is a Gordian knot tied together by four women: a mother, a wife, a lover, and a martyr. Each represents a strand woven through my life, though some are thicker than others. My therapist would have said I place too much importance on these women, and suggested I take responsibility for myself.

No. That's wrong. The Carny would have been the one to say that. My therapist would have simply nodded and jotted a note to himself to Google what a Gordian knot was.

These women dominate my story so much, and yet it's the Carny I keep coming back to, that knotted ball of fetid masculinity whose time had passed centuries ago. Like all substitute father figures, he is both reviled and loved.

My therapist would have had a field day with that.

I'm stalling. It's a quirk of mine and not an endearing one. Where to begin? Rome. Let's start with her.

It's difficult to explain what I felt as the plane descended through the clouds over Italy. I'd been sitting in that seat for nine hours and some change, contemplating three of those women. The fourth I'd yet to meet. My ass had long ago fallen asleep, gone into a coma, and passed on. My legs were so stiff it wouldn't have surprised me if the muscles had been replaced with planks of wood. I was tired, I was hungry, and all I wanted to do was exit that goddamned flying nightmare.

Then I glanced out the window. White clouds, edges scuffed with gray, parted to reveal Rome in all her glory.

A cupola topped a building so large it couldn't have been thousands of feet below us, it had to be right there, a massive dollhouse some joker had glued to the wing of the plane. Thousands of red roofs huddled close together, punctuated here and there by another massive church or monument. The larger piazzas dotted the cityscape like rare flowers, tiny lines of bees buzzing through the streets from one to the other. I glimpsed the Coliseum, looking so much the size of a model I'd seen at a museum as a child. It was as though I sat on Olympus and watched the Eternal City like Jupiter himself.

Miranda would have loved the sight. She would have slipped her arm around mine and pulled herself against me, pressing the side of her head into my shoulder while we stared out the window together.

As we made our descent, the ancient city walls and watchtowers came more and more into view. An aqueduct snaked through the fields outside them, modern shopping malls and apartment buildings shying away from it as if in awe of the ancient wonder. The plane followed the pipeline until it cut to the right and disappeared.

And then we were falling, descending so fast into this new world I still struggled to make sense of it. The landing gear dropped, the plane shook, and we touched down.

A crackle from the loudspeaker and the pilot announced, "*Benvenuto a Roma.*"

Welcome to Rome.

Outside the airport, taxis jostled for position, a hundred horns sounding some bizarre melody not truly appreciated by human ears. Cab drivers threw luggage into trunks, pausing only to curse at one another with a flick of the hand and a speedy string of syllables before slamming the lids and peeling off.

Elderly couples to my right were fought over by a pudgy Asian man and a paper-thin white woman. One couple smiled and snapped picture after picture of the arguing cab drivers as though they were costumed performers at Disneyland.

"Sir? You speak the English, yes?"

I turned to see a bizarre collection of features, like some kid with cutouts of human parts tried to build a cab driver. Fleshy upper arms dwindled to sticks for forearms. A bulbous ass supported by toothpicks wrapped in khaki. He wore a white t-shirt with "U.S.A." stamped across the chest in red, white, and blue.

"You look American." No way his thick accent was Italian. He smiled, his thick mustache reminding me of a bandito from a Sergio Leone flick.

"Sì," I said. "Yes, I'm American."

"Excellent, sir. You ride in my cab, yes?"

He grabbed my elbow and pulled me toward a dented white taxi parked at the curb. The paint was scuffed, and a small crack ran through the windshield. The tires, however, were pristine and new, *Ferrari* printed in bold white letters around them.

"Sure. Yeah."

I shuffled inside and he shut the door behind me. He climbed into the driver's seat and started the engine.

"Where to?"

"My hotel." I pulled my phone out and stared at the spinning circle as my email tried to load. "Sorry. I have an email with the address but my phone's not cooperating."

"Oh, sir. Your phone no work here. American and European phone systems are not compatible."

Of course they weren't. "I didn't know. This is my first time to Rome."

"Oh! Your first time! Is this so?"

"Yeah."

He peeled out onto the road. Tires squealed. Someone slammed on their brakes.

"Oh, sir. You will love the city. Is finest city in the world."

A horn blared as he cut across three lanes of traffic.

"I'm sure."

A car pulled beside us and a young woman leaned out her window, hands waving wildly. "*Io sono caduto miei braccie!*"

The car sped off.

"What was that about?"

He thought a moment, struggling with the words. "She say… eh… 'I throw down my arms at you.'"

"Okay."

"It much worse in Italian. Kind of like…"

"Fuck your mother?"

"What?"

"Like 'fuck your mother'?"

"Yes! Like fucking mothers."

We switched lanes, forcing a Vespa onto the shoulder.

He turned around in the seat and held out his hand. "I am Dimitri."

"The road!"

"What?"

"Could you watch the road? Please!"

He laughed. "Of course. If it make you feel better."

"It does! Please!"

He turned back around in time to slam on the brakes and lay into his horn.

"So. What is name of hotel?"

I gave him the name and gripped the door as he whipped a U-turn to a chorus of horns.

"Yes, yes. Rome is lovely. What is goal here, sir?"

"See the sites. Find some interesting local color. The usual," I lied.

"Ah. Then first thing you do is go to Termini."

"Termini?"

"Bus station. Is real shit hole. Just trash and scum. Awful place. You go there first. Take the 64 Bus. It go to all big sites. Coloseo, Foro, Vaticano, all of them. It filled with tourists. Very popular."

"Oh. Perfect. That sounds great."

"Yes. It is great."

The joy in his voice was thick. I should have paid more attention to it.

***

It wasn't long until I was riding the Number 64 Bus around the major sites like every other tourist too frightened to get out and experience the city. We rocked our way down cobblestone streets already ancient when America was first discovered. Clicks and flashes filled the bus, everyone more concerned with taking pictures of the city than actually seeing it.

For an entirely different reason, I didn't see the sights either.

She sat a few seats up from me on the crowded bus, an old man in a tweed jacket and two large Germans between us. She glanced my way, brown eyes locking onto me as she smiled. The summer sun tickled her dark hair and dusky skin. I damn near lost my breath.

The bus took a sharp turn. I gripped the rail tighter and adjusted my backpack. I'd left the rest of my luggage at the hotel but grabbed the bag for all my essentials. It made me feel like a student again, with the guidebooks and phrasebooks and a change of shoes inside, and maybe that was one of the reasons I felt the stirrings of a summer fling.

She stood, eyes never leaving mine, and slipped through the packed bus with the grace of a dancer. She stopped inches from me, her hand brushing mine where she gripped the rail.

"Hi," she said. "You American?"

She was the very picture of a Bollywood actress and whatever witty retort I concocted died in my throat.

"Um. Yeah," I managed. "Sure am. First day in Rome, as a matter of fact. You?"

She laughed. It was the sound of birds singing. "Also American. Though I've been in Rome a little longer."

The bus took another turn and she fell into me. The smell of fresh spring flowers, lilac and rose and a hundred other blooms, tickled my nose. She placed a hand against my chest and looked into my eyes. Outside, the white travertine of the Coliseum loomed over us, its shadow falling onto the bus as we slowed to a stop, but even that two-thousand-year-old wonder could not tear my gaze from her.

"That's my stop." She patted my chest and made her way back through the crowd.

I felt off-balance, like the first few moments after waking from a dream. She was to the doors and stepping off before I gathered myself.

"Wait."

She looked back, smiled, and exited the bus.

I stumbled forward, squeezing a grunt from the Germans and crumpling the old man's paper as I made my way through the doors. They slammed behind me and the bus shook to life. I scanned the crowd, thousands of tourists milling about and snapping pictures, hoping she hadn't gotten away.

She stood by the Arch of Constantine, a black wallet in her hands. Just like the one I carried.

She flipped it open and fanned through a thin stack of crisp euros.

The realization crashed into me like an out-of-control Vespa. I shrugged my pack off, unzipped the bottom pocket, and peered inside.

I could see straight down to a bit of gum on my shoe. A ragged hole had been cut into the bottom of the backpack.

Right where I'd put my wallet.

"Don't want to lose it," I'd said to myself, feeling all clever as I shoved it into the backpack instead of my pocket earlier. Yeah. Real clever, that's me.

She hadn't even noticed I was off the bus.

"Stop! Thief!"

It came out before I knew what I was doing.

She glanced my way.

And then bolted.

"Thief!"

The other tourists stared, wide-eyed and slack-jawed, the way I imagine cattle stare at one of their own being butchered. I sprinted after her, the girl of my dreams, an angel sent from heaven who had just stolen my hotel key, my credit cards, and my passport, leaving me stranded in a foreign city where I didn't speak the language and knew no one.

It was the best thing that ever happened to me.

***

The decision to come to Rome had been a rash one. I wish I could say I spent hours deliberating, poring over my options, before making it.

There are a lot of things I wish I could say.

After signing my divorce papers I'd scanned the tiny apartment I'd been banished to, exiled to the San Fernando Valley like Ovid to the Baltic. Boxes lined the walls and were stacked to the ceiling. My life spread out before me, trapped in cardboard. Did any of it matter? What was left that was mine? Clothes. Books. Blu-rays.

A picture of my wife sat at the top of the first box I opened. She smiled, the sun behind her, eyes piercing me and reminding me of everything I'd done.

The next day at my therapist's, he asked how I felt about my divorce.

"What do you want me to say?"

"I want you to say how you feel."

"I miss Miranda."

"And your wife?"

I didn't know how I felt about her. Or how she felt about me. Not really. Some people hate their exes, often for good reason. With Chelsea, I don't think she hated me. She didn't care enough for hate. Not anymore. Can't say I blamed her.

The therapist gave me space to answer and, when I didn't, he went on. "Have you tried talking to either your wife or your...?"

"Mistress?" The word was awkward, not a word I would use. It felt like something reserved for sixty-year-old Wall Street bankers who secretly rented a one-bedroom apartment on the wrong side of town.

"She hates me," I said.

He pursed his lips and scribbled something on his notepad. "Does she know about your condition?"

"She knows I'm nuts."

"You're not nuts."

"Listen, Doc. People out there don't treat mental illness the way they do in here. I'm a nut. A whackjob. A dickbag."

"Dickbag." He scribbled. "Go on."

"It doesn't forgive what I did that I have some kind of problem."

"Because you're a dickbag."

"You got it."

"People can be more forgiving than you give them credit for."

I pulled out my phone. "Let me read you a message Miranda's sister sent me. And I quote: 'You are a shitlicking assmouth and a bug-eyed loon. As far as I'm concerned, testicular cancer would be too kind for you. I hope your pecker gets gnawed off by mutant carnivorous mice in your sleep. Do the world a favor and deep throat a shotgun, you lunatic. Yours in Christ, etc."

He scribbled something on his pad.

"What are you writing?"

"Just that bit about mutant mice eating your pecker. That's good."

In Los Angeles, everyone's working on a script.

"I feel like I can't go on, Doc. I don't mean I'm sad and depressed. I mean there are days I just wish I didn't exist. Days where I don't even want to sleep because sleeping means dreaming, means being. I want to stop doing that."

"Dreaming?"

"Being."

He tapped the pencil against his knee. "It's been a rough time for you. Honestly, I'm surprised your episode wasn't worse. You're holding it together remarkably well."

That's what he called it. An "episode," as though Kramer burst through the door during the middle of it.

"Have you been taking your medication?" he asked.

"Yeah."

"And?"

"And what? My workouts suck, my dreams are directed by David Lynch, and I couldn't tell you the last time I got it up."

He set the pad down. "You need a change. Take a vacation. Start a new hobby."

"A hobby?"

"Sure. Why not? Take a cooking class. Learn Japanese. Something to occupy your time and give you a feeling of accomplishment. Something — and this is important — something you don't associate with your wife or Miranda."

"So, you think dusting potato dumplings or conjugating verbs is what I need?"

"I'm not sure you conjugate Japanese verbs."

That night I received a coupon in my email for a free car wash. The header read, "Enjoy your birthday reward!" Was it my birthday?

I checked the calendar and, yep, there it was. For the first time since I was a kid, I had no one to spend it with.

Was there anyone to even get a drink with now? Miranda had long ago changed her number. Chelsea, my wife (ex-wife now), her lawyer had asked not-so-nicely that I stay far away from her. My friends had all been her friends, and so even the ones I hadn't treated like trash weren't answering my calls. Like I'd told my therapist, people don't care what condition you have if you're a bastard to *them*. I had no one.

"I am a shitlicking assmouth," I said. It had a nice ring to it.

My cat meowed for some food. I'd forgotten to buy any. We'd never had a good relationship, me and that cat. Probably would have helped if I'd bothered to even name him. I'd rescued the cat from a kill-shelter, thinking that maybe taking care of another creature might help things. But he wanted nothing to do with me except when his bowl was empty. Don't suppose I could blame him.

"You know what?" I asked.

He gave me an angry meow in reply.

"This was a bad idea."

I opened the door and shooed him outside with my foot. Fuck that cat.

He looked back at me as if to say, "Thank Christ," and trotted off with his tail in the air like he was the happiest feline in the world. Couple of hours later, I heard two cats fucking outside my window, just screeching up a storm, and I was jealous of the little bastard.

After a few beers, which I'd been advised against thanks to my Topamax and Lamictal prescriptions, I picked up the phone again and mindlessly punched in Chelsea's number out of habit. I hung up before it could ring. She'd been my best friend for so long and now?

Shit. She's better off now, I thought, and that's the God's honest truth.

What a goddamned life I'd made for myself. Divorced and alone on my thirtieth birthday.

The guilt came, that old familiar standby, and I wanted to ball up on the couch and cry, to weep like a child. The pressure in my chest was unbearable. The tears were there, but I couldn't pull them out. There are few things worse, I've found, than needing to cry and not being able to.

I dug through the boxes, looking for some movie like *Braveheart* or *The Fault in Our Stars* that would open the floodgates.

The third box was nothing but books. I almost turned away from it. Then the spine of a pink and white notebook caught my attention.

My mother's journal, written when she lived in Rome.

I removed it and slid down the wall. There on the floor, I read through a life I wished I had known.

CHAPTER TWO

AT THE FRONT DESK of the hotel, I was greeted by a teenage boy in a suit two sizes too large and a white pocket-square peeking out from his breast pocket.

"No key," he said, a hint of mustache on his upper lip.

"Please, just look me up. I only checked in a couple of hours ago."

"Sir," he said, and laughed in a way that suggested I was simple, "you could be any person. Any person could walk in here and claim to be this gentleman you say you are, and if I were to give a key to every person who did this, all of Roma would be in this room tonight."

"Okay," I said. Time to change tactics. "Where's the older man who was working the front desk earlier?"

"Fabrizio?"

"Sure."

"Oh, he was rushed to hospital. Heart attack."

I blinked.

"But do not worry. He has had several. He will be fine."

Taking a deep breath, I fought hard not to reach across the desk and throttle him. "Is there any way that I can prove who I am?"

"Simply provide your identification, sir, and I can assist you, as I have explained."

"As I have explained, my identification was stolen."

He shrugged.

"Isn't there a record from when I checked in? A copy of my passport or anything?"

"Oh, surely."

"And?"

"I would not know what Fabrizio has done with this. He has his own system for things. Refuses to use computers. Calls them 'the Devil's Own Boxes.'" He laughed. "We updated our systems here in the fall and the older staff, of which there are many, continue with their own ways."

"Why wouldn't the entire staff be required to use the computers?"

He narrowed his eyes. "That hardly seems fair." The phone rang and he raised a finger as he answered. "Pronto? Oh. Oh, no. Oh, oh, no." His eyes sunk and he cupped his hand over the mouthpiece. "Fabrizio has passed away."

"Poor Fabrizio," I said.

He scowled at me and turned his back. When his conversation finished, he hung up the phone and came around the counter. "I am sorry, sir, but you must leave now."

"Excuse me?"

"I must go to see Fabrizio's family and tell them the news. I only worry about his poor wife. She has gallstones. But I must lock up while I am gone."

"When will you be back?"

"I cannot say, sir. We are in mourning." He materialized a black handkerchief and replaced the white pocket square.

He shuffled me outside and locked the door behind us.

"What will I do?"

"Your room key will let you into the lobby here even when I am gone." He pointed to the electronic lock.

"But I don't—"

"Ciao!" He trotted across the street.

I should have throttled him when I had the chance.

***

After wandering through the streets for hours, I still had no clue what to do. I considered going to the American Embassy, but that would have been admitting defeat. "Excuse me. I'm too stupid to travel to a foreign country and not get taken advantage of. Could you hold my hand, please?"

No, thank you.

Ditto with the police. I thought of Chelsea, but a collect call to my ex-wife also did not seem like the right thing to do.

There is a gulf between who we are and who we think we are. I'd always thought of myself as a survivor. Independent. Resourceful. That illusion was being shattered. The gulf had been spanned and the bridge rocked and swayed in the wind.

Night had fallen over the Eternal City as I stumbled through her streets. The cobblestones were hard on my feet and sent aches up my calves. I stopped at one of a thousand water fountains scattered about. If there was any one thing you could associate with Rome, it was water. As I sipped from the fresh stream, I wondered if the aqueduct I saw that morning still pumped it in. Chelsea had always complained about the filthy tap water in our apartment and those pipes couldn't have been older than twenty years. These could date back two millennia for all I knew.

The cold water felt good on my face and neck. The heat had pulled every drop of sweat out of me. A stone elephant stood ahead of me, an Egyptian obelisk riding its back like Hannibal. I pulled a travel guide from my ruined pack and flipped through it. Bernini had designed the elephant, but the obelisk was brought to Rome during Caesar's time, when the city was obsessed with all things Egyptian.

Dimitri smoked a cigarette beneath it.

The cab driver stood with two other men, both thinner than him but with the same unknowable origins.

I splashed water into my face, shook it off, and checked one more time.

It was him, his misshapen body leaning on the base beneath the elephant like a broken tree propped against a house.

Whatever god or goddess watched over me that night, they had put me on the right path. *La Donna Fortuna*, the Italians would say. Lady Luck. Here she was something more than back home, powerful and substantial in a way the weekend gamblers driving to Vegas had no inkling of, and she smiled down on me.

"Dimitri."

He and his friends turned. He tilted his head like a dog and tried to place me. Finally, he smiled and thrust out a hand.

"Hello, my friend. Good to see you. How you enjoy city?"

"Not very much."

"Oh?"

"I was robbed."

The smile vanished. His two friends whispered something to one another. They waved to Dimitri and peeled off into the dark.

"Robbed? That is harsh. You must be careful in the city, my friend." He dropped his cigarette and ground it under his heel.

"Thing is, I don't know what to do. My money, my credit cards, my passport, they got it all."

"That is shame. You should get money wired from home. The banks open early here."

"I don't have anybody." Admitting it was like a punch to the stomach.

"You have no one can send you money?"

"No. I really don't."

His eyes darted around like he was afraid we were being watched. "I say what. I buy you panino and coffee. That best I can do. I wish I could help you more."

He was hiding something. It was as obvious as the blisters on my feet.

We sat at a café near the Pantheon and watched tourists snap pictures of the ancient behemoth. Local teenagers covered the fountain at the center of the piazza, smoking, laughing, reading to one another, and making out.

The sandwich was delicious, the coffee even better.

"It happened on bus, yes?"

"Yeah. She cut the bottom of my backpack open and slipped my wallet out."

He nodded. Shifted in his seat. "That is shame. Real shame."

That afternoon he had been all smiles and laughs. Now he was tense and quiet.

"Yeah. I don't care about the money. I just want to get my passport back so the embassy will help me get home."

"That is all?"

"Yeah. No reason to go to the police or anything. I don't want to cause any trouble. I just want to go home. Homeless in Rome is not where I saw this trip heading."

"No *polizia*?"

I locked eyes with him. "No *polizia*."

He squirmed in his seat. Lit another cigarette. Stared across the piazza and into the black night swimming between the columns of the Pantheon. "I wish I could help."

I opened my backpack, rummaged through my things, and pulled out a pair of Nikes. I slammed them down by my plate, hoping this wasn't considered an insult in the mysterious and unidentifiable land he hailed from. Coffee splashed onto the saucer.

He eyed them a moment before reaching across the table and fingering the leather along the sides. I'd only worn them once and they were as white as clouds.

"These sneakers cost me three hundred dollars," I lied. I bought them at a going-out-of-business sale for sixty bucks.

"Three hundred?"

"I need my passport, Dimitri. Please."

He finished his cigarette and smudged it out on a saucer. "You not hear this from me."

"I'll never mention your name."

He sighed. Made the sign of the cross. Stared at his lap. "When I growing back home, my father fell in love with woman from Greece. She, uh, cunning man? Is that right word?"

"Conman."

"Conman, yes. When she was done with father, we were homeless. He die before I could save enough money to get us here."

I thought a sentimental memory had overtaken him as he slipped the sneakers from the table, kicked his own off, and slid mine on. He held up his scuffed, brown leather shoes. They were covered in holes.

"I wear these piece of shit since then," he said. "They were my idiot father's." He sat them down before leaning over and tying the tennis shoes. "Good fit."

"My passport?"

"No mention my name?"

"Scout's honor."

He cocked an eyebrow in confusion.

"I swear," I said.

***

The following afternoon, I paced around over-priced restaurants and tourist shops filled with ceramic gladiators before making my way back to the Coliseum. Panic scratched at me and I sat under a tree to think.

Across the piazza stood the Arch of Constantine. There's a carving inside that arch of Roman soldiers carrying away the spoils from one of their many victories. Rome had long plundered and stolen from the people of the world. I was just the latest victim in a three-thousand-year-old tradition.

Dimitri had told me Bus 64 was notorious for thieves and pickpockets. A group of them gave him a few euro every week to put unwitting foreigners like myself on the bus. After dropping the marks off at Termini, he would text the victim's description. During the summer, he said, the woman was on the bus almost every afternoon.

Without money for a bus pass, I'd paced around near the Coliseum all day, watching passengers file off. I was tired, I was hungry, and I was sore. My calves and upper back ached and the bones in my feet felt like they'd been peppered with buckshot. With no place to sleep, I'd hopped around through the city all night, avoiding the police, and trying to steal a nap here and there.

Luckily, Rome had a bustling nightlife. Most of the clubs didn't vomit out their clientele until sunrise. By that time, I'd made my way to the faint impression of the Circus Maximus, curled up on the grass beneath a cypress tree, and slept with my backpack as a pillow. Teenagers playing soccer woke me sometime before noon. I'd hovered near the Coliseum ever since but hadn't caught sight of the thief.

The sun was in its descent and bathed the city in dull orange. This was Miranda's favorite time of day. "The magic hour," she called it, that hour around sunset when she was getting home from work. She would sit on her back porch, surrounded by grass that refused to grow, and sip from a glass of wine while staring at the half-finished subdivision around her. When the glass had emptied, we would make love in her living room, not caring that blinds and windows were open, not worried about who could see or hear.

If she were with me, everything would be all right. The way she handled problems was near divine. Poets could write sonnets about her grace under pressure. There was a time when I was the same. But ever since my condition flared to life...

Condition? What a quaint term for it.

Condition.

There is a strange state of being we sometimes find ourselves in, moments of the deepest melancholy when everything seems useless and meaningless, when your life feels as though it's reached its zenith and you're on the decline at the ripe old age of thirty. These moments are said to open us up for great things. Staring into the setting sun, I felt what the ancients called *kenosis*.

KENOSIS: Greek for "emptiness;" often used in theology (as in "he emptied himself to be filled with God and thus had achieved kenosis").

I was an empty vessel, ready to be filled. Only it wasn't the power of God that waited to rush in. It was...

Well, I had no clue what it was. It had to be big, I told myself. Important. Earth shattering, even. I traveled halfway across the world for it, so it damn well better be.

The crowds shuffling from the bus hurried into the ancient structure before it closed for the night. There had to be forty people forcing their way into line, forty people who came to sneak a glimpse of ancient glories.

And one who slipped toward the street.

She looked back to the bus, grinning as she pulled a wad of cash from a wallet. She tossed the wallet into a trashcan as she darted across traffic. Her white cotton dress left a trail behind her like a photograph taken at the wrong shutter speed.

Or maybe I just needed to sleep.

I followed the pickpocket down the modern street Mussolini had carved from the Forum to his window. As I did, I couldn't help but be distracted by the sights around me. I almost lost her when I spent too long beside the red brick of Trajan's Market.

Focus, I told myself. Time enough to be a tourist later.

She took a winding path up a hill, twisting between thick shrubs and broken columns. I waited for her to disappear over the crest before darting after her.

The trail led me into the Piazza del Campodoglio. I'd later learn how Michelangelo had designed the piazza, how its perfect lines and marble equestrians were painstakingly carved to create a sense of awe and wonder, but at that moment I could only panic.

Hundreds of people filled the square.

Soft notes from violins vibrated the air as Italians wearing clothes that cost more than my car milled about snacking on bruschetta and fruit. An art show of some kind.

My thieving angel was gone. Panic again took hold. There was no way I could find her in this mess. She could have gone into one of the museums or sprinted down to the street.

Or picked someone else's pocket.

There she was, passing through the crowd as smooth and swift as a breeze. She plucked a glass of wine from a server's tray with one hand while palming a money clip with another.

I should bust her, I thought. But watching her work was like watching a magician. Her fingers quick and nimble, her body twisting between marks with an almost supernatural ease. There are few things as entrancing as someone excelling at their craft, and I was lucky enough to observe a master.

In the shadows of sunset, all I could see was the white dress. It twirled and flowed away from the crowd and down into the street. It hurried along the cobblestones, zigging into alleys, zagging down roads. I had no idea where we were. If I'd seen a sign saying we'd somehow ended up in Florence, I wouldn't have been surprised.

Of course, I wouldn't have been able to read it.

Once night had flooded the streets, she slipped down a tiny alley. A sign carved into a wall at the corner read *Via dei Papiri*. The path was cramped and narrow, shadows painting the stones with thick brush strokes. The alley had no exit.

I crouched in the dark and waited.

She stopped at a butcher's shop. A man as ancient as the city itself fought with the locks on the front door. They exchanged a few words in Italian and he held the door open long enough for her to disappear inside. He locked it behind her and made his way toward me.

I crept from the alley and pretended to examine a movie poster taped to the window of a clothing store. The thick smell of organ meats smothered me as he walked past.

When he was gone, I marched to the store front. I'm not quite sure why I hadn't confronted her before she made her way inside. Maybe I thought I'd catch her off guard. Standing in front of the locked door, I had no idea what to do. So, I did the only thing I could think of.

I rang the doorbell.

The shrill noise echoed inside. I stared through the glass and into the dark. Nothing moved.

I rang the bell again and again.

A thin stream of yellow light fell across the floor. Then a ghost glided toward me, the shadows gripping her and trying to pull her back. Finally, the white dress came into view. The lock clicked and the door cracked open.

"*Chiuso*," she said.

"Remember me?"

Her face was blank. "No." She moved to shut the door.

I wedged my foot between it and the frame. "I'd like my things back."

Her eyes moved from my face to my foot and back. She cocked an eyebrow and sighed. "From the bus, right? Yesterday?"

"Yeah."

She nodded.

And then slammed her shoulder into the door and crushed my foot.

"Ow!"

The second my foot was out she had the door shut and fumbled with the lock.

I hit it with my shoulder, a hard shove that sent her sprawling backwards to land on her ass on the gray tile. Stepping inside, I leaned over her.

"All I want is my stuff."

Silver flashed through the black. Cold steel pressed against my neck.

"It's not nice," a man's voice said, "to shove a lady."

His accent was British, thick and street like a thug from an old Michael Caine film. He smelled of oiled leather and slipped an arm around my neck.

The knife hovered in front of my eye, promising pain.

A sharp kick to the back of my knee sent my legs sprawling out. He jerked me backwards and I fell into him, clawing at his arm, fighting for breath.

It was no use. In seconds everything had gone black.

CHAPTER THREE

I DREAMED OF THE first time Miranda and I slept together.

We were in an empty parking lot waiting out a storm. We'd teased each other in the car the entire night, tickling one another's legs and cheeks, whispering what we were going to do. The rain crashed against her windshield as music played, our bodies pressed together in time to Sam Cooke. We fought to stretch out the anticipation the way Italians stretch out a meal, savoring every breath we shared, every time our lips brushed together.

When we finally gave in, our bodies crashed and flowed like they had always been a part of one other. They fit together like two statues carved from the same piece of marble. There was none of the awkwardness of two people being together for the first time, none of the pauses or confusion.

It was perfect.

***

A hard slap brought me to.

"Oy, Casanova." The Brit sat beside me. His eyes were ice and a jagged grin ripped across his face. "You talk in your sleep. It's embarrassing. I shouldn't have listened." He scratched his bare scalp. "Glad to have you back here in the world of the living. Though you may not be here for long."

My cheek stung from the slap. I sat up too fast and cracked my forehead into the stone above me. Sparks flashed behind my eyelids.

The Brit laughed. He had no eyebrows, just pale strips of flesh above his face.

I rubbed my head and let my eyes focus. Gray rock surrounded me. They had placed me in some sort of nook. Dozens of human-sized shelves were carved into the walls. I'd read enough about Rome, seen enough documentaries, to know where I was.

"Catacombs?"

He grinned. "That's right. This is what the Greeks called a Necropolis. You know what that means? City of the Dead. This is where Christian corpses while away the centuries waiting to be resurrected."

He tapped a finger onto the ceiling of my crypt. A fish had been carved there, the same shape adorning thousands of pickup trucks across the United States.

"Do you wish to be resurrected?"

"I just want to get my shit and get out of here," I said.

"No. I think you want more. You came here because you needed something."

"Yeah. *My shit*."

"I know you. We have known one another for centuries, you and I. Since Socrates guided Plato toward self-discovery."

"You're not making any sense."

"How's this for sense? You're a train wreck, mate. A fuck-knuckle. You have nothing and are nothing."

"Go to Hell."

"I hit a nerve?"

"You don't know me."

He tossed my passport onto my chest.

"Age thirty. Recently divorced. Work as a night security guard in hooray-for-Hollywood. Had a few articles published here and there. Some are rather good, others meh, though the last was years ago. Seems you've stopped trying since then. It's amazing what five minutes on Google will get these days."

I shifted my weight and slid from the crypt. He stood and took a step away, his hands behind his back.

"I can't let you leave here as you are," he said.

"What does that mean?"

"I am a shepherd of men. This is my pasture. If I let you go as you are then you'll tell the wolves where my sheep graze. We can't have that, can we?"

Stone crypts surrounded me. A single white bulb hung from a coil on the ceiling, the wires disappearing down the hallway that stretched behind him. There was nowhere to go but through him and one of the hands behind his back surely held that knife.

"Do you desire resurrection?"

I scanned the room looking for a rock, a piece of bone, anything I could use for a weapon. "What are you talking about?"

"You're lost."

"Well, you brought me here."

"In life, mate." He pulled my backpack from a corner and tossed it to me. "Thirty years old and you come to Europe with nothing but a backpack?"

I clutched the bag to my chest. Maybe I could use it as a shield to catch the knife. If I timed it right when I rushed him, it could take the brunt of the damage.

"Divorced," he went on. "That never sits well in a bloke's head. Mind if I play Freud?"

"Be my guest."

"I think you're at a crossroads. Too old for a quarter-life crisis, too young for a mid-life, yet you've fallen apart. You're searching for an identity. A new life. Your old one crumbled in your hands and now you're hanging on like on the bough of a sinking ship, hoping someone will come along and throw you a lifesaver."

I could only stare.

"*Let me be that lifesaver.*" He leaned back against the wall. "It's not easy following Shelley. She's got talents you can't even begin to fathom. And eyes in the back of her skull, swear to Caesar she does. The fact you tracked her here and were able to get in? Well, either you're something special or the gods put you in my way for a purpose."

"The gods? You're crazy."

He shrugged as if that didn't matter.

Now or never, I thought. I threw my backpack at his face and rushed him.

He spun and slammed me to the ground. My back hit hard, the wind going out of me. He crawled onto my chest and flicked open his knife.

"Not to beat the metaphor to death, but I can be said lifesaver. Leave here tonight and you will keep drowning." He smacked me in the face with his free hand. "But no real man dies of drowning. No real man lets himself sink underwater until the cold does him in."

Smack.

"Real men set themselves on fire."

Smack.

"Real men burn to ashes."

He shifted and stood, extending a hand to help me up.

"And then," he said, "from those ashes, a Phoenix is born."

I rubbed the stinging from my face and took his hand. "You mean *re*-born."

He yanked me to my feet. "You hungry?"

"Huh?"

"Big Jim."

A shadow peeled itself from the corner. A tall black man in jeans and a t-shirt had been standing there, so still and quiet I never noticed him. His head was shaved, and a pink scar ran down the side of his neck.

"Come, Dickweed," he said.

I followed him down the hall. The Brit stayed behind.

Music crawled along the walls. As we made our way through the corridor I wondered if I could overpower Big Jim.

He scratched his neck and his forearm flexed like a python. I decided against trying.

Light danced on the ceiling up ahead.

"The Carny likes you. The Carny not like no one." His accent was thick and exotic.

"The Carny?"

"That is what we call him."

"Why?"

His eyes narrowed in thought. "I do not know."

"Okay."

"Do not disappoint him, Dickweed. He not like disappointment."

"He's nuts."

"Nuts?"

"Crazy."

He seemed to consider this for a moment. "Yes. Probably."

The music swelled. It sounded familiar.

The hallway opened onto a giant antechamber. It was twenty feet high if an inch. Wires and pipes crisscrossed it, running down the walls and disappearing into other passages. Track lighting fastened to the ceiling shone on a group of children. They clutched microphones, dancing back and forth in front of a karaoke machine while singing "Psycho Killer." The music blared from two giant speakers on c-stands at their backs.

My pickpocket appeared in front of me. She slammed a fist into my jaw and sent me sprawling.

"No one knocks me on my ass," she said.

Big Jim roared laughter. He grabbed my shoulders and hefted me to my feet like I weighed nothing.

I rubbed my jaw. "You got quite an arm."

"I know," she said.

"What the hell's going on here?"

The children yelled, "Fa-fa-fa-fa, fa-fa-fa-fa-fa, fa."

She made a face. "It's Tuesday. Karaoke night." She walked back into the room as though this were common knowledge.

Big Jim took a seat at a bar running the length of one wall, dark wood with a neon "Cheers" sign hanging behind it.

Others sat in the shadows. A middle-aged woman in a checkered dress took up one corner, clapping her hands in time to the music and grinning. A pale woman with deep-set eyes fiddled with long strands of purple and red hair falling into her face. She passed a bottle of wine to a handsome Mediterranean, shirtless and muscled like Michelangelo's David. The rest were sprawled out on rugs and sofas with stuffing bursting from the seams.

My pickpocket tucked her feet under her on a red leather love seat. The dim light in the room flickered over her face and I couldn't read her expression. I glanced to Big Jim, but he was focused on a bottle of grappa and a deck of cards.

Not knowing what else to do, I sat beside her.

"What's your name?"

She stared ahead at the children. "You can call me Shelley."

"Shelley. All right. I'd say nice to meet you, but…"

"Yeah."

"The, um, Carny? The Carny said there would be food."

A dwarf in a white tuxedo, skin obsidian and a scraggly beard draping down his chest, appeared from nowhere. He thrust a plate of pizza into my hands.

I took a bite. "Oh my God. This is delicious."

He bowed in thanks, face swelled with pride, and vanished again.

Shelley snatched one of the pizza slices.

"My name is—"

"Don't," she interrupted.

"Don't what?"

"Tell me your name. We don't use our old names here."

"We don't?"

She leaned closer, her eyes still focused on the children. "The Carny gives us new names. New names for new lives."

"Oh. So, Jim isn't—"

"Big?" She motioned to his massive form lounging at the bar. "I think he's named after an old action figure. He used to sell knockoff toys, among other things. Not much of a market for that anymore thanks to Amazon."

"Why are you called Shelley?"

She gave me a look dripping with irritation, gold flecks in her brown eyes catching the light. "The poet. I was named after Percy Shelley."

I looked around at the others. "Is one of them Lord Byron?"

"No. Byron left us years ago. I wouldn't bring him up around the Carny if I were you. Sore subject."

The music ended and the room erupted in applause. The children bowed and scampered off stage. They ran to the middle-aged woman. Her giant arms took them all in for an embrace.

"Bravo, my darlings," she said.

A slim Asian woman stepped into the spotlight. She wore a skintight dress, hair teased and makeup fashionably vivid. "The Orphans, ladies and gentlemen." More applause. "And now, one hand clapping against the other makes a wonderful sound for…"

"I'm up." Shelley stood.

"Shelley!"

Applause, whistles, and hoots.

She handed me a bottle of wine. "You might want to have a few drinks."

"Why?"

"You're next."

She took the microphone before I had time to protest. The familiar chords of "Suspicious Minds" started.

Her voice was flawless. I wanted to hate her, I really did, but everything about her drew me in. The way she smiled, how her hips moved when she reached the chorus, the way she closed her eyes and threw her head back when she told us we couldn't go on together, all of it.

The Asian woman sat next to me. She smelled of strawberries. "Hello, handsome."

"Hi."

"Madame Butterfly."

"I'm sorry?"

She ran a finger down my arm. "My name, silly. Can I have a drink?"

I handed her the bottle. She upended it and gulped down a third.

"Thanks," she said, and handed it back. She leaned in and kissed my cheek before walking over and plopping down next to Big Jim at the bar. Glancing back, she blew me a kiss.

I chugged the wine.

When Shelley had finished, Madame Butterfly sauntered over for the microphone. Shelley raised a hand to stop her and kept the mic. Madame Butterfly put her fists on her hips and tapped a foot, pouting.

Shelley cleared her throat. "We have a newcomer here tonight. He's a real—"

"Dickweed," Big Jim yelled.

Everyone laughed.

"Yeah," she said. "A real dickweed. He's penniless, directionless, and nameless. So put your hands together for... *Him*."

Applause. Whistles. Cat calls.

I froze.

Get your ass up here, she mouthed.

I was dreaming. I had to be. This was too strange, too surreal. Whoever choked me out had caused an aneurysm and I was hallucinating.

Shelley came across the stone floor in a few strides and grabbed my hand. She jerked me to my feet and dragged me into the lights.

"I picked out a good one for you," she said.

"I can't sing."

She shoved the mic into my hand and ran off.

The monitor of the karaoke machine turned blue. "Life on Mars by David Bowie" scribbled itself across the screen in gold letters.

The lights shined hot and yellow. The room itself became little more than hazy orange blurs. This is ridiculous, I thought. Throw the microphone down and get out of here. Fuck these lunatics. Go to the police and then to the Embassy. Get the hell out of Rome and on the first plane home.

Sound advice. *Sane* advice.

Instead, I cleared my throat and sang.

CHAPTER FOUR

MY EX-WIFE AND I met at karaoke. After a pitcher or two of beer, I worked up the nerve to sing "Viva Las Vegas." I wasn't kidding when I told Shelley I couldn't sing. I can, however, do a badass Elvis impersonation. I'm talking if you closed your eyes you would think it was the King himself.

My gift, my curse.

While gyrating my hips I caught sight of Chelsea and her friends at a table across the room. They screamed encouragement, beers held high, and I laid it on thick.

Chelsea came over to our table a few minutes later. "Hey, Elvis."

"Yeah?"

"I need a partner for a duet."

I smiled. "Well, I'm your man. What's the song?"

"Under Pressure," she said, and took my hand.

***

After a few more rounds of singing and a few more bottles of wine, the children were put to bed and we played *Pictionary* in the catacombs. It was like I'd crashed someone's family reunion. It was a bizarre gathering of accents and mindsets and not a single soul there could draw worth a damn. We were drunk and heckled each other's art like seasoned critics.

Big Jim came into the room while I scribbled something to suggest "Richard Nixon" and motioned for me. Everyone booed him.

We strolled down one of the hallways, the wine determined to pitch me into the walls, and stopped at a purple curtain. Big Jim lifted the edge and I ducked under.

The Carny sat in a recliner, a pair of gold-rimmed glasses on his face and a book open in his lap. Lou Reed played from an old record player in the corner.

He closed the book and set it on a table next to him. "Hey, mate."

I walked around the room, scanning the spines of books and records shoved together on oak bookshelves. "You know, they have digital music now."

"Shut your fucking gob. I'd rather saw my cock off with a rusty nail file than compress my music into some digital cack." He stood and removed his glasses. "Well?"

"Well, what?"

"Do you get it now?"

"I don't know."

"I think you do. Shall I elucidate?"

"Elucidate away."

"We're misfits. The Misfits of the World. You remember that Rankin and Bass Rudolph cartoon?"

"The claymation one?"

"Think of this as the Island of Misfit Toys. We are the broken tops and the racecars with two wheels. We are the teddy bears that bleed stuffing. We are the detritus of the world, washed up here like so much trash. Take a seat."

I sat on a velvet ottoman. He plopped back in his chair and steepled his hands under his chin.

"Why did you come to Rome?" he asked.

"To sightsee."

"Bollocks. Why did you come here?"

"It's private."

"All right, then. What do you have to go back to?"

Nothing, to be honest. Though I wasn't going to tell him that.

"I been in this city for years," he went on. "There are powerful gods at work here. I don't care if you believe in them or not. They sure as shit believe in you. And they brought you here."

"To the catacombs?"

"You're a misfit. Right? There's something off about you. Your temperament, your view of the world, your bloody personality. You don't fit in."

He had me there.

"I have a... Well, a condition," I said.

"That's what I thought. I took one look at you and said, 'This fucker's a loon, he is.'"

"I'm not a loon. I just have a condition."

"What is it?"

"Borderline Personality Disorder."

"Never heard of it."

"Most people haven't."

"Does it make you violent?"

I swallowed, thinking of that last day at the office. "Rarely."

"Homicidal?"

"No. God, no."

He held up two pill bottles. *My* pill bottles. "That what these are for?"

"Yeah." I reached for them and, with a flourish of his hands like an old stage magician, they vanished.

"I need those," I said.

"We'll see. This disorder, do you struggle with it?"

"I'm learning to get a grip on it now. It got pretty bad for a while but…" I shook my head, the wine blurring my judgment. Why the hell was I telling him any of this?

"No one who thinks they have a grip on it actually does," he said. "Chinua Achebe once said, 'When suffering knocks at your door and you say there is no seat for him, he tells you not to worry because he has brought his own stool.' So, let me ask the uncomfortable of uncomfortables: People judge you for your condition, don't they?"

"Yeah. Of course they do. Of course they fucking judge me. You said I was crazy? Well, then. Doesn't everyone judge a lunatic?"

"We don't." The Carny leaned back in his chair. "We don't judge one another here, mate. We're all one and the same. We're all—"

"Misfits."

He smiled. "This is where we shed all them negative titles the world forces on us. We shed the expectations they have of us. People think you're a nutter? Well, they expect you to act a nutter. That expectation bleeds into you. It twists around your heart and you can't help but be the man they expect you to be. But not here. Here you can be *re*-born." He winked. "It's no coincidence the Renaissance started here. There is a magical quality to Italy what lets you rise from the ashes. I'm offering you the Renaissance of your life, if you're willing to be a part of it."

Maybe it was the wine, but there was a sort of madhouse genius in what he said.

"How did you and Shelley meet?" he asked.

"She picked my pocket on the bus."

"We don't hold down nine to fivers here. We don't work sixteen-hour shifts down factory. We do as the city herself. We take from the gullible and the greedy."

"You're all pickpockets?"

"The tip of the iceberg. There are a hundred cons and scams you'll learn. And whatever you take goes to the flock. That's it. That's all you have to do."

"That's it?"

"That's it. Do your share and keep your mouth shut." He considered that before adding, "And unswerving loyalty, of course."

"Of course."

"What do you say, then? Ready to set yourself on fire? Ready to rise from the ashes?"

This is the point in the story where a normal person would tell him "no, thank you" and march out. But, as you should have gathered by now, I was not a normal person.

I thought of Miranda wrapping her sprained wrist. I thought of Chelsea's signature on the divorce papers. I thought of my boss having security escort me from the building, of my father surrounded by beer cans, of my mother rotting away in a box six feet underground. I had few friends and less family. I hated my job. I hated my tiny, cramped apartment. Hell, I hated Los Angeles, with its smog alerts and choking traffic and privileged dude-bros and seventy-year-old women Botox'd until they looked like mannequins. I hated my life.

I hated myself.

There were nights I lay awake and stared at the ceiling fan spinning, knowing depression would eventually get the best of me. If I didn't want to exist now, if I had times where I wished I could just blink out of being, what would I feel like at forty? At fifty?

Eighty percent of all Borderline Personality Disorder cases report a history of suicide attempts. Ten percent of all cases succeed.

Would I be one of them? If I continued the way I was, would I consign myself to the void, too?

I thought of that other void, the one inside of me, begging to be filled.

Kenosis.

It wasn't a difficult decision.

CHAPTER FIVE

AS A NEWCOMER, I was an Orphan and wasn't allowed a name. Big Jim continued to call me Dickweed but to the others I was "You" or "Guy." That first week in the Necropolis was spent as a non-entity. I wasn't spoken to unless someone demanded something, and I was not invited to participate in karaoke or any other activity again. Most of my time was spent cleaning up after everyone. I was a busboy. A janitor.

"Just until your Rite of Passage," Big Jim had said one night as I washed dishes.

"Rite of Passage?"

"You will see, Dickweed. You will see. After Rite of Passage, you get a name."

"What's wrong with my name?"

"Your name is shit. The Carny give you new name."

Being a non-entity, it was easy to observe everyone without being noticed. I could eavesdrop on political arguments between Dostoevsky and Sappho, or theological discussions between Marco Antonio and Ravenna. I could watch Tolstoy paint still life or Madame Butterfly design and sew her outfits. Sometimes I could even listen to the group laugh in the Family Room while I stretched out on my cot in a small, dank cove wedged between Big Jim's and Miss Fagin's quarters.

Miss Fagin was the middle-aged woman and, I learned, looked after all the children. The children were both actual orphans and Orphans with a capital O. They were always referred to in the collective. Miss Fagin said the Carny refused to give them names until they were older. She collected them from all over the city the way some women collect porcelain dolls. Until my Rite of Passage, whatever that may be, I was considered an Orphan. For most of that week the only conversations I had were with Miss Fagin.

"Sweetheart," she'd say in her Scottish accent, "this will be the best thing that ever happened to you. You must trust me on that. Trust the Carny."

"Why is he called the Carny?"

"I think he fancies the name because it's like his own little carnival down here. We're his bearded ladies and strongmen."

"The Misfits of the World, right?"

"Something like that, love."

Miss Fagin showed me the ropes of life in the Necropolis, where things were kept and what chores needed to be done. She also drew a map of the labyrinth around us. The sections they had navigated so far, at least.

It was a commonly held myth that all the catacombs were outside of the city, most along the Appian Way, but Rome is a city of secrets. Every attempt to build a subway or lay the foundation to a new office building reveals more ruins. There are cities laid atop cities laid atop cities, the modern giving way to the medieval, the medieval to the ancient, the ancient to the prehistoric. I would find that the Necropolis was the same. Every time one secret was unearthed, another would soon be found beneath it.

***

After one of the many parties I was not yet allowed to attend, I was introduced to one of those secrets. Everyone had retired to their quarters and I was busy cleaning up empty wine bottles and dirty dishes. I passed through a long hallway leading to a makeshift kitchen cobbled together from appliances too pristine not to have been stolen.

The ceiling was low, and I crouched under a hundred strands of Christmas lights strung along it. A cold draft swept in from somewhere carrying the scent of ancient dust and stone. At the intersection up ahead, a shadow glided by.

"Hello?" I called.

No answer.

Whatever. No one spoke to me under most circumstances. Why would they start now?

At the intersection I turned left. The catacombs were quiet, the only sound the faint hum of makeshift wiring and my footsteps echoing in my ears. I walked for a good distance before coming to a dead end. The stones bricking up the wall were slick with dripping water.

I'd made a wrong turn. Learning the labyrinth hadn't been easy and, hands filled with plates and bottles, I hadn't been using the map.

When I turned to head back down the passageway, I heard the sobbing.

My first thought was I hallucinated, that the silence and spooky atmosphere conspired to play tricks on me. Stopping to listen dispelled that idea. Someone *was* crying. A chill scurried over my skin and I pressed against the wall.

"I'm so sorry," a voice whispered, faint and trembling.

The crying continued for a few minutes before drifting away into nothing.

God only knows how long it took before I mustered up the nerve to move. I never saw anyone and, by the time I'd made it to the kitchen, had convinced myself I'd heard a ghost.

I'd find out later I was right, though not in the way that I thought.

CHAPTER SIX

THAT WEEKEND, THE CARNY asked me to join him for a stroll. I jumped at the chance, thinking I'd be able to leave the Necropolis and get some fresh air.

I was wrong.

He grabbed a flashlight and we descended into old and unused tunnels winding deep into the earth.

"We don't use these halls," he said, ducking under a sagging archway. "Too dangerous."

"That's comforting."

"Buck up, mate. I thought you was a loon? Loons usually have testicles the size of grapefruit. I do."

"Where are we going?"

"Just exploring. Little hobby of mine. I been mapping these tunnels whenever I get a chance. I know there's something they lead to."

"Something like what?"

"The emperors built pleasure palaces all around the city. Nero's Domus Aurea was found solely because some clumsy shit tripped and fell through the roof in the fifteenth century. These tunnels, there's no telling where they go. Alexander's sarcophagus could be down here. The bleeding Ark of the Covenant could be behind one of these walls. You never know."

We turned right, left, right. I lost my way a few minutes in. The fear of being trapped down here wandering these tunnels until I died of starvation was overwhelming.

"Besides," the Carny went on, "I feel bringing you down here is metaphorically pertinent."

"What do you mean?"

"All good journeys start with a trip to the Underworld, eh?" The Carny smacked the wall. Dust and pebbles rained down on us. "Ooh," he said, "that can't be good."

We exited the corridor and stepped into an open room. It looked like an ancient bathroom, stone benches lining the walls and dotted with holes I can only assume were toilets. The flashlight dancing around the walls revealed vivid frescoes. Theseus battling the Minotaur, if I remembered my mythology correctly.

The Carny sat on one of the benches and lit a cigarette. Sitting across from him, I rubbed my arms to fight the subterranean cold.

He clicked the flashlight off. The only thing visible in the dark was a red nub at the end of his cigarette.

Silence.

His cigarette went out.

Panic took me. "Hey."

No answer.

"You still there?"

"Shhh."

Hearing him shush me was enough to calm down.

"The darkness," he said, "is honest."

"Yeah?"

"I said hush. Just listen a bit. The darkness does not lie. See, dark has gotten a bad rep. It's associated with the bad. With evil deeds. But it ain't evil. It's pure. In the dark, there's nothing but you and the truth. What brought you here? I don't mean why you left the States. You don't have to tell your life story to me. I just want to know why you chose Rome instead of Paris or Cairo."

"My mother."

"A momma's boy, eh?"

"I never knew her. I've got this journal of hers from when she was here, and I thought I would come and check out some of the places she saw. Kind of, I don't know, a way to get to know her, I guess."

"Ah. I see. Just as I thought."

I waited for him to go on and shuffled in my seat.

"I spoke to you about the gods. I won't force my religion on you. But the threads of fate tie you to this place. To this city. To these catacombs."

"I don't know that I believe in fate."

"People look to fate when the good things happen, but when the bad comes along they discount the idea. Maybe fate destroys as much as it brings together, eh? Maybe fate has a larger plan, and that plan involves both exaltation and heartache."

"And that's why it brought me here?"

"Tomorrow's your Rite of Passage. Tomorrow you begin your rebirth. It is a slow, painful thing, but it's why you're here. None of us knew ourselves when we first came here. But we do now. Proper well. And so will you."

If this were therapy, it wasn't the strangest kind I'd ever had.

It occurred to me then that I hadn't taken my medication since coming here. I hoped that wouldn't affect things.

"For now," he continued, "let's just sit in the dark and think about the truth of things, yeah?"

Closing my eyes, I wondered what my Rite of Passage could be. I'd love to say I didn't care, that I was ready to face whatever came my way, but that wouldn't be true. My guts had knotted themselves into a ball bouncing between my ribs and pelvis. If I'd had some inkling of what I was about to go through it might have been different but sitting there in the dark, my mind raced through every horrible possibility I could imagine.

I thought of the scar on Big Jim's neck and hoped it was something he'd had since he was a kid.

My father had been a believer in Rites of Passage. He'd never called them that, of course, had likely never even heard the term and wouldn't have used it if he had. But as an ex-Marine and a good ol' boy, he knew their importance. He put me through a few. They just never seemed to take.

When I was eleven, he took me hunting. We traveled deep into the Appalachian wilderness while he told me how his father had done the same with him, how he had put a bullet through a ten-point buck and then his old man had cut the animal's neck and made my father drink the blood.

We never so much as found a single track that day. I was secretly relieved. The idea of killing a living thing bothered me deeply.

I suppose that's why it's considered a Rite of Passage.

At thirteen, he enrolled me in Golden Gloves. I didn't want to do that, either, was scared horribly at the idea of being punched. But by the sixth week I realized I wasn't bad at it, was pretty good, all things considered. And then, little over a year later, my father drank too much and threw a glass across the room at me. I thought I could stand up to him finally, could really take control of my life for once.

I was wrong.

He kept me out of school for the next three weeks. The flu, he'd said, though I'm not sure who believed him. When I went back, the bruises were easier to hide than I thought they would have been.

I wasn't allowed to do Golden Gloves after that, wasn't allowed to do much of anything for a long time other than read and help one of an endless parade of stepmothers around the house. Whenever I stepped out of line, he'd shoot me that look again, and I'd become the obedient son once more.

I suppose that had been a Rite of Passage as well.

He strove to be a stereotype, some New York writer's idea of a Southern man who drove a truck for a living and flew into drunken rages. He rarely read and, when he wasn't on the road, spent most of his time in front of the television. He didn't understand why I always had my nose in a book, or why I never cared much for football or John Wayne marathons. On the surface, he was a beer-soaked cliché.

Beneath the surface he was a man in deep and unending pain.

Leaving town was the only rebellion I had left to wage. By the time I left for Los Angeles, I'd dropped out of college and squandered most of the chances I'd had at anything resembling stability. And my father had a brilliant way of letting me know it at every turn. Whether a snide comment while watching reality TV or that goddamned look, he let me know.

And so, I left, headed the way of Horatio Alger and the Donner Party, not knowing what was coming, having no idea where the path I'd chosen would lead. It was liberating and exciting and stressful and frightening.

Story of my life, I guess.

CHAPTER SEVEN

A PHOTOGRAPH SAT ON my grandmother's television when I was growing up. The TV was a large floor model, a Curtis Mathis, I think, with the green color tube blown and every actor looking like Oompa Loompas all grown up. This photograph, nestled between a wooden chicken and a lamp the shape of snuggled-up Siamese cats, was taken in front of the Pantheon. My mother in a green dress, hair cascading onto her shoulders like it was placed there by Raphael himself. My father in his Marine dress blues, chest puffed out so the golden buttons caught the light at just the right angle to create several tiny lens flares. He smiled, not yet able to hide his feelings the way he would later in life when the pain became too much to bear.

As a kid I used to sit on the floor and stare at that picture, attempting to recreate what their time together would have been like. That moment, forever captured in an 11x9 Olan Mills frame, was the pinnacle for me of happiness. It was also a symbol of opportunity missed, of a life that could never be. I couldn't formulate these thoughts when I was five or six but, looking back on it, I recognize the melancholy.

After the Carny brought me back up through the catacombs, I collapsed onto my bed and worried more about what my Rite of Passage would be. Pulling out my mother's journal, I revisited why I had come to Rome in the first place. Really poured over it. That was something I hadn't done before, even when sitting down to buy plane tickets for Italy. Self-reflection had never been a strength of mine. At least, not before the Carny.

Next door I could hear Miss Fagin and the Orphans. She sang them to sleep, an Italian song I didn't know the meaning to but made me smile.

Reading the journal, I combined the story inside with what little snippets I'd heard growing up, fragments that had leaked out of my father on the rare occasion he would so much as mention my mother's name.

She was a puzzle I'd spent a lifetime trying to piece together. There were days I felt so close to seeing the entire picture, yet still knew so little. She craved garlic ice cream when she was pregnant with me and listened to the Stones. She liked to dance while she cleaned, her long hair tied up with a ribbon, her stick-thin legs kicking around as she sang along with the tune.

From what I'd pieced together, she met my father like this, dancing around the lobby of the one-star hotel she worked at that allowed her to spend a year in Italy.

He crashed through the front door, drunk, yet sobered a moment when he saw her. He smiled. She smiled back. He took the cue and sauntered over.

"Hi," she said.

He threw up.

The next day, after a hot shower and hotter cup of coffee, he took his soggy and aching brain down to apologize.

"It's okay," she said. "It was a humbling experience."

"Huh?"

"Having someone throw up when they looked at me. First time that's happened."

He shook his head. "That's not why I threw up."

"I know."

She smiled and his heart skipped a beat. He wondered if he had palpitations and made a mental note to see a doctor. First, though, he asked her to dinner. She declined, saying something about how she didn't want to see the meal twice. But he was persistent, my father. He asked her out again the next day and again after his doctor's appointment that Friday.

The doctor, for his tiny part in this story, told my father his condition was either "love at first sight" or bad lasagna. My father chose the former.

After another week of what most women would have considered harassment, my mother relented and agreed to coffee after her shift. "That way," she said, "I'll have the energy to run away if you turn out to be a creep."

"I'm no creep," he said, and smiled.

She clocked out, took his hand, and thought she should see the family practitioner about the fluttering in her chest.

I looked up from the journal at that point in the story to see two of the Orphans in my doorway, their wide-eyed stares impossible to ignore. Neither could have been older than four.

"Hi," I said.

They were quiet.

"What are your names?"

Nothing.

"Um, *parla inglese?*"

The boy started to cry.

"Hey, I'm sorry, I…"

The girl grabbed his arm and dragged him into the hall.

Shelley stepped around them. "Mind if I come in?"

I closed the journal.

"Wow." She motioned around the room. "The Carny really put you in a closet, huh?"

"Yeah."

She leaned against the wall and crossed her arms. "Listen. I'm your guide on your Rite."

"Guide?"

"The Carny will fill you in. But I just wanted to let you know you better not ruin this, okay?"

"I don't even know what we're doing."

"That's what bothers me. Just don't get any stupid ideas about running off or yelling for the cops or anything like that, *va bene?*"

"Sure."

"And do exactly what I tell you. I know it might be weird taking orders from someone younger than you."

"How old are you?"

"Twenty-four."

"How old do you think I am?"

"I don't know. Everyone between thirty and fifty looks the same to me."

I really needed to take better care of myself.

She kicked her heel against the wall twice. "Doesn't matter. Until you get through tomorrow, you're just one of the Orphans, understand?"

"Sure."

She turned to leave, stopping in the doorway to glance back. "If it were up to me, we would have knifed you and threw you into the Tiber. Just so you know."

She left.

So much for my crush.

I clicked off the bulb hanging in the corner and stretched out on the cot that served as my bed.

A tiny hand tugged on my sleeve. I turned the light back on. The little boy who had run from the room crying stood beside the bed.

"Hey, buddy."

He blinked and held a tiny fist out.

"For me?"

He nodded.

"Thanks."

I put my hand under his. He opened his fist, and something fell into my palm. A gift.

Then he ran out.

A dead roach sat in my hand.

I threw it into the corner and wiped my hand on my pants.

When I finally settled down, the thought that I'd toss and turn all night, anxious and excited and uncomfortable, took hold of me. I clicked the light off and leaned back onto the rough fabric.

I was asleep in minutes.

CHAPTER EIGHT

FREEZING WATER SPLASHED MY face.

Jolted awake, I tried to sit but couldn't move. A legion of hands pinned me down. Duct tape covered my eyes, and a rough cloth was shoved into my mouth. It tasted like vinegar.

I was forced onto my stomach. The screech of tape ripping. Wrists connected behind my back. Ankles fastened together.

Then: Airborne.

Someone carried me through the catacombs. I squirmed and fought, but it was no use. It had to be Big Jim. None of the others would have been able to heft me so effortlessly. I felt twenty feet above the ground.

He shifted and spun me. A tug against the tape on my ankles and the hands let go.

I hung upside down by my feet.

High-pitched giggles filled the room.

"Hush," Miss Fagin said.

A throat cleared. "Welcome, you who come before us naked." It was the Carny.

"He's not naked," someone whispered.

The Carny groaned. "Well, cut his fucking clothes off then."

A knife ripped down my pants and shirt. A second later, my clothes drifted to the floor.

"What about his boxers?"

"Don't worry about them. Ahem. You who come before us naked."

"Naked except for the boxers."

"Forget the fucking boxers, all right? You who come before us *almost* naked. You have asked to join us—"

"I thought you invited him?"

"Shut. Up."

"Sorry."

"You have asked to join us and be reborn. Do you still crave resurrection?"

I made a noise into the cloth.

"We must burn out who you were. We must leave all your old fears here on the floor with your sweat and piss and blood."

Blood? I tried to say. It came out as a squeal.

"Your old self will die a violent and brutal death here today."

I squealed more.

"And then you will be a babe, newborn, naked and empty and ready to become."

Feet shuffled.

"How did that sound?" His voice was moving away, exiting down a corridor.

"It was good."

"Sure it didn't come off as tripe?"

"No. Real inspiring."

"I don't want to sound like a wanker."

"You didn't."

Fat fingers pressed into my ears. I squirmed. It took a moment to realize someone had shoved earplugs in.

The pressure in the room lessened and I knew everyone had left. I hung there, sightless, soundless, upside down and alone, for God knows how long.

The Times ran an article once on sensory deprivation. It's used by governments the world over to torture suspects. Even my own government, that supposed bastion of humanity and compassion, has used it from time to time.

No one can ever predict what the results of sensory deprivation will be. There was a study done in Britain where volunteers agreed to be locked in an old bomb shelter for forty-eight hours. The lights were turned off and the rooms made of concrete two feet thick to prevent any external sound from entering.

The mind, it seems, does not react well to lack of stimuli.

One woman complained her sheets were wet. There was, of course, no moisture in the room. Another imagined she saw roaches everywhere. A third swore that a line of oysters washed up at the foot of her bed and sang "Ain't Too Proud to Beg." Those were the more pleasant experiences.

Others were tortured by loved ones. A father watched in horror as his teenage daughter pulled herself from the wall and hacked at her neck with a rusty knife. A mother watched her husband drag their son into the room and beat him. Only twenty percent of the participants did not have a negative experience. Ten percent bore the scars of the experiment for life.

It took far less than forty-eight hours for my broken mind to begin its games.

Water dripped from somewhere. It tapped a rhythm against the floor, soft and steady. I heard this, even though the earplugs kept me from hearing the crinkling of the tape as I swung around.

The growing pool soon filled the room and the top of my head skidded across the surface. The air was heavy with the harsh tang of chlorine.

Something splashed off to my right.

I worked the cloth from my mouth and spat it into the water.

"Hello?"

Another splash.

"Hello?"

More splashing. Whatever it was waded over to me.

"Who's there?"

Lips pressed against mine. They were soft and warm and completely imaginary. I knew it as soon as I felt them and yet couldn't help but play along.

"Miranda," I whispered.

"Hey."

"What are you doing here?"

She placed a cheek against mine, her hair tickling my face. "I needed to be with you."

"Can I see you?"

"No."

More splashing.

"Who else is here?"

"Your wife is with me," Miranda said.

"Hi." Chelsea kissed my other cheek. Her lips were thin and cool. "Aren't you going to say hello?"

"This is awkward," I said.

They both laughed.

Then silence.

"Miranda?"

"She's gone," Chelsea said. "It's just you and me." She shoved my chest and I swung back and forth, back and forth, the top of my head skimming across the water. My hair was soaked. "You know, when I'd said I wanted a break, I didn't expect you to crawl into someone else's bed."

"Yeah," I said. "Me neither."

"I just needed some time away from you. Some time to deal with your condition. Your outbursts. They scared me. The diagnosis. What was it again? Schizophrenia?"

"It's not schizophrenia."

"I thought it was?"

"No. Schizophrenia's worse."

"Hard to imagine that."

Silence.

"Chelsea?"

More splashing.

"Miranda?"

The splashing wasn't either of them. It was heavier and moved with less grace. Whoever else had entered the room stood far away, quiet, and watched me swing.

***

Hours later, Miranda returned.

"Can I ask you something?"

"Sure," I said.

"Why were you so cruel to me?"

"It was my condition."

"Uh-huh." She didn't sound like she believed me.

"I always say I suffer from Borderline Personality Disorder when I tell people but, the truth is, it's the people around me who suffer."

"That's a line from a brochure."

"I hoped you wouldn't notice."

"You treated me like filth," she said.

"I didn't want to."

"I don't care what you wanted. Tell me why."

"I wish I knew. When I was in the thick of it, I hated sunlight and fresh air. I hated people."

"You hated yourself."

"Still do."

"You hated me."

I couldn't think of a lie to answer with. How could anyone decent care for someone like me, anyway? It didn't track. There were times I felt that loving me was a crime worthy of hatred.

***

I waited for Chelsea to return, but she never did. Instead, a swarm of flies buzzed into the room and landed on my chest. They tickled their way over my abdomen and up my thighs. I struggled to shake them off, but it was no use.

One crawled into my ear and rolled little flecks of earwax into a ball. "Two plus two is four," it said through the earplug.

I tried to ignore it.

"Three plus three is six. One plus one... Well, that equals two. But one *times* one is still just one."

"Is that supposed to be profound in some way?"

It ignored me. "Vowels are the backbone of syllables, and syllables ride each other into words. Words daisy-chain into sentences. Continue this and you eventually have the complete works of Virgil and Ovid." It rolled another ball of wax and shoved it against the earplug. "But you would need to read Latin to understand them. Still, the syllables are there if you know how to find them."

My father splashed his way over to me. "You need to do something about this water, son. It'll ruin the floor."

"I know, Dad."

"The sperm and egg are both necessary for the production of life," the fly said.

"When are you going to come visit again?"

"I don't know, Dad. Christmas?"

"The sperm fertilizes the egg. But what fertilizes the sperm?"

"That's good, son. I never see you since you moved to the West Coast. I know things were never great between us—"

"The tail of the sperm is what allows it to swim through the uterus."

"I'm sorry, Dad. The fly in my ear is talking and it's really hard to concentrate."

"That's okay. I'll come back later."

"Sperm will fight each other over an egg, but the egg could care less about which sperm digs its way in."

"Sure thing, Dad. Later."

He splashed away.

***

When the fly had gone to sleep, whoever had been watching from the corner approached.

"Who are you?" I asked.

A soft, feminine hand pressed against my chest.

"Mom?"

I don't know why I said it, but I knew it was true.

She remained quiet.

"Please. Talk to me."

Nothing.

The tears came then. After so long of wishing they would fall, they broke free of whatever dam had been holding them in place. The duct tape over my eyes was soaked. Tears ran up my forehead and splashed into the water.

"I'm so sorry," I cried.

Silence.

"I'm so sorry I killed you."

At that, she turned and splashed away.

CHAPTER NINE

"WAKE UP, RIP VAN Winkle."

My eyelids were strips of concrete mortared shut. My neck ached. My head was heavy and thick. I felt like I had a hangover.

The tape ripped away in several painful tugs. I fought not to scream.

"Come on. We need to get started."

The light was harsh. It took a few moments and several blinks to realize I was outside.

The Virgin Mary stood before me, hands outstretched, a brilliant halo blurring her features and stretching fingers of warm light toward me.

"About goddamned time," she said.

Rubbing my eyes dispelled the illusion. Shelley crouched in front of me, the sun over one shoulder.

"He's up," she yelled.

I struggled to sit. My limbs had a hard time responding.

The Carny's grinning jackal face thrust into view. "Morning."

"How…" My mouth was dry and sticky. I smacked my jaws together a few times to work up spit. "How long was I out?"

"Two weeks," he said.

"What?"

"I'm just taking the piss. Twenty-four hours."

The cobblestone beneath me was wet and cold. I pressed against the wall and stretched my legs out.

"Well," Shelley said, glancing down before turning away, "at least we know he's alive."

Shit, I was naked. I pulled my knees up and covered my groin with my hands.

"Here's the game plan," the Carny said.

"Can I get some clothes?"

"You are as naked as a babe newly birthed into the world. You must fend for yourself."

A cool morning breeze crawled between my legs and I shivered.

"All right, so here's the fun part. You are going to meet with Shelley at the Spanish Steps in two hours. That is the first part of your Rite. The second will be explained when you get there. Understood?"

"How am I supposed to get there?"

"Walk, I suppose."

"Naked?"

"Well, that's up to you, innit? You ever hear of the Spartans?"

"Like the Greeks?"

"Spartan children had a particularly interesting Rite of Passage. As infants they was left out for the elements. Any child what died of exposure or was carried off by wolves was not fit to be a Spartan."

"That's what this is? I'm being left to the elements?"

"Shhh. You talk too much. Let me finish. Later, when they was old enough to join the army, they had another Rite of Passage. This involved them once again being left to fend for themselves, only this time they was instructed to steal what they needed. They had to prove they was cunning and resourceful. Oh, and they had to murder a slave, but we can skip that part."

The Carny patted my shoulder and stood.

"Good luck," he said.

They vanished into the shadows of a nearby street.

Many travelers say they feel naked in a strange city. When you don't know the local customs, the geography, or the language, it's easy to feel exposed. But to feel it in a very literal sense, well, that's frightening in a way I can't even begin to explain.

Standing was slow and difficult. My joints creaked and my muscles weren't entirely awake. I stood in a large alley. It stretched several yards in both directions. Across from me the buildings dipped, allowing the sun to pour in.

I heard children laughing and froze.

An older woman passed by one end of the street. Behind her, a string of students in school uniforms formed a line. They moved like a centipede, keeping a steady pace as they walked by.

When they were gone, I exhaled and stepped out into the alley.

One boy had broken off from the rest and stared in my direction. We locked eyes and, aside from me covering myself, neither of us moved.

The teacher appeared and grabbed the child by the arm. He mumbled something to her, and she looked my way.

Her eyes went wide. "*Aiuto*," she yelled. "*Polizia!*"

I ran.

The other end of the alley opened onto a large piazza. People sat at outdoor cafes and sipped coffee. Women walked their dogs. Across the piazza, past a fountain covered with Italians glued to the screens of their phones, another thin path wound into shadows.

My friend Siggo and I had once sneaked some beers into a football game in high school. We'd hid under the bleachers and drank, taunting each other about streaking.

"You a fucking pussy?" Siggo had said. "You afraid someone will see your junk and laugh?"

"What about you? Why aren't you doing it?"

"Half the people out there seen me naked. You seriously ain't gonna do it?"

"No, man. I don't want to get busted."

"All right." He'd slid his shirt off. "Fine. But if I get caught, I'm telling everybody it was your idea because you wanted to see my dong."

He'd had his clothes off in seconds and slipped around to the end of the bleachers.

Handing me his pants and shoes, he said, "Grab my shirt and meet me on the other side, will you?"

"Sure."

"And don't forget the beer." He closed his eyes and mumbled something to himself.

"What did you say?"

"The trick," he said, "is to haul ass."

"Yeah."

"But don't hide away. You got to puff up like a peacock."

"Okay, okay. You doing it or what?"

He punched my shoulder. "See you on the other side."

Taking a deep breath, I conjured Siggo and took off.

The cobblestones bit into my feet. I had the sudden fear one of my toes would slip into a crack and snap, hobbling me, making me scream out and fall to the ground only to be arrested and thrown in a foreign jail. All around people set their coffees down, put aside their newspapers, and watched in confusion as I sprinted across the piazza. Like Siggo said, I puffed out my chest, held my head high, and grinned. If I had to go streaking, might as well do it right.

I slipped into the alley, took a corner, and stopped to catch my breath. The sun had a harder time filling this corridor and I stuck close to the buildings to stay in shadow. At the end I popped my head out and peered around.

Two *polizia* stood down the street staring into the window of a lingerie shop. The alley continued on the other side.

As soon as their heads were turned, I darted across.

It felt like I'd been naked for hours when I came to a string of clotheslines hung between two buildings. Ducking behind a Smart car, I watched an old woman fill a basket with sheets. She smoked a cigarette, a cell phone wedged between her shoulder and ear. She rattled on and on about something that seemed to piss her off. When the basket was full, she carried it into the building, no doubt to dump its contents and come right back out.

I hurried to the clotheslines. The best I could do was a beige skirt and a white t-shirt two sizes too small. I fought the shirt on, slipped into the skirt, and ran around another corner. Not an ideal uniform for whatever I was doing, but at least I was no longer nude. Italians might appreciate nude statues, but eventually my non-marbled self would have drawn attention.

Sticking to the alleys, I picked up a thick layer of grime and broken glass with the bottoms of my bare feet. Eventually I stumbled across a street corner with a kiosk labeled "Tourist Information." Smoothing my hair back, I marched inside.

A young woman sat behind a folding table in the tiny white room. She read a novel and cocked an eyebrow at me when I entered.

"*Americano*?"

"How'd you guess?" I smiled, trying to be charming.

"Map?"

"*Sì*."

She handed me the map.

"*Grazie*," I said.

She went back to her book.

Outside, it took a few minutes to get my bearings. Map in hand, I had to cut through a few streets before I pinpointed where I was and which direction I headed.

"*Bellissima*!" cried a group of men in hard hats smoking around a hole in the road. None of them seemed to be working, just lounging around this hole like they had nothing better to do.

"*Dové vai, ragazza*?" They all bent over laughing.

Seems construction workers are the same no matter where you are.

I ignored them and turned down another street. According to the map I was in Testaccio in the southern-most part of the city.

The Spanish Steps were in the northernmost section.

I stole a few large gulps from a fountain, rinsed my feet, and took off.

***

The sun was high over the city by the time I burst into the Piazza di Spagna. A thousand people milled about the shops lining the Via Condotti, swarmed around the stone dolphins of the Fontana della Barcaccia, and filled the Spanish Steps. I could feel their eyes on me.

I made my way to the fountain, scanning the area for Shelley. A hand rose at the top of the steps, right under the church of Trinitá dei Monti. She slowly waved her arm about as if she were at a concert.

I weaved around the teenagers on the steps, through the couples and over the tourists, before plopping down next to her.

"With only minutes to spare," she said, and thrust a panino into my hands. She wore a giant pair of pink sunglasses, neon green earbuds in each ear.

I inhaled the sandwich and she handed me a bottle of water.

"I like your skirt," she said. "Really brings out your eyes."

"Thanks."

She patted an envelope on the step between us.

"What's this?"

"I was told not to peek."

"Okay."

"The Carny has a strange sense of humor. Get used to it."

I ripped it open. A Post-It note was tucked inside. In a script small and delicate, it read: *Good job! Next to you is the Keats-Shelley House. There's a first printing of John Keats' poetry in there. CONT'D*

I flipped the note over.

Bring it to me.

The C

Shelley leaned over. "What's it say?"

I handed it to her. She scanned over it and frowned before crumpling it into a ball and shoving it into her backpack.

"Great," she said.

"Well?"

"Well, what?"

"You're my guide. What do we do?"

She lowered the sunglasses onto her nose and cut her eyes at me. It was a simple gesture, one filled more with scorn and irritation than anything, but even now when I think of Shelley this is one of the first moments to materialize: the sun beating down overhead, people sprawled out around us, her skin glistening with a hint of sweat, dark hair draped over her shoulders, and those gold-flecked eyes cutting at me.

"The fuck am I supposed to know," she said. "He doesn't tell me shit."

We watched a couple arguing at the foot of the steps. They had to be Italian. The girl slapped the guy across the face. His response was to grab her around the waist and kiss her. She collapsed into him. Only Italians live with that kind of passion. Try to kiss an American woman after she slaps you and you'll lose teeth.

Shelley dug into her bag and handed me a pile of clothes. "Here. Put these on."

"Where am I supposed to change?"

"Go into the church. Use one of the confessionals." She handed me a few coins. "Put these in the donation box and no one will care."

I stood.

"Don't forget your shoes," she said, and handed me a pair of white Nikes.

They were the same pair I had given to Dimitri.

CHAPTER TEN

SHELLEY WAS RIGHT. I dropped a few coins in the box and no one cared as I bumped and shuffled around in the tight confessional.

She'd brought me a pair of gray slacks and a white cotton dress shirt. I felt very slick, very Italian, putting them on. Though I wondered if Italian men went commando.

The white Nikes threw the whole ensemble off.

How had they gotten the shoes from Dimitri?

I suddenly feared I'd been wrong about these people and had stepped into something dangerous. Sleaze-ball that he was, I still hoped the cab driver was okay.

Shelley waited for me by the church doors. I almost asked about Dimitri but thought better of it.

She slipped an arm through mine. "Okay. Here's the deal. We're gonna go into the museum, just a couple of tourists on vacation, and scout it out. Okay?"

We walked down the steps.

"And then what?" I asked.

"I don't know yet. But we'll get an idea once we're inside and see the thing."

She'd taken her earbuds out and they hung over the front of her shirt. "Don't tell the Carny," she said, referencing the device as "Ob-li-dee, Ob-li-da" leaked into the air. "I'll never hear the end of it."

At the bottom of the stairs a small man jumped into my face. "Beautiful flower for beautiful woman?"

"No thanks."

He shoved it into my hand. "Three euro."

"I said I didn't want it." I tried to give it back, but he took a step to the left, held up his hands, and shook his head. "Three euro, *signore*. Don't steal from me, please."

Shelley stepped forward and rattled off a string of Italian so fast and foul that I couldn't even begin to follow. The color drained from his face and he said "*spiace, spiace*" over and over as he backed away.

"Your flower," I said.

"Keep it!" He turned and went after another tourist.

"What was that about?"

"An amateur scam," she said. "These assholes have no sense of art. No pride in their craft."

"What did you say to him?"

"I told him we were with the Carny and if he didn't fuck off right this second, I would sever his baby-maker and feed it to pigs."

"Oh."

The pink brick of the Keats-Shelley House caught the noon sun and reflected it back onto us. It forced my eyes down as we approached the door. I grabbed the handle and opened it for her.

"Oh, your flower."

She grinned and took it. "I knew you were gonna do that."

"Do what?"

"Give me the flower. Very predictable. Very corny."

She snapped the stem off, removed her sunglasses, and placed the flower onto her ear.

"So, every conman knows the Carny?"

She slid her sunglasses back on. "Most have heard of him, yeah."

"And they're all scared of him?"

"Aren't you?"

She slipped inside.

***

"In November of 1820, John Keats was dying of tuberculosis." The tour guide led us into the main room of the museum. "He came to Rome at the urging of friends and doctors who hoped the warmer climate might improve his health."

The room was large, dark wooden shelves lining the walls, the floor a series of white and red tiles. Books filled each shelf amid framed illustrations of Mary Shelley and the house where John Keats grew up.

"The artist Joseph Severin looked after Keats here," the tour guide went on, "until the poet's death in February of 1821." The guide was a middle-aged woman who fought hard to be the very picture of a librarian: gray slacks, brown sweater over a crisp white blouse, hair in a ponytail. All she needed was a pair of thin and malignant glasses. She was American and her voice pure affectation.

"What's this?" Shelley pointed to a framed illustration of several men and a woman standing around a blackened and smoldering pile of wood and ash.

The tour guide glanced over and smiled. "That's a rendering of Percy Shelley's funeral by Fournier. Never a swimmer, he drowned on an ill-fated boat ride. His ashes are interred here in Rome at the Protestant Cemetery."

Shelley leaned in closer, fascinated with the funeral of her namesake.

"Wasn't there something weird about his heart?" I asked, remembering some trivia I'd heard once.

"Oh. That." The tour guide shifted her weight. "As the story goes, Percy's friend Edward Trelawny snatched his heart from the pyre and gave it to Mary Shelley, who kept it in her desk until she died."

"Macabre," Shelley said.

"There were many strange stories about the Shelleys," the tour guide went on. "Percy Shelley used to see his doppelganger quite often. He thought it a portent of his death. Even stranger was the fact that, a few weeks before he did die, a room full of his friends saw it too." She looked at her watch. "Now, if you'll excuse me, I have a call I need to make. Don't hesitate to find me if you have any more questions. I also suggest purchasing the audio tour." She nodded to punctuate how solid the idea was and then left the room.

"Well?" I asked.

Shelley walked around examining the books. "Well what?"

"What do we do now?"

"I don't know. It's your Rite."

"Then what are you here for?"

"In case you botch it."

"Comforting." I scanned the shelves. "How can I tell which one is a first edition?"

"It wouldn't be here. Not on the shelves."

"Where then?"

"Behind glass somewhere." She glanced through the door. "The display cases we passed on the way in."

The cases she referenced were in the previous room which, I might add, was also where the tour guide's desk was.

Stepping into that room, I pretended to admire the wainscoting. It was beautiful, I suppose, if you're into wainscoting.

Artists' renderings of Keats were framed inside the cases next to letters by the poet. On one side was a plaster death mask. I crouched and stared at his closed eyes and the slight smile on his lips as though, in death, he had learned something of which the rest of us are still ignorant.

A white, non-descript book with a tattered and stained binding sat next to the mask. The cover read: *Lamia, Isabella, The Eve of St. Agnes, and Other Poems.* This had to be it. It radiated age.

Shelley admired a portrait of Lord Byron on the wall.

"Pssst."

She continued to examine the portrait.

I looked to the desk. The tour guide leaned over a notepad, scribbling something as she whispered into the phone.

I tried Shelley again. "Pssst!"

She looked over one shoulder, eyes filled with bored irritation.

Pointing at the case, I mouthed, *I think I found it.*

She motioned for me to get on with it.

I couldn't see where the lock on the case was. Not that I'd have known what to do if I saw it. After a minute of searching, I gave up and approached Shelley.

"I can't find the lock."

She didn't say anything.

"What should I do?"

"Figure it out," she said.

"Thanks. You're a lot of help."

She glared at me. "This is the point of the thing, dipshit. You have to prove your cleverness here. You can't do that if I tell you what I would do. But if you come up with something, I can help you execute it."

Trying to think of what James Bond would do, I considered seducing the tour guide for a moment. She looked up as I stared her way. I waved and smiled.

She rolled her eyes and went back to her notes.

So much for that.

Noticing my shoelace had come untied, I bent over to tie it. The lock stared at me like a scarred eye socket from the underside of the case.

Still kneeling: "I found it."

"Found what?" Shelley asked.

"The lock."

"Okay. What are you going to do about it?"

"Pick it."

"Do you know how?"

"I was hoping you did."

"I'm not a cat burglar, you know. Now stand up. You're being weird."

I stood to find the tour guide watching us. I smiled and, lifting my foot, pointed to my laces.

She again rolled her eyes and turned her back to us.

"See if she has something on her desk," Shelley said.

"Like what?"

"Paper clip, knife, I don't know. Maybe the stupid key?"

"Oh. Right."

Taking a deep breath, I sauntered over to the desk.

"Mama, I told you, he just doesn't know how to kiss." The tour guide, back still to me, tapped her pencil on the desk. Her voice was different, the affectation replaced with a child-like timbre. "It's like a gerbil is scrambling around my mouth trying to pick food from my teeth."

I scanned the desk. There weren't any keys. I guess that was too much to hope for.

"Besides, he never wears deodorant. He smells like grilled onions when he sweats."

A box of paper clips sat by her elbow.

"I don't know why I married him. He had a cute accent and spoke three languages. I know, Mama. Of course I should have listened to you, Mama."

I stretched across the desk, hoping to snag a clip without alerting her.

She glanced down at my hand.

"Hold on." She cupped a hand over the phone, clearly annoyed. "Can I help you?"

"Sorry," I said, and snatched a brochure from the desk. "Just curious." The cover read *Nineteenth Century Child-birthing As Told Through Verse*.

If she could have engulfed me in fire by her gaze alone, I would have been ash.

I returned to Shelley and pretended to show her the brochure. "There are paper clips on her desk."

"Told you. Did you get one?"

"No. She caught me."

Closing her eyes, Shelley shook her head and took a deep breath. "You tried to swipe them while she was at the desk?"

"Yeah?"

"Okay, okay. Fine." Shelley handed the brochure back to me. "I'll take care of her. You get the paper clips. Or better yet, search the drawers for the keys."

I felt like a three-year-old who had just peed on the floor.

Shelley walked over to the desk. "I'm sorry. Is there a bathroom?"

"Hold on, Mama. Yes. One floor down. You'll need a key." She came around the desk and handed Shelley a brass key attached to a small board by wire.

"How do we get down again?" Shelley asked, all smiles.

The tour guide motioned around the corner. "Head this way..." She stepped out of sight and Shelley followed.

I rushed over to the desk.

"Through that door and down the stairs."

Opening the top drawer, I saw a letter opener. I snatched it up, closed the drawer, and rushed away to examine a sketch of a dead tree.

The tour guide came back around the corner and eyed me. I thought for sure she knew I'd been at her desk, but she simply picked up the phone and went back to whispering.

I thumbed the letter opener in my pocket, trying to think of how to distract her long enough to get into the case.

Turns out I didn't have to.

"Oh, shit!" Shelley's scream was followed by a series of loud thumps.

"My stars!" The tour guide rushed around the corner.

I hurried over to the case. Jamming the tip of the letter opener into the lock, I twisted it this way and that.

Nothing happened.

Murmured conversation drifted up the stairwell. I didn't know how much time I had and tried harder.

The tip of the letter opener snapped off in the lock.

"You just need to sit," I heard the tour guide say. "I'll call an ambulance." Her voice was getting louder as she came back toward the desk.

Fuck it.

I jammed the broken letter opener into the crease where the glass met the case and jerked upward.

The intent had been to pry it open. Instead, the glass shattered with the sound of a gunshot. A million little specks of twinkling glass covered the floor.

The tour guide came back into the room and froze.

Shelley rounded the corner. "Oh, Donald," she said. "Not again!" She rushed over to me and pulled me to my feet. "You said 'never again,' that's what you said!"

The tour guide rushed to the phone. Her mother squawking incomprehensibly from the earpiece, she hung up and punched the keys. "*Polizia?*"

"I'm sorry," Shelley said as she walked toward the tour guide, motioning me to the book as she passed it. "He was in a boating accident on our honeymoon. Brain damage."

The tour guide scrambled behind the desk. She grabbed a stapler and held in front of her like a knife. "You stay away!"

Not knowing what else to do, I snatched the book up and sprinted past Shelley.

"Hey," she called, and clomped down the narrow staircase behind me.

I was moving so fast I lost my footing on the tiny steps and fell onto my ass. I skidded down several, a dozen bruises already forming on each check, and vaulted back to my feet at the door.

"Copycat!" Shelley yelled behind me.

My hand on the door, the impact of something heavy slammed into my back. I fell into the piazza on my knees, the wind knocked out of me.

The stapler skidded by on the cobblestone.

"Jesus," Shelley yelled back at the tour guide. "You almost took my head off!"

I made a noise like a cartoon donkey while trying to get my breath back.

"Hurry." Shelley looped her arm through mine and tugged me to my feet.

"I. Can't. Breathe." Each word sounding like I said it through a kazoo.

"Breathe later," she said, and jerked me into an alley.

We ran.

***

We caught the H Line and rode it in silence all the way to Trastevere. I'd found my breath somewhere around the Piazza Navona and worried that the stapler had cracked a rib.

Shelley had placed the book in her backpack and held it in her lap, her hands crossed over the top. She stared out the bus's window at the city going by and, once again, I stared at her.

Later, when I read that book of Keats poetry over and over, I stumbled upon a line from "Ode on a Grecian Urn." I felt I'd found some hidden genius. It wasn't until the Carny talked about the poem that I discovered it was Keats' most famous verse. It read:

Beauty is truth, truth beauty, -that is all
Ye know on earth, and all ye need to know

I felt that truth watching Shelley as she was lost in her own thoughts and oblivious to my spying. That's how I always felt around her.

Close to our stop she caught me looking. She sneered and turned back toward the window.

Her reflection in the glass smiled.

CHAPTER ELEVEN

THE BUTCHER SHOP AT the end of Via dei Papiri had been there for twelve generations. Its clientele had included Frederico Fellini, Italo Calvino, and even Mussolini. The locals regarded it as one of the better butcher shops in a city where food was elevated to an art. The elderly owner, Giacomo, maintained a farm in the Lazio countryside. Every morning he would drive into the city before sun-up with a truck filled with the animals he and his wife had killed the night before, or giant hunks of meat that had been hanging in his smokehouse all season.

Giacomo worried that no one would take over the shop when he was dead. I helped him unload the truck one morning and he bought me a *café corretto*, coffee with a shot of liqueur, and told me all about it.

"My son, he is more concerned with chasing the women in Milan and calculating stocks than with family and tradition," he said. The weight of his years dragged down his face.

I felt for him. This was a common problem for Italians, the fight of tradition versus the modern world. I could empathize. In many ways Italy experienced its own kind of national insanity, a cultural Borderline Personality Disorder that wove its way through Florence and Milan and cut a divide between parents and their children.

Giacomo's shop sat atop our small system of catacombs that remained a mystery to the Ministry of Cultural Integrity and the Italian Tourism Board. In the eighteenth century, his ancestors sold the ancient corpses to Resurrectionists. They were little more than brittle bone by then, but those skeletons might still adorn some medical school classroom. The rest of the items, jewelry and pottery and what have you, ended up in the various museums and galleries around Rome. The catacombs sat empty for another two centuries until the Carny and his original crew slicked Giacomo's palm and moved in.

Ten percent of everything we made went to pay the rent on our little hideaway. Giacomo enjoyed the extra money, I'm sure, but seemed to take a greater delight in thumbing his nose at authority. This is a grand Italian tradition, the distrust of government. Italians are a fiercely proud and independent people.

Shelley and I slipped through the butcher shop and into the storage room. We moved a few crates to the side to reveal the door handle, slid Shelley's key in, and made our way down an ancient flight of stone stairs. They wound back and forth, and it was impossible to tell how far below the earth we went. The temperature rapidly dropped and the pressure in my ears changed.

When the Carny saw the book, he burst out laughing and slapped my shoulder.

"You dirty bastard. I didn't think you would do it, but you did." He turned to Shelley. "He did do it, right?"

She held her hands up. "I didn't give him any more help than Ravenna gave me on my Rite."

"Good girl." He gripped my shoulder with a hand that could crush coconuts and pulled me along. "We must celebrate."

We went into the antechamber where we had sung karaoke. Everyone called it the Family Room. Madame Butterfly stood behind the bar.

The Carny stepped over to the bar and, with another magician's flourish, produced my Topamax and Lamictal pill bottles.

"Oh, thank God," I said, thinking I'd earned them back.

He lifted a trashcan and dropped them both in.

Before I could say anything, Madame Butterfly clapped her hands together in excitement.

"Does that mean what I think it does?" she asked.

"Aye aye," the Carny said.

"Excellent." She pulled a bottle of champagne out and popped the cork. It went flying across the room to shatter a lightbulb.

We drank and I relayed the story of how we took the book as the rest of the gang made their way in. Someone turned on the speakers and played Louis Prima from an iPhone. The Carny shook his head at the appearance of the device but didn't say anything.

There was a dozen of us, not counting the Orphans. I won't go into the roll call. Too many names and it would only confuse you. You'll meet each of them in time, one by one, just the way that I got to know them.

We ate and talked and drank, everyone congratulating me and giving me big hugs. Shelley stayed on the other side of the room, talking to anyone but me, and made a point to move if I made my way toward her.

To Hell with her, I thought.

She confused me. It wasn't that she was bitchy, or cold, or that I thought she secretly had a crush on me, or any of the usual misogynies that men concoct about women to feel better about ourselves. There just wasn't any logic to her behavior that I could decipher.

The Carny clapped his hands and the room fell silent.

"Ladies and gentlemen. Misfits, scoundrels, and thieves." He winked at me. "Raise your glasses in welcoming the newest member of our family. I give you…"

Everyone leaned forward, expectant, curious what name I would be given.

"Keats."

Eyes went wide. Someone gasped. Shelley ran a hand through her hair and shook her head.

The Carny ignored them. "John Keats once said, 'I could martyr myself for my religion. Love is my religion. I could die for that.'" He slammed the book into my chest. "This is yours. Get to know it."

It was easy to see by the expressions of the others that the name bore much more weight than simply an association with the object of my Rite. The air in the room changed. Where seconds ago it had been festive, joyous, welcoming, now anxiety and confusion swept through.

The Carny squeezed my shoulder. "Welcome aboard, Keats. Don't stay up too late celebrating. You start training in the morning."

He walked off.

I turned to the others, but they had set their glasses and plates aside and made their way from the Family Room, murmuring to one another and cutting glances back at me.

I stopped Shelley as she was leaving.

"Why is everyone so upset?"

She glared at me, nostrils flaring as she took deep breaths. She closed her eyes and forced herself to calm. The effort was visible.

"Don't worry about it, okay?" she said. "We'll all get over it."

She stormed off down one of the hallways.

***

That night, after everyone else had dozed off, I sneaked back out into the Family Room to dig my pills out of the trash. Only the can had been emptied.

I'd had trash duty as an Orphan and so knew exactly what dumpsters in which alleys we tossed our bags into. I dove into them, one after the other, a desperate urgency growing in my gut.

A *polizia* officer on patrol walked by as I frantically searched my last dumpster. He cleared his throat and I stopped, looking at him wide-eyed and covered in garbage. Here it is, I thought. I'm off to jail.

He handed me a five euro note and said something in Italian. All I could make out was "dinner" and "bath."

Back in the Necropolis, I showered the stench off and tried not to panic. The Carny knew what he was doing. Right?

I wasn't convinced.

Trying to take my mind off it, I reread the entry in my mother's journal about the Keats-Shelley House. It seemed appropriate.

My parents-to-be had coffee at a little trattoria in Trastevere, talking to one another about their families and the plans they had for their futures. She'd only been eighteen at the time and I suspect her future took up more of the conversation than her past. She'd planned on getting a degree in literature and working in Rome. She was a brilliant girl, my mother, though I suppose most people would say something similar. Children mythologize their parents under normal circumstances. In my case, all I had was the mythology.

I have been to that trattoria — it's in the Piazza di Santa Maria — and can imagine her sitting at one of the tables outside, the sun casting her hair in gold as brilliant as the roof of the third-century church behind her. I can imagine the children playing on the huge fountain that dominates the piazza. Writing this now, I can even see the long-legged Italian women gracefully gliding their high-heeled feet across the cobblestones, walking dogs too large for their tiny frames to control if the beasts decided to dash away. I can see the businessmen in thousand-dollar suits discussing mergers over lunch. I can hear the *click-click-click* of cameras snapping photos as tourists wander about.

"I'm a huge fan of the Romantics," she said. "I'd love to do some work at the Keats-Shelley House. After I get my degree. It's one of my favorite places in the city. I can't describe how amazing it is to sit and read *Endymion* in the house where its author died."

My father smiled at that. "Who's your favorite?"

"That's a tough one. If I were forced to pick, and I hate being forced to do anything, I'd probably say Byron."

He nodded, feigning recognition.

"Have you ever read Byron?"

"Honestly? No. Never even heard of him."

"Really? That's a shame." She finished her coffee and set the tiny little cup down on the saucer. "You wanna walk?"

"Sure."

She slipped her hand into his and strolled through the narrow medieval streets of Trastevere. "So, where are you from?"

"Knoxville, Tennessee."

"I thought I recognized the Southern accent in there."

"You a Southern girl?"

"Born and raised."

"What part?"

"The great state of Virginia."

"I'll be damned. How'd you end up in Rome?"

They'd made their way to the Ponte Sisto and climbed onto the white brick of the bridge. She leaned over the side and watched the waters of the Tiber slap against the banks.

"I always wanted to come to Italy. Well, ever since I started reading. Serious books, I mean. Not just *Dick and Jane* stuff. I'd read a little about Italy here and there, and it sounded amazing. But when I started high school, I discovered the Romantic Movement. The way they wrote about Italy, it was like the Garden of Eden really existed, you know? So, I started working odd jobs and saved every penny. Then last summer I got a job at a hotel and it turns out they had a relationship with that dump I'm at on the Via Cavour. I wrote letter after letter after letter until, finally, they gave in and offered me a job, if for no other reason than to shut me up. School let out, I hopped a plane the next day, and here I am."

"Wow. You really go after it, don't you?"

"Daddy always said I was nothing if not determined. What about you?"

"I'm stationed at Camp Darby, up near Pisa."

"A pilot?"

"Nope. Just a jarhead, like my daddy and his daddy before him. Long line of jarheads, my family. There's a small detachment of Uncle Sam's Misguided Children up at the base."

"Are you AWOL?" she grinned.

"On leave. Me and a couple of the guys thought we'd see Italy."

"Where have you been so far?"

"Just here."

"Where do you go next?"

"They're going on to Naples and Sorrento, then down to Sicily before heading back up."

"They are? Not you?"

"Nope."

"Why not?"

"Well, I've only got seven days left. That's seven more coffees I could have with you."

He grinned and she found it far too easy to imagine kissing him. Though she didn't. Instead, she turned her head, gazing into the Tiber, and smiled down at the bridge's ancient foundation.

CHAPTER TWELVE

MARCO ANTONIO PROPPED A foot on the edge of the Trevi Fountain and smoked a cigarette. His tight black t-shirt, wavy dark hair, and aviator sunglasses were more suited to the cover of an Abercrombie catalog than to a thief.

"It is only a small inconvenience," he said to the two American women in front of him. They were pushing fifty and attractive, if a little too done up. They leaned in, hanging on his every word.

I continued to sketch the fountain behind them in charcoal. Only Pollack could have been proud of my work. I am no artist.

"But I would very much like to join *due belle donne* such as yourselves for, how you say, lunch?"

His accent was thick and dripped Italian machismo. I have to say, it was rather good. Marco was, after all, from Australia.

"Oh! Of course," one of the women said.

"We would love to treat you to lunch," the other said. "I had my purse stolen once and it was just horrible. I know what it's like."

"Besides, you've been so wonderful."

He took their hands in his and kissed the backs of them. "*Grazie. Mille grazie.*"

He turned and tossed his cigarette into the fountain. An elderly British man looked up from his guidebook long enough to scowl.

"I know a place *in vicino* is perfect. You will love." He glanced over at me and slid his finger down his nose ala *The Sting*.

The women hooked their arms together and giggled over some private joke as they followed his swagger through the crowd and into the street.

This game was called **JULIET'S BALCONY**. All the cons were referred to as games and each had some pithy name. Marco told me how this game required all the skill and finesse that Romeo used at Juliet's balcony, hence the name. It went like this:

Marco would sprawl out on the steps in front of the fountain, a favorite destination for tourists, especially women. He took on the stereotypical idea of the romantic and sensual Italian male, lazing in the sun and waiting for someone to check him out. Then, when they inevitably whipped out their phones to take a selfie in front of the fountain, he'd walk up and offer to do it for them. Flirts and seductions would follow as he snapped picture after picture. He'd ask the women their names, give his, and tell how he had been waiting at the fountain all day trying to think of what he was going to do now that his wallet had been stolen.

They fell for it every time.

He had run through the particulars of the game again and again that morning, not satisfied until I knew every beat.

"Go over it again," he said.

I rattled off all the details, including the part I'd be playing.

"Good," he said, and stretched out on the fountain.

"What do we do now?"

"Wait." He lit a cigarette. "You do a lot of traveling, Keats?"

"Not until now. I mean, I've been all over the States. And to Canada, but that doesn't really count, does it?"

"Wouldn't know."

"What about you?"

"Been all over the world. Well, except your neck of the woods."

"What's your favorite place?"

"This," he said, and tapped his finger onto the steps.

"This fountain?"

"Italy. No place like it. There's a magic here I never seen anywhere else. Asia has its own temples and beaches, North Africa and Greece its own ruins, but no other place has Italy's people. Its atmosphere."

"How long you been here?"

He took a drag and scratched his chin. "Three years?"

Three years. That was hard to imagine.

"Course," he went on, "I haven't been with the Carny that long. First few months I was here I backpacked up the coast. Came to Sicily from Egypt and made my way north. My original plan was to head into Germany and meet my girlfriend."

"What happened?"

He smudged the cigarette out and stared across the fountain. The tourists were beginning to trickle in. Only the elderly so far, but it was just a matter of time until the fountain was smothered in foreigners.

"I called her from Naples," he said. "She had met some bludger in Munich. Took forever for her to give me the deadset, but the entire time I'd been making my way up from Cairo she'd been, shall we say, familiar with him."

"Sorry, man."

"Me too. The worst part was that it fucked my head six ways to Sydney. My plans went up in smoke. I was wandering around here, laying it to any woman who'd let me stay the night, when the Carny found me. Said he'd been watching me for a while and appreciated my potential. I don't know how that could be true, but you never know with him. Man's got some serious mojo."

Back at the game, Marco turned a corner with the two women. The next part was where I got my feet wet.

They sat at an outdoor café, sipping coffee and waiting for their food. They were at a corner table, the women with their backs to the street, their purses slung onto the ground between their chairs. Marco slipped the sunglasses onto his head, bunching his thick hair up in a close approximation of what I'm sure it looked like after sex, and flashed his best movie star smile. I was across the street and couldn't tell what he said, but he grabbed their hands every now and then and ran his fingers over their palms. The food came and as they all ate the women twirled their hair and touched their necks and let their bodies reveal every sweaty thought in their heads.

After Marco had finished his meal, he dropped his napkin. That was my signal.

I crept up and slid the purses out from behind them. They were so focused on Marco they never noticed. I was halfway down the street before he yelled.

"*Ladro!*"

He jumped the rail and took off after me. The women looked around, confused. I stalled long enough for them to see their purses in my arms before sprinting down an alley. I took a few turns, just enough to make sure they couldn't follow. Marco jogged around the corner and gave me a high-five.

"Brilliant, my man. Good job."

"Thanks." I dumped the purses out onto the ground.

We scrounged through the mess, pulling all their cash out. One of the women had even stowed jewelry in a zippered pocket. I pulled out the rings and held them up. A wedding band and an engagement ring.

Marco laughed. "Oooh, that's rich."

"I guess this means they like you."

"Seems that way."

I stuffed my pockets with the cash and jewelry. This particular scam involved leaving their credit cards in the purses.

"All right," he said, and stood. "Hit me."

"What?"

"Give me a shot to the face. Don't fuck me up or anything. Just enough to get my cheek red."

I stood and cracked my knuckles. "You always do this?"

"Nah. Just came to me." He closed his eyes and steeled himself for my punch.

I took a boxing stance.

"Oh. Wait." He slid the sunglasses onto his face. "Try to break the glasses. That'll be good."

"Okay. Close your eyes, just in case."

"Yeah, yeah. C'mon."

My fist crashed into his eye. The sunglasses crunched and he stumbled back.

"Argh!"

"How was that?"

The glasses hung awkwardly from his face. The right lens had broken and fallen to the ground.

"Fucking Christ! I said not so hard!"

"Sorry. I pulled it."

"You a fighter or something?"

"I boxed when I was younger."

"Now you tell me." He grabbed his shirt and ripped the collar, twisted his clothes around a bit. He bent and rubbed his palm in the dirt of the alley and smudged it onto his face.

He grinned. "How am I looking?"

"Like you just fought a mugger."

"Good. Now give me the purses and take the money back to the fountain. If I'm not there in twenty minutes, then everything worked, and I'll meet you back at the Necropolis. Got it?"

"Got it."

He smacked my shoulder. "Later," he said, grabbing the bags and jogging back around the corner.

When Marco returned with their purses ("I am so sorry, but the thief took the cash before I could catch him"), the two women would treat him as a hero. He would go back to their hotel with them and get his reward. After he got what he really wanted, he would then go into a sob story about how his brother was in jail and his own stolen wallet had the bail money in it.

He never returned to the fountain, so I assume the women bought all of this. The credit cards stayed in their purses so they could take out cash advances to cover the bail money. Marco said that, between the cash in the purses and what he usually got from the bail story, Juliet's Balcony sometimes netted him as much as two thousand euro. If we had just taken the cards they would have been canceled within the hour.

I went back to my charcoal, trying to capture the marble gods of the fountain as afternoon shadows stretched across them. A young woman leaned over the edge and snapped a few pictures. I sketched her as Miranda would have looked, giant sunglasses on her face and a smile stretching from ear to ear. Or that's what it would have been had I any talent for art whatsoever. Instead, she looked like a bug-eyed clown.

My thoughts kept returning to Miranda and I hated it. But that's how it was. When a relationship ends it's like a sunburn. No matter how much you try not to think of it, you can't escape it. Every time you sit or move or brush up against something, it's a constant reminder of the hurt.

"Hey." Shelley slid onto the step next to me and elbowed my ribs.

"Hey hey."

"How's it going?"

"Pretty good. Marco's been gone a while now, so I guess we should have a decent haul."

"Good."

"You coming to check up on me?"

"Yeah. Sort of." She tapped her foot against the stone.

I sat my charcoal down. "What's wrong?"

"Who said anything was wrong?"

"You're tapping your heel."

"So?"

"So, you do that when you're upset."

"How do you know?"

"I pay attention."

She stopped tapping.

"And," I added, "unless I'm mistaken, I'm not your favorite person."

"True."

"So, the fact that you're here to talk to me means?"

She stared off into the distance. "I was just close by and needed some familiarity. I was hoping Marco was here."

"Why is that, by the way?"

"Why is what?"

"That you don't like me."

She exhaled slowly. "It's nothing personal."

"Everything is personal."

"True."

A group of teenage girls giggled arm in arm at the fountain's edge. They each threw a coin in.

"Wonder what they wished for," I said.

"That's not why they throw coins in."

"Why do they do it, then?"

"It's from an old movie, *Three Coins in the Fountain*. Legend is that if you throw a coin into the Trevi then you're guaranteed to return to Rome."

"Does it work?"

"I don't know. I've never left."

"How long have you been here?"

"Almost ten years."

"Since you were, what, fifteen? Seriously?"

"Mmm-hmm."

"How'd that happen?"

She patted my knee and stood. "I should be going. Last big crowd will hit the 64 Bus soon."

"Hey, Shelley."

She stopped and looked down at me.

"If you ever need to talk, about anything at all…"

"Right," she said and laughed in my face. "Because you *so* have your shit together."

Then she hurried off.

I pulled a coin from my pocket and watched it sail into the fountain.

CHAPTER THIRTEEN

THE CARNY TAUGHT ME how to sharpen knives. He loved knives. He played with them while relaxing the way some people whistle, twirling them around and around like fan blades. He'd collected hundreds, even had one he lifted from an antique dealer on the Aventine that belonged to one of Napoleon's corporals. It was given to the officer by the short bastard himself and had an inscription in French on the handle. I never learned French, but Ravenna swore it said: FROM ONE DIRTY FUCK TO ANOTHER. The Carny loved that knife.

I'd sit around the catacombs, ten or twelve blades laid out in front of me, a couple of stones or a strap in hand. I had to keep those things razor-sharp. We made our livelihood from those blades, after all.

I learned a lot about knives from the Carny. I learned where the best metal came from and the ideal depth of the tang. I learned about oiling, and tightening, and how to hide a knife (not to mention how to use one). Most importantly, I learned the Carny's philosophies on the knife.

"A knife," he'd say while spinning one around in his hand, "is like a person. It's fucking useless if it ain't sharp."

Or:

"Thing about a blade is, some of them only got one dangerous edge."

And my favorite:

"Only a dullard thinks of a knife as simply a weapon. There are a thousand uses for a blade and all of them ain't that obvious."

We never took anything by force or threat of force. That was lazy and sloppy as far as the Carny was concerned, something more fit for the freelancers or Lord Byron's boys. We made our living by wit and cunning. That's why I thought it was weird when the Carny grabbed me by the shoulder one morning and said, "C'mon. Time to learn how to fight."

My stomach twisted as I followed him down a hallway and into a large, open room. Below us, water had gathered for two thousand years and the arches overhead were adorned with figures from mythology. It was an ancient cistern and we squared off on a deck overlooking it.

The Carny tossed me a small blade. It slipped out of my hands and clanked across the floor.

"Watch it, mate. Don't want to lose it over the side. The gods alone know how deep that is."

I snatched it up and examined it. The tip was blunted and the edge a quarter of an inch thick.

"Practice blades," he said. "We'll use real ones later, after you've learned the basics."

That first lesson was a whirlwind of technique. We practiced zoning, angling your body along triangular lines to slice your opponent. We riposted and feinted and intercepted attacks like fencers. We danced like boxers, bobbing and weaving — the one area where, thanks to my Golden Gloves training, I could keep up. We did the flowing energy drills of Filipino kali, like *hubad* and *sinawalli*, before moving on to what he called "Defanging the Snake." This was where you see your opponent's strike as an opportunity to destroy the limb. As they attack, you simply flick your blade into their path. So instead of focusing on the face or gut or all the places most people would think to attack, you're cutting open the limb, the hand, the biceps. The Carny told me that, during the Cagayan battles in the 16th century, Filipino guerrillas used the technique to cut the fingers off samurai whenever they swung their swords.

"All it takes is to graze the skin," he said. "Just brush a sharp bugger across flesh and it'll open like your sister's thighs." He danced in a low crouch, the knife swimming in front of him like an erratic salmon.

One thing I found funny about the Carny was how fluid his speech was. He'd go from speaking like an erudite professor to a back-alley pimp, sometimes even in the same sentence. I felt like one of them was an affectation, but for the life of me I couldn't figure out which. For someone who considered themselves a criminal philosopher, they both served his purpose.

After ninety minutes of panting and sweating, red welts covering my arms from every flick of his practice blade, I asked why we even needed to know how to fight.

"It's just," I said, "if we're living by our wits, like you say, I don't see when we'd even need all this."

He lifted his shirt to his neck. A pink scar ran from one nipple down over his abdomen before disappearing into the waist of his jeans. Several other scars, shorter but nastier looking, intersected it at odd angles across his torso.

"Jesus," I muttered.

"I don't think Jesus particularly cares." He dropped the shirt.

"How did you get those?"

"We ain't the only game in town, Keats. Stick with us and eventually you'll run across some pikeys or," he spat, "Byron and his toads. And believe me when I say that, if they could, they'd gut each and every one of us." He tossed the knife into the air, catching it without looking and spinning it around the back of his knuckles. "Too bad they'd have to get through me to do it."

After the lesson on knives, I was sent out with Ravenna. We walked along the Tiber toward the Vatican and I asked her about the Carny.

"He is powerful man," she said. "He has powerful blood."

"What do you mean?"

"His blood so strong, he have no hair."

"I thought he shaved it off?"

She shook her head. "Alopecia."

"What's that?"

"It mean his blood too strong for his hair."

Ravenna was Eastern European, though I could never place from where exactly. She refused to say. Shelley thought she may have been Romani and survived one of the horrible conflicts in the Ukraine or Chechnya. She came to Rome via Ravenna a dozen years ago and, at that time, had spoken no Italian or English. "Ravenna" was the only thing she said that the Carny could understand, and the name stuck.

We cut across the Tiber and she led me to the Campo di Fiori. It was a beautiful piazza filled with farmers, butchers, and flowers. That's what the name means, actually: Field of Flowers. But it was primarily where tourists went to buy produce so they could tell their friends back home they "lived like a local."

"Okay. What's the scam we're running?"

She handed me a sheet of paper.

"What's this?"

"Grocery list," she said.

We spent the next thirty minutes wandering around squeezing tomatoes and discussing how fresh the cheese was. Ravenna and the vendors were all on a first name basis. I tried to follow their rapid-fire Italian, but my brain was left in the dust.

"How long have you been a Misfit?" I asked, trying to figure out how you determine whether an eggplant is fresh or not.

She snatched it from my hand, making a face at the texture before returning it to the display cart. She grabbed another one and handed a few coins to the vendor. Sliding it into her backpack, she strolled along to a stall of spices and herbs.

"The entire time I live here," she said. She tucked a multi-colored tangle of hair behind her ears and examined the garlic.

"What brought you to Rome?"

"Running."

"Like a marathon?"

She looked at me like I was a moron. "No."

Her tone suggested it was best not to pry any further. "How did you meet the Carny?"

"Miss Fagin who I met. Orphans take my backpack and I follow them and steal back. Then she tell me I should meet Carny, only he not call Carny then."

"What was he called?"

She stared at me for a moment and then shook her head. "Not my place to tell." She shuffled around some things in her backpack and tried to fit the garlic, basil, and onions inside. "Damn. Hold this, please."

"Sure." I stuck my hand out, expecting her to give me the eggplant.

She removed a human skull from her pack, gray with age and missing its jawbone.

Ravenna placed the skull in my palm and I froze.

"Two hands!"

"Sorry." I cupped it with my other hand.

"There." She took the skull back and slid it into her bag. "Okay. We need prosciutto." She hurried over to another stall.

Not knowing how one should react when handed a human skull, I opted not to make a thing of it. I'd ask someone else about the skull later.

"Shelley always want best prosciutto," she said. "And Madame Butterfly best *Parmigiana-Reggiano*. You must learn these things, yes?"

She haggled with the butcher before walking away with several slices of meat.

"I don't think she likes me," I said while she examined the list.

"Who no like you?"

"Shelley."

"Of course, she no like you. You follow her. No one follow her. She is slippery as a meal."

"An eel."

"What?"

"Slippery as an eel."

She stared at me.

"That's the expression."

"That is stupid expression." She shrugged. "Shelley is one who is, eh, how you say, pleased that no one find her ever."

"Did she run from something, too?"

Ravenna looked around and sighed. "She hide."

"What's she hiding from?"

"A man," she said, and walked to the next stall.

***

I learned about the skull from Madame Butterfly a week later. Everyone else was out and she'd caught a cold. I made her chicken noodle soup from a recipe Miss Fagin had given me and brought it to her in bed. It was the first time I'd been in her room and it reminded me more of a Venetian palazzo than a catacomb. The walls had been painted with trees and greenery. Peacock feathers abounded. The bed draped in red curtains.

She made a show of coughing as I entered. Sitting up against the headboard, she shook her head.

"Keatsy. You're the only one who cares about me."

"I doubt that."

"It's true," she said, taking the tray from me and positioning it on her lap. She wore a blue silk robe, her wig on the table beside her. "I'm dying and everyone runs off and leaves me."

"You're not dying."

"How can you be so sure?"

"I've seen worse," I said.

She smiled and patted my hand. "You're a sweet man. I could tell that about you from the first moment you came here. That's why I let you see me like this. Without my hair. I haven't even shaved today. Do I have a five o'clock shadow?"

"You look amazing."

She blushed. "You wouldn't tell me if I did, would you? Of course not. You have the soul of a poet."

"That why he named me Keats?"

She looked up at me, something hard flashing over her eyes. Her expression calmed and she smiled. "Must be." She sipped her soup. "This is delicious."

"It's Miss Fagin's recipe. I'm just surprised I didn't fuck it up."

"You curse too much."

"True."

"You and Shelley. And the Carny, of course, but what could possibly be done about him?"

Beautiful, hand-painted posters lined the room, meticulously framed and hung with care. She caught me looking.

"They're originals," she said. "The operas of Giacomo Puccini. I had the damnedest time tracking them down. *La boheme* and *Turandot* in particular."

"They're gorgeous." I pointed to the poster for *Madama Butterfly*.

"Ah. You've found my little secret. My sister took me to see *Madame Butterfly* when I was young. The lights dimmed and when they rose, Cio-Cio-san—Madame Butterfly—glided onto stage with a grace I'd never seen. I hadn't known such beauty existed until then. I went home and told my father how much I wanted to play that part someday. He beat me with a rolled-up magazine for it. 'Boys don't wear dresses,' he said."

"I'm sorry."

"He's dead now and I wear three or four dresses a day, so I suppose it all worked out. Now: how are your studies going?"

"Okay, I guess. I feel so clumsy with everything."

"It will come in time, don't you fret. You should have seen Shelley when she first joined us. As clumsy as the day is long. But look at her now. The girl is an artist."

"That she is," I said.

She cocked an eyebrow. "You like her, don't you?"

"I wouldn't go that far."

"But you do."

Warmth flooded my cheeks. "You know, when I was out shopping with Ravenna, she said Shelley was hiding from a man."

"Oh, honey, I can't tell you about that. Conversations between us girls are private."

"Sorry."

"So. Did Ravenna show you her grandmother?"

"Hmmm?"

"The skull in her bag."

I shivered thinking of how brittle and rough it had felt in my hands. "Yeah. She even asked me to hold it."

"Alas, poor Yorick."

"That's her grandmother?"

"That's what she says. Says it was the only piece of her family she could smuggle out with her."

"Where's she from?"

"She won't say. Somewhere people collect skulls, I suppose. Do they do that in Turkey?"

"I don't think so."

"I was joking."

"Oh."

She sipped more soup and wiped her mouth clean with an embroidered napkin. "It talks to her, you know."

"What does?"

"The skull."

I laughed.

She didn't.

"You're serious?"

"She claims it does. I've never heard it. But then again, there are stranger things at work down here in these catacombs. Still, she says it tells her prophecy."

"Prophecy?"

"Mmm-hmm. Ravenna is the Carny's own personal Oracle."

"Right. And do her prophecies come true?"

She thought about it. "Half the time."

"Really? Fifty percent?"

"Give or take."

I tried not to laugh again and decided to change the subject. "So, what's your con?"

She shook her finger. "A lady does not reveal her secrets."

"I'll have to learn eventually."

"Oh, I doubt that." She slurped down the rest of her soup, wiped her mouth, and handed the tray back to me. "Thank you again. I appreciate both the soup and the conversation."

"Sure."

I stood and walked to the door.

"You know," she said, "she gets turned on by creative types."

"Who?"

"Don't play coy with me, Keatsy. What's your talent?"

"I don't have one."

"Everyone has one. Look to your namesake."

***

Leaving Madame Butterfly's room, I saw the ghost.

A woman in her forties, dark hair pulled back in a ponytail, black dress draping to the ground.

I froze when I caught sight of her gliding down the hall. She didn't even look at me, vacant eyes focused straight ahead and staring at nothing.

As she passed, I shivered.

CHAPTER FOURTEEN

DOSTOEVSKY WAS A VIRTUOSO with his violin. You name it, he could play it. If he heard a tune once, he could instantly reproduce it. It was magical, watching the bow fly across the strings. It was almost enough to forgive him for the tuning forks.

Almost.

That was Dostoevsky's annoying habit. Habit? Compulsion is a better word. He collected tuning forks. We were all collectors, we Misfits. The Carny collected knives and Miss Fagin collected children and I collected guilt.

Dostoevsky was constantly setting his tuning forks off. Constantly. I'd be reading and *DING* an A minor would go off. Or I'd be sleeping and *DING* a C sharp would wake me up.

One night I asked why he set them off repeatedly.

"There are small differences in each one," he said. Dostoevsky's English was smooth, with only a hint of a Russian accent.

"Yeah. Of course, they're different. They're different notes, right?"

"That's not what I mean. Look." He pulled out two of them. "These are both F Major. Yes?"

"Okay."

"But when I play them..." He dinged one and sent it humming. When it died, he dinged another.

They sounded the same to me.

"See?" he asked.

"No, I don't. Sorry."

He stared at the forks, eyes narrowed in thought. "Well. You either have an ear for it or you don't."

Sometimes he'd set them humming and let Tolstoy grab them. I guess he could feel the vibrations shoot up his arm. Probably the closest he ever came to hearing, truth be told. It was sweet, in its own way.

Dostoevsky and Tolstoy were brothers. Or, at least, I had always thought of them that way. They both had Russian names and Dostoevsky was the only one of us who knew sign language, so I just assumed. Come to think of it, they didn't look anything alike. Tolstoy was short and stocky with dark hair while Dostoevsky was tall, thin, and blond. Dostoevsky was handsome in an Ivan Drago sort of way. Tolstoy, however, was not an attractive man. I feel bad saying that because he was deaf, but it's true.

That's silly, isn't it? That I feel bad for saying it because he was deaf, as though having a handicap means you should be brilliant and attractive, or your flaws should be overlooked. And Tolstoy had flaws. He was a pig, for one. Left dirty dishes all over the place, wore shirts dotted with food stains, and usually looked like he didn't wash his hair. But he was a good kid. Always helped me carry groceries or take the trash out and didn't mind manual labor.

They ran a scam together they liked to call **THE MAGIC FLUTE**. It was a bit of a misnomer as Dostoevsky played the violin, but they loved Mozart so much that I didn't give them too much flack for it.

The rules were simple. Dostoevsky would find a space near heavy tourist traffic to set up. He'd throw his case down, open it, and spread a few bills out inside. Then he would play. Sometimes classical music, but often bluegrass or old Romani songs, something fast and energetic. He'd dance around while he played, a giant smile plastered on his face. The crowds that formed around him would be hypnotized watching the show. He was that good.

Tolstoy would then sneak through, weaving his way in and out, almost invisible, emptying every one of their pockets. No one ever noticed him. They were too enraptured by the show. When he'd fleeced the entire assembly, he'd give Dostoevsky the signal. Dostoevsky would then bow and pack up his violin to thunderous applause.

I watched them work one day. They set up shop by the gates to the Forum. Dostoevsky's bow blurred as he played "The Devil Went Down to Georgia." He even sang. I stood on a rise and marveled at how Tolstoy slipped through the crowd unnoticed. It made me think of how viruses spread.

When they were done, we walked to Marius's Amphitheater. Tolstoy counted the money.

"How much?"

Dostoevsky signed my question to Tolstoy. Tolstoy signed back.

"Four hundred and seventy-six euro," he said.

"For one song?"

He grinned. "We usually clear fifteen hundred a day during tourist season."

I whistled.

Tolstoy's hands flew about.

"What'd he say?"

"He says to tell you the time-consuming part is walking around. We try to play each song in different parts of the city so no one figures it out."

"Smart."

"Tolstoy's idea. It's worked out so far."

Tolstoy and Dostoevsky spent much of their free time with Sappho. The three of them liked to go out drinking most every night. Dostoevsky and Tolstoy would try to pick up women and Sappho would act as their wingman. Or vice versa. The three of them joined the Carny's gang about the same time and, like the new kids at school, tended to stick together. To tell you about the Russians, I feel like I should tell you about her.

Ah, Sappho. She was as though a Botticelli painting stepped down from its canvas and threw on Dolce & Gabbana. The word "sexy" doesn't even begin to do her justice. Nor does "beauty" or "grace." There has yet to be a word invented that truly describes how awe-inspiring she was.

There's a saying in Los Angeles popular amongst guys dressed in Affliction t-shirts who wear too much cologne. "An Oklahoma nine is an LA six." Substitute Kansas or Tennessee or any other state in the Union and you get the drift. Well, an LA nine would go apoplectic with jealousy to stand near Sappho. She effortlessly bore a figure that could have been sculpted by Raphael. A neck a swan would be envious of. Heart-shaped face. Pouty lips. Deep blue eyes, sleepy and cat-like, the kind you lose yourself in while talking to her and forget what you were saying. Hair the red of a sunset and crashing over her shoulders like waves rocking through the sea. Again, my words do not do her justice.

It may sound like I had a thing for her, but Sappho, true to her name, was a lesbian. I don't say that like some egomaniacs who would think, "If she won't go out with me, she must be a lesbian." She was legitimately gay. I found this out the hard and embarrassing way men discover most truths about women: by flirting with her. To her credit, she nipped it in the bud on the very first instance and told me she was not into men.

"I'm gay," she said.

"I can make you gayer."

She laughed and we shared a few drinks and commiserated about lost love. I felt I had more in common with Sappho in that department than I did with any of the guys. She'd been in a long-term relationship that also fizzled out. While visiting her hometown she ran into an old friend. What started off as catching up quickly became a fiery and passionate love affair. Her long-term partner found out.

"Let me guess," I said, referencing my own bullshit. "She asked you to move out."

"No." Sappho stared into her drink. "She killed herself."

Sappho knew her infidelity hadn't been the sole cause of that suicide. No one offs themselves strictly because of a breakup. That's usually just the icing on the cake, the final sign from a cold universe that you're not really wanted here, could you pack up your desk and be out by seven? Thanks.

But it had ruined her. She couldn't face this other woman she'd fallen for without feeling guilty for her girlfriend's death. So, she fled to Italy to eat and pray and forget about love. The Carny himself had found her.

"I hadn't been sleeping. I'd stay up all night and drink too much. Let myself just go to shit. All the clichés, you know? Then he came up to me on the Spanish Steps and said he could tell something had broken in me. It was such an odd thing for a stranger to say that I just sat there with my jaw hanging open and listened. He said grief is cyclical, that the things we do because we're grieving end up perpetuating the grief. He brought me back here, taught me how I'd become a slave to my guilt, to eating and drinking, how my screwed-up sleep cycles were killing me. After all that time, he made me confront what had happened. A year later and I was back to my old self. I'll never forget what happened, or my part to play in it. But I won't let it destroy me again. He guided me through all that."

She was absolutely enamored with the Carny. They all were. To hear them talk, he was a messiah who had stepped into their ruined lives and gave them purpose. What had he said to me? He could be my lifesaver. I think he was everyone's lifesaver. How could you not admire someone like that?

This is how cults start.

Lesbian or not, hot women know they are hot. They can never deny it. They're confronted with it every day. Even if they somehow avoid mirrors, they can't go fifteen feet without some asshole gawking or whistling.

Especially in Italy. We'd take walks on slow days and reminisce about the States. Italian men would lean forward and make gestures with their hands, yelling things like "*bellisima*" and "*caramia*" and whatever foul acts they could think of doing with her. She'd just smile and keep walking.

I tried to defend her once, whirling on a group of men outside a nightclub and demanding they keep their mouths shut. One of them stepped forward, all swagger, ready to throw down. Sappho grabbed my shoulder and pulled me away.

"Don't go all caveman for me," she said.

"Yes," Captain Swagger said, a shit-eating grin on his face. "Listen to your bitch, little man. Scurry on."

Without missing a beat, she revealed a little yellow taser and stuck him with it. There was a loud crack and a *PZZZT*. Then he crumpled to the ground twitching.

His friends rushed over to check on him, but Sappho had already walked away. I hurried after her.

"Insult me all you want," she said, "but no one talks to my friends like that."

Sappho's game was called **GOIN' FISHIN'**. All she would do was hang out in a restaurant or bar and wait for someone to hit on her. Like most of the Carny's gang, she had picked up his belief in fate and swore that when someone approached her it was because the gods or the universe or whatever had brought them into her path. Maybe she really believed this. Or maybe it was a way to absolve her of guilt. I don't know.

Sappho would play the flirt, the American who'd gone abroad looking for a summer romance to tell her friends about. At some point in the evening, she'd lean in and whisper something particularly filthy to the man, something to fire all the neurons in his lizard brain and freeze him where he stood. Then she'd head off to the bathroom, snagging his wallet on her way. She'd climb out the window and head to another bar or restaurant to do it again. I could only imagine how much money she made every night. Hell, I knew she wasn't into men and I'd probably let her walk off with my wallet if she tried it on me.

She and the Russians took to me for some reason. I know why she and I clicked, but I'm not sure what Dostoevsky and Tolstoy saw in me. Maybe it was because Sappho and I got along. Sometimes friendship is that simple.

They always invited me out on their little drinking excursions. I didn't go every time, but I went enough to feel like one of them.

It was good, feeling like a part of something again. Not just them, but the entire Necropolis. I wasn't sure how long it had been since I could say I was a part of something.

Too bad it wouldn't last.

CHAPTER FIFTEEN

THEY CALLED IT THE Wallet-Eater.

The name conjured images of some horrid monster from mythology, something Odysseus or Beowulf might have killed. But the Wallet-Eater had never been defeated. There had never been a hero to come along with enough cunning and courage to fell this beast. If you rode the Wallet-Eater, then you signed up to be a victim.

Shelley took me onto the Wallet-Eater the day I had my first run-in with Byron's boys. She called her game of thievery **BUMP AND GRIND**. It was strange to revisit the site of my own victimization. If Dimitri had told me the 64 Bus had such an endearing nickname, I might have thought twice about riding it that day.

We climbed on near the Castel Sant'Angelo and sat in back. Neither of us brought bags or a wallet.

"What are we doing?"

"Just watching," she said.

"Watching what?"

She elbowed me in the ribs, hard, and pointed to the front of the bus. An Italian businessman in a thousand-dollar suit stood.

"Are we going to rob him?"

"Do you ever shut your mouth?"

The businessman bumped into two elderly British women on his way out. He smiled and said, "*Scusi*," and then was off the bus.

"Did you see it?" she asked.

"See what?"

"He slipped their wallets from their purses."

"The guy in the Armani suit?"

"No, Ronald McDonald."

"Wow."

"Yeah. That's Pietro. He's pretty slick. And who would suspect someone in a suit like that?"

"Is he one of us?"

"No. He's a freelancer."

Freelancer is how we referred to the dozens of thieves and conmen who operated in the city but weren't affiliated with any of the larger gangs.

"And he's okay with you operating on here, too?"

"You see how packed this bus is?" She motioned around. "This is how it always is. Every day, nine to sundown. It's the only bus that hits all the major sites. No matter how many guidebooks warn against hopping on it, almost every tourist in Rome rides it at some point. Most do it out of ignorance, but some actually think they're too smart to get their wallet snagged."

"Are they?"

"Those people, the smart ones? They're the easiest pickings."

An old man with a cane hobbled on-board. He smiled at Shelley and winked. She gave a small wave.

"That's Giuseppe," she said. "He's sweet."

"That old man is a freelancer?"

"Yep."

"He looks like someone's grandpa."

"He is. His grandkids are so cute, you'd just die."

"So, do you guys all have some sort of agreement?"

She brushed a piece of hair from her eyes. "It's kind of like a buffet. First come, first serve. Other than slipping the bus driver some cash, there are no rules. We hop on and off all day long. No way any one person could take this entire bus anyway."

An Asian man in glasses and a dark suit stepped on.

"Recognize him?"

I stared at him. Something looked familiar, but I couldn't place him. He caught me staring and locked eyes with me.

"No," I said. "Should I?"

He blew a kiss my way.

"Holy shit. Madame Butterfly?"

Shelly giggled. "Yep."

"So, this is her scam? His scam?" I was suddenly unsure what pronoun I should use.

"*Her* scam. And no. Everybody takes a turn at the bus. I'm on here all the time, but there's always someone else on here, too. Her scam is... Well, it's different."

"Was she on here the day you got me?"

"No. That was Eleanor Rigby."

"I haven't met her."

"And you probably won't. She keeps to herself most of the time."

"Ah. 'All the lonely people.' That where she gets her name?"

"I would guess."

"What's her story?"

"No one knows. She's been with the Carny since the beginning. Usually just glides through the catacombs in her black dress. It's creepy sometimes, especially at night. She'll appear out of nowhere and slide past you, won't say a word, won't even look at you. It's like we're living in a haunted house and she's our resident ghost."

I only felt slightly better about the phantom encounters I'd had at night.

"You know, some of the freelancers," she said, "they used to be Orphans."

It hadn't occurred to me until then that those children Miss Fagin collected eventually grew up.

"They don't stick around?" I asked.

"Some do," she said. "For a while, at least. But you know how it is. When they grow up, they want to move out on their own. The Carny encourages it. Sends them out as freelancers or to other cities. They send a tithe back to the Carny and he has a little network around Italy he can use as needed."

"Sounds like a franchise."

"They're free to come and go. Whenever they get into trouble, they usually crawl back to the catacombs for a while. Byron took a lot of the older kids when he left. They're all adults now. Rattlesnakes, mostly. Rather cut you than pull a con. Those Orphans, they're not welcome back."

We watched the passengers come and go, the freelancers buzzing among them like flies.

Shelley grinned. "Wanna give it a shot?"

"Uh, no."

"Why not?"

"I'm not that slick. There's no way I could slip someone's wallet out without them knowing it."

"You'd be surprised."

"No. I don't think I would be."

"Chicken."

"I'm just saying—"

"*Cluck.*"

"Haha. It's just—"

"*Cluck cluck cluck.*"

We locked eyes, hers daring me to prove myself, mine wishing she'd stop clucking.

"All right," I said. "Who?"

She patted my knee as she glanced around the bus.

"There." She pointed to a chubby American struggling to hold himself upright against one of the rails.

"What do I do?"

"Odds are his wallet's in his back pocket."

"Why?"

"Well, he's American, isn't he?"

"Yeah, but so am I and that's not where my wallet was."

She shook her head. "Look at him. Black tennis shoes, cargo shorts, Titans jersey. It's in his pocket."

"What if it's not?"

"Stop being a baby about this. Just go bump into him. Lock eyes, apologize, and slip his wallet out while he's distracted. Then hop off the bus before he realizes."

"Right." I stood.

She grabbed my hand. "Wait until we get near the next stop."

She tugged me back down into the seat, not letting go of my hand. Tiny electric shocks tickled their way up my arm and into my chest.

"Okay," she said as we neared the Pantheon.

She patted my hand and let go. The air around my palm felt cold without hers there.

The bus rocked as I made my way toward my fellow American. When I was near him, I faked a fall and slammed into his back.

"Watch it," he said.

"Sorry."

My palms were sweaty, and my stomach could have churned butter. I met his eyes and smiled.

"American?" I asked.

"Yeah." He turned away.

I looked back to Shelley. She raised her hands in a gesture that said, "Well, are you gonna do it?"

I sucked a deep breath and shoved my hand into his pocket.

He spun and grabbed my arm. "What the good goddamn?"

"*Ladro,*" someone yelled. It was taken up as a chant around the bus.

Before I knew it, umbrellas and purses crashed down on my head. A fist collided with my stomach. The chubby man and someone else grabbed me by the arms and tossed me around. It was like being caught in a tornado. I spun and spun and had no way of telling which way was up.

We screeched to a stop and a dozen hands shoved me off. Someone hopped off after me, screaming in Italian and kicking me in the ass over and over.

The bus roared away.

I turned to see my assailant.

It was Shelley.

She doubled over laughing, hands on her knees.

"Haha," I said. "Laugh it up, chuckles."

"I'm sorry, but…hold on…gotta catch my breath. Whew! Just, you getting your ass kicked by the entire bus… Oh, man."

A hundred bruises were already forming. "Yeah. That was awesome. Thank you so much."

"Don't mention it." She slipped her arm through mine and pulled me down the street.

"What went wrong?"

"You suck."

"That simple?"

"That simple. But don't worry. A little practice and you'll be fine."

I touched a knot forming on my skull. "I don't know if I can survive much more practice."

She shoved a wallet into my chest.

"What's this?"

"Cargo shorts' wallet. I snagged it while he was whaling on you."

"I was bait?"

"Not intentionally. But, hey, a girl has to use a situation like that to her advantage." She held up a thin, silver camera. "I also got his camera."

I couldn't help but smile. "You're a piece of work."

"I know. A real Michelangelo, right?" She bumped her hip into mine. "I flipped through the wallet. Not a bad haul. Why don't you treat me to lunch before we hop back on the bus?"

***

We ate lunch at a *tavola calda* outside the Piazza Navona. As we did, she gave me pointers and continued making fun of me for getting kicked off the bus.

"What was your first time like?" I asked.

She sipped her coffee. "Better than yours. Well, you've been on the receiving end of my game. That's pretty much how I've always done it."

"By seducing some poor yahoo like me?"

"Exactly."

"Right. Well. On that note… Can I ask you something?"

"As long as you're not afraid of the answer."

I took a deep breath and watched the water crash out from Bernini's *Four Rivers*. We were having a great day together, even with my screwing up on the bus, and I didn't want to ruin things. But I had to ask.

"I thought you hated me," I said.

"That's not a question."

"Well, I just mean—"

She held up a hand. "Listen. I'm weird."

I waited for her to go on, but she just went back to sipping her coffee.

"Weird," I repeated.

"Yeah." She sighed, irritated that she had to explain. "Look, it pissed me off that you followed me that day. Still does. And… Well, I don't like newcomers. Especially some older man who's just trying to get in my pants."

"You know I'm only thirty."

"Sure," she said.

"And I'm not trying to get in your pants."

"Good. You wouldn't fit, anyway. Your hips are too big."

"Since you're being so open, can you I ask something else?"

"Is there any way I could stop you?"

"Why was I named Keats?"

"You really want to know?"

"I'd like to know why that bothers everyone."

"It's not my place to tell."

"Whose is it?"

"The Carny's. So, let's drop it, all right?"

I finished my *arancini* and worked up the nerve to ask what else was on my mind. "What brought you here?"

"What are you, a journalist? Should I just fill out a questionnaire and speed this along?"

"I'm just curious. Jesus. Ravenna said you were hiding from a man."

Shelley's head snapped up, her eyes boring into me. "Oh. She did, did she? What else did she say?"

I could tell by her tone I'd made a mistake. "That was it."

"Hmph."

We sat in silence for a long while.

"I'm sorry," I said. "I didn't mean to pry."

She pursed her lips and brushed her hair from her face. "My father," she said, and stood.

"Your father?"

"Look, Keats. That's all you're gonna get out of me today. All right?"

I held my hands up in surrender.

"Why are you so interested anyway?"

"I don't know," I said. "You remind me of someone."

"Right. And who do I remind you of?"

After paying, we stood and walked down the street, only now there was a wide space between us. I shoved my hands in my pockets.

"You don't actually remind me of her, but…"

"But what? Spit it out, old man."

"You make me feel the way she did."

She snorted. "And how did she make you feel?"

"Wonderful?" I felt stupid for saying it.

She was quiet for a while. Then she backhanded my chest and skipped ahead.

"We need to hurry if we're gonna hop back on the bus today," she said.

I followed after her.

***

The sun was high above the Coliseum as we made our way toward the dense crowds surrounding it. A tour group lined up to have their photographs taken with three large men dressed as gladiators. We hopped up on a rise and sat waiting for the bus.

Shelley pulled out the camera. "Let's see where Cargo Shorts has been today."

She scrolled through the photos, nothing catching her interest.

"Do you ever feel guilty?" I asked.

She furrowed her brow. "Guilty? About what?"

"Taking these people's things. I mean, taking that camera, it's kind of like stealing someone's memories."

"Someone's a Debbie Downer."

"I'm just saying."

"Did you voluntarily pay taxes?"

"What?"

"Taxes. Back in the States. Did you ever sign up to pay taxes? Or did they just take them?"

"They just took them. But that's different."

"How?"

"Well, the taxes went to pave roads and fund schools and provide—"

"Blah blah blah. Listen, your taxes also went to feed the poor. To put clothes on the backs of people who either couldn't work or refused to. It provided medical care for immigrants."

"Who are you, Tucker Carlson?"

"It's not about politics, jackass. It's about the reality of the world. It's about redistribution of wealth. Even the freest societies on this planet require you to distribute a portion of your wealth to the less fortunate. Corporate loopholes notwithstanding. And it's always been that way. Some cultures do it by taxes, others through tithing to a church, what have you. What we do is no different. Maybe a little more Robin Hood than Karl Marx, but it's the same principle. What? Why are you looking at me like that?"

"That was just a lot more than I expected you to say."

She smirked. "Blame the Carny."

"He's Robin Hood in all this, I suppose? Does that make us his Merry Men?"

"He's more like Socrates. The way he sees it is we're taking our tithe, our tax, from the tourists who come here to spoil and commercialize our city. And hopefully, in doing so, we open their eyes to the world."

"You want to make these people jaded?"

"No. We want to shake them up. Transform them. It could be small, like some college kid having to call his parents and apologize for the way he's been treating them, or large, like you joining us."

"Really?"

"Really."

I snorted.

"What?"

"Just sounds like a justification for stealing."

"Hey, grandpa. You don't like it, you don't have to be a part of it."

"Do you believe it?"

"It worked for you, didn't it?"

She had me there.

"Look at this." She passed me the digital camera. On the screen was a zoomed-in image of a well-endowed woman bending over, her cleavage filling the shot.

"That his wife?"

"I doubt it. There's a dozen of these on here, all different women."

I scrolled through the pictures. One zoomed in shot after another of cleavage and women bent over picking up things sped by. The skin tone changed and the colors of tops, but little else.

She laughed. "'Stealing his memories.' You really are something, Keats."

I spun the camera and snapped a picture of her. Her laughing face filled the screen.

Embracing my silliness, I hopped from the rise and dropped to one knee, snapping picture after picture as though I were some runway photographer. Shelley played along, pulling her hair up over her head and making pouty model faces.

I grabbed her hand and yanked her down. She hit the ground and pirouetted. I kept taking pictures, the crowds behind her pointing and smiling at our antics, as Shelley danced around like a child.

"*Scusi.*"

One of the gladiators had left the tourist group and approached us.

Shelley stopped dancing and spat on the ground.

I lowered the camera. "Yeah?"

"You take my picture," he said, his accent thick.

"You want me to take your picture?"

"No," Shelley said. "He's saying you took his picture." She turned to him. "Why don't you just go back over to the rubes, Maximus? We didn't take your picture and we're not falling for it."

"Fifty euro." He folded massive arms across a chest that would have made Arnold jealous.

"What? Are you serious?"

"He's serious," Shelley said. "Keats, meet Maximus."

"Hi."

He nodded. "Fifty euro."

"His game," she went on, "is to overcharge tourists for his picture and demand money from anyone snapping a photograph of the Coliseum that may have gotten him in the frame."

"Ah. I get it." I held up the camera and clicked the review button. "Well, as you can see, no pictures of you, pal. Sorry for the confusion but—"

He smacked the camera from my hand. It skidded across the stone.

"Fifty euro," he said.

Shelley jumped in his face. "We didn't take your goddamned picture and we're not paying you shit."

"You no get in my face, little girl."

"Then get your ass back over to your pals," she said, refusing to back down.

I had worked security at a nightclub in college. The one thing you always had to keep an eye on when tensions mounted was where a guy's friends were. Luckily one of his pals was getting his picture taken with a tour group, his back to us. I didn't see the other one. There had to be more money over there with the crowds, anyway. So why was Maximus wasting time on us?

"Ah," I said as it came to me. "Turf war."

He cocked an eyebrow.

"That's what this is, isn't it? We're in your territory and you've come over here to piss on our legs."

"That's exactly what it is," Shelley said.

His response was, "Fifty euro." He grinned. "I no ask again."

"Good," Shelley said. "Because I'm getting tired of hearing it." She bent and picked up the camera.

"And I take camera," he said.

She laughed. "This camera?"

And then she snapped a picture of him.

He placed a giant palm on her chest and shoved her. She flew back three or four feet and slammed hard onto her ass.

The next few seconds were a blur.

I remember thinking: *Get out of here right now.* But my body acted on its own. My fists fired into his face, his nose and cheek cracking, my knuckles splitting on his teeth. He stumbled backwards, my fists following him. Guy that large, he'd normally wipe the floor with me, but I remembered something my dad had once said: "If you want to win a fight, just hit first and don't stop hitting."

When Maximus crashed to the ground, his friend's paw came from nowhere and collided with my cheek. I spun, confused, as blow after blow hammered the sides of my face. I was so focused on Maximus, I hadn't even seen the other guy approach. Instinct kept my head down as knuckles crashed into my temples and neck. Bruises from the bus blossomed and screamed. Hot iron filled my mouth.

Shelley yelled, "Stop!"

I fell to all fours and spat a mouthful of blood across the cobblestone.

Through white sparks igniting in my blurred vision, I saw Shelly straddling Maximus, a stiletto pressed against his neck. He was still on his back, eyes wide, and a dab of blood trickled down from the tip of her knife.

The newcomer stepped back and put his hands on his hips. He locked eyes with her.

She stared him down, her gaze wild and fierce.

"Keats," she said. "You okay?"

"Yeah."

"Let's go."

I fought to my feet, head ringing like I'd just gone three rounds with a pickup truck. Shelley hurried over to my side, grabbed my arm, and led me up a hill. At the top, she put the knife away.

"You think you can run?" she asked.

"Yeah. Why?"

She spun. "Hey, shitheads!"

They looked up at us.

"Say 'cheese'!" She snapped a picture.

They started up the hill, but we were gone before they crested the top.

CHAPTER SIXTEEN

"THIS HASN'T BEEN A good day for your face." Shelley tossed me an icepack.

"Tell me about it." I didn't know where to start with the thing. I opted for my swelling jaw.

The Carny sat a cup of water down on the bar and three pills. "Take them."

"What are they?"

"Just take them."

I did.

"How many attackers were there?" he asked.

"Two," Shelley said. "Maximus and Spartacus. There was a third there, but he never got involved."

"Fucking twats." The Carny scratched his skull. "You should have stuck them."

"At noon in front of a thousand people?"

"Yeah, yeah." He motioned to me. "You should eat."

"I'm not hungry," I said.

"Eat."

The dwarf appeared as if from nowhere. He wore the same white tuxedo he wore my first night in the Necropolis, but today his beard was braided.

The Carny patted his shoulder. "Mansa Musa, you wouldn't happen to have anything prepared already, would you?"

A grin on his face, Mansa Musa nodded and walked off.

"Mansa Musa?" I asked.

"A king of the Mali people," the Carny said. "Known far and wide for his generosity. You been enjoying the vittles here?"

"Yeah. Everything I've eaten has been great."

"Our Mansa Musa is an excellent chef. He's been so generous in feeding us, he's earned the name three times over."

"He's mute?" I asked.

"No. He just believes one should only speak when they have something to say."

Shelley nudged me. "You could learn something from him."

I moved the ice pack to the pounding pain in my temple. "All right," I said. "So, what was with those assholes today, anyway?"

"Byron's boys," Shelley answered.

They both spat.

"What's the deal with this Byron? You guys have mentioned him before, but what's the static there?"

They shared a look. The Carny nodded.

Shelley pulled out three shot glasses and a bottle of limoncello. "Lord Byron runs the other biggest gang in town." She filled the glasses.

"I figured that." I took one of the drinks. "I mean, why does he got it out for us?"

"Drink first," the Carny said. "But we need a toast."

He and Shelley stared at me, waiting for me to come up with something.

"Um, okay. Let me see…"

"You been reading that Keats book, mate? A fine man to toast with."

"I haven't been memorizing it, I just—"

"Bollocks. It's impossible to read great poetry and not let it seep into your soul. Take a breath, give a search, and let fly."

Something had come to me. I cleared my throat, and we held our glasses high.

"'Give me women, wine, and snuff
Until I cry out "Hold! Enough!"
You may do so sans objection
'Till the day of resurrection
For, bless my beard, they aye shall be
My beloved Trinity.'"

We downed the neon yellow drink. It was chilled, thick and sweet, and we slammed our glasses onto the bar when finished.

"That was perfect, mate." He slapped my shoulder. "Just make sure you live that."

"Live that poem?"

"Yes. That poem is about grabbing life by the testicular region. It's about squeezing every ounce of living that you can out of every moment." He scrunched up his face as though a foul smell just wafted through the room. "Right, so you want to know why Byron's got a hard-on for us, eh?"

"Yeah."

"He used to be one of us. And not just one of us. Byron and I started this little enterprise."

"The two of you?"

"There were three of us then. But yeah. We found these catacombs, decorated, invented some of the games, and recruited other Misfits."

"What happened?"

"It was supposed to be a way of life. We had ideals then. Honor. Dignity. Byron pissed on all that. He had a different take on how to do things. You saw it today. His dogs are monsters. They're not conmen, they're bruisers. They have no class. His way, no lives are changed for the better. His way, the police will be cracking down on us all before we know it."

He walked around the bar, took my head in his hands, and kissed my crown. "And that's all I feel like saying about that." He walked to one of the hallways and stopped. "Good job on walloping Maximus. Always hated that cunt."

He left.

Mansa Musa waddled in and set a tray of fried artichokes on the bar. He gave me the shooter with his index finger and was gone. The smell was intoxicating. I tore into it like a starving mutt.

"You worked up an appetite, huh?" Shelley smiled.

"I guess so."

She took the ice pack and held it to my cheek. "Thank you."

"For what? Getting my ass kicked twice today?"

"For defending me."

"Yeah. Great job I did there."

"It's the thought that counts. Though, I must admit, you did beat the shit out of Maximus. Where'd you learn to fight?"

"I boxed when I was young. I'm surprised I still got it."

"A poet and a fighter." She brushed my hair from my face. "And not bad looking, when you're not covered in bruises."

We shared a smile. As silly as it sounds, the aching from my fight evaporated.

"Why, Shelley. Are you flirting with me?"

She smacked the back of my head. "Don't be an ass. I'm just trying to make you feel better."

Shelley picked up an artichoke and took a bite. A bit fell from her mouth to roll down her jaw. She grabbed a napkin and wiped it clean.

"So," she said. "What brought *you* here?"

"You stole my wallet."

"No. I mean to Rome."

"Now look who's the nosy one."

"Fine. If you don't want to tell me…"

"Women problems," I said. "Other stuff, too. A whole bucket of other stuff, really."

I slid my shot glass over and motioned for more. She refilled our glasses and we clinked them together. "This is great," I said, and slammed mine back.

She downed hers and wiped her mouth. "A friend of the Carny's in Naples ships limoncello up. Made in Sorrento from a hundred-and-fifty-year-old recipe. I think it holds up."

"Definitely."

"So, the other stuff."

"It's silly."

"Everything that comes out of your mouth is silly. Give it."

"Okay, okay. My mother."

"Your mother?"

"I never knew her. She died when I was little. But she'd spent some time here in Rome. She met my father here, actually. All I have of hers is a journal from when she was here and a bracelet that, for some dumb reason, I gave to Miranda."

"Miranda?"

I didn't mean to mention Miranda and waved it off. "Anyway, I found her journal in a box of things and started reading it and got this dumb idea."

"That you'd come here and get to know her?"

"Yeah."

"That's not dumb. It's sweet."

"Anyway, that was my plan. I was going to go to some of the places she wrote about. Kind of see what she saw, I guess."

"And then I stole your wallet."

"And then you stole my wallet."

She tapped a finger against the bar and stared into a corner, her face serious as she worked something out.

"Sunday," she said.

"What?"

"Sunday we'll take the day off and I'll show you all the places she wrote about."

"You don't have to do that."

"I know."

***

In six years of marriage, Chelsea and I talked about my mother once. Few of my friends had ever heard the story. My therapist weaseled it out of me during our first session and then, oddly enough, rarely mentioned it again. I went out of my way in most cases to avoid speaking of it. This contrasted with my father who, if he drank too much, would cry and tell me how I had killed her. Growing up, that fact was always in the air, hanging between us like cigarette smoke in a dive bar.

There was one day where Miranda and I were in bed, pressed against one another, and I told her everything. I don't know what led up to it, but I stared at the ceiling and told how the infection had set in from my birth and my mother fell into a coma, how her lungs gave out, how they hooked her up to machines. I told how my father had been in the room when the machine malfunctioned and pumped too much air into my mother's lungs. He watched as her body swelled and bloated, her lungs burst, and blood was pushed out through her pores by the air pressure.

He was never the same, was never the fun-loving sweetheart my mother had written of. How could he have been? Even during the malpractice trial, it sounded like he'd been a zombie. Her doctors, Dr. Cocksucker and Dr. Dickfuck, as my dad called them, they and their lawyers ran roughshod over the entire family. My mother's parents had been simple folk, neither having even completed the eighth grade, and were made to look at trial like petty buffoons trying to snatch an easy buck where they could. No one had been emotionally equipped for what they were put through, and it ruined them all for life.

Growing up, my father was ever quick to point out how cheap an abortion would have been. Who says that kind of shit to a seven-year-old, anyway? "A hundred bucks would have scraped you out and saved your mama's life." It's no wonder I ended up the way I am.

But still, in those quiet times at night where only my broken brain could keep me company, I couldn't help but think he was right. What would her life have been like had she snuffed me out in the womb? Would she have ended up at the Keats-Shelley House, pursuing her passion?

The only sound in the catacombs was a soft drip of water from somewhere in the hall. It was late and I was certain everyone else was asleep. I sprawled out in bed and counted the cracks.

Those cracks above me shot through a dull picture, faded to nothing with age, of a man and woman holding hands in a field. It was probably painted by some asshole like me two thousand years ago, some miserable shit pining about his woman running off with a chariot racer.

The Roach Boy stood in my doorway. None of the Orphans had names, but that was how I referred to him after his macabre gift. I had to call him something, after all, and the "no names" rule was already driving me crazy. I couldn't imagine how Miss Fagin dealt with it.

"Can't sleep?"

He shook his head.

I patted the bed and he rushed over to hop up next to me.

"Want to hear a story?"

He nodded. I'm assuming he understood English. Miss Fagin often spoke English to the kids, and he seemed to be reacting to what I said.

I dug through the stack of books the Carny had given me. My studies, he called them. It made my head spin. There was poetry by Keats, Shelley, and Byron. There were the histories of Herodotus and Suetonius and *I Will Fight No More Forever*. Treatises by Mary Wollstonecraft and Simone de Beauvoir. Theological studies by Augustine and Thomas Aquinas. The works of Rumi, Al-Khansa, and Imru' al-Qais. The criticisms of Kabir. The collected works of Rabindranath Tagore, Chinua Achebe, and Bessie Head. Shakespeare and Marlowe. Hemingway and Faulkner. Steinbeck. Fitzgerald. There was also *The Anarchist's Cookbook* and *Steal This Book* and volumes of Voltaire.

He'd given me a bookmark alongside the small library. A Bruce Lee quote topped it in a typewriter-like font, both a guideline from the Carny and a command: "Absorb what is useful, reject what is useless, and add what is specifically your own." Every time I looked at the stacks of books around the room, I thought of that quote and it intimidated the hell out of me.

I wasn't sure what to read the boy. I almost pulled out *The Iliad*, thinking that at least had some fantasy and adventure, when I found a kid's book shoved into one pile. Worn and tattered, I wondered if its placement had been intentional. Some lessons, I suppose, are best learned when children, and maybe the Carny intended it for me after all.

I leaned back and read the title page. "*Where the Wild Things Are*, by Maurice Sendak."

The boy cuddled up against me and I read.

***

Miss Fagin woke us in the morning. "Keats?"

"Hmmm?"

"I need the boy."

I sat up and she nudged him awake, hefting him onto her hip and whispering something before sending him down the hall.

"Sorry," I said. "He wandered in here last night, so I read him a story."

She gave a sad nod.

"What's his name?" I asked.

"They don't have names."

"Yeah. Right. Sorry."

She shuffled around my room, looking at the stacks of books. "You need a bookshelf or two, love."

I couldn't disagree there.

Her back to me, she said, "The boy saw his father murdered."

"Oh."

"I think that's why he likes you. You're around the same age."

"What happened?"

She picked up a book and flipped through it. "He was stabbed by a jealous boyfriend. The boy hid in an alley behind their apartment. That's where I found him." She gave me a sad smile. "Just thought you should know."

"We're all just one big tangle of tragedies down here, aren't we?"

"You don't know the half of it," she said, and returned the book to its pile.

CHAPTER SEVENTEEN

TUESDAYS WERE KARAOKE, AS I've said. Wednesdays were movie nights, usually an American classic with Italian subtitles thrown onto the back wall of the Family Room from an aging projector. Thursdays were called "Book Club" because we picked a new novel or collection of poems to discuss while Mansa Musa tested recipes on us. Fridays were what the Carny called "Star Search," and each of us had to demonstrate some talent or skill, preferably something artistic, though Marco Antonio usually performed physical feats like walking around the room in a handstand or push-ups using only his thumbs.

All the activities were designed to make us autodidactic. Part of the Carny's philosophy was what the Greeks called *arête*, a perfection of mind, body, and spirit. *Gnosis* was another ancient word he bandied about, and I do think a part of him was Gnostic, though he professed to be pagan. It was his firm belief that submission to a higher power did not secure one's place in Heaven or offer enlightenment.

"Wisdom," he'd say. "The constant search for knowledge and experience. We were put here to learn everything we could about this world before we move on. There are countless lessons out there. Lord Byron — the real one, not that fucking cunt — said that 'sensation is the only proof we exist; that is why we crave it.' We cannot find enlightenment in a vacuum. We cannot become divine until we've sucked every ounce of juice from this fruit we call life."

He believed in hedonism and passion, but also knowledge and wisdom. These things may seem at odds, but history's greatest and wisest men, as he'd often say, were lustful, gluttonous, and, addicted to one thing or another.

"It was a lust for life, a hunger for sensation and experience, what pushed them. If only they had learned to temper that with self-control, imagine what wonders they would have accomplished."

Up until that Friday, I had observed the talent show without participating. The Carny had said we all had to find our gift, our art, and until we did, he was not going to force us to perform. But he'd always say this with an undertone of "you just better fucking find it before too long." After talking to Madame Butterfly about Shelley, I had decided to try my hand at poetry.

When I was younger, I'd always imagined I would write one day. After moving to Los Angeles, I even had a few articles published, mostly book and movie reviews. But I'd never taken it seriously, never taken the time to learn the craft. Eventually I gave up and settled into more mundane work. Most people came to Los Angeles with purpose, some dream they wanted to fulfill. I never had a grasp on what my purpose was. But when Madame Butterfly nudged me, I wondered: Had I given up too soon?

I devoured the real Keats and the real Shelley and the real Byron and scribbled a few things down. Much of my chicken scratch was dreadful, but there was one poem I liked. I was proud of it and had decided that this Friday would be the night to show it off.

Looking around the room, I hoped Madame Butterfly would be present, but there was no sight of her. I assumed it had something to do with whatever her secret game was.

Everyone cheered as Marco unleashed a series of cartwheels, back-flips, and spins. He finished his routine and bowed. We all applauded.

"Very good," the Carny said. "Your control over your limbs is astonishing. I remember when you routinely smashed your face into the floor. Your hard work has not been in vain, my son. Now. Who's next?" He sat in a giant leather recliner and spun a knife over his knuckles as he watched us.

Ravenna hopped up with an accordion. She pulled her grandmother's skull from her bag and sat it on a table facing her.

"This was song grandmother love very much."

She began playing her tune.

I only half-listened, too focused on my poem. Reading through it over and over, thinking of which words I would emphasize, I grew excited to hear what both the Carny and Shelley would say about it. I'm not sure who I wanted to impress more.

In my head I could already see their reactions. The Carny would stand and applaud, saying something like, "Bloody brilliant, mate," while Shelley would smile and tell me in her own snarky way how beautiful it was.

The longer I had to wait, the more my legs shook. My foot tapped the floor of its own volition.

When Ravenna finished the song, we applauded. She leaned over and whispered something to the skull, held it to her ear as if hearing a response, nodded, and returned to her seat.

"Ravenna, that was both sad and lovely," the Carny said. "I think you lost the rhythm a bit at the end, but it was quite good."

She shrugged. "It is hard song."

He scanned the room. "Well. Anyone else? Is that it for tonight?"

I cleared my throat and stood. "I've got something."

He grinned. "Keats. Popping the old cherry, eh? Very good. I'm glad. Let's see it."

I walked into the spotlight, catching Shelley's eye as I passed. She theatrically cocked one eyebrow to show her surprise.

"Okay," I said once I was in the light. "I, uh, wrote a poem. I guess. I mean, yeah, it's a poem, but... Well. It's called 'Carving Pygmalion.' So, I guess, um, here goes."

I cleared my throat twice more, as though it were a magical ritual to empower my speech. The lights were hot and sweat already dripped down my face. I held the paper I'd scribbled on in front of me and read.

"Skin drapes like sun-warmed silk across my weary chest.

Marble carved, Olympus spies, Gods give art breath.

Hair, soft as air from quickened lungs, plays across my face.

Eyes flash with welcome fire, clouds part for moonlit grace

Hands trace roads long forgotten along a tender map

Memory makes note of every rise, every dip, every gap

My hands unsteady, my voice so frail

I, the Artist, blessed to see what Gods beheld."

I took a breath and waited for my applause.

It never came.

The Carny leaned forward in his chair. "Is that it?"

"Yeah. Yeah, that was the ending."

"Huh."

Water dripped onto metal somewhere, a slow *tink-tink-tink*.

"What's the form, then?" he asked.

"What?"

"What kind of poem is it?"

"Um, a romantic poem?"

He shook his head. "No, I mean, is it a sonnet, or—"

"Oh. Free verse?" I had no clue.

He put his index finger to his lips and leaned back. "I mean, don't get me wrong, there's something there. Vivid imagery. A very strong emotional moment. Passion, eh?"

"Yeah."

"Right. And it was erotic. I got that. And I dig the reference to Greek mythology, of course. But might I make a suggestion?"

"Sure."

"Study form for a while. Write in the different disciplines. Learn the rules. Absorb what is useful. Then you add what is specifically your own. Got it?"

I shuffled off stage. At the back of the room, I sank into my chair and tried to will the shadows to wrap around and cover me so no one could see how red I'm sure my face was.

It didn't work. The shadows stayed where they were, the bastards.

Shelley stared back at me. I examined my heels as they kicked against the chair. When I looked up again, she was still staring. I forced a smile. She grinned and turned back toward the front.

The Carny hopped up from his seat. "Let me give you a great poem, one like what our boy Keats was channeling. The real Lord Byron wrote this one. Ahem.

"'She walks in Beauty, like the night
Of cloudless climes and starry skies;
And all that's best of dark and bright
Meet in her aspect and her eyes;
Thus mellow'd to that tender light
Which Heaven to gaudy day denies.'"

He went on but I tuned him out. I knew "She Walks in Beauty," had memorized it when I came across it. I'm sure I tried to emulate it with my poem but had gone wrong somewhere along the way.

***

Later, while washing dishes with Big Jim, I recited the poem again.

"Yes," he said. "There is something there."

"Uh huh. But?"

"Well, it is, how to say, unrefilled?"

"Unrefined?"

"Yes. Unrefined."

I nodded and scrubbed a wine glass.

"The Carny," he said, "he just want to push you to do best work, to be best. As he say, mastery of a skill masters the soul."

"Yeah, I've heard that. I know he's trying to push us. I just…"

"You what?"

"I was proud of it. I put my heart and soul into that thing. I mean, isn't that what poetry is?"

"Will heart and soul build a house?"

"What?"

"Will heart and soul build houses on its own?"

"No."

"Then why would heart and soul be all you need to write? Houses fall down in forty years. Good poetry lasts centuries, is this right?"

"Yeah. Yeah, you're right." I handed him the glasses I had just scrubbed.

He went to work rinsing them. "There is saying where I am from. 'Talent will make you good, hard work will make you great, and talent added to hard work will make you legend.' You see?"

"I get it. I just need to bust my ass more, right?"

"Yes. Bust asses. And stop writing about vagina stuff."

"Excuse me?"

"You are vagina who write about vagina stuff. I not try to offend you. I only mean you write about women you cannot forget about. This is correct?"

"This is correct."

"Is vagina stuff, yes?"

"I'm not sure that's what you mean to say."

He shrugged.

"You know," he went on, "we have another saying where I am from."

"Yeah? What's that?"

"When a woman leaves a man, he must take his penis out of her." He roared laughter and slapped me on the back.

"Very profound, Big Jim. Very wise."

"You will see, Dickweed. This woman you write about, she is gone." He looked at me very seriously and gripped my shoulder. "Take your penis out of her. Yes?"

"Okay, man. I'll try."

He picked up a plate and rubbed the towel over it. "And please, for the love of all that is right in the world, do not put it anywhere else."

CHAPTER EIGHTEEN

SATURDAY, I SHADOWED RAVENNA for **LOST AND FOUND**. This scam was one of the most deceptively simple of all the Carny's games. It required finesse, fast-talking, charisma, and a small amount of intimidation. The favored targets were tourists who were lost and nervous, didn't speak much Italian, and had too much cash on them.

Ravenna had filled her backpack with old rings. None were worth more than a few euro, pyrite and brass mostly. But when they were cleaned and polished, they looked like gold. We sat on the fountain at the Pantheon and waited. Most of the games consisted of long periods of waiting. I mentioned this to Ravenna, and she just shrugged.

"It doesn't get to you?"

"No," she said. "I practice *l'arte di non fare niente*."

"What is that?"

"It is Italian philosophy. Very essential to be happy."

"What's it translate to?"

She thought for a moment. "The art of doing nothing."

"So, it's just about being lazy?"

"Do not be obese."

"You mean obtuse?"

"Whatever it is, do not be it."

"Okay," I said. "Then what is it?"

"It is about enjoying the fact that there is not a thing happening. It is about finding joy in the sun on your face, or watching the water in this fountain, or a short nap. It no matter. What matter is being not always having to be busy. Being not always having to do something. Being happy in small moments. Yes?"

"Yeah. Yeah, I think I get it."

"Good." She closed her eyes and leaned back on the fountain.

I did the same. "*L'arte di non fare niente.*"

"Yes."

It was difficult to let go like that. The American way of life is so fast-paced, especially in a city like Los Angeles, and to enjoy moments of nothing was not something we were bred to do. I tried to think of what it was like after eating a giant meal, or making love, or laying on the couch on Sundays and watching TV, but even those moments revolved around an activity: eating, sex, entertainment. To enjoy doing nothing was difficult.

After a few minutes on the fountain, the water trickling behind me, the sounds of footsteps on the cobblestones, the sun warming my face, I thought of these apple trees in the side of our yard when I was a kid. I'd go out there on lazy summer days and curl up underneath one. I couldn't have been older than five or six at the time. Probably looking to get away from my father during one of his moods. I'd sit there for what felt like hours, watching beetles crawl around on the ground or birds zip by. I'm sure I thought of things, but I don't know what. I couldn't have had much to occupy my young mind. Afternoons spent doing nothing.

With those childhood memories refreshed, I finally let go. In that moment, I was enlightened.

The philosophers and zealots are wrong, by the way. Enlightenment does not come as a lightning bolt smacking you in the back and charring your soul. Enlightenment, I learned during my time in Italy, comes in small bursts, brief epiphanies that open you up to some new way of thinking. It's not a state of being, as the founders of so many movements would claim to have achieved. It's a state of learning. Enlightenment comes more as a series of doors you find the keys to and, when you pass through them, the hallway on the other side is a little brighter and more colorful than the one you left behind.

Ravenna patted my shoulder. "We have one."

She pointed to a gelateria across the piazza. A young couple stood with both a guidebook and a map out.

"It's like they're advertising," I said.

"They always do."

It was strange to think of them as tourists and myself as a local. I'm not sure when this change had come about, but I felt it. I belonged. They were the interlopers. There was no kinship between us. Even the guilt I had asked Shelley about had faded to a small whisper in the basement of my mind.

We walked toward them and split up. I stood off to one side and pretended to be confused by all the flavors of gelato. Ravenna circled down to the Pantheon before making her way back up. The ancient temple was so massive behind her and the throngs of tourists trying to make their way inside or link hands as they wrapped around the gigantic columns all looked like gnats in comparison.

She'd slipped me one of the rings from her bag and, as she approached, I tossed it onto the ground. It bounced once before landing a few feet from the couple. They didn't notice.

Watching them study their guidebook, I realized why Americans stood out so much here. The Italians practiced many obscure philosophies. *L'arte di non fare niente* was just one. Another was *la bella figura*. To an Italian, dressing sloppy was a cardinal sin. This was a strange concept to Americans, who might think it a shallow one. But in Italy, dressing well is considered polite to the rest of society. Only someone rude and crass would force everyone they dealt with to view them in ball caps and flip-flops.

Americans, of course, dressed for comfort. This couple was a good example. The man's hair was messy and his gray t-shirt a size too big for even his bulky frame. A pair of baggy jean shorts and tennis shoes completed the look. The woman dressed similarly.

"Honey," he said while pointing at the map, "I don't know if we got time." His accent was Southern and reminded me of my father's.

"We got time," she said. "We can get to the Boar-gay-zee and be back for the Vat-ee-kin tour."

"*Scusi,*" Ravenna said.

They looked up.

"Ring?" She pointed to the ring on the ground.

The couple glanced at it and then back at her.

"Ring," she repeated.

The man bent over and picked it up. He held it out to her. "This yours?"

Ravenna smiled. "You like?"

"Yeah," he said. "Nice ring."

"Thirty euro."

He laughed. "Oh, no. That's okay." He tried to hand it to her, but she held her hands up and circled around.

I thought of the amateur at the Spanish Steps that day thrusting his flower into my hand. I had mentioned this to Ravenna when she explained the game to me and asked why he was an amateur and she wasn't.

"First," she had said, "he play for very little money. Three euro? I wipe my ass with three euro. Next, he no use any brains. He just stick flower in your hand. What if you turn and walk away? He out a flower."

The brains, it turned out, fell on me.

"Please," she said, "do not steal my rings. I sell rings to feed my children. Please. Thirty euro."

The man and woman looked to each other, confused.

Ravenna started to cry. I was impressed. Real tears flowed. She could have given Meryl Streep a run for her money.

I stepped in. "What's going on here?"

"They took my ring," Ravenna said.

"Now, just hold up a minute," the man started.

His wife cut him off. "We didn't take a thing. It was on the ground here and my husband picked it up for her. She refuses to take it back."

Ravenna shook her head, tears flying off her cheeks like a sprinkler. "I tell them thirty euro. They no pay."

"You guys don't speak Italian, do you?" I asked.

"No," the man said.

"First time in Rome?"

They both nodded.

"Listen, people do things differently over here. The culture... Well, it doesn't really make any damned sense half the time. This is why Americans have the stereotype of being rude. We just don't understand how they do things."

"My children," Ravenna wept. "*Miei ragazzi.*"

"Look," I went on, "what's thirty euro, huh? Plus, you'll have a nice souvenir and a great story when you get home."

Between me rattling off as much bullshit as I could in one ear and Ravenna wailing in the other, they forked over the money, apologized, and hurried out of the piazza.

Ravenna wiped her eyes. "Back to the fountain."

"How many times do you do this in a day?"

She opened her bag and counted the rings. "I have twenty-three rings."

"And?"

"That how many times we do today."

"Twenty-three?"

"Yes." She climbed back onto the fountain.

Returning to my previous seat, I'd soon fallen back into *l'arte di non fare niente.*

I could get used to this, I thought.

***

Saturday night, the fly came back to visit me.

"The one constant in the universe is chaos," it said as it squirmed its way into my ear. "Nothing will ever go as planned."

I tried to get it out, but it burrowed deeper. I gave up and let it roll its balls.

"Just when things seem their most stable is when everything shifts and the floor drops out from under you."

Since my Rite of Passage, I had visitors most nights while I slept. Chelsea had visited more than once. My father came one night and lectured me on how to fix the wiring in the catacombs. My mother appeared sometimes, but she'd only stand in the shadows and watch me sleep. I could feel her there, but she never said anything, no matter how many times I begged her to.

Siggo came the previous night and congratulated me on streaking.

"You did me proud," he'd said.

I wanted Miranda to come back but, even in my unhinged fantasies, I'd put her through too much for that.

And so, I was left with the fly.

"Psst," it said. "Pssssst."

"What?"

"Psssssssssst."

"I'm listening."

"Pssssssssssssssssssssssst."

"Christ."

"The walls are filled with cracks. They will soon tumble."

I waited for it to go on.

"They always tumble. They tumble and they fall, and you are left trying to build them back into some semblance of structure."

"Okay."

"But every time they fall you lose some bricks."

SECONDO

He who knows little quickly tells it.
-Italian proverb

CHAPTER NINETEEN

SUNDAY MORNING GREETED ME with the smell of fresh java. I rolled over and blinked sleep away. Shelley sat next to my bed.

"Good morning." She handed me a saucer and a shot of coffee. Italians always drank shots of coffee, what we call espresso. To them it's just *café*. They call the way we drink it *café americano*. Every tiny thing was askew there from what I was used to. Frustrating at first, but if you're forced to look at each aspect of life from a different angle for long enough, you'll start to look at yourself from a different angle as well.

"Thanks." I sat up and sipped the coffee.

"You ready to explore?"

"After a shower," I said.

"Oh. Well, you're going to be disappointed then. There was a problem with the hot water heater. Big Jim tried to fix it, but it busted and now the water's out. I had to use bottled water for the coffee."

I wiped my face, and my palm came away greasy. "Great."

She smiled. "I've got an idea, though."

"Yeah?"

"How adventurous are you feeling?"

If Shelley asked if you were feeling adventurous, it was usually not a good thing.

***

Half an hour later I stood in a fountain in Piazza di Santa Maria wearing nothing but swimming trunks and scrubbing my armpits with a bar of soap.

"How did you talk me into this?"

She giggled. "Just hurry."

I finished and crouched into the spray. Older Italians in fine suits and dresses walked by on their way to morning mass.

"*Buon giorno*," Shelley said to a passing group.

I hopped down and she tossed me a towel.

"Is da wittle boy happy now dat he had a baff?"

The towel was rough and the early morning air freezing. "You enjoy torturing me, don't you?"

"More than you'll ever know."

My change of clothes was laid out on the steps of the fountain and I slid into them.

She plopped down next to me. "How long have you been here, now?"

"This morning?"

"In Rome."

"Six weeks? Maybe seven? Why?"

"Just curious."

I sat and tied my shoes. "Curious why?"

"I never got a visa."

"Hmmm?"

"You're only allowed to stay in the Eurozone for three months without a visa. If I ever get busted for anything it'll be much more serious."

"Well, then don't get caught."

"That's the general idea." She kicked her heel against the step. "I can't leave, either."

"What do you mean?"

"Without a visa I'd be arrested at the border."

"Why would you want to leave?"

She jumped up. "Your shoes tied?"

"Yeah."

"So. Where do we go first?"

That was Shelley's way. Hell, not just Shelley. It was all of them. If they didn't feel like talking about something, there was no power on earth that could get them to. I think they picked it up from the Carny. Privacy was especially important to him and anything that was important to the Carny was sacred to the rest of us.

I pulled out my mother's journal. "You sure you want to do this?"

"I'm out here, aren't I?"

"Okay," I said. "The Borghese Gardens."

***

My parents had walked through the gardens, hand in hand, before coming to a small patch of grass amongst the trees. They laid down a blanket and went to work building their sandwiches. After eating, he placed his head in her lap and she read him poetry from an aging blue copy of Byron's works. It was a beautiful book, the edge of each page lined in gold, the date of printing only a few years after the poet's death, and she cherished it more than anything. She wrote about the book a few times, but I've never seen it. Lost somewhere along the way.

They had been seeing each other all summer, my father exchanging favors to sneak a day of leave here and there. She ran her fingers through his hair while reading *Childe Harold's Pilgrimage*. When she'd finished the first canto, she set the book down.

"I'm pregnant," she said.

They were quiet, my father watching the clouds pass overhead, her watching his face.

"I'm pregnant," she repeated.

"I heard."

"And?"

"What do you want to do about it?"

"I thought about getting rid of it. I mean, I'm so young and I've got my career to think about and… I don't know."

He took her hand. "And what if I asked you to marry me?"

"I don't deal in 'what ifs.'"

"Okay." He rolled his head over and stared up into her eyes. "Marry me."

She smiled. "Why not?"

***

We strolled along the paths through the gardens, the trees growing tall and lush at our sides. Every now and then, a marble statue of a god or athlete would make an appearance.

Shelley tucked her hair behind her ears. "I never knew my mother, either. Not really."

I waited for her to continue. The trick with Shelley, I found, was not trying to force her to do anything. You had to give her time to come to it herself.

"She was a drunk," she went on. "She and my father divorced when I was six and she took off. I never saw her again."

We stepped off the path and walked through a cluster of cypress trees.

"Do you know what happened to her?" I asked.

"No. Don't really care. When I was young, I used to think I ran her off. That she hated being a mother. Hated me."

"You don't feel like that anymore?"

"No. She was just a drunken fickle skank. That's what I think now."

"And your father?"

She was quiet for a long time. We climbed back out onto the path and crossed over into a botanical garden. A multicolored array of flowers spread out around us. The trees had been trimmed to allow the light in and, at this hour, the only shadows came from taller flowers and clouds passing in front of the sun.

"He brought me to Rome," she finally said. "He traveled for business all the time and in the summer would drag me with him. We were here in Rome when he…"

She sucked a sharp breath and turned toward the flowers. Her hand found mine.

"He'd started treating me differently as I got older. Acted more like I was his wife than his daughter. Or his property, I guess. We got into a big argument about school and Mom and I don't know what else. He'd always had a temper, but nothing like that day. He'd been drinking and slapped me across the face. Hard. Something in his eyes, it was like a barrier broke. Like he'd always wanted to do this and had been kept from it. Once he started hitting me, he never stopped. I woke up in a hospital, eyes swollen shut. I heard my father telling the police how a group of Moroccans attacked me outside our hotel. They never even bothered to question me."

I didn't know what to say. I squeezed her to my chest. Her arms wrapped around my waist and she leaned her head against me.

"As soon as I could, I sneaked out of the hospital and hit the streets. I did a lot of shit before the Carny found me. Bad shit. I mean, you name it and… and I…"

She began to cry now, her tears hot and wet soaking into my shirt.

We held each other in the gardens while she cried out everything she had. When she finished, we held each other longer.

"I'm sorry," she said.

"Don't be."

"I shouldn't…" She trailed off.

We fit together so well that I felt broken when she pulled away. She looked up at me, eyes wide. Those little flecks of gold on fire.

When our lips met, the sun broke through the clouds and washed over us.

Shelley jerked away. "I'm sorry," she said again, and ran through the garden.

"Shelley!" I sprinted after her.

She lost me somewhere in the park.

CHAPTER TWENTY

RETURNING TO THE NECROPOLIS, I expected to find Shelley in her room. She wasn't. I asked around, but no one had seen her since we left that morning.

Dostoevsky assured me she'd be fine. "She'll turn up. She always does. Be back here before you know it."

I tried to take my mind off the situation by reading. Even then I couldn't help but picture Shelley in the corner of some piazza out there crying. And if I could get that image out of my head for even five seconds, the warmth of her lips pressed against mine came rushing back. It was a no-win situation.

The Carny knocked on my wall a few hours later. "Hey, mate."

"Come on in."

He stepped through the cramped doorway and sat in the tiny chair next to my bed. "I hear you upset Shelley."

"I don't know what happened."

"What did you do?"

I hesitated, not sure if I should tell him about the kiss or not.

"Ah," he said. "I see."

"What?"

He touched the tip of his nose with one finger and pointed at me with the other. "Listen. Don't worry about her. She's a cracker."

"I don't know what that means."

"She's strong. Stronger than most anyone down here. She'll be fine."

"I know. I just…"

"I worry too. But we have to trust one another." He sorted through my stack of books. "You read any of these histories yet?"

"No. Not yet."

"You should. They're quite good. Why don't you make that an assignment, eh? Read about the emperors and how they governed, how they fell apart. I think it may help you." He stood. "Marco talked Mansa Musa into letting him make pizza for dinner tonight."

"Awesome."

"You only say that because you haven't tried his cooking yet. See you in the Family Room later, then?"

"Yeah. Of course."

He started to walk out.

"Hey," I said. "Before you go…"

He turned back to face me.

"Why does it bother everyone so much that I was named Keats?"

He grinned. "Well, because that was my name once. In the beginning."

He left and I wondered what the hell that meant.

***

Shelley returned after dinner.

We were all sprawled around the Family Room, sipping wine while the Carny sharpened knives and lectured us about personal and social responsibility.

"The problem with government," he said, "is us. They do what we should be doing. We should be feeding our own poor. That's our responsibility. But they have to step in because we muck it up time and again. We're more concerned with fancy new cars and flat screen televisions than with taking care of our own. People complain about taxes even as they step over a homeless woman dying in the street. To these people, poverty is a moral defect. You can't have it both ways. Personal responsibility is needed, yeah, but with it comes communal responsibility. We are each responsible for the health of this community.

"Perhaps it's because so many people lay the cause of their unhappiness at someone else's feet. Maybe there's someone out there to blame. Blame poor people. Blame immigrants and 'sexual deviants' and conspiracy theory boogeymen. It's only when we realize the power we have, when we accept that solutions begin within us, that we can truly enact change.

"Look at our underground utopia here. You think we started this because we accepted the status quo? Or blamed others for our ills? Fuck no! We dropped out of all that and created our own society. Our own rules. We took responsibility for ourselves and one another." He pointed a knife at Marco. "Marco, your problems?"

Marco was sprawled out on a couch, the very image of an ancient Roman dinner party. "What problems?"

"The ones what led you here. Whose fault was they?"

He snorted. "My girlfriend."

"Is that so, my son?"

Marco rolled it around a bit. "I mean, yeah, sure, I made some decisions I'm not too proud of. Sure, I did. But hindsight's twenty-twenty, yeah?"

"Indeed, it is. Keats."

I wasn't used to being called on during these speeches and sat up straight. "Yeah?"

"Your divorce. Whose fault was that, eh?"

I knew I was being put on the spot, that this was a test, but I didn't know how to answer. Had it been my fault? We were trucking along perfectly, I thought, when I was diagnosed. When I needed Chelsea the most, she needed a break. Everything with Miranda, that all came later.

"I don't know," I said.

He grimaced. "You have to start taking responsibility for your part in things."

"I do."

"I don't think so. You talk a big game about how you done fucked up, but you still treat it as something that happened to you rather than something you did."

I fought to keep my voice calm. What the hell did he know about my life?

"So," I said, "you're saying nothing that happens to us is ever outside of our control? That we're to blame for everything?"

"No matter what road you go down in the end, all the choices you made brought you there. If you encountered roadblocks along the way, you should have chosen another path. And if you now find yourself at a dead end, the only one who can reverse and take another road is you."

I was trying to formulate a rebuttal when Shelley walked in, her clothes and hair wet. It must have been raining out.

"Shelley," I said, and took a step toward her.

She took one back.

We stared at one other across the now silent room.

Feet shuffled behind me and I knew most of the others had left.

"I'm sorry," I went on. "About today. I didn't mean…"

She raised a hand and cut me off. "I don't want to talk about it." She walked toward her room.

I stepped in front of her. "Shelley."

"I said I don't want to talk about it."

Miss Fagin was having a difficult time wrangling the children. As for the Carny, he pulled his legs up all criss-cross-applesauce and continued sharpening knives. It seemed privacy was only important when it was his.

"You never want to talk about it," I said. "Maybe if you did—"

"Who are you, fucking Freud?"

"I just want to know what's going on."

One of the Orphans giggled and leaped over a chair. Miss Fagin grunted and dove for him. He laughed and ducked behind the bar.

Shelley crossed her arms. "What's going on, what's going on… I'll tell you what's going on. You're trying to use me."

"What are you talking about?"

"I know your type, Keats." She shoved a finger into my chest. "You're hung up on some woman and you think getting between my legs will solve things."

The Carny whistled. I ignored him.

"You're not making any sense," I said though, deep down, I knew she made perfect sense.

"Oh, yeah? Well, who's Miranda, then?"

It took me a moment to understand what she had asked.

She went on. "Is she your wife?"

"I'm not married anymore."

"Was she?"

"No."

"Then who is she, huh? Some poor girl like me you fucked to get through your depression?"

"This is ridiculous, Shelley. I don't know what the hell brought this on, but—"

"You brought this on," she said. "In the park."

I felt something ugly bubbling up inside of me. Something angry and horrible and all too familiar. I tried my damnedest to push it back down.

"I'm sorry, Shelley. I went too far. I didn't mean to—"

"Tell me. You just bounce from one vagina to the next, hoping one of us will make things better?"

"Shelley, listen—"

"You going to fuck me and then take off to India or some shit? Just move on, try to get your head straight?"

"I would never do—"

"Then you can pine over me to get the next piece of ass. Right?"

"Stop interrupting me!" I slammed my fist into a lamp. The shade crumpled and the bulb burst, the stand falling to the floor.

The ugliness rushed up the back of my throat. My mind sank inside of me to take a backseat and watch as the Freak came out to play.

The Freak is what I called that *other* me, that vicious bastard that pretended to be me, that wore my flesh and spoke with my voice, but was something else. This is what it felt like when I had an "episode." It was like being in the audience while a movie played of your life, only now instead of the hero, you were the villain. You didn't even recognize the actor playing you.

I grabbed the broken lamp from the floor and hurled it across the room.

"It's not fair," I yelled for some reason I'm still not sure of.

She shoved me. "Life's not fair, you privileged, self-righteous shit." Her eyes twin balls of fire.

The Carny motioned toward us with a knife. "Wiser words have never been spoken," he said, before going back to sharpening his blades.

The Orphans froze with fear. Miss Fagin was finally able to round them up and herded them down one of the halls.

"Life's not fair," I said. "Life's not fair?" I kicked a sofa, scooting it several feet across the floor. "You don't think I know that?" I flexed and unflexed my fingers. The fly's warning echoed in my ears: *The walls will tumble.*

"You don't know what it's like," I went on, "to have everything snatched away from you because something in your head went sour."

Shelley laughed in my face. "You mean kinda like what you're doing right now?"

"It's all stolen from you because of something beyond your control and you'll never get it back. Just fucking brain chemistry or bad genes or I don't know what the fuck. I didn't choose to be like this! And all this fucking bullshit about personal responsibility and rebirth and adopt what is useful—"

"Shut up!"

Eleanor Rigby appeared, God only knows from where, and rushed across the catacombs. She Spartan kicked me in the chest, and I tumbled back like a bag of trash thrown into the Tiber. She stood over me, lips quivering, tears streaking her face.

"You make me ill," she said, an aristocratic flair in her voice. "You want to know unfair? You want to know out of control brain chemistry? I loved my husband more than anything. And I *murdered* him."

And with that sentence, I was enlightened.

Our problems are relative. What is catastrophic to us is pitiful to someone else. What is devastating to another person is meaningless to us. Here I'd been whining about my broken life and it meant nothing compared to what some of the others had experienced. My tragedies were not the center of gravity here.

Eleanor Rigby snatched one of the Carny's knives and rushed back to me. "I have listened to you babble on and on about how you destroyed your life like a petulant child. You're so sick of your life? Please. Allow me to end it for you." She lunged.

The Carny uncoiled and sprang in between us, gripping her arm and twisting it behind her back. She roared.

"Eleanor. *Eleanor.* Drop. The. Knife."

Her fingers relaxed and it skidded to the floor. The anger drained from her face, leaving sad confusion behind.

She looked down at me, eyes trembling.

"I'm sorry," she said, tears dripping from her chin. "I'm so sorry."

The Carny released his grip and she rushed down one of the halls.

"Gods be damned." The Carny turned to us. "You two think you can keep from wrecking this place for ten minutes?"

It was a rhetorical question. He was gone before we could answer.

I rolled onto my knees to stand. Shelley kicked me in the ass and I skidded back onto my face.

"Don't talk to me like that again," she said. "Ever."

The Freak and I wrestled while I lay there, my newfound enlightenment giving me the edge. It was a small enlightenment, not the kind that would make of me an Aristotle, but it was enough. Even after weeks without my medication, the Freak went back into his cage. He rattled the bars and gnashed his teeth, and I was afraid he might throw the door open at any moment, but I was in control.

For now.

"I'm sorry." I stood and dusted my hands off. "I don't want to be like this. I just… I don't know. I wish I could explain it."

"Yeah," she said, and took a deep breath. "I shouldn't have said what I said, either. I didn't mean it. Not really. I get scared sometimes. Angry. Paranoid, I guess. I'm just a little messed up too, you know?"

"Yeah. I guess we all are."

"I don't want to be with anyone," she said. "Not down here, not after everything. But here I've been, thinking of your dumb ass ever since we sat on the Spanish Steps that day."

"I thought you hated me."

"I do. That's what sucks about it all."

"If it makes you feel any better, I've thought about you since you stole my wallet."

She looked up at me, the fire in her eyes still there but burning a different shade.

I thought of that day on the Steps, too. I thought of the Italian couple arguing. The woman smacked him, and he kissed her. I'd thought only Italians could be that passionate. None of the tourists around them could have mustered that kind of intensity.

I didn't think of myself as a tourist anymore.

Slipping an arm around Shelley's waist, I pulled her to me. Our lips pressed together, tongues dancing, my fingers tangled in her wet hair, her hands digging into my back. The smells of the city in her damp clothes enveloped us, rain and exhaust and flowers and wet linen.

In my bedroom, we fumbled with each other's clothes. We knocked the furniture around. We laughed and fell about the room before collapsing together onto the bed. We made love there in the catacombs. It was awkward and filled with pauses and confusion.

It was not perfect.

But it was right.

CHAPTER TWENTY-ONE

WE LAY IN THE dark, limbs wrapped together, and listened to one another breathe.

After a long silence, Shelley leaned over and lit a candle. She paused on her way back and stared down at me.

"What?" I asked.

Smiling, she kissed me and laid her head on my chest.

I ran my fingers up and down her back. "Good."

"What's good?"

"I thought you might regret this."

"I expected to. But no. I don't." A pause. "Do you?"

"Well…"

She pinched my nipple.

"Ow! I'm kidding."

"You better be, you prick."

Quiet. I watched wax run down the side of the candle and cool in a heap at its base.

"What are you thinking about?" she asked.

"I feel like I should tell you everything."

"What do you mean by everything?"

Next door, one of the Orphans cried. Miss Fagin shushed the child back to sleep.

"What happened to drive me here," I said. "The things I did. Though you won't think much of me after I tell you."

"I don't think much of you now."

I curled her up in my arms and kissed her again. Staring at the two lovers on my ceiling, I took a deep breath and wondered where to start.

Should I start with how I lost my job when I blew up on a client and hit a door so hard it broke free from its hinges? Or maybe the depression that set in after, when Chelsea had given up her burgeoning music career to take an office job because I couldn't pull myself off the couch for weeks. How we did nothing but fight and then didn't even do that anymore.

When Chelsea wanted to go out, I'd create a thousand excuses why we shouldn't. When she was invited to a party, I would claim exhaustion or stress and click through the channels, never landing on anything, never actually desiring any program, simply content with surfing. Should I tell Shelley about that? About how I thought it was all standard, that this is what marriage became?

Or the money problems. I could start there. Breaking my hand on a wall and my Borderline Personality Disorder and the medical debt we incurred because I'd lost my health insurance. My car getting repossessed. How the exorbitant interest of a single payday loan ensured I had to take out another, and another, never getting my head above water again until after the divorce.

Or the graveyard shift work I took out of desperation. That might be a good beginning. Not seeing the sun for a year changes you in profound ways. I knew it had done so to me when I started showing up at the Metro station earlier than my 7:40pm train necessitated, early enough that I could sit on a cool metal bench and stare into the deep black of the tunnel. Early enough that I could watch the trains whip by and think about how easy it would be to walk to the edge of the platform as one came rumbling out of the dark, leaning forward until I fell into the path of its bright light.

Siggo had done that. Maybe I should start with him. Michael Sekowski. Not a train, but he'd made the choice all the same. Siggo was my best friend growing up. As graduation finally approached, we planned to move in together. I wanted to get away from my father so bad, and Siggo had found this apartment in the middle of nowhere. Creepy place, a former hospital, I think, but it was cheap, and I really didn't care about anything else. I mean, I was going to be living with my best friend, right?

Only Siggo's mother found him hanging in his closet the weekend after we graduated. He'd never even seemed depressed. Not Siggo. He was the life of the party. But the note he left said he'd been in a dark place for a long time. He never felt like he could talk to anyone about it. I still wonder what I'd done to make him think he couldn't talk to me.

"I'm broken," he had written, "and this is the only way I know to fix myself."

I could start there.

Or how about with my father, that miserable bastard, calling to tell me stepmother number six was expecting. I was about to be a big brother. His voice was so filled with joy, a joy I'd never heard growing up as he routinely smacked the shit out of me and called me a fairy and told me I murdered my mother. Where was this loving man when I had needed him?

That got to me more than I thought it could.

I was arrested twice. I could begin there. Though that came toward the end. Maybe better to work up to that.

Or Miranda. How that, in the history of the world, there could only have been a handful of women who had a smile such as hers. Helen of Troy. Maybe Cleopatra. Not many more.

It's common for people with my condition to pour their attention into another human being. Shelley wasn't wrong there. It's much easier to tell yourself that the person you're currently with (or the absence of a person) is the cause of your ills and, by simply finding a new love, you can fix what ails you. I never intended to cheat on Chelsea, to fall in love with someone else, yet there it was, as much another symptom as anything.

That's an excuse, and a horrible one at that. I refused to feed Shelley such bullshit.

Therapy, then? My diagnosis? The drugs? How I destroyed what few friendships I had, some with threats of violence? How Chelsea signed us up for couples counseling at the same time Miranda asked me to leave my wife? How I exploded and trashed Miranda's place, threw dishes, put my fist through the wall, and shoved her across the room? How I threw a similar tantrum in Chelsea's car days later, cracking the dashboard and ripping the rearview off?

It was the fear, I think, that bothered me most. That I could make these people I'd laughed with and joked with and loved afraid of me. None of them would ever look at me the same again.

God, there was so much. And that wasn't even getting into the worst of it.

"I don't need to know," Shelley said, and squeezed my hand. "All of that, that was from before. This place, it's a new beginning. The past is dead. Let it stay that way."

I had heard my whole life that the best way to deal with something was to talk about it. Teachers and guidance counselors said so. Chelsea and Miranda and my therapist, they all urged me to talk it out all the time, to spill every dark thing inside of me onto them in the hopes I'd get better.

And now, here was someone telling me to forget it all. To keep my mouth shut and leave it behind. That she didn't care what sins I'd committed, what baggage I carried. She only cared who I was now.

I loved her more in that moment than I ever thought possible.

CHAPTER TWENTY-TWO

I'LL LEAVE THE RASH sentimentality aside for now. The Reader's Digest version of it all: Shelley and I had found something in each other, and we became inseparable. We spent the days performing our various games, sneaking off to have lunch or grope each other in a dressing room somewhere, and our nights cuddled up together. We came together in a way that only two broken people could, and it was glorious.

Los Angeles plagued my thoughts less and less and my troubles seemed to evaporate. Shelley had been right on that account.

But the fly still came to me at night. Chelsea and Miranda and Siggo and my mother had all gone on vacation somewhere, but the fly wouldn't leave me alone. It reminded me that, when the wall fell this last time, there was no way I could have pieced it together into a solid mass again.

"There are bricks missing," it would say. "I just know it."

***

Miss Fagin took the Orphans to the Spanish Steps and let me tag along. Her game was called **SHOCK AND AWE** and was the most chaotic of all the scams. It was also one of the more lucrative.

We sat on the steps and watched the Orphans mill about. They were less like children and more like bees. They would meander lazily around the fountain until called into action. Then they became a frantic swarm.

The Roach Boy balanced on the edge of the fountain, walking its length like a tight rope. He smiled and waved up at us. I gave him a thumbs up.

Miss Fagin unwrapped the sandwiches she'd made that morning.

"Those look good," I said.

"They are. I roast red pepper and layer it with salami, prosciutto, basil, and provolone."

"You're a woman after my own heart."

She wagged a finger. "I'm a bit too old for you, love."

"You're not that much older."

"I'll be fifty-three next month."

"Bullshit."

She smacked me on the mouth. "Watch your tongue."

"Ow!" I rubbed my stinging lips. "Sorry."

"It's true. Fifty-three." She watched the children skip around and play.

"Do you, uh… do you have…"

"Any children of my own? I did. Years and years ago." She handed me a sandwich and raised her own in a toast. "Car accident," she said before I could ask.

"I'm sorry."

"Me too."

The sandwich was as delicious as it sounded. I was lost in the flavor for a moment before she tapped my knee.

"All right, love. Watch and learn."

A pale man in an expensive suit paced around the fountain, sipping a bottle of water. He was probably American or British, in the city for a meeting and using his lunch break to see the sights.

Miss Fagin locked eyes with the Roach Boy and gestured two fingers toward the businessman. The Roach Boy pulled a newspaper from his back pocket and whistled. The other Orphans stopped what they were doing and watched as he skipped over to the mark.

The Roach Boy unfolded the paper and held it up to the businessman. The mark read the headline, trying to figure out what the boy wanted.

As he did, the swarm attacked.

They swept in behind the man and, in seconds, had run off with his wallet, watch, and cell phone.

The Roach Boy lowered the paper and scampered off.

The Orphans were gone down an alley before the man realized what had happened. He yelled, ran one way, then another, before darting down the wrong alley.

"Wow," I said.

"I'm so proud of them. That was even faster than usual."

After enough time had passed for the man to be long gone, they buzzed through the piazza and up the stairs. They handed their spoils to Miss Fagin, who slid them into the folds of her dress. She pulled them all into one giant hug.

"Oh, my darlings. You did so exceptionally good."

Then they were off again, playing around the fountain and waiting for the next victim.

The tourists looked like the ones I saw every other day. Shorts, t-shirts, and ballcaps. Some old, some young. I counted how many pairs of tennis shoes trotted down the street.

A large man stood at the corner of an alley and stared up at us. He looked familiar, but I couldn't quite place him.

Suddenly it hit me. "Shit," I said.

"Keats, if you don't watch your tongue…"

"It's Maximus."

"What?"

"Maximus. One of Byron's boys." I pointed down at him.

When she caught his eye, he smiled and walked off.

She stood and clapped her hands. "All right, children. Time to go."

"We're leaving?"

The Orphans ran up the Steps.

"Yes, we're leaving," she said, huddling them around her. "I'm not the Carny or Big Jim. I can't protect… Oh. No no no."

"What?"

"We're missing one. Where is he, children?"

I scanned their tiny faces. The Roach Boy was not among them.

The kids pointed to the alley that Maximus had ducked down.

I was off the Steps and across the piazza before Miss Fagin had time to yell.

The Roach Boy walked hand in hand down the alley with a tall, thin woman in a red dress.

"Hey," I said, wishing the kid had a name.

He turned and waved. The woman smiled and lifted him onto her hip.

Maximus stepped out in front of me.

"*Buon giorno*, Keats."

"Didn't recognize you without the S&M outfit, Max."

"It's Maximus."

"What are you taking him for, anyway?"

"What is the American expression? To fuck with you?"

"Yeah. That's it."

He popped his knuckles. "I fuck with you now, I think."

He shrugged his jacket off. When it reached his elbows, his arms pinned at his sides, I broke his nose.

Stumbling back, he still fought with the jacket, his arms useless, and I laid punch after punch into his face. He dropped to one knee, face slick with blood. A hard kick to his chest sent him toppling over.

"Maximus, buddy, I hope you're a better lover than you are a fighter."

He coughed and spat blood onto the cobblestones.

The woman mounted a Vespa at the end of the alley. The Roach Boy hopped on behind her and slid his arms around her waist.

My legs pumped hard to reach them, feet pounding the cobblestones in frantic rhythm.

She started the Vespa and turned the handlebars.

I was almost on them—

—when another woman stepped around the corner and head-butted me.

My nose split, a thousand stars exploding in my vision, and I fell backwards. The Vespa roared away down the street.

"Fuck!" I cupped my hands around my nose as blood gushed like an open faucet. "You broke my nose!"

She smiled. It was like looking at a reflection of the woman on the Vespa. Same pale skin, same freckles, same lanky build. The dress was the only difference. Hers was blue.

"What a mouth you got on you," she said, her accent thick like the Carny's.

Then she was gone.

***

The Carny went apeshit.

"Those fucking twats!" He roared and stomped around the Family Room like he was crushing roaches. "This is crossing the line. They bloody well know what happens when they cross the line."

Everyone watched his rampage in awe. Well, everyone except the Orphans. Miss Fagin had herded them off to their room.

Ravenna sat in the corner and whispered to the skull.

The Carny took a deep breath. "Big Jim."

"Yes?"

He grabbed a notepad and scribbled something so furiously the pencil broke in his hands. He growled and grabbed another to finish, then thrust the note into Big Jim's hands.

"And take Keats," he said.

I followed Big Jim up the stairs. The bandages on my nose were beginning to itch.

The Carny's voice floated up after us. "Fuck! Those shit-sucking sons-of-whores!"

"Where are we going?" I asked.

"Bloody cunts!"

Big Jim looked down at me. "Do not worry, Dickweed. We go to roof."

"I'll ass fuck the lot of them!"

We walked from the storeroom in the shop and around the customers waiting in line, down a hall and to another staircase. We took it up to the roof. Giant pigeon cages spread out over the tile, the shade from an apartment building keeping them out of the scorching sun.

"Carrier pigeons?"

Big Jim ignored me and went over to one of the cages. He petted a large gray bird on the head. All the pigeons began cooing.

"Feed them," he said.

A large bag of feed leaned against one of the cages. I took a handful and tossed it onto the floor. The air was filled with fluttering wings as the birds descended.

Big Jim picked up the one he'd petted in both hands. "This one I call Steve Perry."

"Why?"

"He like the songs of Journey."

"Oh."

"He is trained to go to Byron."

A small leather case was attached to the bird's leg. Jim rolled the note up and placed it inside. Then he tossed the bird into the air and it was off, soaring over red roofs and around church bell towers before disappearing into the sun.

"Where do they stay?"

"We do not know. That is one thing the Carny so angry about. They know we are here because Byron used to live here but we not know where they are. Byron send Steve Perry over with a letter one day. I tried to follow the bird once but could not keep track."

He crouched into one of the cages and petted another bird, leaning over and whispering to it. The cages were pristine, only a small amount of bird shit splattered on the floor and down the perches. The birds were healthy and fat. It was easy to see how much Big Jim cared for them.

He checked the water and fed the birds in the other cages.

"Now what?" I asked.

"Now we wait."

***

The response didn't come until the next morning. Big Jim pulled out a boombox that looked like it had been on the roof since nineteen eighty-six and we listened to Parliament-Funkadelic and Curtis Mayfield cassettes to pass the time.

At sundown Shelley brought up bowls of *cacio e pepe* for dinner. She cuddled with me in one corner and we watched the sun sink behind St. Peter's.

Big Jim finished his pasta, smoked a cigar, and then fell asleep. His snores were high-pitched and whistling, not a noise I would expect to come from such a large man.

"What's gonna happen?" I asked.

Shelley pressed closer and tickled the back of my neck. "I don't know. The Carny's pretty pissed off."

"Is there gonna be a gang war?"

She looked up at me and cocked an eyebrow. "A gang war? Really?"

"What?"

"You watched a lot of TV growing up, didn't you?"

I pinched her hip. She squealed and smacked my chest.

"Well, then," I said, "what will happen?"

"Do you think any of us can predict what goes through the Carny's head?"

"Good point."

"All I know is that he and Ravenna snuck off to the Temple to see what her grandmother has to say about it."

"What's the Temple?"

"You haven't been?"

"Man, just when I think I've learned everything…"

"You'll never learn everything, *caramia*. Even if you could, what would be the fun in that?"

I kissed the top of her head. I don't know what she washed her hair with, but it smelled of a hundred exotic flowers.

Something had been nagging at me for quite some time now.

"Do you know what happened to Dimitri?"

"Dimitri?"

"Yeah. The tennis shoes you gave me at the Steps that day."

"What about them?"

"They were mine."

She looked up at me and scrunched the side of her mouth up. It was Shelley's "you're an idiot" face. "What are you talking about?"

"That's how I found you. I gave Dimitri those tennis shoes and he told me you were on the bus almost every day."

Her body went rigid in my arms. "Dimitri told you that?"

"Yeah."

"That piece of shit."

"Where did you get those shoes?"

"The Carny gave them to me."

"And he didn't say anything about Dimitri?"

"No." She took a deep breath. "But he wouldn't have hurt him."

"Has Dimitri texted you since then?"

"He did tell you everything, didn't he?"

"Has he?"

"No. But that doesn't mean anything. He disappeared around this time last year for a few weeks. Met some woman who lived in Sperlonga and spent all his time at the beach."

I wasn't so sure.

"Look," she said, "if it'll make you feel better, we can go down to the airport after this whole mess gets sorted out and you can check up on him. All right?"

"Sure."

"Now shut up and let's enjoy the view." She kissed me and went back to watching the sunset.

It was a beautiful sight. Michelangelo designed St. Peter's to instill the wonder and awe of the divine in anyone who viewed it. The sinking sun glowed orange behind the cupola and shot red veins through the purple sky around it. It was easy to forget my worries and watch, especially with Shelley pressed against me.

The realization that I hadn't been inside the Vatican hit me hard. I ticked off a list of the other sights I hadn't visited. Falling in with the Carny's gang, I became a local so quickly that I never enjoyed being a tourist. When all of this was over, I'd have to remedy that.

"Keats?"

"Yeah?"

"Do you think this will last?"

"Well, the sun has to disappear eventually. But don't worry. It comes back."

"No, you jackass. You and me."

"I'd like to think so."

"Me too."

Sitting there holding her, all I could picture was a wobbling wall.

***

"Dickweed."

Big Jim shook us awake when the pigeon landed. Shelley jumped to her feet, yawned, and stretched. My body had been in a much worse position all night and it was a fight to stand. I rubbed my neck and tried to get the feeling back into my legs.

"We have an answer," Big Jim said.

CHAPTER TWENTY-THREE

"GATHER AROUND, CHILDREN."

The Carny hopped onto a chair and crossed his hands behind his back. Head high and chest puffed out, he could have been General Patton. We crowded around and waited for our marching orders.

"There will be a salon," he said. "Five of them, five of us. We will meet tomorrow at noon in the gymnasium of the Baths of Caracalla. Volunteers?"

Feet shuffled all around me. The anxiety in the air was so thick I almost choked.

"*Audentis fortuna juvat*," the Carny said. "Fortune favors the bold."

What the hell? I stepped forward.

"Keats. That's my man. Who else?"

Shelley joined me with a sigh. "This is a bad idea," she whispered.

"Why?"

She shook her head.

"Shelley," the Carny said. "How fitting."

No one else moved.

"All right," he went on, "if no one else will man up, I nominate Big Jim, for obvious reasons."

Big Jim snorted.

"And Miss Fagin, to explain our case."

Later, while trying to fall asleep, I asked Shelley why no one wanted to go.

"These salons always go wrong."

"Salons?"

"The Carny's archaic term for a meeting. Salons used to be where artists and philosophers came together to discuss their fields. For us they usually involve a lot of arguing, a few bribes, and a bit of blood."

"Oh."

She fell asleep in my arms and I examined that fresco above me again. One of the cracks now ran between the man and woman, separating them.

Had that always been there?

***

The Roman Empire could be divided into two periods. The earlier period, the Principate, was founded by Augustus and at least operated under the pretense that the Republic still stood and the Senate had some kind of power. The Dominate, by contrast, declared the emperor all-powerful. Caracalla came to power during the Dominate. Standing in the ruins of his baths, it was easy to imagine the power he wielded. Even in decay the complex was awe-inspiring. The towers still standing rose as high as most modern office buildings.

As we walked into the gymnasium, I marveled at the frescoes that remained. Roped-off areas of the floor were pieced together by millions of tiny multi-colored squares. Other frescoes on the walls showed sprinters practicing with weights or wrestlers running through drills.

We arrived twenty minutes early, the Carny's idea being to "claim the high ground" and achieve some type of intangible control. It might have worked, too, if they hadn't beaten us there.

They stood against one of the towering red walls. The twins were there, though today they wore blue jeans and matching white t-shirts. One of them held the Roach Boy on her hip. Spartacus was there as well, standing next to a stocky man with a Neanderthal forehead whose name I never learned.

In the middle of them all was Lord Byron. There was no mistaking him. True to his namesake, he wore a long red coat reminiscent of a corsair even though it had to be ninety degrees out. A loose linen shirt was unbuttoned beneath it, his torso covered in pink scars like the ones the Carny bore. Sandy blond hair draped over his shoulders as he leaned his weight onto a jewel-tipped cane.

He bowed as we approached.

"Ladies and gentlemen," he said. "Thank you for coming." He extended a hand.

The Carny took a step forward. They locked eyes and grasped forearms. "Thank you for having us."

Their "thank yous" were said with all the graciousness of snarling dogs.

"It seems," Byron said, "there is an issue we must resolve."

I learned later that the twins were called Janus. The one with the Roach Boy on her hip stepped forward. To avoid confusion, I thought of her as Janus A and the other Janus B.

"Which one of you fucks took my boy?" Janus A said.

We all turned to Miss Fagin. She was quiet, her eyes wide in confusion.

"Wait," the Carny said. "What are you blathering about?"

"Dylan," Janus A said. "He's my son."

"She lies," Miss Fagin said. "He was orphaned. His father was killed in a knife fight."

"I know," Byron said. "I killed him."

The Carny laughed. "Well, ain't this fucked?"

Byron cocked an eyebrow. "As elegantly put as always."

The Carny stared him down.

Byron was the first to turn away. He nodded toward me. "Is this the new Keats, then?"

"Yeah." I hated how weak my voice sounded with the bandages on my nose.

"You have put quite the damper on Maximus's love life, you know."

I couldn't even pretend to be sorry about that.

"Though I hear Spartacus roughed you up rather well. What were you saying about that, Sparty?"

"I fuck him up," Spartacus said.

"Ah. Yes. He 'fuck you up.'"

Shelley snorted. "And then he pissed his pants when I pulled a blade. Didn't you?"

Spartacus glared at her.

She turned away and exchanged a look with Byron. It was brief yet charged and, in that moment, it was painfully evident they'd been close once. How close I wasn't sure. But close.

"All right," the Carny said. "We could measure our pricks all day. Miss Fagin. Is this her son?"

Miss Fagin stared across at the boy. "No," she said.

"You're a fucking liar," Janus A yelled.

The Carny raised a hand, and everyone went quiet. "It appears," he said, "we're at an impasse."

Janus A rushed over to Byron. "She's not stealing my boy."

Byron didn't take his eyes from us as he leaned over and whispered, "We're not even sure that's Dylan."

She held the boy at arm's length and examined him. "He could be," she said.

The boy smiled.

"I mean, don't you think?" She held the boy toward her sister.

Janus B shrugged.

"Third blood?" Byron said.

The Carny smiled. "Third blood."

The two groups backed away from one another to confer.

"What's third blood?" I said.

Big Jim shook his head. "Just what it sounds like."

"Ready to get your feet wet, Keats?" The Carny grinned.

"What are you talking about? What's he talking about, Shelley?"

She kissed me. "Be careful."

"What's going on?"

The Carny handed me a knife. "You'll go to third blood."

"Waitaminute."

"The first to bleed from three wounds," he said, "loses."

"What about first blood?" I stammered. "That's a thing. That's all we need, really. First blood's good. It's solid. That's where Rambo came from. First blood."

Miss Fagin laid a hand on my shoulder. "Thank you."

"Hold on a just a sec, here."

The Carny leaned in close. "It don't always end at third blood, mate, so just be careful."

"What?"

"Don't turn your back on them and you'll be fine." He patted my shoulder. "I have faith in you, Keats."

He walked off.

Janus B stepped forward and glided a knife through the air in front of her with enough grace and speed to make me want to vomit. My stomach pumped so much acid it could have dissolved a corpse.

She grinned. "How's the nose?"

"Been better."

"Looks like it just broke on the bridge."

"Yeah."

"That means it should heal all right. Won't mess up your looks."

"That's good."

"So, I guess I have to fuck up your face now," she said.

I swallowed.

She feinted twice and I jumped back both times. Her footwork was good, quick and smooth, and she danced around me. I'd had about two dozen lessons with the Carny so far, but those had always been with practice blades.

And he'd always kicked my ass.

I gripped the knife so hard my knuckles ached. I tried to remember the different nuggets of advice I'd been given. "Knife fighting ain't boxing," the Carny always said, and most of the advice seemed counter-intuitive to every bit of training or instinct I previously had. Take a deep breath and relax. Shift into a slight crouch and fold in on yourself until you're as compact as possible. Move erratically so your opponent can't match your rhythm. Neither hand, knife or empty, should ever remain still.

A tour group stepped through flashing pictures and speaking German. We hid the knives behind our backs and pretended to examine the frescoes. I'd hoped they'd stick around for a while, but they weren't all that interested in what they saw.

When they left, we resumed our dance. Janus B lunged, flicking the knife at my neck. Reflexes took over and I slipped the attack like we were boxing. She arced the blade and brought it right back down my chest. I wasn't quick enough, and she nicked me, a quarter-sized patch of blood welling up on my shirt.

Her compatriots cheered and she kept the pressure on, the knife swimming in the air in quick Xs as she kept moving into me, pushing me back.

The Carny's voice echoed in my ears from one of our lessons.

Defang the Snake.

My back now against the wall, she came in again, the knife swinging straight at my face.

Darting to the left at the last second, I put my blade in her path and she sliced herself on it. She sucked a sharp breath, her knife clattering to the stone as she jerked her hand back. Blood streaked down the meat of her palm.

Not taking any chances, I shoulder butted her, knocking her back several feet, and kicked her knife out of the way.

"All right," I said. "We're done. Okay? Third blood or not, I disarmed you."

She glared at me as she licked the blood from her hand.

Then she pulled another knife from her waistband.

"Oh, come on!"

She came at me again, this time angling back and forth, the knife no longer moving. I danced around her, my Golden Gloves footwork kicking in, but soon realized it was no good. The space was too tight, and her movement didn't match the kind of rhythm boxers trained for. She faked a stab to one side then shifted, bringing the knife around for my throat. I turned, my blade meeting hers, my free hand on her wrist, our arms all bunched up with her knife glinting right in front of my eye.

I jerked her knife hand down and brought my blade up toward her face, but she slipped the movement and head butted me. Then she stomped on the top of my foot and dragged her knife across my stomach.

Oh God, I thought. She just opened me up.

I shot a knee into the side of her thigh, elbowed her biceps, then planted a foot into her stomach and kicked with everything I had. She flew back several feet, buying me a moment to check on my intestines.

They were still inside of me. Blood slicked the front of my shirt and I'd need stitches when this was over, but I was alive, at least.

For now.

She sprang to her feet and I quickly weighed my advantages. I was stronger and could take a harder blow than she could, but that doesn't do much against the edge of a knife. Everyone's skin opens just as easily, after all. She was quick, but I was quicker. The problem was that she was simply better. More aggressive, more skilled, more confident. Fucking meaner than I was. All she had to do was nick me one more time to win.

And I could tell by the look in her eye the next cut she delivered would be fatal.

We rushed one another.

She lunged and flicked the knife at my face. I angled and parried, my blade grazing her forearm. She recoiled, sucking in breath, blood soaking her arm.

Then she whipped her hand back out to strike me in the jaw with the butt of the knife. It hurt like a bitch and hot blood welled up in my mouth. My instinct was to spit it out, but if I bled once more, she'd win.

So, I swallowed it.

It still stalled me a beat. She took advantage of that to swing wide, this time trying her damnedest to spill my insides. I shuffled back and she followed through, cocking her arm over the other shoulder to backhand slice across my torso.

I laid a right cross into her jaw with my knife hand. My knuckles hit hard, the knife in my grip giving some extra weight to the punch, and she fell onto her ass.

Dazed, she swung wildly in front of her, eyes unable to focus. She tried to stand but her legs had to gone to jelly.

I crouched beside her, careful to stay away from her knife hand. She tried to swing it across her body at me anyway, but it was a slow and sloppy blow. I easily grabbed her wrist and twisted just enough the wrong way for her to grimace and drop the knife.

"Do it then," she said, eyes coming back into focus.

She tilted her head back to offer me her throat.

Everyone watched in silence, waiting to see what I would do.

I raised my knife over her neck.

And poked her nose.

It was just a little poke, not much of a thing at all. She looked at me, confused.

Then a drop of blood welled up on the tip.

"Third blood," the Carny said.

Janus B leaped to her feet, ready to throttle me. But Spartacus grabbed her by the shoulders and pulled her back. She hissed like a feral cat as he ripped a piece of his shirt off to tie her wounds.

The Roach Boy was sent running over to us. Miss Fagin held out her arms for him, but he ran straight to me and jumped up, throwing his hands around my neck.

"Be careful." I laughed and hoisted him. "I'll bleed all over you. "

The Carny took his knife back and wiped the blood on his jeans before slipping it into his jacket. "Good work, mate."

Janus A scratched her scalp. "Maybe it wasn't Dylan after all."

Shelley kissed my cheek and slipped her arm around my waist.

"And that," the Carny said as we backed out of the gymnasium, "concludes today's salon."

"Next time," Byron said.

Janus B stepped forward and thrust a bloody index finger at me. "Watch your arse, Keats!"

Another tour group made their way into the gymnasium and we hurried out before Byron changed his mind.

CHAPTER TWENTY-FOUR

WE CELEBRATED THAT NIGHT like never before. A victory over Byron and his gang, I learned, was always cause for a party. Even Mansa Musa got wasted, stumbling naked through the room and singing Marvin Gaye. He rarely spoke but, boy, could he sing.

Turns out, I did need a few stitches after all. Madame Butterfly rinsed my wounds with grappa and sewed me up. Eighteen in total; six on my chest and a dozen on my stomach. They hurt like a bitch going in. Drinking the rest of the grappa helped.

"You're lucky," the Carny said. "Looks like the cloth bunched up here." He presented my cast-off shirt, pointing to a little distressed spot to the side of the tear Janus B cut in into it. "Kept the attack shallow. Another few millimeters and we'd be dumping your body in the Tiber tonight."

Ravenna tried to teach everyone else a dance from her homeland while Dostoevsky played, but they were too clumsy and too drunk to learn it. She eventually gave up, telling us all we were uncouth pigs better served by digging through slop in a barn than trying to be cultured. We laughed and poured her more wine.

Tolstoy and Marco stood in the center of the room, each three sheets to the wind. They had their shirts off and their hands on their heads. Sappho stood before them.

"Are you sure about this?" she asked.

Tolstoy took several quick, loud breaths.

"Just do it," Marco said.

She tased Marco. *PZZZZZT!* He yelped and hit the ground.

Tolstoy doubled over laughing. Then she tased him and he dropped, too.

Big Jim dragged me to the bar where he poured some clear, foul-smelling liquid into metal containers. Then he lit it on fire. Blue flames danced atop it.

"Wait for it," he said.

"I don't know about this."

"Now!"

He saw whatever cue he'd been waiting on and we quickly downed the drinks. I wasn't sure what burned more, the hairs on my upper lip or my throat when it went down.

Several of the others danced by, Shelley kissing me as she passed.

"You didn't take my advice," Big Jim said.

"What advice?"

He took on a very stern look. "You put it somewhere else."

Sappho grabbed my shoulder just then and pulled me away, saving me from the reprimand.

"Dance with me," she said.

"What about my stitches?"

"If they rip, we'll sew you up again. Come on!"

I was drunk enough that this sounded like an excellent plan.

She played Billy Idol's "Rebel Yell" over the speakers and even the Carny went nuts. Madame Butterfly snatched the microphone up and sang along, a wild rock star in the making.

As the night wore on, the Carny had me tell the story again and again, each time urging me to color and embellish it. By the fifth or sixth time, I was a pro.

"Her knife cut through the air past my face. It whistled as it sliced by, coming so close that it clipped the end of a hair on my eyebrow. I could feel the way she moved, could sense the air vibrate with her intention, and put my blade in her path."

No matter how many times I told it, everyone hooted and hollered and applauded.

After Mansa Musa passed out upside down in a recliner, I went down to our wine cellar, really just a crypt outfitted with shelves, and grabbed a few more bottles. On my way up I saw Eleanor Rigby. She passed in her usual ghostly way.

"I'm sorry," she said.

I thought she was playing out her MO and ignored her.

"I'm sorry I tried to stab you."

I stopped and turned. She stared my way, eyes quivering, and played with the tail of her dress.

"That's okay," I said. "We all have our issues."

She nodded and was gone.

**

When everyone else had passed out, I dragged Shelley to her room. We took one another again and again, then lay head to toe on her bed and talked in slurred words.

"You were amazing today," she said.

I thought she meant the sex. "You're not so bad yourself."

"The way you cut that bitch's arm open!"

"Oh. Yeah." I probed my aching jaw with my tongue. "I think she knocked a tooth loose."

"They'll be gunning for you now."

"It's over. What can they do to me?"

"Just be careful. Byron holds a grudge."

"What's with the two of you, anyway?"

"The two of who?"

I tickled her foot, and she kicked my shoulder.

"You and Byron," I said.

"There's nothing between us."

"There was a look."

"What look?"

"Just a look I saw."

"You jealous?"

"Just curious."

She sat up and looked at me. "When I first came here, right before Byron left the Necropolis..."

"Yeah?"

"We were lovers." She lay back down.

"Lovers?"

No answer.

"Shelley?"

She began to snore.

"Lovers. Hmph."

CHAPTER TWENTY-FIVE

THE VITTORIO EMANUELE MONUMENT was built by Mussolini, his intention being to incorporate the best techniques of the Baroque artists. But, like most despots, Mussolini's design went unchecked. Romans have not appreciated the overindulgence. "The Wedding Cake" and "The Typewriter" were only two of the nicknames for the building; it resembled giant versions of both. Covered in statues and gaudy columns, it looked a little like the rest of the city vomited all its treasures onto this one spot.

The Carny called it "Benito's Tumor."

Big Jim and I crawled over the steps with digital cameras and tried to pass ourselves off as tourists. This wasn't a game he cared much for. He called it **SLOPPY EATER**. Big Jim was not as creative as the others.

The rules were simple. He would buy an "American Dog," as he called it, from a vendor who parked a food truck nearby. These food trucks were all over Rome and I wouldn't have taken a starving dog to one. Unlike the food trucks in Los Angeles known to serve gourmet vittles, these peddled microwave dinners bought from a grocery store and never fully heated. I had a knack for always finding the icy spot in my first bite.

Armed with his hot dog, a food simultaneously exotic and despised in Rome, he would play the part of the tourist. When someone stood close as he snapped his pictures, he'd pull a packet of mustard from his pocket and rip it in such a way that, when he squeezed it onto the hot dog, a little stream would shoot out the side and land on this poor person's clothes.

"Oh, goodness," he'd say. "Very sorry." Then he'd ask them to hold his things while he wiped the mustard clean with a napkin. He'd tell some horribly convoluted story about how strange his day had been and how he wasn't in his right mind. Between his accent and his size, they'd be thoroughly captivated by whatever bullshit he spun.

And, as he wiped the mustard clean, he'd take their wallet.

I'd spent most of the morning trying to perfect his technique for opening the mustard packets. All I had to show for it were a series of yellow stains running down my shirt.

"I can't do this," I said as I marched over to him.

"You have mustard on chin."

"Huh?"

He handed me a napkin. "On chin."

I wiped it off. "How the hell do you do this?"

"Maybe you do not have dexterity in fingers."

"I probably don't."

He scanned my shirt. "You cannot play game with shirt like that. You look like a stinky garbage can. No one believe you."

"Yeah. I figured."

Crossing his arms, he looked around the monument until it came to him. "Come. I teach you different game." He tossed his hot dog in the trash.

Twenty minutes later we exited a bus near one of a hundred Santa Marias. The piazza in front of it held another giant obelisk.

"Where are we going?"

"To see a movie," he said.

We crossed the piazza, moving in a zigzag pattern to avoid the freelancers with their chintzy little flower scam, and bought tickets for a superhero film. Inside the theater I strolled down the aisle.

Big Jim whistled from behind me. "Dickweed. Here." He said it like I was a dog.

I walked back up and plopped into a seat beside him at the back of theater.

"What are we doing?"

"Wait."

Another fifteen minutes passed, and the theater filled with people escaping the heat. The lights dimmed and the projector started.

Once the opening credits had rolled, Big Jim pulled himself from his seat at the pace celestial bodies change course and dropped to his belly.

"What are you doing?" I whispered.

He waved his hand back at me to shut up.

I loved war movies when I was a kid. Everything from *Bridge Over the River Kwai* to *First Blood*. My friends and I used to run out into the woods behind my house and play our own little war games, building forts and setting traps and pretending to mow each other down with broken sticks. Today those woods are gone. Someone came along and thought, "More trees? Don't we have enough of this shit?" and replaced the entire thing with yet another drab, cookie-cutter subdivision. Southerners, it seemed, now demanded to live in houses identical in every aspect to thirty of their neighbors.

Anyway, one of the things I'd always noticed while we played Vietnam or World War II out in those woods (or sometimes Vietnam with Nazis; we were kids, not history professors) was that none of us could manage the army crawl very well. No matter how hard we fought to stay low and move smoothly, our asses would cock in the air like a cat begging to be petted, or we'd crash around destroying any pretense of stealth. It was something I'd assumed at a young age you had to do over and over for a long time to do right.

And here was Big Jim, slithering on his stomach like a snake, not a single soul in the entire theater noticing his massive form on the floor. I'd wager he was ex-military. Whatever country in Africa he'd fled from, he had trained and drilled to be able to move like that.

It made me wonder about that scar on his neck.

He crawled right up to a big, golden purse sitting at an Asian woman's feet. I knew he was going to get busted. This was too ballsy, too risky. There was no way she was not going to see a giant man rifling through her purse.

I was wrong. She didn't so much as glance his way.

He backtracked to our seat and revealed a wad of cash.

"Nice work," I said.

Grinning with pride, he shoved it into his pocket.

"What's this game called?"

He thought for a moment. "I never name it."

"Really? Why?"

"I only do it by myself until now." He ruffled my hair like I was a child. "Why do you not name it?"

"Yeah?"

"Yes."

I scrolled through my mental encyclopedia, trying to come up with the perfect name. "How about **SISKEL & EBERT**?"

"Siskel?"

"And Ebert."

"What is this?"

"Couple of movie critics back in the States when I was a kid."

He scratched his chin. "Very well. Siskel and Eggbert."

"Ebert."

"Yes."

A warm sense of pride bloomed in my chest. I imagined this was how someone felt when they named their first child.

"Your turn," he said.

The fear rinsed the pride away. "No way. I can't do that."

"Why can you not?"

"I can't move like that."

"No. But you will be fine. Go."

Looking around the theater, all I saw were hundreds of dark heads laughing as Italian subtitles scrolled across the bottom of the screen.

"Who?"

He pointed his finger down the aisle. "That one. Red purse."

I didn't move, just sat there staring at her as though I could use the power of my mind to make her to throw her purse at me.

Big Jim slapped a massive hand onto my back, lurching me forward.

"Do not become poultry," he said.

"You mean chicken?"

"Chicken, turkey, duck. Do not be any of them."

Okay, I thought. He's right. I can do this. I can.

Deep breath.

Exhale.

And go.

My chair creaked louder than any chair has ever creaked in the history of creaking chairs. I dropped to all fours and tried to mimic Big Jim's slither. I only had another week for my stitches to be removed, but the movement tugged at them all the same. I ignored it. At least the bandage was off my nose.

The floor was disgusting. Halfway down the aisle I'd already gotten my elbow wet by a spilled drink, had popcorn bits stuck to my shirt, and collected three pieces of gum. At least, I hope it was gum.

A little girl met my eyes while I crawled by. She waved. I winked.

I was directly behind the purse when a skeletal hand thrust down from the seat to dig around inside. It pulled out a small bag of smuggled candy, vanishing again before anyone could see.

Another deep breath. This one I held, afraid that even a small exhale would give me away. I plunged my hand into her bag-

And something bit me.

Yanking my hand back, I clamped down on my tongue to keep from yelling. Blood trickled down a small, silver pin sticking out from beneath my fingernail. I removed the pin, closed it, and pocketed it. Sucking on my finger, as any child will tell you, eased the pain.

Back into the purse. There was more junk in this woman's bag than in Chelsea's closet. I'd almost given up when I felt that familiar crinkle of paper money. I pulled it out, stuffed it into my pocket, and made my way back up the aisle.

The little girl gave me two thumbs up, so I guess I did a good job.

Crawling in reverse wasn't working so well. Eventually I gave up and stood, walking the last several feet back to our aisle. Big Jim shook his head.

"What?"

"Nothing," he said.

I plopped into my seat and pulled the cash out.

"How much?"

"Hold on," I said. I counted it and recounted it. "Shit."

"What?"

"Six euro."

"Six. Euro."

"And a coupon for Starbucks."

He burst out laughing. No one paid attention because the entire audience soon followed suit.

CHAPTER TWENTY-SIX

"BECAUSE I DID THEM last week."

Shelley didn't seem to care. She put her hands on her hips and gave me one of those long-suffering looks of hers. It made me feel like we were a sixty-year-old married couple killing time between visits from the kids.

"Me and Big Jim," I went on, pressing my case, "we did them. So, by my calculations, it should be you and Sappho."

We were discussing the dishes. Everyone in the Necropolis had to take their turn at the various chores. Somehow it seemed Big Jim and I washed up after everyone's meals more than we should have. Probably because neither of us complained about much. Well, Big Jim never complained about much, anyway. A true Stoic, that was Big Jim.

"I'm not doing the dishes," Shelley said. "I dirtied a single wine glass. Look at this pile you and Dostoevsky made."

She pointed to all the pots and plates stacked in the sink, casualties of our experiments in the kitchen that evening. Dostoevsky had developed a taste for Calabrian cuisine lately, while I'd really gotten into Tuscan cooking. They were at opposite ends of the spectrum and, while the average American might call them both "Italian," they had about as much in common as hamburgers and sushi. Mansa Musa had given us free reign to cook that night and we tried making something each of us would like, which created what Shelley called the Leaning Tower of Dishes.

"Point taken," I said. "But we also fed everyone."

"I would have been happy with takeout."

I wasn't going to win this one. I could tell by the way she brushed her hair from her face with a giant flick of the wrist, as though she flipped a spider from her forehead.

How many relationships have ended because of dirty dishes? Quite a few, I'd wager.

"Dostoevsky went out," I said. Before she could say "Not my problem," I leaned in and kissed her. "So, what's say I wash, you dry?"

"Give me a backrub later?"

"Deal."

Backrubs had become a form of currency between us.

"You know," she said as she grabbed a stack of dirty plates, "we don't know much about each other."

"Sure, we do."

"Yeah? What do you know about me?"

I took too long to answer and she laughed.

"Wait," I joked. "Gimme a minute."

"We only know all the bad shit that's happened."

"That stuff's important, isn't it?"

"Yeah, it is. But what about the normal stuff? The stuff people topside would talk about on a first date?"

Pursing my lips, I took on my dorkiest white-guy voice. "Well, I'm an investment banker into long walks on the beach. I own the entire catalog of *The Eagles* on compact disc and my favorite spice is mayonnaise."

"Ha ha."

"Seriously, dating topside ain't all that great."

"Still. I don't even know what your favorite song is."

"'American Pie' by Don McClean."

"Really?"

"Yeah."

"Huh." She didn't seem impressed.

"What?"

"I dunno."

"You don't like 'American Pie'?"

"I like it fine. But favorite song?"

"Oh, c'mon. The lyrics are pure poetry."

"I guess."

"What's yours?"

"'Fuck the Police,'" she said.

"That probably says a lot about us."

"Probably. Okay. I like this. This is fun. What's your favorite movie? Mine's *La Règle du Jeu*."

"Oh. Yeah," I said, no clue what she was talking about. "Great flick."

She cut her eyes at me. "You've never heard of it, have you?"

"No."

"I swear, Americans just refuse to watch foreign films."

"You're American," I said.

"Point taken. How about my second favorite film, then? *The Princess Bride*."

"Now that's a solid choice."

"I think I just like the idea of having a handsome man around to say 'as you wish' to all my demands. So, what's your favorite movie? *Porky's 1* or *Porky's 2*?"

"Haha. Mine's *Casablanca*. I know it's cliché, but I could watch it over and over."

"I've never seen it."

"You've never seen it?"

"Nope. I mean, I know about it. It's the archetypal romantic movie. Which, by the way, I knew you were sappy, but c'mon. Be original, at least."

"Never?"

"No, never."

"I call bullshit."

"Why is that bullshit?"

"Because, my dear Shelley, women have been known to lie about seeing *Casablanca*."

"Why in the fuck would we do that?"

"So that the guy you're with at the time will feel like he was the first one to show it to you. Showing a woman *Casablanca* ranks up there with your first crush or first kiss."

She snorted. "Think what you like, grandpa, but I've never seen it. No bullshit."

"You're serious."

"As an STD."

"Hmmm."

She laughed. "You don't know if you believe me."

"It's not that, it's... Okay. It's exactly that."

"You got me. I got nothing better to do here than lie about whether I've seen an eighty-year-old movie or not. That's what my life has come to. Now toss me that dish towel and accuse my entire gender of some more ridiculousness, will you?"

***

After paying my back rub debt, we both fell quickly asleep. But something woke me in the middle of the night, and I rolled over to find Shelley sitting up in bed.

"What time is it?" I asked.

"Shhh."

She stared at the doorway.

"Someone's there," she said.

I crawled out of bed and fumbled the lamp to life.

The doorway was empty.

I stepped out into the hallway, but no one was there, either.

"Just a bad dream," I said, and crawled back into bed.

"Yeah. I guess." She didn't seem convinced.

"Who was it?"

"It was…" She shook her head. "You're right. It had to be a dream."

We slept with the light on the rest of the night.

CHAPTER TWENTY-SEVEN

IF YOU'RE GOING TO steal from anyone in Italy, you steal from tourists. It was an unspoken code that you never stole from Romans. Now, this didn't always pan out. If you were hungry and broke you might swipe a slice of pizza, or steal bus fare, but in practice it was a good idea to stay away from the locals.

Part of this was common sense. Most tourists would not press charges even if you screwed up and got busted. Pressing charges meant sticking around for the trial and, in the notoriously bureaucratic Italian legal system, this could take months. No tourist wanted to be stuck in the city for that long. Italians, on the other hand, would most certainly press charges.

Another reason, and maybe the more practical one, was that tourists were easier marks. They were awe-struck by their surroundings and easily distracted. They didn't know the streets and so couldn't chase you very far. They also carried large amounts of cash in easy to reach places.

Americans were the easiest. The typical American male carried all his money in a wallet in his back pocket. Sometimes they'd try to get sneaky and hide the wallet in their jacket pocket (which, honestly, made it even easier when playing **Bump and Grind** to snag it) or slip it into their backpacks. This is where the knives came in. A few quick slices and we'd walk away with wallets, phones, and whatever else they had in their bags. I was walking proof of how well that worked.

American women carried everything in their purses. Again, a few flicks of the knife were all it took. Occasionally you would run into a savvy traveler who had read *Rick Steves* or *Lonely Planet* and hid their cash in a money belt, but this was as rare as spotting a tourist with good fashion sense.

After Americans, Australians and Canadians were the best. They practiced many of the same bad habits as Americans. Japanese tourists were good, too, but for different reasons. They were often warm and optimistic, the idea someone would steal from them being a truly foreign one. I always felt bad for robbing them. The Japanese usually gave up great toys, too, mostly cameras, but sometimes tablet computers and smart watches.

Fashion was also an indicator. Americans have the worst fashion sense in the world, followed closely by Australians and Canadians. Again, they all dress for comfort, making them stand out in crowd. I'm not sure why, but the worse a person's fashion sense the easier they were to steal from.

Cash was the number one thing to get, for obvious reasons. The British pound was the highest prized currency, followed by the euro, the American dollar, and on down. Jewelry was always good, as were electronics. Any of these items, as well as some of the stranger things we nabbed (I slipped a diamond studded Mickey Mouse pendant from an old woman on the bus one day; Ravenna's got me beat, though - she nabbed a crystal dildo from a backpack) ended up on display at our booth at the Porto Portese.

The last Sunday of every month we set up shop at one of the world's largest and oldest street markets. The Porto Portese is what I imagine Heaven would be like if God was my ex-wife. The market started at the ancient Roman gate from where it got its name and spread out forever. It took me an hour and a half to travel from one end to the other. It seemed the entire city had a table there selling everything from leather jackets to kitchenware to cashmere scarves.

Our table was covered in the most eclectic and bizarre array of items imaginable. Anything we couldn't spend, eat, or drink ended up at the market. We worked in shifts. Ravenna and Marco Antonio took the first shift, followed by Dostoevsky and Tolstoy, and then Shelley and me. Sappho and Madame Butterfly would relieve us. Then Big Jim came by to close everything at sundown.

Between customers, Shelley and I played a little game we made up called "If This Were a Movie."

"If this were a movie," she said, "we'd be played by two models who can't remember their lines and you'd have a better haircut."

"If this were a movie," I countered, "plinky, plunky music would be in the background to show just how *zany* we are."

"Awful, but true." She counted the money in our cash box. "I wish things would pick up. This is probably the slowest it's been out here in I don't know when."

"If this were a movie," I said, "a dozen extras who weren't allowed to speak would be picking up merchandise from our table and smiling way too big."

"I wish," she said. "If this were a movie, a wealthy Saudi prince would buy everything at our table and not care what he paid for it."

"If this were a movie, we'd be selling artisan desserts and landscapes you painted by hand."

"If this were a movie," she said, "I'd be white."

"You win."

Two young guys approached wearing Liverpool jerseys. One of them picked up a portable DVD player we'd nicked from an American church group.

"Oy," he said. "What's this run, then?"

"Sixty euro," I said.

"Bah," his buddy grumbled. They both had red hair and pockmarked faces and I wondered if the same ugly bastard had sired each of them.

"Give you forty for it."

"I don't know," I said, and made a face. "I paid close to that. Not much of a profit." I pretended to consider the offer. "Fifty-eight."

"Fifty-eight? For this shite? Who even watches DVDs anymore?"

"You do," Shelley said. "Otherwise, you we wouldn't be having this conversation."

"Pfft," he said, not denying it. "It's all dented. It even play?"

"Of course, it plays." I snatched it from him, turned it on, and shoved in the *Fireproof* DVD that had been inside when I snagged it. After a few seconds, Kirk Cameron's face filled the screen.

"All right," he said. "Forty."

"Forty?" Shelley shook her head. "You guys might as well be on your way. There are some real pieces of shit down at the next stall for that price. Of course, they'll stop working before your flight leaves."

This was another skill I was learning: the art of the haggle. Haggling was a national pastime in Italy. Back home the price was the price. Whatever an item was labeled, that was what you paid. But here it was more of a suggestion, a starting point that the buyer and seller could use to determine the actual price.

The four of us finally settled on fifty euro, though I would have let it go for forty-five if they had kept up. But they weren't that good at it and went off to no doubt watch a match somewhere and get tanked.

"If this were a movie," Shelley said, "they would have dropped a flash drive filled with secret spy codes."

"No, not those guys," I said. "It would have been a man in sunglasses and a polo shirt. He would have hidden the flash drive in the DVD player and when the Soviets came, they'd kidnap you and I'd have to track those guys down to get it back and save you."

"Ugh," she said. "The damsel in distress thing is so played out."

A high-pitched tinkling sounded from somewhere.

"What's that?"

"My cell." She slipped it from her pocket.

"I didn't know you had a phone." I don't know why that seemed strange to me. Her earbuds had to be connected to *something* whenever she listened to music.

I guess because we lived under the radar. Didn't Dimitri say he had sent texts to her describing me and the other marks he put on the bus? I'd just never seen the device before.

"I don't use it that much, mainly to..." She stared at the screen and the color left her face.

"What?"

"Shit. I'll be right back."

She jumped up and darted off.

Before I could say anything, a group of elderly Italian women had marched up to the table and were fondling the electronics like they were artifacts taken from a crashed spacecraft.

My Italian was poor. Piss poor. Shelley had been giving me lessons in the evenings, but I'd had a difficult time of it. Probably because most lessons ended when one of us gave the other that "I could eat you alive" look and we'd forgo the language lessons for another Italian pastime.

The women asked me a string of questions that I could barely comprehend. I tried to answer but my replies only served to shock and confuse. They waddled off, shaking their heads and mumbling under their breath.

I tried to work out what I said. I think it might have been something about lemons being out of season, I'm not sure. Shelley ran back up and broke my train of thought.

"I have to go," she said, and kissed my cheek. Her eyes were red and puffy.

"What's wrong?"

"Nothing. Don't worry about it." She took off again.

"Shelley!"

She spun and blew me a kiss.

If this were a movie, I would have followed her and learned her big secret. Instead, I stayed seated and waited for her to come back.

I didn't see her again for three days.

CHAPTER TWENTY-EIGHT

"ENLIGHTENMENT?" THE CARNY ASKED.

"Yeah."

"Seems you're on the right path, mate."

Trying to take my mind off Shelley, I'd sat down with the Carny that night and told him about my tiny enlightenments over a few glasses of wine.

Everyone from Marco to Madame Butterfly had told me not to worry about Shelley. It seems this was par for the course with her. She'd disappear for a few days and then come back no worse for wear. No one ever pried when it came to these "vanishings," as Miss Fagin called them. It was yet another of the Necropolis's secrets.

I avoided mentioning it to the Carny. I'm not sure why, but I never felt comfortable talking to him about Shelley. It was like talking to your parents about sex. Not that Shelley and I were a secret. Far from it. But still.

The Stones played from his record player. I recognized the song. "Midnight Rambler," a blues number telling the story of Albert DeSalvo, the Boston Strangler.

"Is this *Let It Bleed*?" I asked.

The Carny grinned. "It is, it is. Surprised you recognize it. In this age of Spotifuck, the album seems to have gone the way of the dodo."

He slid the record from the shelf and handed it me. A birthday cake hovered above a vinyl record on the cover. A group of plastic figurines I assume were Mick and Keith and the gang played tiny instruments atop the cake.

"It's the artwork I miss the most," he said. "When we was boys, Byron and I'd walk down to the local record store with a jar of change and buy whatever we could afford that week. We'd share the things, trading them back and forth every Friday. I'd sit in my rubbish bin of a room while Dad was down factory and Mom got pissed and just stare at the artwork as the record played."

I handed it back. "My dad had this one. Said Mom had stuck with LPs as the rest of the world moved on. It was one of her favorites."

"Your mother had good taste." He slid the record back onto the shelf. "How's your studies coming along?"

"Good."

"You read about them emperors yet?"

"Oh, yeah."

He sat, leaned back in his chair, and sipped his wine. It was a very regal gesture, something that made me think of academia, thrown off only by his ripped and stained shirt, scars and tattoos running up his arms. It was like David Niven and Syd Vicious had a child.

"Tell me about them," he said.

"Which ones?"

"Pick your favorites. You've got the noble ones, the heroic ones, the ineffectual ones, the insane ones. Your choice."

"The insane ones are fun."

He laughed and tapped his temple. "You really are one of us, Keats. The insane ones it is."

I recounted some of my favorite bizarre stories. Most had to do with Nero.

Nero Claudius Caesar Augustus Germanicus slowly succumbed to madness like a man sinking in quicksand. He liked to perform poetry and play music in front of crowds that weren't allowed to leave. He kicked his pregnant wife to death and then mourned her for the rest of his life. At a party, he saw a slave boy that reminded him of her and had the boy castrated there on the spot. He killed his mother and then swore he saw her ghost until the day he died.

My favorite one, though, was when he tried to convince the Senate that the way to deal with the rebellious Gauls was to sing to them.

When the Praetorian Guard, those purple-robed soldiers that protected the emperor, finally had enough, they forced him to open his own gut. As he fell, his dying words were, "Oh, what an artist dies in me."

The Carny grinned. "Now that is the way to go. Do you know about Caligula?" He didn't give me time to answer before going on. "His name means 'Little Boots.' That's what the soldiers called him when he was a boy and would follow them around in a little soldier's get-up. Sounds so cute I almost vomit. When he became emperor, the entire Empire rejoiced. He was loved, levelheaded, and brilliant. But then he fell ill. No one knows from what exactly. Some vicious type of mind-altering flu, I reckon. But when he came round again, his mind was gone. He butchered and killed and had conversations with statues of the gods claiming he was one of them. Then he got his own sister pregnant and — now this is truly sick, mate — in imitation of the Titans, he pulled his baby from his sister's womb and ate it."

"Jesus," I said.

Who knows if any of this was true, about Caligula or Nero. Their histories were written by people who had a vested interest in destroying their legacies. Still, the stories were all we really had.

"The Praetorians skewered him, too," the Carny went on. "That was part of their duty, I suppose. To not only serve the emperor but to cut him down if need be."

"Thank God for the Praetorians."

"Theirs was indeed a harsh duty." He sipped his wine and nodded in thought. "Would you have been able to do that?"

"Do what?"

"Kill the emperor. I mean, here's a bloke you have served and loved with all your heart. And then to see him fall apart like that. Would you have been able to end him?"

"I don't know."

"You fell apart. I mean, the way you snapped in the Family Room that night. You've done that before, right?"

I didn't like the way this conversation was heading. "Yeah?"

"It was worse then, wasn't it?"

"Yeah. Yeah, it was worse. And it went on for months. What's your point?"

He leaned forward and set his wine on a table between us. "Now imagine if you lost it like that, if your head spun round and round and you couldn't get it back straight. If your mind was permanent chaos."

"I have imagined that. It'd be a living hell."

"Right." He patted my knee. "Right. Now, would you want someone to put you down?"

"Yes." I didn't even hesitate.

He sat back in the chair. "The Praetorian Guard." He laughed. "You're like my Praetorian, Keats."

I was quiet, not sure what he meant.

"Ravenna's grandmother has told me things about you."

"What kind of things?"

"All in due time, my son. There are strands of fate that tie us together."

"You keep saying that. What aren't you telling me?"

"You'll see. Hopefully not for a while. But you'll see."

"Hence naming me Keats?"

He grinned. "You will be my successor, you know that?"

"Are you planning to retire?"

"You'll carry on everything I've done here, all the good I've accomplished. You'll do that, won't you?"

"Sure. I guess."

He was quiet for a long while. Then he pulled a cigar from somewhere, bit the tip off, and lit it. Closing his eyes, he took a few puffs, smoke drifting into the air.

"In the beginning," he said, "it was me — called Keats then — Byron and Shelley." He waved his hand before I could interrupt. "Not your Shelley. Eleanor Rigby's husband. We all grew up together in Luton. Town's rubbish. Only thing it's got going for it is an airport. We had this idea one year as brats to travel the globe, right? So, when we was out of county school, we stole a few hundred quid and hopped across the Channel. We kept stealing, right down to Rome."

I was quiet, afraid to disturb him. I knew I listened to something rare, something the others might have never heard. If I disturbed him, he might change his mind and the history lesson would be over.

"Thick as thieves, we were. Nothing could tear us apart. We was young, our heads filled with all the shite ideas the young develop with no clue how to put them into practice. Shelley, he was the first to come up with the games we played. Byron and I, we just took what we wanted, but Shelley saw an opportunity for something more. That we could elevate ourselves, even in our thievery. He pushed us to be better men. It wasn't long until others began to flock in.

"Then we found this place, our very own Villa Diodati. We only planned to stay here a few weeks, high on the notion of living in a secret catacomb. But then Shelley met Eleanor. Course, she weren't called Eleanor then. She was called Mary, obviously.

"He'd always been popular with the ladies, never had any problems getting company for the night. Bit like Marco, but with more panache. Yet when he and Mary first locked eyes on one another... Well, that was the end of the line for his bachelorhood. Our new family settled down here and quickly grew.

"The idea right from the start was to have a kind of Utopia. Something like Plato might have envisioned. All us Misfits coming together in the shadows, a place to escape the outside world with its judgement and hypocrisy. That was the ideal. And as we devised more games, that ideal grew to spread a little chaos into the world. You know, the Chinese view chaos as opportunity. We wanted to give an opportunity to all these boring tourists flocking here and refusing to experience Rome, refusing to treat this city as anything other than an amusement park, give them fuckers an opportunity to change. To open their eyes."

He opened his own and smiled.

"To experience enlightenment, no matter how small," he said. "To become *reborn*, if they wished it."

He picked up his glass and swirled the wine around inside. "That's what you have to remember, Keats. We loved life and we wanted to experience it unhindered. We wanted others to wake up and see what a beautiful and interesting world they was in. We were the Romantics." He downed his wine.

"What went wrong?"

He picked at a loose thread on his jeans. "It was a house of cards. One strong wind blew it all down."

"Byron?"

"That's where it started. He began hanging with those bruisers he runs around with now, brought some of them back here. They didn't fit in. Couldn't hear the music. Men like that, they have no philosophy. They only understand hierarchies of abuse. Our little Utopia rotted from within. There is a difference between hedonism and animal excess. Between passion and debauchery. Their path was the latter. They had no care for the greater good, for community. Hell, even consent was a foreign concept. Things fell apart around here so fast, everyone squaring off and choosing sides.

"When Shelley was killed, that's when it really went to hell. I tried my damnedest to hold it together after that, but Byron…" He trailed off, unable to finish.

"I'm sorry," I said.

"I tell you this because you must know. This is what you would be stepping into. It's no piece of piss running things. But this place needs its new Keats and its new Shelley and, eventually, even a new Byron. The Misfits will need new leaders, new Romantics to show them the way. Can you dig it?"

I wasn't sure what to say. What he told me was absurd and tragic and noble and overwhelming. I didn't know if I wanted that kind of responsibility when he left. Hell, I wasn't sure I wanted to stick around if he was gone.

He stood. "Let me show you something."

CHAPTER TWENTY-NINE

THE TEMPLE OF DIONYSUS Ascendant sat at the end of one of the unlit corridors I'd never ventured down. It wasn't a long walk, but I refused to explore any path not outfitted with electricity. The last thing I wanted was to be caught in one of those shafts when an earthquake came, and two-thousand-year-old walls crumbled and trapped me in the darkness.

The Carny's lighter sparked, and a torch came to life. He lowered the flame to a trough that ran along the wall and fire raced across the oil pooled inside. In seconds, the room was as bright as if Apollo himself had manifested.

Beautiful paintings covered the room, their colors far too vivid and vibrant to have avoided maintenance in two thousand years. Green trees and vines ran along red walls, gold borders framing the scenes. Portraits of Dionysian revels were everywhere. Here a group of naked women danced around a fire while a satyr played the lyre, there men drank wine from amphorae and wrestled. Plays were performed, poetry recited, and carnal passions indulged.

At the other end of the Temple stood a statue of the God of Wine and Revelry himself. Carved from stark white marble, he stood fifteen feet tall if an inch. A lyre was slung over one shoulder with a leather strap. His left hand clutched a vase of wine while his right stretched up over his head holding a bunch of grapes. A wreath adorned his curly hair and, though his face was tilted up to eat the grapes, his eyes were focused across the room at us.

The Carny slipped his shoes off. His feet seemed to glide over the bright blue mosaic floor. He knelt in front of the statue, pulled coins from his pocket, and placed them on a small table. There were other offerings there, fruit and crisp bills and iPhones. He spread the coins out before them, picked up a small porcelain bowl and a bronze knife, and slit his palm. Blood filled the bowl.

He replaced the items and removed a Snoopy Band-Aid from his pocket. He slapped it on his palm, whispered something in Latin, and bowed three times before standing.

"Keats," he said. "Meet He Who Guides Us." His grin almost split his face in two.

I stared into the marble eyes for a long while.

"You have a religion, Keats?"

"I've never really claimed one."

"Nothing wrong with that. But you need to know that Dionysus watches over us and guides us. When I'm gone, you'll still need to bring offerings to Him, whether He chooses to speak to you or not. Think you can do that?"

"Yeah. Sure."

That seemed to satisfy him.

"Why is he Dionysus," I asked, "and not Bacchus? I'd thought you'd use the Roman name."

"It wasn't my decision. Besides, names are mutable things. As you well know."

Hard to argue with that.

He gripped my shoulder. "Nothing I said today leaks from here, eh?"

"My lips are sealed."

"Even to Shelley."

"Of course."

"Good." He stared back at the statue. "Good."

Then he slipped his shoes on and left.

The flames sent shadows dancing over Dionysus. It was a trick of the light, I'm sure, but it looked like he was laughing.

***

Shelley didn't come back that night. I borrowed Marco's phone and called her. It went straight to voicemail. I tried not to let it bother me, but all that kept running through my head was her and Byron. Ridiculous, I know. And I've never been a jealous man. But when I spread out on my cot and tried to read, I could only conjure images of the two of them together.

So they had been lovers. Big deal. Their relationship didn't mean anything now. How many women had I been with in my life? I trusted Shelley. We were together.

He was so much older than her, too. She joked about our age difference, but it wasn't much. We were still both part of the same generation, at least.

Her lips kissing their way down Byron's scarred chest flashed into my mind.

"To Hell with this."

I got up, tossed a jacket on, and went out for a walk.

***

Rain sprinkled the dark cobblestones of the Piazza Navona. I stood under the eaves of a closed gelateria and watched a young couple sip coffee through Bernini's Four Rivers. The man's face looked fragile nestled between the Danube's marble triceps and its back. Or was it the Nile? The Baroque had never been my strong suit.

I tried to picture the day that Shelley had stolen my wallet, but the thoughts came to me cloudy, like I swam through murky water and tried to make out something floating on the bottom.

Where the hell had she gone? I smacked the wall so hard the bones in my forearm ached.

The Freak sidled up next to me.

"She's fucking him," he said.

"Piss off."

"If not him then someone."

I tried to ignore him, but the bile rushing up burned my throat.

"You heard what she said about her father. You think a girl who's gone through something like that can have a normal relationship? And then whatever she had to survive as a teenage runaway? Shit, man. Get with it."

The rain bit into my face as I took off across the piazza. I had to move. The burning spread to my limbs and I wanted to lash out at something, at anything. If I kept moving, if I didn't stop to think about things, I would be fine.

"You ever wonder who Miranda's been fucking?" the Freak said, keeping pace with me. "God, that girl loved to fuck. She's probably spreading her legs all over the city right now."

"Shut the hell up."

An old man dumping trash in front of a *tabaccheria* shot me a strange look.

"And Chelsea. Shit. She just woke up and looked at you one day, saw how pathetic you were getting, and said 'I can't do this anymore.' Whoever she's fucking right now, I bet she started before she even told you she didn't love you anymore. And how emasculating is that, anyway? How pathetic does that make you that your own goddamned wife had to take a break just when you got diagnosed with mental illness? In sickness and health, my ass."

This was how the Freak worked. You thought you were handling all the stress. You seemed calm. Hell, you felt calm. Then one major thing would happen and he'd show up and try to convince you to let him out and play.

I took deep breaths and ran through all the mental exercises I'd learned to keep him in check. I counted slowly to one hundred. I played through all the good images in my head, focused on Shelley and my new family and everything I had going for me now.

An image of my pills came to me. Topamax and Lamictal. How long had it been since I'd taken them? I suddenly missed those pills, missed them almost as much as I missed Shelley.

My walk became a jog before exploding into a sprint. I dashed down slick alleys and across wet streets. I darted around a couple kissing under a dull yellow lamp at the Ponte Garibaldi and rushed across the Tiber. This was another trick for dealing with my condition. All that nervous and angry energy had to go somewhere. It was better to spend it through exercise than to scream and break furniture.

All these things worked for me. They did. I pushed the Freak back. Tonight, I would win.

My lungs seared, my throat scorched from sucking harsh breath, I tried to come to a stop, but my feet slipped out from under me and I crashed hard onto the street. My ass took the brunt of the impact.

I fought to my feet and hobbled over to a wall to catch my breath.

Someone applauded.

I looked up to see Janus A.

"Great," I said.

Janus B slid up next to me and slipped a knife between my ribs. Three quick jabs. I felt the skin part, felt the pressure of the blade, but no pain. Not yet.

She kissed my cheek and then she and her sister skipped off arm in arm, giggling. I could only watch them go, too shocked to understand what had happened.

The pain hit after they rounded the corner. It dug deep into my flank. Snaked through my guts. I patted my side and my hand came away thick with blood. Clutching the wound, I hobbled back toward the Necropolis.

"Help," I managed. I don't think anyone heard me.

I passed out somewhere along the way.

CHAPTER THIRTY

THE FLY BUZZED IN my ear. "Three hundred fifty-six, three hundred fifty-seven, three hundred—"

"What are you doing?"

"Counting the bricks. Don't interrupt me. Three hundred... Three hundred..." It sighed. "Goddammit. One. Two. Three."

It was dark. I was on a bed, warm and soft, the smell of vanilla candles drifting in from somewhere.

I reached over and flicked on a lamp.

"Shit."

Miranda's bed. Her room was just as I remembered it. Her dresser ran the length of the wall to my right. Her closet was on my left. A door opened into her bathroom in front of me. A TV sat next to that, the door to the living room across from it.

Cold raced through my body. What was I doing here? Was she going to enter and think I had broken in, that I'd turned into some psycho stalker?

As if on cue, she stepped into the bedroom. She wore the same yellow dress she had the last time we'd seen one another.

"Hello." She smiled and sauntered over to the bed.

"Hi."

The fly continued. "Fifty-six, fifty-seven, fifty-eight..."

I ignored it.

She sat next to me and caressed my face.

"I hate you," she said. "I hate you so fucking much." She said it with the same soft voice she used to tell me she loved me with. "If I heard that you died from this, that her knife had punctured your lung and you drowned in your own blood, I'd throw a party."

Tears leaked from my eyes and down my bare chest. I'm not sure how long I'd been naked, but I realized I was. The tears turned red as they ran off my side and a pool of blood spread across her bed.

"Shit," she said. "I'll have to dry clean that."

I tried to explain to her about the Freak, tried to make her know that I hate myself for what I did to everyone and that I beat myself up over it every goddamned day.

"Good," she said. "You should hate yourself. But let me tell you something." She leaned in, her familiar smell grabbing me and pulling me into a hundred memories. Her hair draped over my face, tickling my cheeks in a way I thought I'd forgotten. "You will never be able to hate yourself as much as I hate you."

"Is there a way I can make it up to you? To anyone?"

She thought about it for a moment and then cut her eyes at me. "There is one thing you can do."

"Name it. I'll do anything."

"You can die," she said.

The wound in my side yawned wide and blood escaped in torrents.

"Two hundred seven, two hundred eight…"

She left the room.

The light in her bathroom clicked on. Shelley stood in front of the sink in a short skirt, hands on the counter and ass angled out toward me. She caught my eye in the mirror and grinned.

Byron stepped up behind her and put his hands on her hips. He kicked the door shut with his heel.

"You're pathetic." Chelsea leaned against the closet, her arms crossed over her chest. She wore her wedding dress, but the cloth was gray and soiled.

"I know," I said. My blood dripped onto Miranda's floor and I thought: I should rent a steam cleaner when all of this is over.

"I don't know what Shelley saw in you," Chelsea said. "I guess the same misguided affection I had. But, Christ, I was over you a few years in. It just took a while to work up the nerve to tell you."

"Two hundred sixty-one, two hundred sixty-two…"

"Why?" I asked. "What happened between us?"

The Carny walked into the room. He went up to the bathroom and knocked. Byron opened the door and greeted him with a smile. The Carny fumbled with his belt as he stepped inside and shut the door behind him.

"Well, look at you. You think you deserve anything long-lasting? Let me tell you, it will be like this every time. You'll either have a breakdown and push them away, or they'll sleep with everyone you know behind your back, or they'll be like me."

"And what's that mean, exactly?"

She shook her head. "You're an idiot. You know what that means. They'll grow bored with you. You think you can inspire any kind of passion?"

Marco and Spartacus walked through the room laughing at some joke. Marco winked and gave me the shooter. They crowded into the bathroom and closed the door.

"That's why Shelley ran off," she continued. "She's sick of you too. Took her much less time to realize it is all. Hell, you're bleeding to death and she's in the bathroom taking as many men as can cram into her."

Chelsea slipped her wedding band from her finger and tossed it at me. It bounced from my chest before skidding across the bloody comforter and landing on the dresser. It spun a few times, blood flicking up onto the mirror, before coming to a stop.

"You make me sick," she said, and spat on the floor.

Then she left.

"Three hundred twenty-four, three hundred twenty-five..."

Siggo and my father and my high school English teacher and an Armenian mechanic I had used once all sauntered into the room. Siggo knocked on the bathroom door. Byron stuck his head out.

"It'll be a bit," he said. "She's a real tiger."

"That's why we're here," Siggo said.

Byron closed the door.

The rest of them formed a single-file line heading out into Miranda's living room. I heard feet shuffle and some mumbling and knew the line was getting longer.

Miranda came back with a six-pack of beer. "You guys thirsty?"

"Thanks." Siggo slipped one out. "Great way to kill time."

"I've got some pizza rolls in the oven. Shouldn't be much longer," she said. She paused at the door on the way out and nodded at me. "You dead yet?"

"It's coming along."

She sighed and looked at her watch. "My boyfriend will be here in about twenty minutes. Think you can be done by then?"

"I'll try."

"I just don't want to explain this to him."

"I'll make sure I'm a corpse before he gets here."

"Thanks," she said.

There was a crash and a moan from inside the bathroom. Miranda whistled.

"Sounds pretty crazy in there," she said. "Why is that, anyway? That the worst thing you could imagine right now isn't that she's lost or hurt, but that she's fucking other men? What does that say about you?"

Before I could answer, a timer buzzed from the other room.

"Ooh, my *petit fours*!" Miranda rushed out the door.

"Well," the fly said, "there are twenty-seven bricks missing."

"Twenty-seven?"

"Give or take a few."

"What's that mean, exactly?"

"It means you're fucked."

The light bulb exploded and darkness flooded the bedroom.

The fly crawled from my ear and flew off.

The room was silent.

"This is fitting."

"Mom?" I'd never actually heard my mother's voice, but I knew it was her.

"You've been reading my journal," she said. The voice my broken mind conjured was soft and girlish, the voice of Meg Ryan in the eighties.

"Yeah," I said. "I have."

"That's private, you know."

"Sorry."

I felt her weight as she sat on the foot of the bed. "This is what it comes to, huh?"

"What?"

"Bleeding to death. Kind of how I went."

"I'm sorry."

"You say that a lot. 'I'm sorry.' You think you have an awful lot to be sorry for?"

"Yeah."

She gave a derisive laugh. "Don't do that. Don't try to be a martyr. Don't play the tortured soul. Not with me."

We were quiet for a long while.

"You should have done great things," she said. "I died to bring you into this world and instead of making my sacrifice worthwhile, what do you do? You thrash about like a wounded animal and hurt everyone that cares about you. And then, when the dust settles, you run halfway across the world to hide from it." Her weight shifted and the springs creaked as she stood.

"You should have died in my womb," she said.

CHAPTER THIRTY-ONE

"KEATS. KEATS?"

Pulling myself awake was like swimming through wet concrete. When I managed to open my eyes, Madame Butterfly sat over me. She dabbed my forehead with a damp towel.

"Oh, thank God," she said. "We thought you were done for." She smiled and held the towel up. "I don't know if this is doing any good, but they always do it on TV."

"It's...good..." My voice sounded like it was broadcast on a weak signal through blown speakers. I tried to sit up and some bastard shoved a red-hot poker into my side.

"Stay still," she said, and placed a hand on me.

"What..."

"What happened? You'll have to tell us, darling. Ravenna swears her grandmother sent her out looking for you. She came across you bleeding in an alley behind Santa Maria." She handed me a bottle of water. "You should drink that. The Carny had a doctor in here to stitch you up. He left some pain killers and antibiotics you need to take." She leaned over and kissed my forehead. "I'm going to tell him you're up."

Sappho came rushing into the room. "Jesus Christ, Keats." She squeezed my hand. "I've been so worried. You okay?"

"I think so. I don't know. Is Shelley here?"

Her jaw stiffened. "Don't worry about her right now. Just get better."

A few minutes later, she left to get me soup and the Carny stepped in.

"Well, mate. You're a bit of a mess."

I could only nod and even that hurt.

"*Il dottore* said you were lucky you didn't puncture a lung. You did lose quite a bit of blood. We was afraid we'd have to take you down hospital for a transfusion. We would have had to leave you there. The *carabinieri* would have been all over you. Glad it didn't go that way." He set several bottles of pills on the table next to my bed. "You should go ahead and take these."

I reached for the bottles and squeezed a groan out.

"I'll play nursemaid for now, Keats." He counted out a handful of pills and dropped them into my mouth. I downed them with a large gulp of water.

"So," he said. "Who did this?"

"Janus."

"All right." He scratched his scalp. "Very well."

"Is Shelley here?" I felt groggy and wondered if it was the pills or the blood loss.

"Hmmm?"

"Shelley?"

He shook his head. "No one's heard anything from her. Ravenna left a voicemail, but it seems her phone's off."

"Fucking...Byron..."

"Don't worry, that twat and his gang will pay for this."

"No... I mean..." Before I could say anything about Shelley and Byron, the dark came to claim me again.

***

The Roach Boy stood next to my bed when I woke. He held my hand in his tiny fingers.

"Hey, buddy. How long you been there?"

He giggled and ran off.

Miss Fagin came in a few minutes later. "Has the boy been in here?"

"Yeah."

"Which way did he go?"

I pointed.

"Thanks." She was off.

The pain had faded to a dull throb if I kept my breathing shallow. If I inhaled too much or twisted too far in one direction it was like being stabbed again. Fighting out of bed was an ordeal, but once I was standing it wasn't so bad.

Marco stood in the kitchen eating an apple. I dug around in the fridge and pulled out the ingredients for a sandwich.

"You look like the walking dead."

"Thanks, Marco. I feel like it. How long was I out?"

"Couple of days."

"God, I'm starving."

He bit into the apple and juice ran down his chin. He wiped it away with the tail of his shirt. "That's good. Means you aren't dying."

"Has she come back yet?"

"Nope."

I pieced together my breakfast and tossed the ingredients back into the fridge. Leaning against the counter to eat hurt a little more than I thought it would, but I'd been in bed for two days and the last thing I wanted was to sit.

"Anyone hear from her?"

He shook his head.

"You're a real help, Marco."

"Just telling it like it is. What else you want?"

"Nothing."

The hole inside me hurt worse than my stab wound.

"Man," the Freak said. "She must be getting fucked good to be gone this long."

I ate in silence.

Marco finished his apple and tossed it into the trash. The trashcan was covered in "Hello Kitty" stickers. A sign hanging above it read *Buon Sapore – Great Taste.*

"The Carny's planning something," he said. "Something big."

"What do you mean?"

"To get even."

"I don't want any trouble on my account."

"It's not just you, Keats. The fact they tried to murder you in an alley, the Carny can't let that go unanswered."

"So, what's he planning?"

"I don't know. But the last thing he said to me was 'The Tiber's going to run red, Marco. I swear to the Gods it will.'"

***

Everyone was out running their games and I sat alone in the Family Room. I was sinking back into an episode, I knew I was. The last thing I wanted to do was go outside and breathe fresh air or feel the sun on my skin. I wanted darkness. Loneliness. An old print of *The Shining* sat in the Carny's collection of film canisters and I threaded it up to watch Jack Torrance lose his mind.

I should have been fighting it. I knew what giving in would mean. I'd felt these episodes creeping up on me before. After I was diagnosed and learned all the warning signs, I had fought them off, but not taking my medication since God knows when and wondering where Shelley had gone, imagining her and Byron sleeping together, getting fucking stabbed and left to bleed to death in an alley, all these things fed the Freak. And you know what? I didn't care. Hell, letting the Freak step in and take over for a while might be a blessing in disguise. It would be nice to not be responsible for anything for the next few days.

"Unless those days become months again," the Freak said.

"No. I won't allow that."

"You sure you can stop it? Once I'm in the driver's seat I'm gone, baby. Zero to sixty in under a second."

Jack Torrance bounced a ball against the wall over and over again.

All work and no play…

What was I even doing down here? This wasn't the real world. My dream-mother was right. I was hiding. Maybe I should board a plane and go back to Los Angeles before someone really got hurt. Or even back to Tennessee and move in with my dad for a few months, deal with that bullshit and meet this little brother of mine that had turned him into a loving father thirty years too late. Get my head screwed on straight.

God, how pathetic. Thirty years old and entertaining the idea of moving in with daddy like some college kid. Dream-Chelsea was right, too.

I needed a drink.

Hobbling over to the bar, I thought I heard the door open upstairs. I didn't pay it much attention. A half-empty bottle of grappa sat on the shelf. I sent the cap sailing across the room to disappear in a corner and upended it. When it was gone, I grabbed a bottle of red and headed to my bedroom.

On the back wall, Jack Torrance laughed at one of Grady's jokes.

I plopped onto my cot and downed the red so fast a quarter of the bottle ran out the sides of my mouth and down my chest. The puddle that formed reminded me of the blood-tears in my dream.

You'll never be able to hate yourself as much as I hate you.

"I wouldn't be so sure of that," I said.

"Keats!" Shelley's voice was faint drifting through the halls.

I ignored it and killed my light.

"Keats!" Her footsteps echoed outside my room.

Quiet. The darkness cradled me, wrapped around me like a blanket.

When the light flicked on, Shelley's face was a sheet of tears in the doorway.

"OhmyGodbabyOhGodOhGodI'msosorry." She lay next to me and kissed my jaw. "As soon as I turned my phone on and got the message I came straight back here. I'm so sorry."

I wanted to hold her tight and kiss the tears from her face and make love to her. The Freak said I should tell her which circle of Hell she should relocate to. We split the difference and I wrapped my arms around her, staring at the ceiling in silence.

She kissed me. "Are you okay?"

The Freak snorted. "Ask her where she's been."

"I've been better," I said.

She placed a hand over my bandages. "Is this it?"

"Yeah."

"I'm so sorry I wasn't here."

The crack on the ceiling seemed larger, deeper. A harsh black line forever separating the couple in the field.

"Who was it?" she asked.

"Janus."

"Those fucking bitches."

She talked some more, but I was drifting away and didn't listen.

CHAPTER THIRTY-TWO

SHELLEY BROUGHT ME BREAKFAST in bed the next morning. A flaky, sweet brioche with fresh strawberries and a cappuccino. She never did anything that could be interpreted as waiting on me. Something was up.

"After you eat," she said, "put on something nice. Like that Armani suit we stole."

"Why?"

"We're going to get you a visa."

"In case you've forgotten, I was just stabbed."

"Which is why you're getting one." She tapped a heel against the wall. "If they had to take you to the hospital…"

"What are you getting at?"

"I mean, if something worse happens and the *caribinieri* or *polizia* come sniffing around, I don't want you getting in trouble. That's all."

I couldn't help but laugh.

She made a face. "What?"

"You're protecting me."

"And that's funny?"

I sipped my coffee.

"Why's that funny?"

"It's just, I'm the guy and I'm older and—"

"Didn't realize you were such an old-fashioned misogynist."

I thought of my dream centered around Shelley's sexuality and realized with a start that maybe I was. Keats the Old-Fashioned Misogynist. Not all enlightenments were pleasant, it seemed.

"All right, all right," I said. "I'll get a visa."

She came back in later, her bag in one hand and the suit held high in the other. Charcoal gray, soft, thin, stylish lines, and, well, Armani. It would have easily cost three thousand dollars back in the States.

"When you finish your breakfast, get dressed." She put a hand on her hip and stared at me, chewing her bottom lip.

"What?"

"Your hair. It's a little shaggy." She dug through her bag. "I'm gonna grab some cash from the piggy bank."

This wasn't one of our odd names. There was a giant porcelain pig about the size of Cujo in the corner of the Family Room. We deposited our cash into a hole in its anus.

"Get enough for a good lunch, too."

"Guy gets stabbed and thinks he deserves the star treatment." She grinned and skipped out of the room.

Her bag sat next to my bed.

The Freak leaned over and went through it.

"What are you doing?"

He shushed me. "Ah. Here we go." He handed me her phone.

"I can't."

"Hurry. Before she gets back."

The curiosity fired into my fingers and they scrolled through her call log. Three days ago, the day she disappeared, she had called Byron.

Byron.

I rummaged through her text messages. She had received a text from him before the call. It read: I NEED YOU. CALL ME ASAP.

The room pitched one way and then the other, as though I were on a ship sailing through stormy seas. I dropped her phone back into the bag.

"Told ya," the Freak said.

"Shut up."

He held his hands up like he was innocent and smiled.

Shelley ducked her head back in. "You're not dressed."

"Sorry."

"Well, hurry up." She winked and was gone again.

***

"It's none of your fucking business."

I was just about to put my shoes on when I heard Shelley's voice. I stepped out into the hall, the floor cold against my bare soles.

She bounced on the balls of her feet and shoved a finger up into Sappho's face.

Sappho smacked the finger away. "He's my friend," she said.

Shelley laughed. I'm not sure why that was funny.

"And he was *stabbed*, Shelley. He almost died while you were out there—"

"I know what happened. That's why I rushed back."

"Did you even consider him before you left this time? Did you consider anyone but yourself?"

"I did it, Sappho. It is what it is. You want me to apologize some more? Fucking put on some tears and cry a bit?"

"So, you don't even have an ounce of shame?"

"I don't do shame. Not anymore."

Sappho caught my eye. I could only imagine what I looked like.

Shelley whirled on me, her face less the angel I'd seen on the 64 Bus that first day and more Medusa. I wouldn't have been surprised to see a snake poke out from her hair and spit venom at me.

They both gave me a look that said, "Can you believe her?"

Mentioning Byron's text and call was not a good idea any time soon. Not unless I wanted to start World War III in the catacombs.

"We've got places to go," Shelley said. "And I don't have time for you to dig your nose into my life."

She stomped back over to me.

"You ready?"

"Almost."

Sappho looked to me and shook her head. She was disappointed, I could tell. But I'm not sure her disappointment was directed at Shelley.

***

Italian bureaucracy is notorious for its red tape. No one is ever in a rush for anything and nothing is ever quick or easy. There's no need, as far as the Italian government is concerned. Or the Italian culture, for that matter. Why rush anything? Rushing is antithetical to *l'arte di non fare niente*, after all.

We waited to fill out forms. Then we filled out forms to wait. Then we filled out forms to request the forms that we needed to fill out in order to get the forms we needed for a visa application to be issued. When it was all said and done, we spent six hours and some change at the government office only to leave with little more than "you should receive the final forms in a few weeks, give or take."

It wasn't quite the cause for celebration we had in mind, but we still stopped at the sushi restaurant on the Via Cavour.

"Well," Shelley said, "it's a start."

"Yeah. Better than nothing, I guess. Think they bought it?"

They had asked me questions about why I was staying in Italy and I gave them the story Shelley and I had concocted. I was a writer finishing a book on the beauty of Rome. They were less impressed than I thought they'd be and kept advising me I should have gone through the US consulate before leaving Los Angeles.

"They don't get paid enough to be suspicious," she said. "Though I still think we should have gotten you a haircut."

Smart cars zoomed by on the street. They might as well have been the official cars of Rome. They were everywhere. I'm surprised they weren't on the flag.

Shelley put a hand on mine. "You okay?"

"Huh? Yeah. I'm fine."

"You don't seem fine."

I thought again about bringing up Byron but didn't feel right doing so. Not yet. I'm not sure what I waited for exactly. Maybe it was just that I'd gotten so used to waiting that I couldn't stop.

"I've got a surprise planned for you," she said as she fought with her chopsticks.

"Oh? What kind of a surprise?"

"Well, if I told you it wouldn't be much of a surprise now, would it?"

"Good point."

She fought a giant piece of fish into her mouth.

"Hungry?" I asked.

"Starving."

Aside from a comment here or there, we ate in silence. It reminded me of the dinners Chelsea and I had in those months leading up to the end.

When we'd finished the meal and left, Shelley rushed up to me and pulled herself against my ribs.

"Ow!"

"Shit! I'm sorry." She switched to the other side. "I forgot."

"It's fine."

She led the way down the Via Cavour.

"Where are we going?"

"I found something the other day," she said. "Something very interesting."

"Yeah? What?"

"You'll see."

We walked from the business district and into the hotel district. For a moment I thought she'd gotten us a room somewhere. But we kept walking past the five-star hotels and into the grungy, rundown places farther along the street.

She pulled away and spun on the sidewalk, striking a pose in front of one of the rattier buildings.

"Ta-da!"

The sign read *La Capra Rossa*. "I don't get it."

"This place wasn't always called the Red Goat."

"Okay."

"It used to be *Il Cielo Celeste*."

The Blue Angel.

That was the hotel where my mother had worked.

The glass doors behind Shelley revealed a dimly lit lobby carpeted in red. Was that where my mother danced while she vacuumed?

Shelley put a hand on my chest. "Well?"

"Well what?"

"We going in or what?"

***

The building smelled of cigar smoke and roasted garlic. It was a far cry from the scent of fresh roses my mother described in her journal. An old man sat in a stained oak chair in front of a portable television. And when I say old, I mean ancient. I would not have been surprised to learn he'd been a pallbearer at Caesar's funeral. He craned his neck toward us, a waddle of skin large enough to hide the TV's remote dangling from it, and smiled. He had no front teeth.

"*Bua jer oh*," he said.

He lifted a fat, soggy cigar to his gums and puffed.

Shelley grabbed my elbow and dragged me over to the front desk. A woman who looked like she could be that man's mother leaned against a cane behind it and scribbled in a ledger. Shelley rattled off something in Italian. The woman nodded. They talked a moment before a grin spread over Shelley's face.

"This is Signora Trombetta. She says she's owned this place since nineteen sixty-eight."

"Sixty-eight?" A knot formed in my throat. "So, she knew... Did she know..."

Shelley and the woman spoke more. The woman smiled and motioned with her hands. Italians spoke two languages: one was Italian, the other some bizarre form of sign language. I had a better time deciphering the sign language than I did the spoken language. Her hands said she was happy about something and glad to speak about it.

"She says she knew your mother. She liked her very much. She was a polite and beautiful girl and helped out around here quite a bit."

I couldn't speak. Shelley squeezed my hand and went on.

Signora Trombetta had even met my father. My father she didn't like as much. She had come to think of my mother as a part of the family and thought my father was just trying to "do the evil that all young men do," as she said.

"She means sex," Shelley added.

"I got that."

She spoke of my mother the way someone would talk about their own daughter and I wanted to come across the desk and hug her. To Italians, family was the most important thing in the world, more important than jobs or money or politics. It was touching to hear my mother had been considered part of their family.

The old woman coughed and spat something green into a handkerchief. Limping around to us, she took my hand. When she spoke her breath almost floored me. To compare it with rotten garbage would not have done it justice.

"What did she say?" I asked Shelley.

"She said she thinks she has some of your mother's things."

***

The basement was a museum of the twentieth century. Any bizarre piece of technology that had come and gone was stacked down there. Dusty typewriters sat atop broken freezers. Dictaphones were shelved next to busted toasters. There was even one of those weird weight loss machines from the fifties, the one with the vibrating belt. It must have taken a genius to market and sell those things.

Cardboard boxes were stacked everywhere. Traveling through a maze of them reminded me of the warehouse at the end of *Raiders of the Lost Ark*.

Signora Trombetta rummaged through a pile against the back wall. Finally, she mumbled something and pointed to a single box. I bent over and opened it.

There, atop a stack of clothing, sat the blue, gold-rimmed copy of Byron's poetry I'd read so much about.

I lifted it, flipping through the pages, and a small Polaroid photograph slipped out. Shelley caught it as it drifted to the ground.

It was a picture of my mother with two other girls in front of the Coliseum.

"She was beautiful," Shelley said.

"*Bella*," the old woman repeated.

The clothes hid a pile of records. *Let It Bleed* was the third down.

"This is what she listened to while here," I said. "It's so strange."

"What is?"

I didn't know how to put it into words.

Carefully, I removed the records and set them next to the box. Beneath them, hiding in a scattering of fliers for concerts and theaters she may have attended, was a small piece of paper wadded into a ball. I unfolded it. Its left edge was jagged.

"Whatcha got there?"

"It looks like a piece of paper ripped out of her journal. But it's in Italian."

Shelley snatched it from my hand and scanned over it.

"Well?"

"Oh, Keats."

"What?"

"It's, um… It's a letter."

"To whom?"

"To you."

"What?"

"Not really, but yes. Let me just read it to you."

Signora Trombetta leaned against a stack of boxes and coughed into her handkerchief again. Then she lit a cigarette and puffed away.

Shelley cleared her throat. "To my daughter." She laughed. "She's not too far off there."

"Haha."

She went on. "I think you're going to be a girl. You feel like a girl. I need to be honest with you. I don't know that I want you. You see, everything is going well for me right now and I think that having you might not just complicate things but completely derail them."

And here it is, I thought. Every fear I've ever had, every piece of guilt revolving around my mother, every horrible thing my father ever said to me, it would all be validated here. And not in my words. In hers.

"Keats?"

"Huh?"

"Do you want me to go on?"

I nodded.

"I don't know that I want you. But I don't know that I don't, either. You see, knowing that you're growing inside of me is strange. I wish I had a better way to describe it, a more profound adjective, but strange is all I've got. I'm too young to be a mother. And I have dreams of my own. Having a child now could destroy all of that. Well, if not destroy it then at least set it back further than I'm comfortable with."

How long had it been since I last visited her grave? This woman gave her life to bring me into the world and I couldn't even be bothered to bring her flowers every year.

"But," Shelley went on reading, "bringing you into the world means that a piece of me will always exist. No matter what happens to me down the road, your life sprang from me at this moment in time, at this point where I'm happy and in love and the entire future is laid out before me. That's the most spectacular thing I could ever ask for.

"No matter where I go and what I do, you will have come from the best part of my life. Every smile you give me, every laugh, will in some way be an echo of now.

"That sounds self-centered and I don't mean it to. It's wonderful and amazing. Is this what they mean when they call it 'the miracle of birth'? You'll always be a reflection of the good and the innocent, the wondrous around me. I can't think of a better reason to call you a miracle.

"I'm excited, my miracle. I can't wait to meet you."

Shelley handed the note back to me. I held it in silence, staring at the perfect script dancing across the page.

"Well," I said.

I packed my mother's things back up and hefted the box. We thanked Signora Trombetta and were about to leave when she stopped us and said something.

"She wants to know how your mother is doing," Shelley said.

I smiled. "Tell her she's doing fine."

***

After dinner we strolled through the city arm in arm and listened to its sounds. Rome is a city of music. Whether it's the rhythm of feet on cobblestones or the melody of water flowing through the fountains, there is a musical undercurrent to *La Citta Eterna*. There's also the very real music flowing through the city, the violinists and guitarists and flute players wandering the streets, smiles on their faces and cases open for spare change.

We eventually came across that strange elephant of Bernini's with the obelisk on its back.

"We never went looking for Dimitri," I said.

I felt her stiffen at my side. "He's in Sperlonga."

"Again?"

"Same girl, I think."

"Really?"

"Yeah." She broke away from me and darted over to a fountain in the piazza.

She was lying. I knew she was, but I refused to trust my gut and pushed the cab driver from my mind.

Shelley hopped up on the fountain's edge and balanced like a gymnast. Three kids chased a ragged dog past us and followed the mutt down an alley.

"Late for a school night," I said.

"Have I told you I love you?" She didn't look at me but concentrated on her feet as she made her way around.

"No."

She simply nodded.

"Me too," I said.

"Will you still feel that way when you go home?"

"I'm not going home. I am home."

"What you came here for, what you needed from Rome, is that done now?"

I didn't know how to answer that. Instead, I answered with, "I love it here. Why would I leave?"

She shook her head. "Love isn't a ring only one person can wear."

"What are you talking about?"

"I don't know." She jumped down from the fountain. "Negative Capability, I guess."

"Negative what?"

She rolled her eyes. "John Keats. It was his philosophy. Don't you read those stacks of books on your nightstand? The basic gist is that an intelligent person should be able to hold two seemingly opposite thoughts in their head at the same time. Like believing in both God and evolution. Or that you can be in love with two places, even two people, at the same time. Negative Capability."

"I don't get it."

She groaned. "I can't believe he named you 'Keats.' Might as well have given the name to a dog." She smiled and punched my shoulder.

I shoved her into the water and then went in after her. We laughed and wrestled, sprinting down an alley when the *polizia* came.

CHAPTER THIRTY-THREE

"WHERE WERE YOU?" I said.

We had fallen onto my bed with a bottle of wine when we came back. When we finished with the wine (and each other), we lay there curled together, my fingers caught in twisted strands of her hair, and I couldn't wait for an answer any longer.

She was quiet.

"When you took off. Where did you go for three days?"

"I do that sometimes."

I waited for her to continue but she didn't.

"That's not an answer," I said.

"It is what it is."

"Is that your new phrase of the day?"

"Maybe."

"Did you get it from a fortune cookie?"

"I don't want to talk about where I was. Okay?" She kissed me and rested her head on my chest.

"No. It's not okay."

"Keats. Please?"

"Were you with Byron?"

I could feel the sharp breath she took even if I couldn't hear it. "No. Why would I be with Byron?"

The dripping of water from somewhere in the room filled the silence. I counted each drop until I reached one hundred.

"I looked at your phone," I said.

She sat up. "You did what?"

"This morning when you left your bag sitting here. He texted you to call him and then you disappeared."

She kicked her heel against the bed.

"Wanna tell me why?"

Shelley stood and slid her dress on. "I think I'm gonna sleep in my room tonight." She was gone in a few seconds.

The crack above my bed swallowed all the light. I couldn't even see the couple anymore.

I gave her enough time to get situated before making my way to her room. She had already killed the light and I stepped into the dark and hovered over her. The urge overtook me to kick her bed as hard as I could, but I fought it off.

She took a deep breath. "What?"

"We need to talk about this."

"Okay, then. Let's talk. Why were you going through my shit?"

"Huh?"

"Why did you feel the need to look at my phone instead of just asking me?"

"I did ask you."

"After you played James Bond."

"Shelley, I just now asked you and you just now lied about it."

She didn't have an answer for that.

"Are you fucking him?"

She flicked on the light. She was sitting up, red-faced and trembling with anger. "You're an asshole."

"Not an answer."

"How's this for an answer? Fuck. Off." She flopped hard onto the bed and rolled her back to me.

This time I did kick the bed. It scooted across the floor to hit the wall. I regretted it even as I did it.

She was off the bed before I could blink. "Don't you dare come into my room and start kicking shit around like you own it." She shoved me hard, and I fell back into the wall, my skull cracking hard against the stone.

"This is *my* room," she went on. "Not our room. *Mine.* Now get the hell out."

The Freak put his arm around my shoulder. "She ain't gonna tell you shit."

"Get out!" She shoved me again. This time I tumbled into a small bedside table.

"You don't know how to handle this," the Freak said. "Let me."

I tried to refuse, tried to force him out of the room until we had hashed this out, tried to dig deep for composure or self-control. But it was too late. He was driving.

And like he said, zero to sixty in under a second.

"Stop pushing me!" The Freak grabbed the small table in one hand and hurled it into the hallway. It shattered against the wall.

"Tell me the truth," he demanded. "Was it worth it? Huh? Is fucking him so good that anytime he hits you up with a booty call you're out the door?"

"I don't need this shit." She grabbed her bag and started shoving clothes into it.

He snatched it from her and launched it into the wall. Something inside broke with a loud crunch. "Fucking answer me."

She nailed his jaw with a right cross.

He fell as she took her bag and stormed down the hall.

I could tell you the rest but it's more of the same. More yelling. More name-calling. More shoving. Shelley called him a lunatic and he pounded up the steps after her and stood in the alley screaming as she stormed off into the night.

She may have been crying, I'm not sure. The entire scene is blurry, like a movie shot in soft focus with a gauzy filter.

Piecing together my episodes was never easy. Episodes? Hell, let's call them what they were. Tantrums. Maybe that's not the medical term, but that's how I felt. They were the result of reality intruding upon my self-absorbed, privileged view that I *deserved* things. And when life didn't kowtow to me, when other people didn't give me what I felt I deserved, then the tantrums came. It's no wonder trying to remember those times with the Freak in charge was like recalling the details of a night of binge-drinking. Scattered moments, hazy details, and a guilty sense that some important information was just beyond my reach.

Eyes watched from the dark, the other Misfits, as the Freak stomped back down into the Necropolis. He took a bottle of whiskey from the bar and flopped onto my bed.

"Well," he said, "that was tiring work. I'm gonna take a rest. Enjoy the whiskey."

Then he was gone and it was just me, alone with my friend Johnny Walker, pondering fate and choices and Negative Capability. I thought of the circular nature of my life and of snakes that devoured themselves.

Ouroboros. The serpent eating its own tail represented as an unbroken circle. Plato wrote the following description of it:

"The living being had no need of eyes when there was nothing remaining outside him to be seen; nor of ears when there was nothing to be heard; and there was no surrounding atmosphere to be breathed; nor would there have been any use of organs by the help of which he might receive his food or get rid of what he had already digested, since there was nothing which went from him or came into him: for there was nothing beside him. Of design he was created thus, his own waste providing his own food, and all that he did or suffered taking place in and by himself."

I was Ouroboros eating my own tail. I had no need of eyes or ears. There was nothing worth seeing or hearing around me. There was no atmosphere to breathe. And all I suffered took place in and by me. The whiskey burned on the way down through organs I had no need for.

The fly came again that night. It didn't say anything, no matter how many questions I asked. It just rolled its balls and hummed.

***

Nine days later, the earthquake hit and everything changed.

TERZO

If you want things to stay as they are, things will have to change.
-Giuseppe Tomasi di Lampedusa

CHAPTER THIRTY-FOUR

LYING WAS THE FREAK'S favorite pastime. He practiced it the way some might practice piano or do push-ups. He was an artist, and I couldn't help but wonder if he'd already painted his masterpiece or if the best was yet to come.

The story he gave around the Necropolis involved Shelley getting drunk after seeing her father by Trajan's Market. She needed to disappear for a few days, he said, and I was trying to get her to let me join her. She snapped and stormed off.

There wasn't necessarily any rhyme or reason to the Freak's tales. I think he just got off on manipulating people and feeling like he got away with it. Or maybe he tried to protect me in some strange way by disguising the fact that my girlfriend had been sleeping with the enemy.

Me?

I just missed Shelley.

***

"Again with the enlightenment?" The Carny patted his ottoman.

I sat. "Just a question. Your opinion, anyway."

"Go on."

"Do finding these little enlightenments mean that you shouldn't be able to screw up?"

"I don't follow."

"Well, if you're on the path to enlightenment, shouldn't you act, um, *enlightened*?"

"You mean, should you act like some racist stereotype of a Chinese monk, as though you can never be rattled?"

"Yeah."

"That's bollocks, mate. A combination of bad kung-fu movies and good PR. You ever read the *Tao Te Ching*?"

"In high school."

"Who wrote that?"

"Lao Tzu."

"And what does Lao Tzu talk about?"

"He talks about how you should let the world go and not be so involved with—"

"Lao Tzu talks about how fucking enlightened Lao Tzu is. That's it. It's like Tony Robbins before the age of television. It's a bleeding infomercial. He goes on and on about how he has the secret and you don't but, if you listen to his words, you might find the secret too. Madison Avenue types use the selfsame cack to sell detergent and mouthwash."

"So, he wasn't enlightened?"

"I don't know. Never met the man. But anyone who speaks so highly of himself is more than a little suspect in his motives, if you ask me. Then the other Great Teachers, from Socrates to Muhammad and Jesus and the Buddha, the only accounts we have of them were written by their followers who, guess what, all had agendas to push. Advertising, Keats. That's it." He leaned forward and punched my chest.

"Listen," he said. "We're all human. Socrates was human. The Buddha was human. Even for those who believe in the divinity of the carpenter from Nazareth, he was still part human. Look how he flipped out on them moneylenders, eh? Or his fear on the cross, asking God why he had forsaken him? Even the various hadith and sīra agree that the Prophet was simply a man. So are we all. And, as human beings, we will all fuck up from time to time. No one is a fount of pure calm and wisdom. It's impossible. Even divinity couldn't bring that to the Greek Gods or the Abrahamic God. Power of the universe in their hands, and they was still angry and spiteful things.

"We are animals, my son. The only thing that separates us from other animals is our inability to accept that we *are* animals. We eat, we shit, we fight, we fuck, and we sleep. You show me a man who has done away with all that and I'll show you this ridiculous fortune cookie idea of a Wise Man you're babbling about."

It was the Carny's idea that all religions and philosophical schools since the pagan era fell had been based on trying to distance ourselves as much as we could from that animal side, from our instincts.

"Look at all the trouble this causes," he said. "All the guilt. We are programmed to fuck and then we beat ourselves up for doing so. Why? Because some asshole who died thousands of years ago said we shouldn't have a go? Or worse, we lie about the fucking. Maybe to whom we're fucking, maybe to ourselves.

"Now, some Buddhists and Christians might tell you it's all an illusion, a test to see if we're worthy. That God manufactured dinosaur bones in the Earth to make us believe in evolution or what have you. But here's my take on that: If the Powers That Be in the universe are trying to trick us or test us or throw illusions up at us, then they are cunts and should be ignored.

"All these philosophies only serve one purpose: to hide away from the world. They are the ideals of the weak. The ideals that men who weren't strong enough to meet the world on Her own terms devised to justify their cowardice and convince others of their superiority. It's no coincidence the major religions all fear women and sexuality and freedom. These are the fears of petty men writ large across the canvas of history. They sell their ideas of enlightenment so that we continue to feel inferior and must follow them for salvation, or glory, or even just self-improvement. Don't fall into that trap, Keats. Better to be a lion of your own making than a lamb of God."

I wasn't sure how any of this applied to my question and tried to bring it back around. "So, the fight Shelley and I got into…"

"Learn from it. You should no more be a slave to your own faults than you are to those stifling ideologies. But you will never excise the animal in you. You must find when to feed it so it doesn't attack from starvation. There's a reason the Shaolin monks went to war. It was because they was men and went mad every now and then and needed to break shit, just like the rest of us. Warrior Monk. Pfft. As though meditating three hours a day washes the blood from your hands."

This was par for the course with the Carny lately. Whatever he thought was going to happen, he believed would happen soon. He was grooming me, teaching me everything he could as fast as he could. It made my head spin.

"Remember what another Chinese philosopher once said: 'Before enlightenment, chopping wood and carrying water. After enlightenment, chopping wood and carrying water.'" He grinned. "How's that for your fortune cookie?"

I rolled these things around in my head while writing another poem. I'd borrowed everyone's cell at one point or another and left who knows how many messages for Shelley. She hadn't called back. The frustration brewed in me like a bitter tea. I didn't know what to do. I pounded out push-ups until my shoulders ground to dust in the sockets. I read until my eyes blurred. I walked around the city until my feet ached and my shins threatened to split open. None of it worked.

And the shit the Carny filled my head with confused me more often than not. He'd quote the Koran or the Bible or the Bhagavad Gita, then turn around and rip them to pieces. He'd rail about personal responsibility, but then say we're just animals and need to let go of our guilt. Was that the Negative Capability Shelley tried to tell me about? I felt out of my depth.

It had only been a few days since she'd left, but I hadn't slept more than an hour at a time. And when I did, I dreamed about her. The insomnia was frustrating because all I wanted to do was sleep. While dreaming I could at least fool myself into thinking I was with her. But an hour, that was the best I could hope for. The only thing I thought to do was write about it.

I scratched the last few words down on the pad and then sat back and read it over.

> Sunrise comes and tears us apart
> and I hold fast to memories.
> Yet light even forces them to depart,
> leaving half-remembered fantasies.

"This is shit," I said. I hadn't learned any of the lessons the Carny tried to teach me.

I wadded the poem into a ball and tossed it across the room.

CHAPTER THIRTY-FIVE

AH, LOOK AT ALL the lonely people.

A thunderstorm blew outside and water leaked from the crack above my bed. I'd never had a problem with leaks before. I hoped my dripping ceiling didn't hide some larger problem. I got up to grab a few garbage bags from the kitchen in a vain attempt to keep my bed dry.

Eleanor Rigby sat at the kitchen table and sipped a glass of wine.

"Oh," I said. "Sorry. Didn't know anyone else was here."

"That's all right," she said. "Have a seat."

I stood there trying to decide what to do long enough for the awkwardness to swell.

She pushed the chair opposite out with one foot. I grabbed a glass and sat. She filled it.

I'd never known anyone quite so lonely as Eleanor. She was troubled, that played a part, but she took the grand prize regardless. I knew loneliness, you see. When I first moved out of the place I'd shared with Chelsea, I'd been consumed by it. Working nights, the entire world seemed a far away and ridiculous notion I had cooked up after a few drinks one evening. Everyone I knew was awake while I slept and slept while I was awake. I would go weeks without having any kind of significant social interaction. A cloud hovered around me that entire time.

Eleanor's cloud was thick and dark.

"Keats," she said, and raised her glass. "Good name."

"Thanks."

"You know what he said about love?"

"About dying for it?"

"Dying for love. How many people do you think have actually done such a thing?"

I thought it a rhetorical question and kept quiet.

"How many?"

Obviously not. "I don't know."

"Shelley's dead, you know."

A hand squeezed my heart. It didn't let go until I realized she meant her Shelley. The original Shelley.

"I killed him," she said. "Right out there in the Family Room. Stabbed him like I tried to stab you."

I expected her to cry, to wail, to lose it, but she didn't. It was just a sad memory told matter-of-factly by a woman with too many regrets.

"Why?" I asked.

She finished her wine and poured more. "If I knew that…"

We listened to the sounds of the Necropolis, to dripping water and snoring children.

"Do you believe in forgiveness?" she asked.

I had to think about that one.

"Might there be acts too horrid to be forgiven?"

"I don't know," I said again.

She held her glass with both hands and stared into her wine. "I like to think that, if two people loved one another, then some part of that remains. It never dissipates, not entirely. If that's true, then surely there's the hope of forgiveness, isn't there?"

"He forgives you," I said. I'm not sure why.

"I do hope so." She downed the rest of the glass in one gulp. "But I don't know that I forgive him."

She stood and placed her glass in the sink.

Then she was gone again.

As I finished my own wine, I wondered how close I was, how close any of us were, to becoming Eleanor. How close we were to letting our sins eat us whole and becoming ghosts haunting the places important to us when we still felt alive.

Where did all the lonely people belong? Right here, it seemed. In the Necropolis among Misfits and the ancient dead.

"Shit! The garbage bags!"

By the time I made it back to my room it was too late. The bed was soaked. I threw the bags down anyway and slept on the couch.

***

"Have you seen the Carny?" I asked.

Miss Fagin slid rubber boots onto the Orphans so they could go splash in puddles. I wasn't positive, but I think her collection of children had grown since I first arrived.

"I believe he's in the Temple, love."

"Thanks."

I ran into him in the corridor outside it.

"Keats. I'm glad you found me." He had a backpack slung over one shoulder and a flashlight in his hand.

"Where are you off to?"

"Working on my map. I'm going to try a different route today. Walk with me a bit?"

"Sure."

He clicked his light on and we walked down one of the unlit hallways.

"How you feeling?" he asked.

"I don't really know."

"That's better than bad, I suppose."

"Can I ask you something? It's been weighing on me since last night. Why did Eleanor Rigby kill the first Shelley?"

"Ooh. Here for some light conversation, are we? I wish I had the answer to that, Keats. I truly do."

"You're not afraid she might do it again?"

"We don't judge here. You know that. She may be broken, but so are we all."

"Do you think she's dangerous?"

"To you lot? No."

"Even though she tried to stab me?"

"She didn't, though."

"Only because you stopped her."

"You say that as though none of us need one another." He stopped, his eyes boring into mine. "Without one another, we would all be the worst versions of ourselves. You know that, right?"

"Yeah. I guess. I just—"

"Don't guess, Keats. If you only learn one thing from me, let it be that. The man who fights alone will never stop fighting."

I wasn't sure what he meant, not exactly, but he had continued walking so I hurried to catch up.

"Why are you so interested in Eleanor all the sudden?"

I was trying to get at something, but I couldn't quite make sense of what.

"But," I said, hoping if I kept talking it would come to me, "if she could do something like that to someone she loved—"

"It is a sad fact of the human condition that we are more comfortable damaging those we care about than we are complete strangers."

We walked in silence a bit longer. There was so much I wanted to ask him, and I didn't even know where to begin.

"Keats," he said. "Can I confess something to you?"

"Sure. Anything."

"I'm afraid."

Chest high, eyes focused, he didn't look afraid.

"Of what?" I asked.

"It's a small matter." His voice soft.

We reached an intersection and he gripped my shoulder.

"This is the point of no return, mate. I only got the one torch."

"Right."

"I may be gone a while. Couple of days. You're in charge until my return."

"Me?" The butterflies in my stomach doing barrel rolls.

"We'll talk more when I get back. Right?"

"Yeah. Sure. Of course."

He stared down the dark passage. "See you then."

I watched as he walked away, slowly swallowed by the black.

CHAPTER THIRTY-SIX

CAMPO DI FIORI CAME alive at night. While crowds visited to shop when the sun was up, at night everyone between the age of seventeen and fifty flocked there to drink and dance at one of the clubs.

Sappho, Tolstoy, and Dostoevsky invited me to join them for a night out. I had the impression they'd all gotten together and talked about how miserable I was and decided it would be good for me.

And it did the trick, as much as I hated to admit it. It was difficult to be too down in such an atmosphere. The club had been a Renaissance palace once upon a time, its structure and decor both gorgeous and ancient with lavishly painted walls and classical columns. The crowd danced to a pounding soundtrack as multi-colored lights cut through machine-made smoke all around them. It seemed everyone wore a smile.

That was another of my favorite things about Italy. People enjoyed themselves without worrying about looking cool. Back in Los Angeles, people were too concerned with appearing aloof and jaded to really cut loose in public. Italians were the opposite. Even with *la bella figura* they cared more about having a good time than what anyone might (or might not) think of them for doing so.

The four of us sat at a corner table and downed drinks while swapping jokes. Every man in the place made a pass at Sappho before the evening was over. They were the butt of most of the jokes.

We were having such a great time and I wished Shelley could have been with us. I tried to ignore the idea. Thoughts like that were termites. No matter how great my mood, they would munch their way in and destroy whatever joy I felt.

Tolstoy and Dostoevsky signed back and forth.

Sappho wagged her finger. "Now, now. What are you two talking about?"

Tolstoy smiled.

"There is a young lady at the bar," Dostoevsky said. "She keeps checking out Keats."

I turned. "Where?"

"At the end of the bar. Purple skirt."

She smiled. It wasn't a Helen of Troy smile, but it wasn't bad, either.

I smiled back and returned to my drink.

"She's cute," Sappho said. "I'm jealous."

"Well, you can go talk to her if you want."

"You're not going to?"

"I'm with Shelley," I said.

Sappho groaned and rolled her eyes.

"You're a better man than me," Dostoevsky said. "If she smiled at me like that, I wouldn't care if I were with Cyndi Lauper."

Even though his English was great, Dostoevsky's pop culture references were not up to date.

"Keats, look." Sappho reached across the table and took my hand. "I'm not trying to be a bitch here, but do you think Shelley would give you the same kind of consideration right now?"

"Yeah," I said, sans conviction. "I mean. Why wouldn't she?"

"Byron, for one."

That stung.

"We shouldn't talk about that," I said. "Don't want the Carny getting the wrong idea that she betrayed him or something." I wish I'd never told Sappho about reading Shelly's texts.

"Besides," I went on, "I don't even know what happened there. Not really."

"Don't you?" Dostoevsky cocked an eyebrow. "Why would she not tell you what happened between them?"

"I don't know. She has her reasons."

"Then she should have told you those reasons," Sappho said. "That's not a crazy request for you to make. And for her to just leave like that…"

"That's my fault. I shouldn't have acted the way I did. I was a raging asshole."

"Yeah. You fucked up," Sappho said. "But stop conflating it all. Your behavior is a separate issue, and one I've already torn you a new asshole for."

"Three or four new assholes," I said, thinking of how Sappho put a finger in my chest when she lectured me on respect and physical power dynamics.

"Damn right," she said with a smirk. "But your behavior doesn't change what Shelley did."

"Yeah, I know."

"Or what she's doing right now."

And there it was. She gave voice to the ugly feeling in my stomach. Shelley may have been with Byron right at that moment. As I pined for her, as I thought of all the thousands of ways I could apologize, she may have been in his bed.

"He's the enemy," Sappho went on. "There is no scenario where she rushes out to see him that involves a pure motive. With their past? He took advantage of her when she first came to the Necropolis as a teenager. Did you know that?"

I hadn't, and I don't know why. The timeline of Shelley's arrival and Byron's expulsion could only mean that their relationship had been when she was high school age. She always joked about the age difference between the two of us, but it seemed such a trivial amount of time compared to the one between her and Byron. Especially if she'd only been a child at the time.

"It was the straw that broke the camel's back," Sappho went on, "and why the Carny finally kicked him out."

God, what Shelley had gone through in those first years in Italy. Byron surely knew and took advantage of her anyway. My fingers curled into fists thinking about it. If Byron had walked through the door right then, nothing could have prevented me taking how I felt out on his face.

"He has a power over her, Keats. A disgusting, manipulative power. And what better way to get revenge on you for that knife fight than getting Shelley to—"

"Can we change the subject?" I interrupted, not wanting to hear where that sentence ended. "I thought we came out to have fun."

Sappho squeezed my hand once before raising hers and ordering another round of drinks.

Tolstoy signed something and Dostoevsky laughed.

"What?" I asked.

"He wants to play a drinking game."

Sappho leaned in and grinned. "That sounds fun. What game?"

"It's a Russian game. 'The Bear Has Come.' I don't think it's a good idea."

"Sure, it is," I said, looking for any path to take us far away from Shelley.

Dostoevsky raised his eyebrows and took a deep breath. "Okay, then."

He ordered a bottle of vodka and started the game. The way it worked was each of us put a one Euro coin on the table. He'd fill our shot glasses, we'd down them, and then he'd yell, "The bear has come!" We'd all scramble underneath the table. After a moment, he'd yell again.

"The bear has gone!"

We'd all crawl out from under the table, put another coin down, and then drink another round. The bear would come again, and again we'd crawl beneath the table. Last man standing took all the coins.

"I think I put my hand in gum," I said on the second time under the table.

Sappho scrunched up her face. "That's not gum."

"The bear has gone!"

And up we went again. All the down and up, down and up, combined with the vodka to make me sick. On the sixth round, I stayed seated when they all went under the table.

Sappho tugged on my pants leg. "The bear has come!" she repeated.

"Fuck the bear," I said, the room starting to spin. "The bear can kiss my ass."

I lost, obviously. I drank two bottles of water while they continued to play, then stumbled to the bathroom and emptied my stomach. I sat there for several minutes until my head stopped swimming, then splashed cold water onto my face. After rinsing my mouth several times and eating a handful of mints, I felt like myself again. A tipsy version of myself, but myself nonetheless.

As I passed the bar on the way back to my table, the woman in the purple skirt stopped me.

"Hi," she said.

"Hey."

The button nose and full lips meant I had to at least have a conversation.

"Why didn't you come talk to me?" She smiled and, even though I only just met her, I could tell she'd had a few herself. "I mean, that's the first time I've ever smiled and waved at someone in a bar. I'm not one of those girls, you know?"

"What girls?"

"Those girls who pick up guys in bars."

"I didn't know that was a type of girl."

"Oh, yeah. They chain smoke and have HPV."

I laughed. "HPV?"

"Human papillomavirus. It's the most common STD, you know. Eighty percent of the whole world has it."

"Is that so?"

"It sure is. So, you see why I wanted to know. Since I'm not one of those girls, I don't know if guys routinely turn away when you approach them in a bar or what."

"You didn't approach me. You just smiled."

She tucked her hair behind her ears. "I'm approaching you now."

Her name was Jessica, though her friends called her Jess. She had come to the bar with about forty of them. They were expatriates, graduate students to the last, and had met one another on Reddit. Most were American or British. Jess was Canadian.

"From Vancouver," she said. "Born and raised."

"What did you do there?"

"What did I really do, or what did I want to do?"

"How about want."

"It's silly."

"I'm a silly kind of guy," I said, and smiled.

"I want to be a poet."

It was a done deal after that.

She hadn't read much Keats and I'd had enough drinks to quote him and Byron to her. She, in turn, quoted Langston Hughes and Rita Dove back to me. When we were closer to sunrise than midnight, she asked if I'd walk her back to her apartment. By that point, Dostoevsky had passed out on the table and Sappho and Tolstoy sat staring at the floor, swaying back and forth. They barely waved when I said I was leaving.

"Watch out for the bear," Sappho slurred as we left. "He's coming for you."

At the door to Jess's place in the hipster Pigneto neighborhood, she kissed me. Shelley was a good kisser, and Miranda had been amazing, but I don't think I'd ever been kissed by anyone the way Jess kissed me that night.

I argued with myself over whether to go inside. One side of the argument took place in Sappho's voice, but between the drinks and Jess's perfume and that kiss, I don't remember which side Sappho took. I don't even remember what the points were. I do remember thinking of Shelley, which almost turned me away.

But then I thought of her with Byron and followed Jess inside.

***

It may seem like there was a ridiculous amount of sex going on in Italy, but it seems that way for a reason: there was. The entire country oozed sensuality. It leaked it into the air like an odorless gas. Fifty-year-old couples groped each other on fountains. Teenagers tongue-wrestled on the backs of Vespas parked in front of churches. And anyone passing simply smiled and said, "*Bella.*"

When I first heard of the Italian siesta, that period in the afternoon when the shops close, I equated it to the Mexican siesta I was familiar with in Southern California. During that siesta, everyone took a nap and rested. I mentioned this to Giacomo once and he laughed.

"That is not what siesta is for," he'd said. "Siesta is time to go home and make love. Everyone in the country make love every afternoon. Is why we so happy as a people, yes?"

I love Italy.

When we had finished that morning, Jess went to take a shower. She invited me along, but I told her I needed to rest a minute. The truth was, I needed to feel like an asshole and that required being alone.

I didn't care that Shelley had cheated on me. Hell, that wasn't even a definite fact. Even if it was, it didn't make me feel better for having gone home with Jess. Oh, I know. I still slept with her. The Carny might have reiterated that I was an animal and simply followed my instincts. He might have said that if I were in a room with a beautiful woman who wanted me, it would be hard to resist.

And maybe he was right. Maybe I just felt like such an asshole because of a lifetime of Puritanical American moralizing. The Pilgrims had really done a number on my whole society, after all.

This is how not to cheat, by the way. The trick has nothing to do with willpower. Willpower will always crumble. The Carny is right about that. We are programmed to fuck. It's the most powerful urge we have and it's harder to deny than the urge to breathe.

The trick, then, is to never put yourself in a situation where you need to refuse it. Men who remain faithful do not walk alone into the apartment of a woman who wants to sleep with them after drinking too much any more than someone trying to lose weight doesn't keep bags of cookies in the pantry. Temptation will always win out.

I could have stayed faithful to Shelley if I had walked away from Jess at the bar, but the second she kissed me, hell, the second we left the bar together, it was over. My instincts would never let me turn down full lips and deep brown eyes and what I'm sure were incredibly powerful pheromones.

What else had the Carny said? We all needed to take responsibility for ourselves. Even if all that shit about instinct was true, I still made the choice to go home with her. Me. I tipped that domino over knowing exactly what would happen if I did. That was on me no matter what.

The urge to sneak out of Jess's apartment while she was in the shower was a strong one. I even stood and gathered my things, but that would have only made me feel like even more of an asshole. Instead, I got dressed and put some coffee on.

She came out wrapped in a towel, wet hair looking almost purple in the light. I handed her a steaming cup.

"Thanks," she said.

"I'm seeing someone." It came out just like that. It was like a sneeze, really. Just *achoo* and there it was. I'm surprised she didn't say, "God bless you."

She looked down at her feet and sipped her coffee. "Someone you care about?"

I thought that was an odd question. "Yeah."

She met my eyes, hers filled with empathy. She still wore her smile, but it had faded a little, like a painting left out in the sun.

"Wanna tell me about it?" she asked.

I don't know why but I did. I told her every detail about Shelley I could without mentioning the Necropolis or the Carny or any of our less than legal pursuits. I changed Byron's to Barry to avoid explaining our unique names.

"I'm seeing someone, too," she said when I'd finished. "Back in Vancouver. We've been together since undergrad."

"Oh."

After an awkward moment of quiet, we both chuckled.

"Well, all right," I said.

"He slept with someone else, too. It was about a month ago. Not that that's why I talked to you last night."

"That's not why I came home with you, either. Not entirely. I mean, my friends had been ragging on me about it and I'm sure it played some part, but I think you're incredibly attractive and—"

"It's okay," she said. "Don't dig the hole any deeper."

I finished my coffee and put the cup down. "So, what do we do now?"

"I guess we go our separate ways."

"We'll always have Paris."

"Huh?"

"*Casablanca.*"

"I've never seen it."

"Christ." I kissed her cheek. "I guess I should go, then."

"You, um…" She tilted her head to the side and grinned.

"What?"

"You don't have to go *just* yet."

The towel fell to the floor.

We didn't see each other again after that, but we saw enough of one another that day to last a lifetime.

CHAPTER THIRTY-SEVEN

THE WALLET-EATER WAS intimidating without Shelley to guide me along. I wasn't familiar with the freelancers and found myself in constant fear of sticking a hand in one of their pockets by mistake, but I felt it was my responsibility to take up her game. Maybe it was because I ran her off. Or maybe it was because we were a couple, I don't know. Hell, it could have been some strange way to feel close to her, running the scam she always ran, doing what she had been doing the day we met.

Or maybe I was just addicted to exhaust fumes.

I was no longer clumsy when it came to **Bump and Grind**. No one yelled "*Aiuto! Ladro!*" until I'd exited the bus. I didn't get my face beat in anymore. Not to toot my own horn, but I'd gotten damn good at picking pockets.

Madame Butterfly floated on and off the bus. She had again become someone else, a stiff professional man in a wrinkle-free suit. That may have been the identity she'd been born with, but it wasn't her. Madame Butterfly was who she really was. This man was just an act. Was that act part of whatever her real game was? I still had no clue what she did when she wasn't on that bus or in the catacombs. No matter how often I asked, she'd remained tight-lipped.

I bumped into an elderly Australian as we approached the Vatican. A few pats told me his wallet wasn't on him, but a flick of the knife found it in his backpack. I stuck a water bottle in the bag and knew it would only be a matter of time before he felt it leaking. Wallet in hand, I hopped off the 64 Bus and hurried into the crowds surrounding St. Peter's.

I remembered promising myself a day as a tourist. With Shelley gone, my head just wasn't in the game, so why the hell not?

Michelangelo designed the Vatican to be approached from a certain angle. Unfortunately, this isn't the angle tourists approach it from today. Even with that inherent flaw, the sight is still enough to snatch your breath away. I suppose that's doubly true if you're Catholic.

Not that I was. I'd never been convinced of the existence of a higher power and, even if I had, the real-world sins of the church couldn't be ignored. But the tradition appealed to me, I suppose. The sense of wonder and mystery. Maybe it was the contrast to that unique brand of Protestantism found in the Southern United States, with its white-walled churches and preachers sounding like used-car dealers. Hard to feel any awe or mystery while shitty faux-rock bands play and the preacher broadcasts his face on giant flat-screen televisions.

Yet when walking through the massive doors of St. Peter's, it was easy to see how the throngs of faithful felt God here. The sheer massiveness of the building was difficult to comprehend, even when standing inside. The only thing I could compare it to was standing at the edge of the Grand Canyon, but even that didn't do it justice. After all, the Grand Canyon was formed over a million years by natural forces. This was built in a lifetime by simple men who didn't even have the benefit of power drills or AutoCAD.

Massive statues filled the place. My favorite was Michelangelo's *Pieta*. It's an emotionally wrenching sculpture of Mary holding Jesus after he was pulled from the cross. What plucks at the heartstrings with a maestro's finger is the absence of religious or spiritual connotations. The statue is simply of a mother mourning the loss of her son. It's behind a sheet of bulletproof glass today thanks to some asshole in the seventies who attacked it with a hammer.

"Hello, Keats."

I turned to find Byron. It was like my worries about Shelley had summoned him.

"Remarkable piece," he said. "Did you know that someone actually had the nerve to attack it?"

"Yeah. I was just thinking about that."

"Monstrous. Some brutes just can't stand to see true beauty untainted."

We stared at the sculpture in silence for a thousand years. Empires rose and crumbled while we pretended to admire the *Pieta*.

"Your stabbing," he finally said.

"Yeah?"

"I didn't authorize that."

"Well, shucks, Byron. That makes me feel much better."

"Janus has a certain...*impetuousness* that they encourage in one another. Sometimes it's endearing. Often sexy. But then when they do something like that... Well, it's very unattractive."

"Is it, now?"

"Mmm-hmm." He took my elbow. "Mass is beginning. Will you join me?"

I could see what Shelley saw in him. His green Anglo eyes were as wide and lovely as her brown Bengali ones, the lashes long and feminine.

"Please?" he continued. "Don't make me beg now."

"You don't seem like the begging type."

"No. I certainly am not."

Why not? It's not like anything could happen to me here in the Vatican.

I wondered if all the popes assassinated over the years had that same thought.

The altar in St. Peter's didn't have a cross. What it did have was a massive sculpture representing Heaven. Clouds of solid gold parted as beams of light shot from a stained-glass center past a hundred angels. A single dove in the glass represented Christ, I suppose. The entire piece seemed the size of the house I grew up in.

Mass was in Italian. I was a little disappointed. I'd hoped it would be in Latin. Not for any type of ultra-conservative pre-Vatican II reason. I simply wanted Latin so the picture would be complete and I could feel transported to another time and place. I'm not sure what that says about me, that religion is just escapism.

Hell, maybe that's not just me.

Byron answered all the prompts and hit his knees at all the proper times. I followed his lead, up and down, up and down. How did Catholics remember all this? It was like being in the Army.

A nun in front of us who was about the size of a six-year-old, even though it had been a hundred years since she'd seen that age, was pushed to the edge of the bench by a group of French teenagers who arrived late. They played with their cell phones through most of the service.

When mass ended, Byron said something to the teenagers in French. Their eyes went wide and they apologized to the nun, who seemed to neither understand nor care.

"Lovely service," he said as we made our way out.

"What did you say to those girls?"

"It's not important. They're French."

"What's that have to do with anything?"

"The French are still trying to milk the pride they gained from Baudelaire and Napoleon. Someone should tell them their time has passed."

"Wasn't Napoleon actually Italian?"

"Indeed, he was. Corsican. Which is technically Italy, even though the French will never give it up. *C'est la vie.*"

We stepped outside, the sudden rise in temperature jarring.

"The only culture worse for living in the past are you Yanks. You're still thumping your chests for bringing the wall down and outlasting the Soviets while letting the rest of the world pass you by."

"Don't forget beating the Nazis," I joked.

"Yes, as though you did that all by your lonesome as well," he said, not finding it funny. "As quick as you are to partner with others, you're even quicker to take all the credit when it's done. But who am I to talk? I'm British and our greatest successes were a century and a half ago, built on the backs of every civilization we could run roughshod over."

"Progress is always made from the suffering of the little guy, I suppose."

"Yes," he said sadly. "I suppose. Stroll with me a bit?"

We walked in silence through the tiny country of Vatican City. It didn't take long.

"Shelley," he finally said.

My stomach knotted with the terrible possibility of what he was about to say.

"What about her?" I asked.

"I know where she is."

"Oh?"

"And I wanted to tell you why I'd asked her to call me."

A red rage built in me. I swallowed it and held up a hand for him to stop. "I don't want to know."

"She said you thought we were rutting."

"Rutting?"

He sighed. "Making the beast with two backs."

"Fucking."

"To be vulgar. Yes. Fucking."

"Weren't you?"

"Not for a long while, much to my chagrin. I've tried. She's magic between the sheets, as I'm sure you well know. You could rut for a hundred years and never stick yourself inside such an artist again."

I didn't rise to the bait, even with the Freak telling me all the ways I could ruin his handsome face.

"Someone taught her well," Byron added.

"What's your fucking point?"

"Gelato?"

Before I could answer, he peeled off into a shop. He returned with two cups and handed me one.

"I hope you like vanilla," he said. "You seem like vanilla."

We walked through the city and ate gelato like two people on a date. I'm sure it was very cute.

"If you two weren't sleeping together," I said, "why did she come running when you called?"

"I can show you, if you'd like."

It wasn't an intelligent move, I admit, but curiosity trumped my judgment.

***

Capuchin monks were a strange lot. The order started in 1520 when Matteo da Bascio became "inspired by God." He felt the Franciscans of his day weren't living the type of life that St. Francis had wanted them to. Matteo thought they should return to a life of solitude and penance. So, he donned a brown robe and set off with some other monks, killjoys from the sound of it, and founded an order. Incidentally, those brown robes are where cappuccino gets its name.

Flash-forward eight years. Some merchant or pilgrim brought crates of soil back from Jerusalem. Everyone wanted to be buried in earth from the Holy Land then. It was the fashionable thing to do, like wearing culottes in the summer or getting highlights. As the ground began to fill up, the Capuchin monks were presented with a quandary. Too many people were dying and there wasn't enough earth to bury them all in. They had two options. The first was to send someone back to Jerusalem to get more dirt. That would have been expensive, and taken a few years, and been a bit of a hassle all around. They went with the other obvious choice.

Digging everyone up and making artwork from their bones.

The sight today is both macabre and morbidly beautiful. Byron had brought me to Santa Maria della Concezione dei Cappuccini on the Via Veneto, just up the street from the movie theater in Piazza Barberini where Big Jim liked to run **Siskel & Ebert**. We strolled through the crypts beneath the church while Latin chants were piped in. There were other tourists, but no one spoke. I couldn't blame them.

The walls were lined with skulls, dotted here and there by flowers assembled from pelvic bones. Chandeliers pieced together from femurs and ribs cast ghastly light onto the entire scene. There were even full skeletons, monks in their brown robes, positioned in prayer or standing in corners as though they watched us all. Bits of mummified flesh still clung to some of their faces.

"Beautiful, isn't it?"

"Why did you bring me here, Byron?"

"This way."

We reached the end of the crypt. The skeletons of two children adorned the wall, ribs spreading out behind them like angel's wings. A young couple admired the spectacle. We waited for them to walk off.

"There," Byron said. He pointed to the back corner where a monk was propped up.

"So?"

"Look closer. Doesn't it seem strange?"

It was odd that this one monk would have kept his body fat in death. The rest of them, even the ones with flesh still covering them, had been through a process akin to mummification. Or at least I assumed they had with their leathery skin, but this bulbous monk with his bushy eyebrows and—

Oh shit. Could it be?

"Dimitri?" I asked.

Byron nodded.

"How?"

"You know how."

"The Carny?"

"What do you think?"

Another batch of tourists made their way over and Byron grabbed my elbow. "You look ill. Let's get some air."

Outside we walked at a brisk pace. I had to move fast, or the Freak would assert himself. We passed a group of Alitalia workers picketing an office building and barking angry gibberish with signs held high.

"Tell me what you know," I said.

"Dimitri was a friend to both our little groups. We hadn't heard from him in a few weeks and I went by his flat to check on him. I found him there, throat slit from ear to ear. He'd been dead for days."

"Jesus."

"As much as our two gangs hate one another, we also protect one another from the authorities. Last thing any of us need is for the government to know we exist. So, when I found Dimitri, I called Shelley and suggested we clean up."

"You put him in the crypts?"

"He always said he wished he could be preserved there. Why, I don't know, but we both felt we owed him that much, at least. Luckily, it made for a convenient way to dispose of the body. Who would find him there? If you hadn't met him before you would never have known anything was amiss."

"And Shelley helped you?"

"Yes. We used to break in there at night when we were together and have candlelight dinners among the dead."

And I thought I was romantic.

"And that took three days?" I asked.

"His body had to be prepared. You do not want to hear the details of that, I assure you."

I'm sure I didn't. I sat on a bench and tried to keep my head from swimming.

"It was my fault," I said. "I got him to talk."

"I know. Shelley said as much."

"Why are you telling me all this?"

He sat next to me and picked at an invisible piece of lint on his pants. "I hurt her when I left. I don't apologize for anything I've done, but… Well. She met me at my worst and I'll always regret that. I owe her. And she's enlightened enough to forgive me on some level for what I did. Not that we'll ever be romantic again, or even friends, for that matter. Our relationship is more complex than that, I suppose."

"Yeah," I said, thinking of what Sappho told me, "I suppose most abusers think of their victims that way."

We both let that hang there as we watched a pigeon snatch bits of a discarded ice cream cone from the sidewalk.

"She cares about you, Keats," he went on. "A great deal. Perhaps this is my way of paying her back for all the pain I caused."

"Where is she?"

"Naples," he said. "She goes there when things are their roughest. She has a friend who runs a bed and breakfast not far from the National Museum."

"Is she coming back?"

"All she said was that she was going." He stood. "And now I've told you."

"And the Carny?"

"What about him?"

"Dimitri."

"Oh. That. Listen. The Carny's losing it. Been losing it for years. One of the reasons I left."

"I thought he kicked you out?"

He waved that off. "Sometimes his old brilliance comes out, but other times the man can't listen to reason. You're on a sinking ship, Keats."

"If any of this shit is true."

"Why would I lie?" He considered that and laughed. "All right, so there are a hundred reasons I'd lie, but you know I'm not."

Could he be right? I wondered.

"You should jump before the ship goes down." He turned and stepped away. "We could use someone like you, you know. A true Romantic."

And then he was gone, vanished into the crowd of picketing airline employees.

The Freak sidled up next to me. "Boy, you actually got someone killed this time. Nice work. My hat's off to you."

"Shut up."

CHAPTER THIRTY-EIGHT

TREMBLING. THAT'S HOW IT started. A shaking so small I thought it was a spasm in my calf. Then a low rumbling rose from under our feet like some prehistoric beast growling beneath us.

The Family Room shook. Dust rained down on us. Books fell from shelves. Glass broke. The children screamed and cried and clutched Miss Fagin's thick legs. Ravenna froze, eyes like softballs. Big Jim pressed against the wall and steadied himself. I pitched back and forth on the couch like it was a wild horse.

The rumbling grew louder.

A crash from somewhere.

Then everything settled.

Coughing fits hit us as we worked up the nerve to stand and examine the catacombs.

Everyone else trickled in. Even Eleanor Rigby stepped out to check on us.

Marco scanned the room. "Is everyone okay?"

Miss Fagin tried to calm the children.

"Yeah," I said. "I think we're fine."

The lights in the room flickered.

"I will check on that," Big Jim said. "Marco, make sure plumbing is good."

"Right."

The earthquake had hit the entire city. It wasn't a big one, especially for a former Angeleno like me. Reports varied between 3.5 and 3.9 on the Richter scale. Most of Rome didn't even feel it, and where it was felt it was a topic of mild conversation for the day and then forgotten. That's how it went for the surface dwellers.

For those of us underground, any earthquake, no matter how small, could be disastrous.

"The Carny," I said, thinking of him mapping out those dark corridors.

I grabbed a flashlight and rushed down the hallway. Footsteps pounded behind me as the others followed. Clicking on the light didn't do much for visibility; the air was so thick with dust I couldn't see. It tickled my throat and burned my nostrils.

The intersection where the Carny had left me, where he had patted my shoulder and said, "This is the point of no return," had collapsed.

"This is the way he went," I said. "The Carny. This is the path he'd gone down."

"No, no, no, no," Dostoevsky murmured.

Madame Butterfly shot past us and tugged chunks of rock away.

"Come on," she yelled. "Goddammit, come on!"

The rest of us dove in, removing stone and handfuls of dirt. We worked for hours, Marco and Jim peeling away at points to check on the rest of the Necropolis, Ravenna and Mansa Musa bringing everyone water. Miss Fagin stayed with the children. Sappho, Madame Butterfly, and I never left the intersection.

None of us spoke more than was necessary, but we each wore the fear on our faces. It was impossible to know how far the Carny had gone into the tunnels. He could be crushed under a thousand tons of earth at that moment, little more than bloody dust beneath stone, or trapped somewhere, starving and injured.

Hours into digging, our backs and arms exhausted and faces filthy, we heard the sound. A faint and far-off keening that ended before we could clear the opening. When we could finally crawl over the debris and into the tunnel, we were met with silence and a deep, impenetrable black.

CHAPTER THIRTY-NINE

DEBRIS HAD BEEN SCATTERED about the tunnel. Every tiny pile we came to was searched for signs of a body underneath. Big Jim and I hurried from one pile to the next, yarn tied to our belt loops and strung back to the entrance to find us in case the collapse wasn't yet complete. Tolstoy had pieced together a makeshift stretcher and Big Jim had strapped it to his massive back.

A rumbling sounded overhead, and we froze. Dust fell around us like early snowfall. It ended and we moved forward, hoping it had only been the Metro.

"Keats," Big Jim said.

I followed the trail of his flashlight. The beam came to rest on a bit of paper jutting out from a pile of rock. I cleared away enough stone to tug it free.

The Carny's map.

We dove into the rock, throwing it to the side, knowing we would find his corpse.

"Over…here…fuckers…"

Our lights shined down the passage to find a pale hand waving from an intersection.

The Carny was half-buried beneath a collapsed arch. A giant gash ran down the side of his head, blood streaking his jaw and neck. His breath was strained, and I worried his ribs might have broken.

"About…fucking time," he said, and passed out.

We cleared the debris and unfolded the stretcher. Carefully, as though lifting a Fabergé egg, we placed him onto it.

***

Back in his room, we laid him on the bed. Sappho ran out to fetch the doctor while we cleaned the obvious wounds and tried to bandage him as best we could. The gash on his head was bad. The stone had hit his skull dead on before dragging down the side of his face.

When the doctor came, the same old Italian with a crinkled mustache and wet eyes that had seen to my stabbing, he shooed us out of the room. All we could do was wait.

No one was particularly pleased with that. Marco couldn't sit still and so went for a walk. Ravenna made her way to the thankfully still intact Temple to pray and consult her grandmother. Miss Fagin took the Orphans out for gelato. Tolstoy and Dostoevsky went for a drink, while Sappho cleaned the dust from her skin in a long shower that steamed the hallways. Mansa Musa busied himself cleaning and repairing everything in the Carny's crushed bag.

Big Jim took position outside the Carny's room like a sentry. His face was neutral, but I could tell by the slump of his shoulders how worried he was.

Wanting to help and not knowing went to do, I decided to get out of everyone's way. In my quarters, I plugged in an old record player I'd found at the Porto Portese. I paid five euro more for it than I should have, but it worked, which was a rarity for anything I purchased there. I sorted through my mother's records before settling on David Bowie.

The Carny had told me something like this would happen. He didn't know what, or when, but he knew somehow it was coming. I had agreed to the responsibility of taking over when he was gone. Even if he recovered, and I so desperately hoped he would, I could feel it. We had reached a turning point. Turn and face the strange.

Was this his karma for murdering Dimitri? I felt bad for even thinking that, and then felt bad for feeling bad. Who deserved my sympathy here? Dimitri? The Carny? Dimitri was just a poor cab driver trying to earn a little on the side. He didn't deserve to have his throat cut.

But the Carny was the Carny. The architect of our subterranean Utopia. He had given me a home, a family. A new identity and a chance to redeem myself.

I didn't want to think about any of that right then. I sank into the bed, closed my eyes, and just listened to the music.

My mother had listened to this album while lying in her room at the Blue Angel. I wondered if she had sensed the changes coming her way, too.

It was odd, listening to her record, even with everything else going on. I felt I'd made a sort of peace with her. It was the letter, I think. But seeing a few of the places she'd been, where she had stayed and worked, I think all these things came together. For so long she'd been an empty canvas that I painted ideas of her onto. Now I knew her in some small way. And I knew how she had felt about me.

Letting that pain go, that guilt I'd lived with my entire life, was both comforting and frightening. When you live with a pain that long it becomes a part of you. Letting go of it is like cutting a piece of yourself away.

My family had changed since coming to Rome. I had brothers and sisters now, Marco and Ravenna and Big Jim, Dostoevsky and Tolstoy and Sappho. I had aunts, Eleanor Rigby and Miss Fagin. I had nieces and nephews in the Orphans.

And I had the Carny.

Keats. That had been his name before it was mine. We were one and the same, we two Misfits.

"Life on Mars" leaked from the record player. Wasn't that the song Shelley made me sing at karaoke that first night?

I should have been anxious, afraid, depressed. Yet a strange calm washed over me and sent me drifting along to sleep. I dreamed, dreams free for once of the fly and Chelsea and Miranda and all the guest stars who usually made an appearance. For the only night since Shelley had left, I slept through until dawn.

CHAPTER FORTY

KEATS.

I looked up to see the marble God in my doorway.

"Yeah?"

Dionysus extended a hand.

I took it. It was warm and felt like flesh. He pulled me to my feet and let go.

I followed him down the hall.

All the rooms we passed were empty. No one was inside and most of their things gone. Dresser drawers hung open and bedside tables had toppled over onto the floor. They had fled, abandoning the Necropolis.

When we made our way to the Family Room, I was surprised to see the karaoke machine out. We walked past it and over the shattered pieces of our collective piggy bank. I didn't know what had happened to it, but the God of Wine and Revelry paid it no attention.

In the Temple, he paused and motioned for me to step forward. The troughs of oil engulfed themselves in flame and lit the room.

Blood filled the bowls on the altar. More of it streaked across the wall and floor. Still wet.

"Where is everyone?"

They have fled. His stone jaw creaked up and down as he spoke. The voice that came out had the timbre and pitch of a Tectonic shift. *They have scattered.*

"What happened?"

It has all burned to ash. It waits for you to give it rebirth.

I didn't understand what he was getting at.

No real man dies of drowning, he said.

Then he stomped across the floor and shoved me.

I fell back, fell so far into the dark and cold. I hit water, freezing and stale, and plunged deeper still. In the black, I felt at peace. The water seeped into my lungs, but I refused to let it take me. I floated there, alone and whole, and waited until I was again pushed into the light.

***

Il dottore's name was Paulo. Before he would tell us anything, he made his way to the bar and poured himself a drink. He swallowed it in one gulp and poured another.

"*Mio papa*," he said, "he spent entire life as *dottore*. He live in Abruzzo. All the people for kilometers know if they are hurt, they come to Ezio. He make them better. Broken legs, stomach aches, *raffredori, mal di testa…*"

"What's your point?" I said.

He eyed me, a giant vein on his temple throbbing. He took a deep breath and sucked down his new drink. Hands shaking, he poured a third. "The point is my father could make the Carny better."

"Where is he?"

"He pass on fifteen years ago, God rest his soul." He made the sign of the cross.

"What's wrong with him?"

"His skull is, eh… *come si dice*? Fracture. He come in and out from wake to sleep for many days, I think. Very high fever. He need to go *ospedale*."

"We can't take him to a hospital," Madame Butterfly said. "You know that." She wiped her eyes with the back of one hand. It came away stained with mascara.

"I bandage him. Give him ibuprofen and ice packs for the fever. He bruised in many other places. Two ribs are cracked and a foot broken, I think. I wrap and leave Percocet. If he make it…" Paolo shook his head. "*La Donna Fortuna* is only one who can say."

When he was gone, we sat there, silent, and stared at one another, hoping someone would have the balls to say, "Fuck it. Let's take him to the hospital."

No one did.

This wasn't cowardice or self-preservation. Not entirely. The Carny had been living off the grid for God knows how long and was likely wanted by the police somewhere for something he'd done. If we took him in, he'd be in the hands of the authorities by sundown.

Everyone was confused. Frightened.

I cleared my throat and stood. "Well, then. We wait," I said.

They all murmured agreement.

Eleanor Rigby pulled herself from the shadows. "I'll watch him," she said.

No one objected.

"All right." I clapped my hands together and looked over the group. "Eleanor will look after him. The rest of us will take the day off to recover.

Marco and Big Jim will double-check the plumbing and wiring, make sure there's no other disaster waiting in the wings. Miss Fagin, do you think you could cook tonight? Give Mansa Musa a rest?"

The chef was stained white with dust. I thought he would object, but his bloodshot eyes met mine and he nodded thanks.

"Tomorrow we'll meet back here first thing. We should take inventory of anything that's broken, as well as whatever supplies we might need. Ravenna and Marco can then go and find whatever's on that list. The rest of us will go out and carry on with our games. We still have to make a living, after all. Now, get some rest."

They murmured agreement and shuffled from the room.

My first act as leader. I had expected an argument the first time I stepped up, some kind of resentment or one of the others feeling they had earned the right to lead until the Carny recovered. Yet, they were all so scared and lost and needed someone, anyone, to give them direction.

I wished Shelley were around to give me a little.

CHAPTER FORTY-ONE

BY THE END OF the week, I was tired. I was tired of checking in on the Carny only to find nothing had changed. I was tired from not sleeping, from tossing and turning all night in a cold, empty bed. I was tired of giving everyone direction. Most of all, I was tired of missing Shelley.

We'd taken more damage than our initial assessment of the earthquake had identified. Everything from broken dishes to clogged toilets were brought to me in what seemed like fifteen-minute increments, the other Misfits needing to know how we were going to get back up to speed.

As I made a list of general supplies we needed, Big Jim and Marco walked up.

"We need to redo all plumbing," Big Jim said.

"All of it?" I asked.

"All of it."

Marco nodded. "We got a lead, though. A truck filled with pipes and other plumbing supplies. Maybe even some copper wire, which we could also use."

"Whoah whoah whoah," I said. "Are you suggesting we knock over a hardware truck?"

They both just shrugged.

"God, the Carny's gonna kill us."

"It will not be violent," Big Jim said. "I know the driver. He will leave the truck parked at a truck stop outside city while he eat a long lunch. We take what we need and he will report it stolen. Very clean."

"Fine," I said. "Do it."

Marco grinned and they took off up the stairs.

I suddenly felt like a gangster in the sleaziest of ways.

While repairing a crack in the bar, Mansa Musa approached. I waved, expecting him to echo the gesture and continue on.

"Keats," he said, and I was so surprised to hear his voice I dropped the wood glue I'd been using. "How you holding up?"

His accent was American. Not sure why that surprised me so much.

"Good," I said.

"Don't lie to me, man. You got the weight of the world on your shoulders right now. It's all right to be stressed. Scared, even."

He climbed onto a barstool and I sat next to him.

"I'm just, I'm not cut out for this," I said.

"The Carny thought you were."

"Yeah. Well. Maybe the Carny was wrong."

"He may have been. But I don't think so. I seen you around here since day one, asking questions, helping out, taking care of folks when they sick or hurt. You ask me, you got the number one trait any leader should have. You give a shit."

"That can't be enough, though."

"I tell you, man, it's more than what most people got. You from LA, right?"

"Tennessee originally, but yeah."

"Atlanta," he said, and thumped his chest. "Most of the people I ever met in leadership positions there didn't care about nothing but themselves. Teachers, city councilmen, the police. Shit, especially the police. They didn't lead people because they wanted to do better for them. To take care of them. Most times, was the other way around. Because they was authority, they expected people do shit for them. Make them rich. Make them famous. Defer to what piddly ass power they had. It's why the world is the way it is.

"The Carny, one of the reasons I stuck around is he gives a shit. That's what makes him a great leader. And that's what you got, Keats. Everything else, you can learn all that shit. But if you got the foundation in here," and he thumped me over the heart, "it don't matter how great you are at giving speeches."

Then he hopped from his barstool and headed into the kitchen.

It was a long time before I heard him speak again. It was like he only had so many words he could use in a day and he saved them for when they were needed most. I was thankful he'd used some of them on me.

***

The Carny woke the next day.

Eleanor Rigby came and tugged on my arm. I could tell what had happened by the smile on her face, a sight as rare as a unicorn. I rushed into his quarters to find Big Jim on one knee by the bed, the Carny grinning.

Big Jim turned to me, the remains of a tear he'd wiped away still shining on his cheek. "He is awake."

"I see that."

The Carny gave a low, throaty laugh. "As astute as always, Keats."

"How you doing?"

"I'm alive, aren't I? I thought it was the end for a bit."

I still wasn't so sure. I sent Dostoevsky and Tolstoy out for Paolo. After a lengthy examination filled with the Carny cursing him for every prod and poke, the doctor nodded to us.

"He is fine," he said. "Unless there is bleeding or swelling in brain."

"Then what?" I asked.

"Then he die. No warning." Paolo snapped his fingers. "Just dead."

"Bah," the Carny said. "I feel fine."

I called everyone into the Family Room for celebratory drinks while the Carny stayed in bed. He demanded one, but we gave him chilled orange juice and told him it was a screwdriver. He knew we were lying, but I think he appreciated the effort.

"Shelley back yet?" he said when I handed him the glass.

"No."

He gave me a look and I knew he was thinking the same thing I was.

"Shelley has been gone for a while now," I said to everyone when back in the Family Room. "With the Carny awake and everything else that's been going on, I think we should go to Naples and bring her back."

No one said anything.

"Not all of us, obviously. Eleanor will stay here with the Carny. But I'm going to go and…" I let it trail off, hoping someone would volunteer to come with me.

No one did.

"I'd like it if someone went with me."

Marco crunched on an apple. Big Jim filed his nails. Miss Fagin rocked an infant to sleep in her arms. Dostoevsky and Tolstoy signed back and forth. Sappho shook her head slowly as though it were the dumbest idea in the world while Ravenna held a strand of red hair in one hand and a strand of purple in another and compared them.

"It would be good for us," I said. "Get away for a bit. Have a little break."

Big Jim glared at me. "You leave the Carny while he still recover?"

"No. That's not what I'm saying. I'm just…"

I had lost them. Lost them, that is, if I'd ever had them. Maybe I didn't. This was harder than I thought.

"Look," I said. "I miss Shelley, all right? I need her. And I'm asking for your help to go with me and find her."

Marco leaned forward. "Why didn't you just say so?"

"How do you know she's even in Naples?" Miss Fagin said.

"She told me," I lied. "When she left. She said she was going to Naples." There was no way I could mention my day spent with Byron, not with the Carny having only just come back from death's door.

"Why didn't you ever mention that before?" Sappho asked.

The lies were already beginning to snowball.

"She'd only said it in passing and said it in Italian. It didn't click until the doctor came." I don't know what that would have meant exactly, but I hoped it was confusing enough that they'd just let it go if I kept talking. "I need your help. Okay? Please?"

"I'm in," Marco said.

I could have kissed him.

"I too will go," Ravenna said. "It may be fun."

"Big Jim?"

He shook his head, his mouth pulled tight. "No, Keats. I will not leave the Carny."

"I have the Orphans," Miss Fagin said.

"I don't like Naples," Sappho said, as if we were discussing a weekend vacation. I knew what she really meant: she didn't think it was good for me to traipse all over the country after Shelley.

She was probably right.

Tolstoy and Dostoevsky signed back and forth. It seemed they argued about it. I don't know who wanted to do what, but they decided with simultaneous shakes of the head not to go.

"Well, just the three of us." Marco stood and stretched. He sent his apple core sailing across the room to land in a trashcan. "Should be a helluva time."

***

Trenitalia does not have the most efficient website. We gave up and hopped a bus to Termini. I fought with a kiosk for fifteen minutes before getting three round trip tickets to Naples.

It was a few hours by train down the coast and into Campania. Marco brought a deck of cards and we passed the time trying to teach Ravenna to play poker. She did not take to it.

"Is stupid game," she said. "With stupid rules."

"So, Keats," Marco said as he dealt another hand. "What brought you here?"

"I'm sick of talking about it." And I was. That felt good, to be tired of talking about it.

"Fine, fine." Marco laughed. "I've heard enough of the bits and pieces to put it together, I guess. Seems like we got a bit in common there."

"A tale as old as time," I said. "What about you, Ravenna?"

She shook her head.

"C'mon, what brings you down into *La Bella Paese*?"

"No," she said, and stared at her lap. "I no talk about it."

"Fair enough."

Outside the window, the baby blue of the Mediterranean rushed by.

Marco beat me again. He swept up the cards and shuffled. "What's the plan when we get to Napoli?"

"You know, I hadn't really thought it out."

He grinned. "I figured as much. The Carny has a mate down there, guy named Coleridge."

"The limoncello guy?"

"Yeah. That's him. Used to be a part of the crew back before my time. He can get anything and find anyone. If Shelley is in Naples…"

"She is." She had to be.

"Well, if she is then she's been in touch with Coleridge. He'll know where she is."

"I hope so."

Marco leaned forward and put his hand on my shoulder. "We'll find her, Keats." He stood. "Now, I gotta see a man about a horse."

He stumbled out into the aisle. It took him a moment to get the feel for the rocking train and I thought he was going to pitch over.

When he was gone, Ravenna grabbed the deck of cards and fanned them out in her hand. "My grandmother told fortunes with cards."

"Tarot cards?"

She shook her head. "No. Cards like this. We no afford tarot."

"Tell me my fortune."

"I never learn how. She always say she teach me one day but even now she does not do it." She turned to stare out the window. "I am scared," she said.

"Scared? Of what?"

"If I know it not frighten me so much." She placed the cards back in Marco's seat. "I no like change. I like things way they are."

"Everything changes. Eventually."

The coast had swelled out into a stretch of farmland. Sheep grazed on the edge as we sped past.

"Everyone I ever know is dust now," she said in a soft voice. "I do not want to haul more skulls around."

Before I could ask what she meant, Marco returned. "Right. I think it's time for some Texas Hold 'Em."

"Yee-haw."

"Ever been to Texas, Keats?"

"I've driven through it. Gigantic."

"My ex-girlfriend, the one I was coming to see when I found the Carny, she's from Texas."

"Oh, yeah? I thought she would have been Australian."

"Nah. Never been one for Ozzies. Mostly Kiwis and Yanks. Not sure why. Just always played out that way. She travels the world. Oil money, I guess. I never asked. But she talks about how beautiful Texas is all the time."

I noticed the present tense. "Talks? As in currently?"

"We still email." He grinned and leaned back into his seat. "I don't know. Hard to kick somebody out of your life when they were that important. Even if they fucked you up sideways for a minute."

"And the guy in Munich?"

"She's still with him. They're gonna get married, it seems."

This was why we were all Misfits. Look at the music we listened to, the movies we watched, the books we read. We were anachronisms. None of us belonged to this age. The world moved on and left us behind.

"He's okay with you two talking?"

Marco picked at the remains of an old sticker on the window. "Yeah. I wouldn't be if I was him, but he babbles on about trust and goes out of his way to show what a better man he is than me." He snorted.

"That's big of him."

"Big of him? He's a fucking prick with his stupid German name and his stupid German hair. His name is fucking Helmut. Helmut! Can you believe that shit?" He shot forward and slapped my knee. "You know what he said to her once? I got drunk and wrote her that I still think about her all the time. And she tells me he said I would do that. I ask what the fuck that meant and she writes that he said, 'One day he'll wake up and realize how much he loves you. On that day you'll wake up next to someone who already did.' What kind of pretentious bullshit is that? I mean, who talks like that, huh? Like a fucking Instagram meme come to life." He deflated back into his chair and glanced at Ravenna. I think he'd forgotten she was there.

She had nothing to say.

"Fucking prick," he repeated.

I knew in that moment that Marco's story of the wounded heart making his way to his lover only to find she'd left him for someone else was only half-true. The Carny had accused us of refusing to accept responsibility for our lives and I could see that was correct. Marco wasn't ready for it. Not yet. He would be. We all are, eventually, but I don't think that's something you can really help someone with. You could nudge them a bit, be an ear for their rants or a shoulder to cry on, help point them in the right direction. But Marco would have to learn it himself like the rest of us.

"You know," Marco said, "we have the reputation for being pricks. We men, I mean. We're supposed to jump from woman to woman while women are supposed to sit around and pine for us. But it ain't true. Women move on much easier than we do."

"This again," Ravenna said and rolled her eyes.

"You think so?" I asked, not sure I agreed.

"Oh, I know so. See, when you fall in love it's like you take everything in your heart and box it up and give it to the woman. And she does the same. She probably decorates her box, though. Hearts and cherubs and shit. You just use whatever cardboard the bottle shop's tossing. But when it's all over she takes her box back *and* keeps the box you gave her. Then when she meets some other guy, she gives him the same box she had given you. Meanwhile your box sits in her closet and keeps you from moving on.

"And the new guy, he has this box that has all the good times she shared with you inside of it. She just passes all those feelings along to him. Twenty years from now, they'll be sitting on a porch somewhere and she'll say, 'Remember that trip to the beach we took?' and he'll say, 'We never went to the beach,' and she'll be confused. She had that experience with you but gave it to him.

"Meanwhile, you're left to make a new box for every woman you're with because she won't give you that box back. So three, four, fifteen women later you're still remembering how much you shared with her while she's thinking the guy she's with now is the only bludger she's ever been head-over-heels for."

He closed his eyes and shook his head, not quite content with his one-sided realizations.

I almost argued with him, but thought better of it. He had been one of the only Misfits to agree to help me, after all.

There was one thing I thought he needed to hear, though.

"You should stop talking to her," I said.

He opened one eye and stared at me like I'd just spoken in tongues.

"She's moved on. The only thing keeping in touch with her does is prevent you from doing the same."

He sat forward, eyes open, and looked like he was about to argue. I expected him to draw some parallel with the three of us racing south to find Shelley.

But he didn't. Instead, he slumped back into his chair, a look of defeat on his face.

Man, I thought. If only I'd been around to give myself this advice months ago. Maybe I wouldn't have slumped around whining like an asshole all the time.

We were nearing Naples. Ships filled the sea outside. In the distance, Mount Vesuvius rose toward the sky.

Marco gave up on his diatribe. He dealt a hand and explained the rules of *Texas Hold 'Em* to Ravenna. She still didn't care for it.

CHAPTER FORTY-TWO

NAPLES IS NOTHING LIKE Rome. It's how I imagine Mumbai or Bangkok to be. The streets are narrow and ancient, dating back to the Greek city of Neapolis. Each one is lined with stalls, merchants selling Christmas ornaments and nativity scenes year-round next to knockoff Gucci bags and fish mongers chopping heads from the day's catches. Laundry runs from building to building on makeshift clotheslines overhead. As you make your way down these narrow and cramped streets, you constantly have to throw yourself against the wall as a car or group of motorcycles zooms by.

Which brings us to possibly the craziest thing about Naples: the traffic. There are lanes and lights, but not a single soul follows them. Cars head straight at each other in rush hour only to find they're playing some bizarre slow-as-hell game of chicken. Then they creep and crawl and angle themselves to get out. People drive on the sidewalk. Seriously. Five hundred pedestrians will be on the sidewalk and an Audi will pop two wheels up onto the curb and speed to an intersection, or Vespas will cut right down the middle and God help anyone who isn't quick enough to jump out of the way.

They say as you go south, Italy intensifies. That's for damn sure. In the north, cities are quieter and more pristine than in Rome, while Naples runs screaming in the opposite direction. It's dirty and smelly and filthy and chaotic and covered in grime.

I was instantly in love.

Ravenna did not feel the same. "I hate this fucking place."

"Why?"

"Look around."

Fair enough. It wasn't everyone's cup of tea. In fact, I think I would have hated it a few months earlier myself.

"The gods here," she said, "are mad."

Marco chuckled. "Aren't we all?"

She considered it. "Yes, but is different with gods. When gods go mad no good can come from it."

Mad or not, the city had a pulse to it. It was a living thing all on its own and that energy bounded from the cobblestones and straight into me.

Naples claims to be the birthplace of pizza and we stopped to try some. Many places hold that claim, but Naples has the strongest case for it. Having tasted pizza from New York to Rome, I'd give the prize to Naples every time.

"What kind of games do they run here?" I asked around a mouthful of buffalo mozzarella and fresh basil.

"No games," Ravenna said.

"None?"

Marco slurped on a glass of fizzy water. I never understood why Europeans prefer their water carbonated. There's nothing refreshing about it.

"*La Camorra*," he said.

"The camera?"

Ravenna lit a cigarette. "No. Is like mafia in Napoli."

"They run everything," Marco went on. "Pretty rough guys. Make your boys in the States look like schoolgirls. Almost all the scams here go through them at some point."

"Should we, like, introduce ourselves to them or something? Let them know we're here?"

Ravenna looked at me like I'd grown a second head. "Why?"

"I don't know. I wasn't sure how they did things."

"It'd probably be better not to let them know we're here," Marco said.

"Is Coleridge with them?"

"Freelancer," Ravenna said.

Marco swirled loose cheese around on a fork. "I'm sure he works with them in some capacity. But he's pretty much independent."

I made the international sign for "check, please" and the waiter sauntered over at a snail's pace to drop it off. I threw some cash down and he thanked us and scampered off.

"Okay. So where do we find Coleridge?"

Marco smiled. "That's the fun part."

***

Forty minutes later we were being ferried out into the Bay of Naples on a small motorboat. Giant yachts and ferries surrounded us, and a warm breeze blew down from Vesuvius. The water crashing against our hull managed to be both neon-blue and crystal-clear. I hadn't gotten the concept yet, but it seemed the water understood Negative Capability.

LIFE ON THE 64 BUS

"They say she erupt again," Ravenna said, and motioned to the dormant volcano.

"You mean soon?"

"She no erupt since World War Two. No big erupt since she bury Pompeii."

"Well, that's comforting."

"Pliny say Romans grew good grapes on the slope. Make best wine in ancient world. When she erupt, all the grapes killed. The wine vanish. Poof." She tossed her head back, closed her eyes, and enjoyed the sun on her face. "Is tragedy."

Marco tsked. "I'd think the tragedy would have been all those people who died."

"People die," she said. "People always die. Nothing to do about that. But good wine is...how to say...good wine is art, yes? Is always tragedy when art die."

"I think," Marco said, "the people of Pompeii may have disagreed with you on that."

"They be dead now no matter what, yes? But if she no erupt we might drink best wine tonight."

An old fishing trawler floated ahead of us, the kind of diesel-driven beast you didn't expect to see outside of New England. Paint chipped from the sides and rust crawled along its length. It reminded me of Quint's boat from *Jaws*. *Cristabel* was painted on the side in bright red letters.

The faint sounds of "Lake Shore Drive" drifted down to us from the deck.

Our driver pulled up next to it and honked the horn. After a few minutes of listening to the waves slap the boat, he honked again.

Finally, a man with the build of an under-stuffed scarecrow popped his head over the side.

"Eh, ye feckers! What the feck are ye honking for?"

He was Irish, I guessed, from all the "fecks." He grinned. Two of his front teeth were missing.

"Marco," he yelled. "Ravenna! The feck didn't ye say who ye were?"

Marco waved up at him. "Throw the ladder down already!"

He disappeared and a moment later a rope ladder dropped over the side. Marco told our driver he could go, and we scurried up.

Coleridge embraced him. "Fecking hell, it's great to see ye." Then he pulled Ravenna to him and lifted her into the air for a quick embrace.

"Hi," I said.

Hands on his hips, he stared at me, my reflection filling his mirror-shade sunglasses. His skin was burned the color of an apple.

"Who the feck's this, eh?"

"He's new," Marco said. "His name's Keats."

"Keats? Feck me running." He raised the sunglasses. His left eye had been replaced with unmoving glass, pitch black and shining like a gem. "Never thought I'd see the day."

He hugged me so hard I thought he was going to crack a rib.

"Nice to meet you," I said.

He rubbed his hands together and bounced back and forth on the balls of his feet. "Well, come on now. This deserves a fecking drink."

***

Eight shots of limoncello later, we finally got to why we came. We sat around a card table in a room filled with junk while Coleridge demanded we report on everything. Including the Carny.

"May the Devil make a ladder from my spine!" He shook his head. "Hate to hear it. But don't ye be worrying about that gobshite. Rough as the sea, he is. Still, I'll ask Poseidon to watch out for him." He squeezed a blob of aloe into his palm and rubbed it on his chest.

"Did Shelley come by here?" I asked.

He poured another round. My head was already feeling it.

"Aye. That she did. Said she needed to get away from a man. I reckon that's you?"

"Yeah. I reckon so."

"Ye got that look about you."

"What look?"

More aloe. He moved to his arms this time. "Ye know what I mean. You're addicted to love. Like that dryshite Robert Palmer. Everyone has an addiction, Keats. Mine, if it weren't obvious, is drink, like the pox bottle I am. Usually whiskey, but as long as it warms the gut I don't much care. You? It's love. I can read it on your face."

I couldn't argue.

"Sex, maybe. I'd peg ye as a serial cheater from that cheeky little grin ye got there. But mostly love. And, like all addictions, someone gets hurt. They always get hurt."

Ravenna had passed out on a threadbare couch with stuffing poking free all over it. Marco stared past me in that way drunks do. I don't think he could hear us. I would have been just as bad if I weren't larger than him.

"And what about you?" I asked, my hackles up. "Who got hurt with your addiction?"

"Good God, the head on you. The topic is Shelley, ye narkey hole. And that girl is like family to me. So, I want to know why the hell should I tell the fecker she's running from where she is."

The Freak leaned in and gave me a hundred lies I could tell. I must admit, they were pretty good, but I didn't feel like lying about this one.

"Because I love her."

He laughed and slapped the table. "The bleeding state of you! That's what I'm talking about. She's your drug."

"I just want to tell her I'm sorry."

"Ye can do that on mobile."

Marco leaned into the table. "She won't talk to me on the phone, you know. Only email."

I patted his shoulder and pulled him back into the chair. He nodded thanks before rushing to the side of the boat to vomit.

"I don't want to call her," I said. "I want to look her in the eye and tell her I'm sorry."

He stared at me, one gray eye and one black gem boring into me. After an eternity of listening to the ship creak, Ravenna snore, and Marco throw up, I thought he'd tell me where to stick it.

"All right," he finally said. "I reckon every fella deserves the chance to look a lady in the eye and tell her how bad he fecked up. As long as she wants to hear it. She doesn't, I'll drag you out by the neck." He stood and propped a bare foot on the table, squirting aloe onto his shin and smearing it in. "We should probably wait for Ravenna and Marco to rejoin the land of the living, though, eh?"

As if on cue, Marco yelled, "You fucking bitch!" across the sea.

"Yeah. Probably a good idea."

"Listen. I got Nintendo in the other room. The old one, I mean. *Bionic Commando* and *Contra*, if you're game."

"Up, up, down, down, left, right, left, right, B, A, Select, Start," I said.

He laughed and slapped my back. "The best part of ye may have run down your mama's leg, but you're all right, Keats."

I stood and had to catch myself on the table. Those eight, no, *nine* shots had gotten to me more than I thought.

"Haha! Ye fecking yanks always think ye can drink like men, but ye can't. It's that fecking watered down piss ye call beer. Never been trained right."

I held onto the table as I made my way around it. The smell of aloe smacked me in the face.

"Hey, Coleridge," I said, suddenly thinking of something I'd almost forgotten about.

"Hey, Keats."

"Marco said you're the kind of guy that can find anything."

"That is what they say about me."

"Can you find something for me?"

He threw an arm around my shoulders. "If it's in Naples, I already know where to get it."

CHAPTER FORTY-THREE

MORNING ON THE BAY of Naples did not rise, nor did it fall. It crept, a slow and uneasy crawl from the horizon across the sea to the terraced hills of the coast. The ships rocked where they were moored, and the city had gone quiet less than an hour before. A few small fishing boats drifted out from the shore, but the other inhabitants were silent, sleeping next to lovers or cradling children or nursing hangovers.

I had passed out sometime around midnight. After Marco threw up everything in his guts, he curled onto the floor and was gone. I fell asleep in a lawn chair in front of a thirteen-inch television playing through *Castlevania II: Simon's Quest*. Coleridge was still drinking when I conked out.

My neck felt like someone had broken it during the night and then tried to twist it back into place before anyone could tell me. I lumbered through the boat, careful not to wake anyone (though I'm not sure even Vesuvius erupting could have done that) and propped myself on the railing.

The sun trickled over the sea and reflected from the ships around us. Yet Naples was still dark. It was strange to see the actual line of light creeping along the water toward her. Looking up the dock, past medieval castles and watchtowers, over modern office complexes and grungy apartment buildings, I could feel Shelley out there. She couldn't sleep either, I knew. She stared at her ceiling and asked herself what was going to happen. I hoped I had the answers.

***

Coleridge fired up *Cristabel's* engine. It rattled and chortled and coughed plumes of black smoke into the sky before struggling along to the dock. We hopped off and waited while he argued with dockworkers about whatever fees and bribes were necessary to keep it safe until we returned.

We stopped at the Galleria Umberto I for breakfast. An enormous cross-shaped mall, it had been open since 1891. A glass dome supported by steel ribs covered the structure. It was a gorgeous piece of architecture. As we ate,

Coleridge confirmed what Byron had told me. Of course, I kept it quiet that Byron had been the one to relay that information. But Shelley was indeed staying at a B&B on Via Supportico Lopez close to the Museo Nazionale. She had visited Coleridge when she first arrived for some hard-to-find jwala peppers and a bottle of his limoncello.

After breakfast we made our way up the hill and through a labyrinth of twisting lanes and narrow alleys. A street performer juggled meat cleavers as an ancient CD player held together with duct tape boomed Louis Prima's "Buona Sera." We stopped and watched while Ravenna shrugged her backpack off and dug through it for a tube of lip-gloss. The scene was almost too perfect.

Then the Vespas came.

Vespa is the Italian word for wasp. The little contraptions were named that because their shape resembles the body of the insect, but if you spent any time in Naples it'd be easy to think they earned the name from how they tended to travel in swarms.

Tinny engines buzzed as they cut down the street. There were twelve of them, at least. Pedestrians jumped and dodged as they flew by. One of the drivers slowed to reach out and snatch Ravenna's backpack as he passed. She jerked forward, trying to hang on. He cut one strap with a knife and she stumbled and fell. Throwing the intact strap over his shoulder, he sped off.

"NOOOO!" She was on her feet in a flash and, before we knew what was happening, raced after the Vespas.

The three of us stared at each other.

"Shit," I said, soft, as though I'd dropped a euro.

We took off after her. It was no use. She had vanished down one of the alleys.

"Dammit!" I kicked a garbage can. It toppled over and rolled down the hill. No one seemed to care. "Now what the hell do we do?"

"Nothing we can do," Marco said. "There are dozens of those gangs around here, riding Vespas around and stealing backpacks and purses. It's impossible to even know who the hell they were."

"Not entirely," Coleridge said. He removed his cap and rubbed his chafing scalp. "All them ballbags pay a tithe up the chain with every robbery. There's one mealy fecker in the Camorra who they all go to."

"Who?" I asked.

"Raffaele Sibillo. He's a right poxy bastard. Wouldn't give ye the steam off his piss if ye was freezing. He won't help for free, mind."

"Fine," I said. "Whatever. I'm not leaving Ravenna here."

"Forgive me if I don't see the problem, though," Coleridge said. "It's just a bag. And she knows where we're going."

Marco shook his head. "It's not just a bag."

"Her grandmother's in it," I said.

He gave us a look like we'd lost our minds.

***

The B&B was located down a grungy street barely wide enough for the three of us to walk down. It sat across from a butcher shop, a table out front filled with plastic laser guns and remote-control trucks. The guy working the table leaned back in his chair, asleep. Two children slipped a truck and its remote right from under his nose and ran off.

Before we could find Ravenna, Coleridge needed to make a few phone calls. We hadn't been far from the B&B and so he suggested we go there and I set about making amends with Shelley while he tried to arrange a meeting.

"We have to be careful here," he said. "This isn't like dealing with the manky chancers conning tourists outside the Coliseum. They feed feckers straight to the pigs here."

I wished Ravenna had left her damned grandmother in Rome.

The door to the B&B was gigantic, ten feet tall and made from oak that had collected enough grime over the centuries to look like a wall of soot. A smaller door was cut into it. Coleridge rang the bell.

A decade later an old woman in a red shawl opened it and eyed our trio with what I can only imagine was a desire for us to burst into flames right there on the doorstep.

Coleridge rattled off a string of Napolitano. In Naples they speak a different dialect. Well, everyone says "dialect" but let's be honest: it's a completely different language. Napolitano has entire letters and sounds the standard Tuscan dialect doesn't.

She answered and stepped aside. We ducked our heads to pass through the tiny door and walked into an open tower. The sky was bright above us, more clotheslines stretching out from side to side. Water pooled on the slate floor.

"Fifth up," Coleridge said.

As we made our way to a rickety glass elevator climbing the center, another old woman leaned over the railing and dumped a bucket of slop onto the floor. I jumped back but it still splattered onto my shoes.

What kind of place had Shelley escaped to? I imagined her in a burned-out room, graffiti covering the walls, the acrid smell of piss in the air as punk music drifted in from the crack addict's room next to her.

We stepped off the elevator and walked to a bright red door. Coleridge knocked three times and it creaked open. A beautiful woman in a white dress smiled in the doorway, her red hair tucked behind her ears.

"Coleridge," she said. "What brings you around these parts?" Her accent was also Irish, though softer and kinder than his.

"Hello, Diana." He removed his hat. Was he blushing? "We, um, we were looking for Shelley."

"Oh? And who are we, dear?" She eyed Marco and me.

Coleridge introduced us.

"Keats, is it?" She looked me up and down. The smile stayed on her face, but the warmth had gone from it. "Well, come on in, then."

My imagination had gotten the better of me. The B&B was gorgeous, a pristine oasis tucked away in the chaos of Naples. The furniture was modern and the atmosphere serene. Verdi filled the air, though I couldn't name the piece. The sound complimented the smell of rose and lilac haunting the entryway.

Two large bay doors opened from the living room out onto a balcony. A cool breeze blew in from the sea and white lace curtains danced into the room. Shelley sat in a wicker chair and stared out over the city.

I looked to Diana. She nodded, though she didn't seem happy about it.

Crossing the room was one of the longest journeys I've ever taken. It was years before I stepped through those doors.

A glass of milk and a plate of chocolate chip cookies sat on a table beside her. It was too easy to imagine what she looked like at six or seven, a young girl with the comfort of homemade sweets and no men to have come along yet and harden her.

That's what we do, we men. It's one thing we're all too good at, one ability we've nurtured and refined to perfection: the power to ruin women, to abuse them, to steal away a bit of the innocence and wonder they have and callous them the way a boxer's knuckles roughen over time.

"Hey," I managed.

"Goddammit." She didn't even look my way.

"Should I go? I don't want to—"

"Just sit. And be quiet. I'm enjoying the view."

I grabbed another chair from the corner and pulled it up beside her. We sat there for a long while before she offered me a cookie.

***

Night crept in at the same pace morning had. We sat next to one another for who knows how long, quiet and munching cookies. The sounds of activity behind us came and went. I heard the faint lilting rhythm of Coleridge's voice on the phone several times, but I couldn't make out what he was saying. I don't know where Marco and Diana had gone. I don't know if there were even any other guests at the B&B. There was only Vesuvius. It was impossible to not be in the shadow of that volcano. It dominated the skyline the way St. Peter's did in Rome. That seemed important in some way, some kind of symbolic destruction and rebirth thing, but I didn't care about puzzling it out. Shelley had reached over and grabbed my hand and I could think of nothing else.

"You're an asshole," she finally said.

"I know."

"And don't give me that 'Freak' bullshit, either. That's a goddamned cop-out if I ever heard one. That's you refusing to own up to your actions."

I didn't say anything. She was right in a way. It's not like the Freak really was a separate personality. That would have been a different diagnosis altogether. He was a monster I had created, a Boogeyman to stuff away in the closet and pin all my guilt on. I wished it would make that side of me go away to admit it, but I had the feeling it wouldn't discourage him in the least.

"Byron and I never..." She didn't finish.

"I know."

She didn't ask how and I let it hang there. It was a little like lying, I guess, the implication being that I'd changed my mind on my own. But in that moment, I felt the distinction to be a small one.

She stood and walked to a bedroom door. I thought I'd said something wrong and stayed where I was.

"Well?" she asked.

"Well what?"

"If you don't come with me right now, I'm going to change my mind about everything."

"As you wish," I said.

CHAPTER FORTY-FOUR

COLERIDGE SAID EVERYTHING WAS in motion and he simply waited for a call back. He seemed nervous about it, fidgeting and pacing around the B&B, and that didn't do much for my own confidence.

When I'd told Shelley what had happened, her face went pale.

"This isn't good," she said.

"I know."

"No, Keats, I'm serious. We do not run our games here and we sure as hell stay out of the *Camorra*'s way. The last thing we need is to get on their radar."

"I figured as much. Coleridge is pretty nervous."

"After what happened to Wordsworth? Of course he is."

"Hold up," I said, knowing we'd just uncovered another secret. "Who's Wordsworth?"

Turns out, Coleridge had indeed been a part of the Carny's gang years back. When Byron first started bringing some of the brutes and bruisers in, a small group of Misfits fled south. Coleridge, Diana, a few Orphans turned teenagers, and three or four others. All following Wordsworth. Shelley thought Diana and Wordsworth may have been a couple, but she wasn't sure.

"Diana doesn't really talk much about those days," she said.

Wordsworth had been this charming, hilarious Maori, one of the first to join up with the original crew and the man responsible for wiring the catacombs for electricity. He'd been wanted for forgery in New Zealand and fraud in England, so he fit right in. He'd been the one to recruit Coleridge and acted as his guide on his Rite of Passage way back when.

So, when Wordsworth said he'd he wanted to create a little satellite version of the Necropolis, the Carny (still Keats then) had given his blessing.

"Take the Misfits on the road awhile," he'd said. "There will always be a place here for you."

His little group ended up in Naples and set up shop. They played their games on the tourists at the Castel Nuovo and the Royal Palace, even treating the train to Pompeii the way we treated the 64 Bus. They kicked ten percent of everything they made back to the Carny as a sort of franchise fee and everyone was happy.

Except the *Camorra* did not appreciate the unauthorized competition. They told Wordsworth in no uncertain terms to pay them their cut or stop altogether. He chose to stop.

For a while.

Being as clever as he was, he thought he could simply tweak a few things and stay under the radar. He changed the games they played. The times and places. Every little detail was tweaked to keep them invisible. They all thought it was fun, trying to hide from this new element. None of them took it seriously.

A month after they resumed their games, Wordsworth was found dead behind a strip club. His torso had been wrapped in gasoline-soaked towels and then set on fire. As if that weren't horrible enough, the flames had been extinguished after only a minute or so and the charred remains of the towels ripped away. His flesh came with it.

They dumped him like that in a back alley to die a slow and excruciating death.

"Jesus," I managed when she had finished. "No wonder Coleridge is nervous."

"Promise me you'll be careful," she said.

"We have to get Ravenna back. I'm not leaving her with people like that."

"Just promise me."

I promised, though I didn't need to. After hearing the story, I don't think I'd ever been so scared in my life.

***

The meeting was scheduled for midnight. As we neared the address, we passed from ancient brick buildings stained with centuries of dust to modern glass towers reflecting the lights of the city.

I asked Coleridge if he knew the guy we were going to meet.

"Never met him personally," he said. "Always dealt with his underlings. But I heard about him."

"And?"

"And what? He's a fecking monster, like all of them." He pulled a roll of antacids from his pocket and thumbed three into his mouth. "They say he was born here, grew up in London with his ma, then came back when his father died to take over his slice of things. He's eccentric, they say. Unpredictable. Heard he once bit a man's tongue out in a fight."

"Seriously?"

"That's what they say. Hard to know what's true. Men like him, they use the stories about themselves as sword and shield."

What happened to Wordsworth was fresh on my mind and I almost asked about it, but the way he chewed those antacids made me think better of it.

I expected our meeting to take place on the top floor of one of the office buildings and was surprised when we found the location.

"This is it?" I asked.

Coleridge looked down at the paper in his hand and scratched the stubble on his cheek. "This is it. Why?"

I pointed to the sign hanging over the door. "It's a co-working space."

"I don't follow."

"You know, where college kids and freelancers rent an office by the day? Like AirBnB for office spaces?"

"So?"

"Never mind." I pushed the buzzer.

A moment later, the heavy-set security guard at the front desk waddled over and opened the door a crack. He and Coleridge exchanged a string of Napolitano and then he led us through the lobby. The place was packed with comfy seating, vending machines, and air hockey tables. Two hipsters in sleeveless shirts with scarves around their necks played ping-pong in the back.

"You sure this is the right place?" I asked.

"Aye, it's the right fecking place already."

We were instructed to take the elevator to the third floor. When we exited, we stood directly across from a large, glass-walled conference room. The lights were off, candles burning on the table, and Coleridge and I exchanged a worried look. Was this some ancient mafia ritual?

After a moment of waiting, Coleridge took a deep breath and knocked.

A shape rose from the table and opened the door.

"Raffaele Sibillo?" Coleridge asked.

The man motioned us in.

There were seven men seated around the table and they all stared at us with unblinking expressions. Not a man there looked like he hadn't killed someone before.

Which is why it took me a moment to realize what they were doing.

The man at the head of the table, who I could only assume was Sibillo, leaned over a three-paneled piece of cardboard standing in front of him and rolled a handful of dice. When they came to a stop, one of the other men leaned over them, groaned, and marked something on a piece of paper.

"Are they... Are they playing *Dungeons & Dragons*?" I asked Coleridge.

Sibillo whirled on me, eyes narrow. "No, we are *not* playing *Dungeons & Dragons*," he said in a baritone, his British accent posh and perfected.

I held my hands up, afraid I'd offended him. "Sorry. I didn't mean—"

"We are playing *Vampire: The Masquerade*."

"*Vampiro la Mascherata,*" one of the men at the table shouted and pumped a fist into the air.

"And you fucking well ruined that scene." Sibillo clicked on the lights.

The other men blinked as the fluorescents came to life above them. I could now see the scantily clad fanged women pictured on the three-paneled cardboard. A city map stretched across the other end of the long table, several finely painted miniatures of men in trench coats and large wolves positioned atop it.

"Right, I'm going to take five," Sibillo said to the other men. "While I'm gone, you lot decide how you're going to handle the Prince. And I swear to fucking Christ, Lorenzo, you move those miniatures around while I'm gone and I'll feed you cock first to a chimpanzee, you fucking degenerate."

He motioned us out the door.

"I'm sorry if we disturbed you," I said.

"It's fine." Sibillo opened another office and ushered us in. "Only the climactic scene of a year-long chronicle, that's all. Do you know how difficult it is to hold their attention for that long? Here I am working my magnum-opus and every third game has to revolve around tits and pegging or they sod off to Toma Gilder's *Warhammer* nights. That *fucking* loan shark."

He smoothed down the front of his expertly tailored silk shirt and propped himself on the edge of the desk.

"Either of you wouldn't know how to edit a PDF, would you?"

Coleridge and I exchanged a glance.

"Never mind. Now. I'm told you're looking to move a fuckton of MDMA. Not my forte, but I'm not one to judge. I've had a love-affair with old Molly myself. Drug trafficking's not usually my bag, but money greases wheels *and* assholes, as my father used to say."

"Um, I'm sorry," Coleridge said. "I think there's been a misunderstanding?"

Sibillo pointed two fingers at us. "You're not looking to move Molly?"

"No," I said. "We're trying to find someone."

He pulled a black day-planner from his pocket and flipped through it. He scrunched up his face reading.

"What day is it?"

"Saturday," I said.

"Hmmm. Looks like I missed that Molly meeting. Oh, well. Now. This here says you're looking for a girl." He shoved the planner back into his pocket. "Not my forte, but I'm not one to judge. Money greases wheels and—"

"No," I interrupted. "We're looking for a friend of ours who went missing."

"Fuck!" He ran both his hands through his thick, dark hair. "Sorry. You'll have to excuse me. I'm tripping balls right now. Turns the game into a virtual reality experience. You're the ones who ran afoul of the wasps, then? Is that right?"

"Yeah, that's us," I said.

"Right. Well, I know where your friend is. Seems she caught up to the pricks who stole her bag and they have her at their place. I'd usually say, 'Tough titty, she should have left well enough alone.' But they're late on this month's payment to me, so fuck them."

"Great," I said. "Thank you."

"We're not there yet," he said. "Fuck them, yes, but what about us? What about *me*? What do I get out of this?"

Coleridge and I exchanged a look. We'd discussed this on the way over. I didn't have much in the way of cash. I could always head back to the Necropolis and raid the piggy bank, but I didn't want to leave Ravenna here with them while I did. Coleridge was already kicking ten percent of everything he made to the *Camorra* to keep them off his back and the only thing he owned was *Cristabel.* Not only was the boat not worth much, but I doubted he'd ever part with it.

All I could say was, "Whatever you want, we'll do it, Mr. Sibillo, sir."

"Please, call me Raffaele. But not Raf. Never fucking Raf." He looked us up and down. "Which one of you is Coleridge?"

My companion meekly raised a hand.

"Right. And you're fucking Edgar Allan Poe, then?"

"Keats," I said.

"Whatever. Your stupid fucking names. I should strangle the both of you just for having names like that. Fucking weirdos. I can tell by looking at you that you don't have shit for me. Except, maybe, that boat."

"Me boat?" Coleridge asked in utter surprise.

"Yes, your shitty, shitty boat. Thing is, that boat, no one ever gives it a second look, do they? Such an obvious piece of shit. Just worthless. Real trash. Yet somehow runs like a Ferrari. You go in and out of ports all up and down the coast and I bet the police have never once searched it, have they?"

A sad look on his face, Coleridge nodded.

"There's a lot I could do with a boat like that."

"It's yours, then," he said softly.

"Coleridge," I said. "No. We'll find another way."

"You can fuck right off," Sibillo said to me, pointing again with those two fingers. "You fucking toilet." He turned back to Coleridge. "Offer accepted."

I put a hand on Coleridge's back. "I'm sorry."

"Don't look so glum," Sibillo said. "You can keep living on the boat. Working on it. All by yourself, even. You can even have full run of the thing to do with as you please. The price for that, though, will be to make these little shipments for me personally. Think you could handle that?"

He swallowed. "Course I can."

"Corsican? What the fuck does that mean? You insulting me?"

Coleridge cleared his throat. "Of course I can, I meant," he said slowly, emphasizing each syllable.

"Oh. Yes. Precisely." He pulled a sheet of paper from his planner, scribbled on it, and handed it over to us. "That," he said, "is where you can find these cock-holes. Be warned that they'll as soon stick you as look at you. If I were you, and thank Christ almighty I'm not, I'd break in while the gobby poncers are out on those shitty bikes of theirs."

"Good advice," I said.

"Of course, if it were me, I'd just send those men at the table back there to set them on fire while they slept."

He eyed me intently and I got the impression he wanted me to ask for just that.

"Now," he continued. "You should know I told them not to hurt your lady friend, but that and the address is the most help you'll get from me. *Capisce*?"

"Understood," I said. "And thank you. We really do appreciate it."

"Damn right you do. Now you can fuck right off." He popped his knuckles. "I've got a game to finish."

CHAPTER FORTY-FIVE

COLERIDGE RETURNED TO THE B&B the next morning with several sheets of construction paper in hand. He'd gone to scout out the address Sibillo gave us as soon as we'd left the co-working space. I'd offered to go, but he insisted I get back to Shelley.

"Ye need to enjoy each other before ye feck it up again, eh?"

Great purple circles ringed his eyes and his skin looked sallow when he walked in. Diana took one look at him and, without so much as saying good morning, started the state-of-the-art DeLonghi machine in the kitchen on a double-sized cup of coffee.

"Gather everyone round," he said.

Shelley and Marco soon joined us around the dining room table. Coleridge laid out the construction paper. He'd drawn maps on each in crayon.

"Working on your shapes and colors?" Marco asked.

"It was the only thing I could find to buy in the middle of the night."

Diana returned and handed him a steaming cup. He thanked her, his good eye lingering on her a moment too long as she took a seat with her own cup.

"Now, this here... Wait." He moved the papers around, sliding them into different positions. "It looks like... No, that's not..." Finally, he threw up his hands and sighed. "I've forgotten where they all go."

We all took a crack at the puzzle, arguing over where walls lined up and alleys continued.

"That's it," he said when we were satisfied. "Now. This here's their garage. There are three apartments up top, couple of bedrooms each. Best I could tell, ten or twelve of them live there."

"And Ravenna?" I asked.

"About two hours before sunrise, she starts yelling at one of the manky bastards, saying the pizza they brought her had the wrong toppings and if they couldn't even get her pizza order right, they might as well go ahead and stab her in the neck. Woke up the whole damn neighborhood. She was in this room here." He tapped an area on one of the papers indicating a corner room.

"We should just wait them out," Marco said. "This time next week, they'll be paying us to take her back."

"Why do they still have her?" I asked. "I mean, I know Sibillo had said not to hurt her, but he didn't really seem like he was going out of his way to do us any favors."

They all stared at me with long faces.

Shelley placed a hand on my arm. "To sell her," she said.

The urgency I felt at bringing Ravenna home ignited like wildfire.

"When can we go?" I asked.

***

The Vespas rocketed out of that garage every day around lunchtime. That was when the crowds grew and the traffic made it impossible to chase them down.

Yet somehow Ravenna had. I had to hand it to her on that front.

We sipped coffee at a cafe down the street and watched their graffiti-covered garage door. Coleridge had fallen asleep at the table as soon as we sat, and we let him enjoy his little power nap.

Even Diana had joined us. She stood at a stall directly across the street from their building, pretending to admire the used books being hawked, as she looked for a sign of Ravenna. After twenty minutes or so, she entered the cafe.

"She's in the same room," she said. "Third floor up. Window's open, but there's no way to climb up or down. One of them just came with a bottle of water and then locked her in."

We'd rented a little Fiat Panda that morning on a stolen credit card. Marco leaned under its hood at the curb near the garage, socket wrench in hand pretending to fix some problem. With the jacket Coleridge had loaned him and his Mediterranean looks, no one batted at eye.

Finally, what sounded like a dozen lawn mowers rumbled from inside the garage. The door rose and the swarm fled from their nest. They immediately took the corner and were gone.

The door descended on its track. When it was almost closed, Marco sprinted over and rolled beneath it.

I smacked Coleridge on the shoulder and he damn near jumped out of his seat.

"It's time," I said.

Shelley and I hurried down the street to the building's front door and waited for Marco to open it. Diana returned to the book stand while Coleridge walked around the corner to lean against the wall like he hadn't a care in the world. Those two were our lookouts and if that swarm returned, they were to signal us.

I'd planned the entire thing down to the letter and felt rather good about it. Maybe I could lead these people after all.

At the door, Shelley asked if I was nervous.

"Nah," I said. "Cool as a cucumber."

"Really?"

"You don't believe me?"

"It's just that the massive sweat stain on the back of your shirt doesn't look very cucumberish to me."

"Haha."

She bumped my hip.

"Glad to have you back, Shelley."

"Glad to be back, Keats."

I couldn't help but kiss her. Marco opened the door right then.

"No time for love, Dr. Jones," he said, and motioned us in.

We took the stairs two at a time to the third floor. I rushed down the hall, trying to work out which one was Ravenna's room, and knocked.

"Ravenna," I said. "It's me. Keats."

No answer.

"We're here to rescue you."

"I do not need you to rescue me," a voice said from behind.

I whirled to see Ravenna in the open doorway across the hall. I'd gotten turned around and knocked on the wrong door. She held a fork in one hand, the tongs bent, and a butter knife in the other.

"Stupid men do not think a woman can pick a lock," she said.

Just then, someone outside broke into a coughing fit. We all looked at one another in confusion.

"Is that Coleridge?" Marco asked, and hurried to Ravenna's window.

"I don't know," I said. "I told him to signal if he saw something, but I forgot to say what the signal should be."

"Cough-cough-cough-cough-cough," Coleridge said, clearly giving up any pretense of incongruity.

Marco stuck his head out the window. "Is that you?"

"Yeah, it's fecking me," he yelled back up.

"Why are you just saying 'cough-cough-cough'?"

"It's a signal. A fecking signal."

Just then, those lawn mower engines rumbled from up the street.

I ran over and stuck my head out the window next to Marco's.

"Why are they back already?" I asked.

Shelley grabbed the neck of my shirt and yanked me out of the room. "Who cares? We need to go."

"Not without my grandmother," Ravenna said.

"Ravenna," I started, "if they find us here—"

"Not. Without. My. Grandmother."

I knew that, if we didn't find the skull, she wouldn't go.

"Coleridge," I said, leaning my head back out the window. "Stall them."

"What?"

"Stall them!"

"Stall them? Feck you, stall them!"

We darted around looking for Ravenna's bag. Stealth was no longer a concern. We knocked over cabinets, threw cushions from sofas, and generally trashed each apartment as we made our way down the stairs.

One floor down we heard the crash outside. People screamed and horns honked.

"What the hell did he do?" I asked.

"You didn't leave much of a choice in thinking things through," Shelley said as she tossed clothes out of a closet.

"Oh, so this is all my fault?" I put my foot through a locked armoire trying to kick it open.

"Yeah, Keats. That's exactly what I meant." Her voice dripping with sarcasm.

"Found it!" Marco yelled.

We came running down the stairs to find him in the garage. He held Ravenna's backpack in one hand and stuffed items from an open trunk into it with the other.

"My grandmother," she yelled as she sprinted across the room. "Is she here?"

Marco held up a skull. Ravenna took it and hugged it close.

"We need to go," I said. "Now."

She stuffed it into her bag and followed.

We hurried outside to see traffic piled up, horns still honking, people yelling and cursing both inside and outside of their cars. The book cart that Diana had been browsing was now in the middle of the street, toppled over and destroyed, books everywhere, pages floating around in the traffic.

Coleridge fast-walked over to us.

"I didn't know what else to do," he said.

Diana wasn't far behind him. "We need to go. Now."

We hurried over to the Fiat and climbed in. As we did, the Vespas had decided to abandon traffic and drove up to their garage on the sidewalk. They all carried white plastic bags heavy with takeout food from some restaurant.

"That is my calamari," Ravenna said, and motioned to the bags.

I pushed her into the car. Coleridge took shotgun. It was a tight fit with everyone else squished together in the backseat, Ravenna draped across their laps. Marco handed me the keys.

"I don't want to drive," I said.

"Just do it," Shelley barked.

"But the traffic here—"

"Fecking drive already!" Coleridge yelled.

I cranked the engine. As we crept by the garage, the Vespas crowded out front waiting for the door to open, Ravenna leaned over and rolled the window down.

"You were not very good hosts!" she yelled. "There is place in Hell for you and your shitty food!"

They turned their heads toward us in surprise and I floored it. The Fiat shot forward into the mess of traffic. In the rear view, I could see the Vespas backing up and turning to come after us.

"Fuck it," I said and, feeling like a local, whipped a U-turn and drove the wrong way down the street.

CHAPTER FORTY-SIX

WE HAD A CELEBRATORY dinner on the balcony that night with the only other guests of the B&B, an Egyptian couple who didn't speak English. We went over the entire ordeal again at dinner, laughing and cringing.

The Vespas had chased us for a few blocks as I white-knuckled it into oncoming traffic. I thought for sure we'd wreck, or at least get pulled over, but every other driver simply maneuvered around us as though this were the most normal thing in the world. With traffic the way it was in Naples, it may have been.

The Vespas stayed on our ass, Coleridge and Shelley yelling at me to slow down all the while, until we finally jumped a curb at the police station. The Vespas sped on past.

Two *polizia* stood outside eating sandwiches from paper wrappers. One of them idly walked up to the car and I thought for sure we would be arrested.

"You cannot park here," he said. "Not without permit."

"Oh," I managed. "Sorry."

Everyone else in the car gripped their seat wide-eyed and tried to catch their breath.

"It is fine," the *polizia* said. "We have not yet put up a sign. So, really, it is our fault."

"I get it. You're probably very busy."

"Eh. Not really." He patted the roof of the car twice and then returned to his buddy to finish his sandwich.

As we retold the story over a spicy curry, we cackled like madmen. The Egyptians could only smile and raise their glasses to us every time we found something funny, or frown and shake their heads if we found something tragic.

Guessing someone's age had never been my strong suit. I don't know how those carnival barkers did it. If I were forced to say, I would have pegged Diana as being in her early fifties. Her skin was smooth but every now and then she would smile too wide and the wrinkles around her eyes and mouth would give it away. Not that those wrinkles decreased her beauty in any way. Quite the opposite, in fact. Every time they revealed themselves, it lit up her face in a new way.

She was named after the Greek goddess. Her real name, she told us without fear of reproach, was Hester. I think the name the Carny had given her was far more appropriate.

Coleridge hung on her every word. He even refrained from saying "feck" during dinner. Well, aside from when the Egyptian woman knocked a glass of wine over onto his plate, but he apologized for that.

It was almost cute, the way he fawned over Diana. I say almost because it was obvious she was not and never would be interested in him. Even the Egyptian couple had to know. In fact, the way they whispered to one another all night, I'm sure they did.

He knew, too. Somewhere inside he knew there was no chance of the two of them ever being together. But that's love, isn't it? It's hoping the sun won't set tomorrow. Even though it has for the last billion days, tomorrow may be the day it doesn't.

Was she what had brought him to Naples to begin with? Maybe it hadn't been Wordsworth he had followed, after all.

After dinner, Shelley and I went for a walk through the bustling Neapolitan nightlife.

"Where are you taking me?" she asked.

"It's a surprise."

"What? You're surprising *me* now?"

"Quid pro quo."

"I don't think I can take any more excitement. Not after your driving today."

"I think I did pretty good, all things considered."

"Sure," she said, and patted my back like I was a moron.

There was a tiny one-screen theater about six blocks from the B&B. Coleridge had indeed proved he could get anything in this wild city. He'd given me directions and I hoped to God I hadn't heard anything wrong. Getting lost in Naples at night was not an experience I wanted to have.

Thankfully, I found it. I knocked and a tiny woman with a mustache thicker than my father's answered.

"*Chiuso*," she said.

"Coleridge." His name was all he told me to say.

She held out her hand and I placed a hundred euro in her palm. She let us inside.

Shelley seemed suspicious. "What's going on?"

"You'll see."

We shuffled into the theater and sat. The lights dimmed and an old film projector hummed to life above us. In seconds, the first reel started.

"*Casablanca*," she said.

"Yep."

She slipped her arm through mine and pulled her head against my shoulder as Peter Lorre ran through the streets toward the Café Americano.

***

After the film, we strolled along the docks and I asked her about Diana.

"I don't know much about her. She's pretty quiet about personal stuff."

"Really? You guys seem close."

"We are. One of those people you just immediately feel a connection to. She's always been there for me."

"You been down here ever since you left?"

"Yeah. Where else would I have gone?"

"I don't know. Sperlonga?"

She released my hand and sat on the edge of a dock. I sat beside her.

"Why would I go to Sperlonga?"

"I hear the beach is nice."

"Don't be a jackass. You know, don't you?"

"Yeah."

"How?"

"Byron."

She kicked her heel against the dock. "That son-of-a-bitch. What else did he tell you?"

"That you were in Naples and that the two of you weren't an item."

"An *item*? What are you, eighty-five?"

"Okay. 'Rutting,' I believe he said. That you two weren't rutting."

"And you believed him?"

"Why wouldn't I?"

"You believed him but not me?"

"Shelley, let's not—"

"No, I want to know. Why would you believe him but not me?" Her hackles were up. She was like that. If she wanted to fight, then there was no power on earth that could calm her. And, in truth, I had it coming.

The Freak plopped down next to me and tried to convince me to scream at her and storm off. I took a deep breath and managed to ignore him.

"You never told me," I said.

"What?"

"When I asked, you got mad and never said anything. If you had told me you weren't, I would have believed you."

She was quiet for a while. Finally, she took my hand and looked at me. "I didn't, did I? I don't know why. I think I was just so mad you went through my things. I'm sorry. Shit, that had to convince you that we were."

"I'm sorry I went through your things. I had no right. And the way I acted?"

"It's fine," she said. "Do it again and I'll put your face through a meat grinder. But we're past it now."

"I know that he took advantage of you when you were young."

She didn't respond to that, simply stared out across the dark sea.

"Just thinking about it," I went on, "kept me up all night. I don't know how you can stay in contact with him."

"No," she said. "You don't get to do that. You don't get to steal my pain."

"I'm just trying to say, I get what you're going through, but—"

"No, you don't get it. My trauma isn't yours. Okay? What I did, the things that happened to me, don't you dare make it about you."

"I'm sorry. I wasn't trying to."

"How I choose to deal with it all, to deal with Byron, that's my decision. Mine. Okay?"

"Of course."

She squeezed my hand and we sat listening to the wood creak beneath us in time with the tide.

After a few minutes, I asked, "Why didn't you tell me about Dimitri?"

She snorted. "What would I tell you? That the man we both follow probably cut his throat because he told you where to find us?"

"Why would the Carny do that? I mean, I joined you guys. I became an acolyte or whatever. A Misfit."

"He has strong ideas on loyalty. I'm sure he still saw it as a betrayal."

"And we just let that slide?"

"What should we do? Hightail it back to Rome and beat him to death?"

"No. That's not what I'm saying."

"Then what are you saying?"

I wasn't sure.

"He's not a monster," she said. "He's a great man."

"But he's also a murderer."

"He did what he thought he had to do. For all of us. That's why he did it. To keep *us* safe. Not himself."

"So, that's that? Dimitri's just a casualty, then?"

"It's not like the Carny kills people all the time, Keats. He had his reasons." She stood. "Look, I feel shitty about Dimitri, too. But what's done is done." She walked a few feet away. "You coming?"

Dark waves crashed against the dock.

"Keats? Please." She stretched her hand toward me and wiggled her fingers.

I stood and took it.

***

I wasn't comfortable with Shelley's dismissal of Dimitri's murder. It put the Carny on the same level as Sibillo and made us little better than that bastard Vespa gang. We were talking about a human life, snuffed out simply because he needed a new pair of shoes. What she would call pragmatism in her view of it I called callousness.

She had thrown up strange defenses in her life, I reminded myself. Her mother leaving, her father's abuse, those first years alone here spent doing God knows what. Byron. You would have to create a distance between yourself and the world around you just to get by.

With Shelley you could only accept this. What was even the point of bringing it up anymore?

***

Ravenna sat on the balcony when we got back.

"Ravenna? Are you okay?"

She held the skull in her hands. "Yes. I am good." She tilted the skull and examined it with one eye closed. "Only…"

"Only what?"

Her head shook like a dog trying to dry itself. "Nothing."

I kissed the top of her head. "I'm glad you're okay."

"You worry?"

"Yeah. I worry quite a bit."

She smiled. I don't think I'd ever seen a genuine smile from her before. With her crooked, stained teeth, it was almost lovely.

"Thank you," she said, and went back to staring at the skull.

***

Naples won their *futbol* match that night. Shelley and I climbed up to the roof, a blanket wrapped around us as we watched the city explode. Children beat pots and pans together. Impromptu bands formed on other rooftops and belted out Renato Carosone tunes. Fireworks lit up the sky. I've never seen such a celebration before. The next day we would board our train and head back to our lives and our problems, but that night we lost ourselves in the abandon.

CHAPTER FORTY-SEVEN

COLERIDGE WALKED US TO the train station.

"I hate to see ye feckers go. Sure ye don't wanna stick around a few more days?"

I shook his hand. "We really need to get back and check on the Carny."

"Understood." He pulled me into a hug. "Ye better fecking take care of our Shelley, mate. I'll come for ye myself if ye feck up again."

She punched his shoulder. They shared a laugh and a hug and everyone else boarded the train.

"I'm sorry about your boat," I said.

He gave a slow nod. "Could be worse, I reckon. It's mine in all but deed. I just ain't too keen on being under their thumb. That rarely ends well."

"Look, you ever need anything, anything at all, you let me know."

He grabbed the back of my neck and pressed his forehead to mine.

As I boarded the train, he called to me. "Hey, Keats."

"Yeah?"

"That was one for the fecking books, wasn't it?"

"You're goddamned right it was."

We all took our seats and I watched Coleridge through the window as he shoved his hands in his pockets and walked away. Living on that boat, we were probably the first real interaction he'd had in a while.

I could only imagine he thought of Diana as he walked away. She might as well have lived in Istanbul, as far as he was concerned.

I put my arm around Shelley and pulled her close.

***

I'd thought we'd all jabber non-stop on the train ride back, but it was quiet. We had so much fodder for conversation between Coleridge and Diana and Sibillo and Ravenna's little adventure, even just with Naples herself, but Marco wadded up his jacket against the window and went to sleep. Shelley leaned against me and followed suit.

Ravenna sat and stared at the skull, her brow furrowed.

"What's wrong?"

"This no my grandmother," she said.

"What?"

She sighed and sat the skull on her knee. "It no my grandmother." She threw her hands into the air in exasperation.

"Of course it your grandmother. It's, I mean." Christ, I was starting to talk like her.

"No. It not."

"So those guys just happened to have another skull lying around they pawned off on you?"

"All I know is it no her."

"It's a skull, Ravenna. How can you tell?"

"I can tell." She picked it up and pulled it right to her face. I thought she was going to kiss it. Then she shook her head and shoved it into her bag. "It no her."

She huffed and crossed her arms.

***

The Carny was up and making lunch when we got back. A bandage ran around his head and another along his ribs. The scabs on his face were beginning to peel.

The smell of burnt toast filled the air. He hugged us and kissed Shelley and me on the cheeks.

"Good to have you back, children."

"Good to be back," I said. "What are you making?"

"Fried peanut butter and banana sandwiches. Elvis's favorite."

You can't get peanut butter in Europe, which was only one reason I thought this was weird. I picked up a jar of Nutella on the counter.

"You got me. Nutella and plantains. Might be good."

Marco stuck his finger in the jar and licked it clean. "How you feeling?"

"Better than ever, mate. Now you children go unpack and rest. I'll bring you lunch when I'm finished."

We dropped our bags in Shelley's room.

"Well," she said. "He seems fine."

"I guess."

"What?"

"That was just a weird scene."

"What was?"

"The kitchen."

"You're being paranoid. Don't worry about it."

That was everyone's mantra these days. *Don't worry about it. It's fine. You worry too much.* Maybe I had to worry so much because no one else seemed to.

I almost said this to Shelley, but I knew she'd be dismissive and it would turn into an argument. Sometimes keeping your mouth shut is the best thing you can do for a relationship, no matter how much therapists advised talking. Talking, in my experience, created problems. If a mouth opens, something bad is likely to come out of it. Better to keep quiet and enjoy the small moments. *L'arte di non fare niente*, right?

***

After lunch I offered to do dishes. While I scrubbed, Madame Butterfly came in for a glass of juice. Her face was tired and sagged. Black circles ringed her eyes.

"You're back," she said, and kissed my cheek.

"How have things been?"

She glanced over her shoulder like an informant in a Scorsese film. "Not good," she whispered. "We need to talk later."

"What's wrong?"

"Not here. Meet me in the piazza at sunset."

"Why?"

She poured her juice and glanced around again. "The Carny has lost his goddamned mind," she said.

CHAPTER FORTY-EIGHT

THE SETTING SUN REFLECTED across the piazza from the gold roof of Santa Maria di Trastevere. I sat on the fountain and ate gelato while parishioners filed past for evening Mass. A few of them cast strange looks my way. They must have recognized me from my all-too-public bath that one morning.

Was that Shelley moving through the crowd? What could she be doing here?

I took a few steps toward her, trying to get a better look. Something about the way she moved was off, stilted, not her usual loose and delicate gait. Her skin looked pale and sickly.

She vanished into the crowd. Maybe it wasn't her after all.

"You're punctual," Madame Butterfly said from behind me. "No one could say otherwise."

We both sat. "Well?"

She drummed her fingers on the stone as she watched a little girl walk a puppy into the restaurant across from us. "It started the day after you left," she said. "He asked me for a bowl of soup and when I brought it to him, he accused me of trying to poison him."

I couldn't help but laugh. She had to be joking.

She turned to me, eyes dull and vacant. I could see how it all wore on her. Then she lifted her wig, something she never did outside her bedroom, to reveal a scabbed-over gash running up her scalp.

"He threw the bowl at me."

"Jesus. This was the day after he woke?"

"Yes."

"Maybe he was still coming around. I mean, he was pretty banged up."

"Just yesterday, he punched Big Jim. Said he had been sending out messages with the pigeons."

"What kind of messages?"

"Things to Byron, to the police, whoever. Big Jim thought he was joking and laughed. The Carny punched him right in the jaw and walked off."

"Shit."

"He thinks everyone's out to get him."

"We should take him to Dr. Paolo."

"He won't go."

"Maybe we should go to Paolo ourselves?"

"I'll do it," she said. "You've been gone, and I know what's been happening."

"I'll go with you."

"Thank you." She took my hand. "I don't like being around him right now. He scares me."

I squeezed her hand. "I'm sure he'll be fine," I said. "Probably just needs some medication."

I don't know if she believed me or not. She pretended to, at least. I think we both needed that.

***

The Carny didn't seem unstable to me at first. Well, more unstable than usual, anyway. I watched him closely all night as we sat in his room, drinking wine and listening to The Stooges' *Funhouse* album as I told him all about Naples. Aside from the bandages, it was like nothing had happened.

When I finished, he said, "I miss Coleridge, the old git. Loyal as the day is long. Wish he would have stayed up here."

Dimitri had been on my mind the entire night. I wasn't sure if I should bring it up, given what Madame Butterfly had told me.

I decided to come at it sideways.

"This is good," I said, and swirled the wine around in my glass. "What is it?"

"Barbaresco. This one's from a little town outside Alba."

"I had a cab driver recommend Barbaresco to me. He was definitely right." Dimitri never said anything of the sort. It wasn't the sliest way to bring it up, but there it was.

The Carny stared at me over his glass. "Did he now?"

"Yeah."

"A man of taste," he said. "Italian?"

"I don't think so. Slavic, maybe? His name was Dimitri."

"The cab driver."

"Yeah. You know, I ran into him again after Shelley robbed me. Traded him my tennis shoes for information on how to find her."

"Is that how you did it?"

"Yeah."

"Those same shoes you got on right now?"

We locked eyes and he was on his feet before I knew it. Our glasses shattered to the ground as he yanked me from my chair. Straightening a leg, he tripped me over his calf. I fell face first, instinct turning my head and covering my face with my forearms to avoid losing teeth.

The Carny snaked onto my back, one arm around my neck, his heels digging between my thighs. Then he rolled onto his back, his legs locked around me as he held me in a half-choke. His free hand pulled my shirt up and slapped around my belly and chest.

"Where is it?" he snarled.

"Where's…what?" I managed, his forearm digging into my throat.

He snaked his hand into my waistband and groped around my underwear.

"The wire, the wire, the fucking wire!"

He stopped, not finding anything, and removed his hand from my pants. He kept his limbs around me a few seconds more. Considering the situation, I guess. Then he released me.

Gasping for breath, I scrambled away on all fours and stumbled to my feet.

He stood effortlessly. "Sorry, mate," he said. "I had to be certain."

Mansa Musa stepped into the room, the look on his face asking what the hell all the noise was.

The Carny clapped his hands together like Mansa Musa was just who he needed. "Do us a proper, mate, and fetch the broom. Some towels, maybe. Bit squiffy and had us an accident."

Mansa Musa cocked an eyebrow in irritation and disappeared again.

The Carny took a step toward me and I shuffled back, hands up and out in a "keep away" stance.

"What. The hell. Is your—"

"Shhh," he interrupted, and placed a finger to his lips.

Mansa Musa returned with a broom, dustpan, spray cleaner, and towels. The Carny tried to take them from him, but Mansa Musa wrestled them back and cleaned the mess himself as though we were children who'd just make it worse.

When he was done, he took the bottle of wine, sighed theatrically, and then left again.

"I thought it might have been you," the Carny said. "I had to know."

"What might have been me?"

"Someone here has been meeting with Byron."

I swallowed. "Byron?"

"I think they're trying to set me up."

"Why would anyone do that?"

"Byron's wanted me gone a long time. *Poof!* If I vanished, he'd run everything. So, when you started in on that muppet who sold us out to you..." He leaned forward, eyebrows raised, hands out in a wild-looking gesture I assumed was supposed to finish the sentence.

"It doesn't make sense." I adjusted the half-wedgie out of my underwear. "Why would anyone here help him?"

"Well, that's the question, innit? He must have something on one of them. Or found the right carrot."

He stared at the floor and nodded to himself. He seemed to have forgotten I was there for a moment before looking back up and grinning.

"I'm sorry, mate. I should have known it wasn't you. You were the one Ravenna's grandmother foresaw, after all. The one Dionysus chose. Keats would never betray Keats, would he?"

"No. No, of course not."

"You're probably the only one I can trust," he said.

"I don't think that's true. Everyone here—"

"Until I know otherwise, it's just you and me, yeah?"

"Sure," I said.

"Now." He walked over and straightened my shirt, smoothing the wrinkles out with one palm. "Promise me something?"

"Of course."

"Keep an eye out around here for me. They all trust you. One of them's bound to let something slip. They'll have their guard down around you."

"Whatever you need."

"We will smoke this traitor out, we will." He extended his hand.

I gripped it and we shared a smile.

Madame Butterfly was right. He was gone.

CHAPTER FORTY-NINE

"HE NEEDS TO BE in hospital," Dr. Paolo said.

Madame Butterfly and I sat in his office. It was decidedly American. A computer on the desk, pictures of his wife and kids surrounding it. The furniture a dark wood. It reminded me of my therapist's office back in LA.

"You know he won't do that," she said. "If we even suggested it, he would blow up."

Paolo leaned back in his chair and twirled a pencil between his fingers. "Is what he needs. He needs X-ray and scanning cats and many things I cannot bring into the catacombs." He was very focused on that pencil.

I leaned forward and snatched it from his hands. "What does it sound like to you?"

"It sound like brain damage. There is term for it. I cannot remember."

"You can't remember?"

"It no matter. Only name."

This was the downside to *l'arte di non fare niente*, by the way.

"How do you treat this thing that you don't know the name of?"

"It require hospital. Maybe surgery. But first X-rays. I can do nothing without these things."

"And if we could get him into the hospital?"

"He won't go," Madame Butterfly said. "He'd never go."

Paolo threw his hands up. "*Va bene*. But if he did there still might not be a thing we can do. It may be serious brain trauma. But if swelling or clot we can operate."

On the bus back to Trastevere, we discussed our options.

"He doesn't have any ID," she said. "No passport, no visa. He's in the country illegally. And I suspect he's wanted for some crime here or back in England. As soon as he went into the hospital the *carabinieri* would show up and haul him off."

"At least he'd be alive."

"He's alive now."

"You know what I mean."

"He might get treatment if he got arrested. Maybe. But this isn't the States, Keats. Odds are they'd throw him in jail and not worry about it."

"They'd probably do that in the States these days, too."

"Really?" She shook her head, her face long like the whole world had gone mad.

"Where are you from, anyway? I've never asked."

"Hong Kong." She stared out the window. "But I haven't been there in almost twelve years."

Twelve years. That hit me hard and I wasn't sure why.

"Let's not tell the others," she said. "Not yet. I don't want to worry anyone."

"They should be worried."

She shook her head. "If we tell them, then every little thing he does will seem like a symptom. We'll bias the entire Necropolis against him."

"But don't they have a right to know?"

"If they know, they will doubt him. Do you think that would make anything better right now?"

I didn't have an answer for that.

When I walked into the catacombs, Shelley threw her arms around me and kissed me.

"It came," she said.

"Huh?"

"Giacomo brought it down earlier."

"Brought what down?"

She handed me an envelope. One end was jagged.

"I couldn't resist," she said.

The contents were in Italian. My grasp of the language was improving, but I still bungled every fourth or fifth word. Shelley walked me through it.

It was an approval letter for my visa.

She jumped into my arms, wrapped her legs around me, and kissed me again.

"Let's celebrate," she said.

Scrambling around onto my back like a monkey, I carried her into the Family Room. Tolstoy was asleep on a couch. Only Tolstoy could have been; Dostoevsky had six or seven tuning forks laid out in front of him. He waved without looking up from them, as though one might jump up and down if he looked away.

Sappho stood in the middle of the room wearing sweats, hair pulled back in a ponytail as she swung a kettlebell up and down, up and down. She looked our way and smiled.

Shelley ignored her and went to the bar.

I mouthed, "Sorry."

Shelley went to work mixing martinis and I trotted over to help.

Sappho was having none of it. She put the kettlebell down and walked over to the bar. "What are you guys celebrating?" She grabbed a towel and wiped the back of her neck dry.

Shelley focused on the shaker cup.

"I got approved for a visa today," I said.

"Really? Congratulations!" Sappho smacked my shoulder. "Most of us don't have one. Probably not very smart on our parts."

Shelley slammed two glasses down and poured her concoction.

Sappho cast me an exasperated look. I didn't want any part of this. Finally, she placed a hand on Shelley's and I went rigid. Last thing we needed down here was more fighting.

Shelley glared at her.

"Shelley," she said. "I didn't mean to get into it with you that day."

Shelley continued glaring.

"Keats is my friend and… Well, I let myself get a little too worked up about everything."

She knew she didn't get too worked up. I had to bite my tongue to keep from saying that I felt her reaction was rather subdued, all things considered.

"Sometimes," Sappho continued, "I can be overprotective. But I'm still on the outside of your relationship looking in." She stuck her hand out. "So, I'm sorry."

Shelley considered the hand a moment before shaking it. "Apology accepted. Now, looks like we need more vermouth. Giacomo has a bottle in the storeroom, I think. I'll be right back." She came around the bar, patted Sappho's shoulder, and ran up the stairs.

"That," I said, "was the biggest load of horseshit."

Sappho laughed. "You and I both know how I feel about it all. But you've forgiven her. Even if I think it's an asinine move on your part, I support you. As long as she doesn't run out on you again."

"Thanks."

"And if you ever need to talk about it, I'm here."

"You know, Sappho, if you weren't into girls…"

"Hey, you could always borrow one of Madame Butterfly's dresses."

What was weird about life in the Necropolis, if you hadn't gathered by now, were moments like this. Normal moments. The kind of regular moments that regular people shared in their regular lives. This conversation could have taken place at a college dorm in Tennessee or a bar on Bourbon Street or on the back lot of Warner Brothers. This is not, however, a conversation that fit neatly inside of a two-thousand-year-old underground burial space populated by thieves and conmen from all over the world who weren't allowed to use their real names. I tried not to think about it too much. Thinking about it made me feel like a bit player in a Fellini film.

"And Jess?" I asked.

"Who?"

"The woman from the bar that night."

"What's done is done. It happened, you learned something from it, and you moved on, right?"

"Yeah."

"I'll never mention it, if that's what you're worried about."

It wasn't. Not entirely. I worried more about what it said about me.

Sappho leaned over the bar. "But you do have to give me details at some point," she whispered. "That chick was delicious."

Shelley came back with the vermouth and pulled out a third glass. The three of us shared a drink and I was happy to feel the tension had eased.

"Where's the Carny?" I asked.

Sappho wiped her mouth with the back of her hand and said, "He went out."

"Out? When?"

"This morning."

"He say where he was going?"

"No. Why the interest?"

I didn't like that, him being gone. Our leader, our lifesaver, and I couldn't trust him to go for a stroll anymore.

The truth almost came spilling out of me right then and there. It's comforting to confide in people, no matter how horrible the truth is, and if they knew then we could gather everyone up and go look for him.

Madame Butterfly walked through the room on the way to the kitchen. She cast a worried look my way.

I kept quiet.

CHAPTER FIFTY

THE ROACH BOY WOKE me that night by poking my face.

"Hey," I said.

He poked me again.

"I'm awake. You can stop that."

He tugged on my arm, trying to get me to come with him. I grabbed my pants from the floor and fought them on under the blanket.

Shelley squeezed my leg. "What are you doing?"

"It's okay. I'll be right back."

The Roach Boy led me out into the Family Room. He was scared, that was easy to see. He sucked his thumb and pointed toward one of the hallways.

"What is it?"

He shook his head and ran back to Miss Fagin's room. I stared into the black for a moment. There was nothing there. He must have had a nightmare.

"Stop squirming." The voice was faint but unmistakable.

The Carny.

I grabbed a flashlight from the bar and made my way down the hall.

His grinning jackal face appeared in the black. "Boo."

"Christ!" I clutched my chest and sucked a breath.

"Come on." He grabbed my shoulder and pulled me along.

"What are you doing down here this time of night?"

"You'll see."

We stepped into the Temple. Someone knelt in front of Dionysus and prayed. Or that's what it initially looked like. When I got closer, I could see it was one of Janus, bound and gagged, the prayers I'd heard merely moaning coming from her tear-streaked face.

The Carny put a hand on my shoulder. "Is that the one?"

She stared up at me, eyes wide and pleading. One cheek was red, swollen, and blood stained the edges of the duct tape covering her mouth.

"Keats?"

"Huh?"

"Is that her?"

"Her who?"

He gave a condescending little laugh like he was trying to teach a child long division. "The one who stabbed you?"

"I don't know. I can't tell them apart."

I knew in my gut he'd brought her here to kill her, but I was too shocked to know what to do about it.

"Let's see what she has to say then, eh?" He ripped the tape from her mouth.

"Please," she whimpered, "let me go. Please."

He slapped her. "Listen, you munter. I am not moved by your whining and pleading, you understand? Now tell me, did you stab my man Keats here? Eh?"

"No…no…"

He tsked. "Phew. Well. We're in a bit of a pickle, we are. Because your sister said the same thing."

"My sister?" The confusion on her face would have been comical under different circumstances.

"Yeah. That tart said *you* stabbed Keats."

We were all quiet.

"Of course," he went on, "she won't be saying nothing no more, if you catch my meaning."

She did. She lowered her head and sobbed so hard I thought her bones would shake themselves apart.

He replaced the tape and turned to me. "What do you think we should do with her?"

The Freak rushed up from nowhere. I hadn't heard from him in a while and had hoped he'd gone for good. I should have known better.

"You remember how she laughed?" the Freak whispered in my ear. "You remember how she slipped that knife between your ribs and left you to bleed out in that alley? You should slice her throat yourself."

God forgive me, I almost agreed with him. It was a powerful temptation in that moment. And the Carny wanted me to do it. I could see it in his eyes. And Janus deserved it, didn't she? Isn't this the path she chose for herself with every decision she'd made? How many others had she stabbed and left to die? How many more would she stab in the future?

"Let her go," I said.

The Freak slipped back into the darkness.

"What?" The Carny cupped a hand to his ear as though he hadn't heard.

Janus stared at me, eyes filled with hope.

"I don't want anyone to die because of me," I said.

The Carny leaned down to her. "Will you excuse us a moment, my dear?"

It wasn't rhetorical and he waited for an answer. Finally, she nodded.

"Thank you." He grabbed my arm and led me into the hall. "Are you daft? I can't let her go."

"Why not?"

"Well, first of all, she's a prisoner of war, isn't she? If I let her go, she'll take the secrets she's learned to the other side."

"What secrets?"

"Well, that I killed her sister, for one. Besides, I promised blood for what they did to you, Keats. I never break a promise."

"It's okay. I don't want their blood."

"I didn't promise *you*. I promised Dionysus." He leaned against the wall and scratched his scalp. "And he does want her blood, I can assure you of that."

The catacombs at night were cool, even in the middle of summer, but a trail of sweat ran down my spine and pooled in the seat of my pants. The Carny was dangerous and unpredictable when he was sane, but now he looked at me with eyes cold and dark.

"Let's leave her with him, then," I said.

"With who?"

"We'll leave her with Dionysus in the Temple for the next day or two and let him decide what we do."

I was grasping at straws. I had no idea where I was going with that suggestion, but I needed something, anything, to get the Carny to wait until I could come up with something.

He drummed his fingers against the wall behind him. He was thinking. I didn't know if that was a good sign or a bad one.

"And how will we know what he chose?" he asked.

"He'll give us a sign. You know he will."

The Carny grinned. "It's good to see you finally believe, Keats. Come on."

I followed him back into the Temple. He walked to the altar and snatched a knife up. Janus wailed into her duct tape and tried to fight to her feet, but the ropes knotted around her wrists and ankles forced her onto her side.

"Calm down," the Carny said. "You'll hurt yourself."

He slit his hand and bled into one of the bowls. Then he turned and held the knife out to me.

I didn't move.

"Your turn," he said.

"Excuse me?"

"If we want him to guide us, we must give him an offering."

There was no way out of it. Not if I wanted to keep the Carny invested in the idea.

I took the knife, wiped it clean on my pants, and held it to my palm. The blade was cold. I stood there for an eternity trying to work up the nerve.

The marble God stared into my eyes.

"Go on," the Carny said.

I took a deep breath and slid the knife across my palm. God, it hurt. I gasped and the Carny held the bowl out. Blood streamed through my fingers as I made a fist and squeezed it into the bowl. He replaced it on the table and muttered a prayer before tossing me a strip of cloth. I tied it around my wound.

"Now we wait," he said, and kicked Janus in the ass.

***

Shelley draped an arm around me when I crawled back into bed, but I couldn't sleep. The pain in my hand was excruciating, but it was the numbness in my stomach that kept me up. A few hundred yards from me someone sat waiting to be executed.

Around dawn I crept back into the Temple. Janus had fallen asleep on her side. When I shook her, she screamed into the tape.

"Be quiet," I whispered. "I'm not going to hurt you."

I cut the rope from her arms and legs. She ripped the tape from her mouth.

"He'll kill you," she said.

"No. Not me." I didn't know if that was true. I doubted it, in all honesty.

She grabbed the knife from the altar. "We should off him now, Keats. In his bloody sleep."

"No." I grabbed her wrist and pulled the knife away. "I'll take care of him." I replaced the knife and gathered up the rope. "Let's just get you out of here."

We crept through the Necropolis. She led the way and I had to remind myself that much of Byron's gang used to live down here. What a horrible mess this family had become. Is this what divorce does?

Good thing Chelsea and I never had children.

Outside on the Via dei Papiri, I followed Janus to the piazza and tossed the rope into a trashcan.

"I'm sorry about your sister," I said.

"He'll pay for that." She folded her arms across her chest and tried to look angry, but her trembling, tear-streaked face undermined it.

"Listen to me. This has to stop, okay? I'll do what I can with him, but you have to stay out of it. All of you. Got it?"

"You think I'll just let him fucking—"

I grabbed her hand. "Janus. I just saved your life. You owe me this."

She sucked a sharp breath and closed her eyes. When she opened them, she had calmed. "Why?"

"Why what?"

"I stabbed you, Keats. Why would you save me after what a cunt I been to you?"

"I haven't a clue. But why don't you stay the hell away from us all until you and I can figure it out, okay?"

She didn't agree to do so or spew more threats of vengeance. She simply turned and walked away.

I crept back into bed and prayed I could think of a plan to keep all this from blowing up in my face.

CHAPTER FIFTY-ONE

SHELLEY AND I MET for lunch by the Trevi and it didn't take her long to pick up on my anxiety.

"What's wrong?"

"Nothing," I said. "Don't worry about it."

She studied me as though she'd never seen a human face before and was curious how it worked.

"You know what your problem is, Keats?"

"No. What's my problem?"

"You have a Christ complex."

"What?"

"You take responsibility for the entire world and when things don't work out the way you think they should you let yourself drown in the guilt."

Real men don't drown. They set themselves on fire.

"That's my problem?" I asked.

She speared a piece of chicken with her fork. "More or less."

"And what am I guilty about now?"

"Who knows? Probably some girl from middle school whose pigtails you yanked and still feel bad about."

She was right, of course. She was usually right with her observations about me. That was simultaneously the most wonderful and annoying thing about her. Only this time I *was* responsible for everything. I was responsible for Dimitri and the Carny and Janus and Coleridge and everyone in the catacombs. I was Keats, after all.

"The Carny has lost his mind," I said.

I laid out the entire story as I knew it, from the flying soup bowl to letting Janus escape. When I'd finished, Shelley put her fork down and stared out into the street.

"Oh, Keats."

"I know."

It felt good to relate everything to someone else, to have someone on my side. Especially Shelley. We were partners, after all.

"You shouldn't have done that," she said.

"What?"

"You shouldn't have let her go."

I was too shocked to speak. She leaned across the table and took my hand. "Baby, Janus is a sociopath. The first thing she did when she got back was to rally the troops. She loves bloodshed. They all do. They're not people. They're animals."

"I couldn't let him kill her."

She opened her mouth, closed it, and opened it again. Not being able to find whatever words she needed, she looked down at her plate and squeezed my hand.

"We have to let the others know," she said.

"No, that would be too dangerous. They'll think I betrayed them, or want to take the fight to Janus, or both."

"Byron and his gang may come for them. Any of them. They need to know."

"I'll talk to him."

"Out of the question. They'll kill you."

"I saved Janus's life. They at least owe me a talk."

"I don't know."

"Trust me. Just this once, okay?"

She chewed her lip and tried not to show how upset she was. Her heel kicking against the chair gave her away.

***

Byron answered the phone on the first ring.

"Shelley. *Caramia*. I'm glad you called."

"It's Keats."

Quiet.

"Hello?" I said.

"I guess you found her, then?"

"Yeah."

"You're welcome, by the way."

"We need to talk."

Quiet again. There was a shuffling sound. Murmuring. Someone shushed someone else.

"Yes," he said. "Yes, I think we do. Three o'clock inside the Mamertine. Alone."

He hung up.

***

The Mamertine Prison was where ancient Rome threw her enemies to rot. A tiny room underground with a single hole in the ceiling from where food, water, and prisoners were lowered. An altar added later ran along one wall. Tradition said it was the spot where St. Paul prayed and a well sprang up so he could baptize the other prisoners.

My favorite of its prisoners (if you can say such a thing) was Vercingetorix, King of the Gauls. When Julius Caesar began his conquest of Gaul, it was nothing but a hundred warring tribes. Vercingetorix, through sheer force of will, rallied all the tribes under his banner and almost managed to defeat the legions. Of course, Caesar's cunning was unmatched in his time or ours and his massively outnumbered legion defeated the Gallic forces. He marched Vercingetorix into Rome as part of his triumph before throwing him into the pit. Imagine that, a king in the same cell as petty thieves.

I came alone, which caused a massive argument with Shelley. That was a pattern between us. When that kind of fire burns inside, it's difficult to live life at a whisper.

She eventually relented, though I suspected she was somewhere outside, keeping an eye on things.

A few minutes past three, Maximus walked into the room.

"Hey, Max."

He scowled. At least, I think he scowled. Hard to tell with a face like his.

"Where's Byron?"

Maximus walked over and grabbed me. I shoved him away.

"Need to search for weapon," he said.

"Oh. Right." I raised my arms and he patted me down. When he reached my hips, I said, "Watch it, handsome."

He snorted and finished.

"Satisfied?"

"Follow me."

We left the Mamertine and walked around to the entrance of the Forum. When we reached the ticket booth, he slipped his hands in his pockets and leaned against the wall. I shook my head and forked over the price for two admissions.

"You," I said, "are definitely not getting lucky tonight."

We strolled through the marble, past ruined temples and overgrown storefronts, until we made our way onto the main drag of downtown Ancient Rome.

Byron stood with his hands behind his back staring up at a giant hunk of marble. He smiled when I approached and motioned to the block. "That's *the* Rostrum, you know. Where Marc Antony gave Caesar's funeral speech."

"Friends, Romans, Countrymen, and all that?"

"According to the Bard, at any rate." He turned and motioned to a metal lean-to with a pile of dirt beneath it. Flowers were scattered atop. "Right there is Caesar's grave."

"Yeah? That dirt?"

"Mmm-hmm. You know, when Caesar was in Hispania with the legion, he came across a statue of Alexander the Great. He was thirty-one at the time, the same age Alexander had been when he conquered the world. Caesar fell to his knees and wept, for what had he accomplished at that age? He then went on to become the man whose very name is synonymous with conqueror. Ruler. Should say something about ambition."

"I always liked what Shakespeare had to say about that."

He laughed as though it was absurd I could teach him anything. "And what was that?"

"Imperious Caesar, dead and turned to clay, might stop a hole to keep the wind away. Oh, that earth, which kept the world in awe, should patch a wall t'expel the winter's flaw."

He grinned. "Very good. My favorite has always been the simpler: Look on my works, ye mighty, and despair."

Byron slipped his arm in mine and we took a casual stroll through the ruins. We stopped at the House of the Vestal Virgins and stared at the flowers growing in the courtyard.

"We didn't come here to cite poetry or discuss philosophy though, did we?" he asked.

"No."

"It's a shame. You do surprise me, Keats. I enjoy being surprised. It doesn't happen often these days, I'm afraid." He shook his head. "The Carny surprised me."

"Me too."

"Dimitri's murder… Well, I hesitate to say it made sense, but it was at least within the bounds of civility."

"Civility?"

He waved it off as though I was a child who couldn't understand. "Killing Janus, and then kidnapping Janus? That was too far."

I wanted to ask if it confused him as much as it did me that they shared a name, but didn't feel it appropriate.

"There will be war," he said. "There can be no other outcome."

War. It sounded ridiculous, especially there in the Forum surrounded by tourists and families and lush greenery, but I had seen the glee in Janus's eye when she stabbed me, saw the blood lust in Maximus and Spartacus that day at the Coliseum, and knew all too well the madness the Carny carried around. These were gangs of criminals, I reminded myself. It was easy to forget that fact when we sang "Car Wash" at karaoke or while sitting around playing *Trivial Pursuit*, but we made our living illegally and always with the threat of violence hanging over us.

If there was a confrontation, there could be no doubt of the outcome. Madame Butterfly and Tolstoy could not handle themselves. And then Miss Fagin and the Orphans? No. Byron's boys would swoop in and make a disaster of us.

"What can I do?" I said, trying not to sound as desperate as I felt.

"I suppose there is one way we can stave this off."

"How?"

He turned to me and placed a hand on my shoulder.

"You must kill the Carny," he said.

CHAPTER FIFTY-TWO

IN THE NECROPOLIS THAT night, I watched everyone perform their various acts and wondered if I could go through with it. Dostoevsky, innocent Dostoevsky, who loved nothing more than to play music, began a soft tune on his violin. Childish Tolstoy, with his dirty shirts and lopsided grins, clapped his hands in time to a tune he could not hear. Sappho, my closest friend, who had cried over me when I was stabbed and confronted Shelley on my behalf, stood and sang. It was too easy to imagine the three of them, their throats cut and bodies floating face down in the Tiber.

The Carny slapped my knee. "You all right, mate?"

"Yeah. I'm fine." I wondered if he had discovered Janus's escape yet.

"If you need to talk, I'm here for you."

It seemed sweet, gentle even. But how could I trust anything that came out of his mouth?

Is this how people back in Los Angeles spoke about me?

Everyone tried to get me to read another poem, but I didn't have anything. Nothing worth a damn, anyway. Big Jim grabbed my hand anyway and yanked me to the stage.

"Recite someone else's then," he said.

The room erupted in cheers and applause.

This was my family. I loved them and they loved me. How could I ever put them in danger?

"Here." Big Jim thrust a book of Shakespeare's plays into my hands. He flipped through it until he found what he wanted me to recite.

The St. Crispin's Day speech from *Henry V.*

Of course.

"I don't know," I said.

They all chanted, "Keats! Keats! Keats!" How could I turn them down?

The part of that speech that got to me is near the end.

"*This story shall the good man teach his son;*

And Crispin Crispian shall ne'er go by,
From this day to the ending of the world,
But we in it shall be remembered-
We few, we happy few, we band of brothers;
For he that sheds his blood with me
Shall be my brother..."

When I finished, the Carny stood and applauded. "One helluva reading, mate. Your performance, the way you teared up on 'we band of brothers,' was truly breathtaking."

I wish it had only been acting. Henry had given that speech, after all, on the eve of war.

***

The Freak and I argued for a long while over what to do.

"Fuck them," he said. "Get the hell out of here and don't look back."

"I can't do that."

"Sure you can. You've got your visa. Head down to Naples and hang out with Coleridge. Diana was giving you the eye, you know."

"I can't leave my family."

"These people aren't your family. They're a bunch of goddamned criminals who have made you like them. They live in a fucking crypt, for crissakes."

"They've given me purpose. I can't abandon that."

"If you stay and you can't work up the nerve to kill the Carny, you'll just have to sit here and watch them bleed."

"I can't do that, either."

The Freak drummed his fingers against his chin. After a few minutes he smiled. "I got it," he said.

I hated when he smiled.

***

"Where is she?"

The Carny pounded into the Temple and scanned the room. Drool flecked his lips.

"Dionysus came to me," I said.

The Carny spun, his eyes wide. "To you?" He looked up at the statue as if he expected it to shrug.

"Yeah. In my dreams."

"Dreams are powerful things."

"He said she needed to be executed in the old way. Like Vercingetorix."

The King of the Gauls had been strangled in the Forum to the delight of the crowd. I knew that would resonate with the Carny.

He stared at me in disbelief. Then his eyes narrowed. "The old way. Of course."

"In the Forum," I said.

"You don't think I fucking know that? Of course, in the bloody Forum."

"He wanted you to have the honors."

"Me?"

"He said he would gift you with the light of the midnight moon." What I said was nonsense, pure and simple, but the Carny loved nonsense.

He looked up at the statue and his shoulders straightened. His entire being crackled with pride.

I felt like George leading Lenny into the woods.

"When I return," he said, "we'll have a celebration to end all celebrations." He kissed my cheek and sprinted off.

I followed him as far as the butcher shop so Shelley's phone could get some type of reception. Then I fired off a text: *He's on his way.*

In a few seconds I received a reply: *You've done the right thing. The Misfits are yours now.*

I didn't feel like I had done the right thing. I felt like I was going to be sick.

CHAPTER FIFTY-THREE

I SPENT THE NEXT hour vomiting. I vomited in the hall outside the bathroom. I vomited in the toilet. I vomited while showering vomit off me. After lying in bed for a couple of hours while Shelley read to me and pressed damp cloths to my forehead (what is that even supposed to do, anyway?), I thought I could eat a sandwich. I threw that up in the kitchen and again in the Family Room.

I had sent a man to his death.

Not just any man, either. I had sent the Carny, our leader, our mentor, *our fucking savior*, to be murdered. It didn't help to remind myself that he had lost his mind, that he was dangerous, that it was him or everyone else. I had still made that decision. I'd played God.

With all this throwing up and hating myself going on, it didn't hit me that I hadn't seen Big Jim all night.

***

"Keats." Shelley's voice was small. It pulled me from my sleep all the same.

I'd been dreaming again. This time there was no wall and no fly. I had instead dreamed of the waters in the Bay of Naples at night, the moon heavy in the sky, Shelley rising from the waves.

"Keats," she repeated, and shook me.

"Yeah, I'm awake."

A single tea candle burned from the bedside table, its orange glow revealing Shelley's face. I had never seen such terror on another human being. She stared at the doorway and gripped my arm so tight her fingernails drew blood. Eyes wide and rimmed in tears, she couldn't take her gaze away.

I looked to the doorway. The hall beyond it was the dark of ocean depths. I couldn't see anything beyond the weak glow of that candle.

"What is it?"

"Can't you see?" she whispered.

I looked again, ready to dismiss it as another bad dream. But something was off.

Was someone standing in the doorway?

"It's me," Shelley whispered.

"What?"

"She's just been standing there. Staring."

I fumbled in the dark for her phone. The screen came to life and I turned it to shine onto the doorway. I caught a glimpse of a pale, feminine calf as whoever stood there walked down the hall.

"Ravenna?" I called, and climbed from the bed.

Shelley grabbed me and pulled me back.

"Don't go," she said.

"It's fine." I slid my pants on. "Probably just someone sleepwalking."

Shelley sat in bed, covers pulled to her neck, chewing on her bottom lip and trembling. My first instinct was to hold her tight.

Instead, I stepped into the hall.

A white dress almost identical to the one Shelley wore the day she picked my pocket glided down the hall to disappear around a corner. The cell phone's screen lighting the way ahead of me, I hurried after it. If it was Ravenna or Sappho sleepwalking, I should wake them. The direction they were heading went deeper into the unmapped sections of the catacombs and they'd never find their way back.

The dark of those tunnels was thick and murky. The meager light of Shelley's screen didn't do much to illuminate it. I fought with her home screen until I found the flashlight app. The white light erupting from the back of her phone was stronger, cutting through the black and lighting the tunnel several yards ahead of me.

Again, that calf and the swoosh of the dress took another turn.

"Sappho," I called, "is that you?" My voice echoed from the stone around me. "Ravenna? Madame Butterfly?"

Silence.

Like the dark, the quiet deep beneath the earth was almost a physical thing. The catacombs felt ravenous in that moment, a hungry beast that devoured light and sound.

I quickened my pace, the hairs on my arms standing. Nooks lined the walls now, the withered husks of ancient bodies filling them.

"Eleanor?" I called, knowing it wasn't her.

I took the corner and froze when I saw who stood a dozen yards away, staring back at me.

"Shelley?"

It was her, there was no mistaking it. Only she was pale, the color drained from her skin to match that white dress. Her face was gaunt and her eyes empty and hollow.

We stared at one another from a distance, my heart racing, my hands trembling.

Then she turned and headed deeper beneath the earth.

She wants me to follow her, I thought. But I knew that if I did, I'd never find my way back.

Shelley had turned all the lights on when I returned to the room. She sat in bed, a lit cigarette trembling in her fingers.

"I didn't know you smoked."

"I don't. Not really. Just, when I'm nervous or scared or…" She trailed off and took a drag.

I stood there watching her, not knowing what to say. Of all the strange things I'd experienced in the catacombs, I did not have the vocabulary for this one.

"Close the door?" she asked.

We never slept with it open again.

CHAPTER FIFTY-FOUR

SAPPHO SCREAMED.

Shelley and I bolted awake and ran into the Family Room.

Big Jim carried the Carny's limp body in and laid him on the sofa. Both were beaten and bruised, their clothes torn, blood staining their skin.

They know, I thought. Everyone knows. He's dead and Big Jim knows and he told everyone else.

They'll come for me next.

Big Jim barked orders. He needed alcohol and bandages and a thread and needle. He needed a lighter and pain pills and a shot of vodka. They all scattered.

I approached the sofa, ready for whatever condemnation Big Jim would lay on me.

"Keats," he said, "hold this." He put my hands on a bloody scrap of shirt pressed against the Carny's biceps. "Is worst wound."

"What happened?"

"I was coming back from Siskel & Ebert when I see Carny walking by himself. Before I can say a word, I see Spartacus and Janus follow behind him. Maximus and Byron and I do not know who else all rush out and attack him."

"Jesus."

"He fight like madman. I come to his side and then the knives come out. There were so many of them. We almost not get away."

Sappho rushed back with vodka and the needle and thread. The others trickled in with their items. The Roach Boy scurried up to me and stood at my side until Miss Fagin herded him and the other Orphans off to their room. That was her primary job, it seemed: to keep the Orphans away from all the arguments and accidents and violence that occurred down here. I suppose that's any mother's job.

Big Jim went to work sterilizing the needles and thread and sewing the Carny's wounds. He didn't seem to suspect anything, and I breathed a tiny sigh of relief.

The Carny opened his eyes not long after. Those twin balls of ice bored into me. He never said a word the entire night.

***

We had agreed to watch him in shifts, but I refused to leave. Everyone thought it was out of worry (and a part of it was), but it was primarily paranoia. If and when my deception came out, I needed to know. I did not want to suspect everyone in the Necropolis of plotting against me.

God, I bet that was exactly how the Carny thought.

Around dawn, as I sat reading *Melmoth the Wanderer* and sipping coffee to stay awake, the Carny spat at me.

"Oy," he said. "You the traitor, eh? It's been you all along?"

I stayed silent. I doubted reasoning would work, anyway.

"You and Byron... Keats and Byron... 'Twas the Quarterly that killed Keats. But what killed the Carny, eh? Ambition? Impatience?"

His face collapsed and he began to sob. I didn't know what to do. After a few minutes, I held him until he cried himself back to sleep.

***

In the morning he was gone. I don't know when I'd fallen asleep, but he crept away and out into the city. Marco received a phone call from him that afternoon. He wanted us all to ride the 64 Bus en masse that Sunday. He said there was something huge in the works, something that would change our lives forever. Miss Fagin argued about staying with the children, but he'd have none of it.

"Leave the children in their room," he said, his voice tinny and distant as it blared from the speaker on Marco's phone. "But everyone else must be on that bus."

I wanted to confess what I had done, but I could see by how worried they were, by how Sappho cried when he vanished and how Big Jim had risked his life for the man, that I would not be able to persuade them.

Even Shelley, when I had told her of my original talk with Byron, had accused me of switching sides. It was a snarky, meaningless comment, but if even she could throw it out as a way to get a rise out of me then what would the others, the ones who weren't in love with me and didn't sleep with me every night, think of my betrayal?

Wasn't the final circle of Dante's Hell populated by traitors?

***

Stealing Shelley's phone from her bag, I snuck out of the catacombs and down the street. I made my way to an isolated corner down a slim alley, a place where I could dart my eyes around and make sure no one eavesdropped, and called Byron.

"What happened?" I asked.

"That goddamned Big Jim came from nowhere. The man fights like a fucking bear. Maximus may never get the feeling back in his arm."

"And where does that leave all of us?"

"Listen, Keats. You did your part. I'll make sure you and Shelley are spared."

"No, Byron. That's not the deal. We can't—"

"The fucking deal," he said, his voice suddenly empty of the control and civility it usually had, "was that you kill that cunt. You took the coward's way out and sent him to us and that got fucked all proper like. You want to slice his throat, we'll be done with it. If not, then your friends will bleed."

"He's gone."

"What?"

"He took off. Left us a weird message to meet him on Sunday."

"Then we'll see where we are on Monday, Keats."

CHAPTER FIFTY-FIVE

SUNDAY CAME TOO FAST. I tried to will it away, tried to alter the universe so we could go straight from Saturday to Monday just this once, but it was no use. You can't sidestep destiny, as the Carny would say.

Speculation filled the halls that morning as we each showered and ate breakfast.

"Byron knows the Necropolis too well. I think we're moving," Sappho said. She had complained more than any of us about the dampness and the drafts in the catacombs and I think she would have been thrilled if we scooted off to some villa in the countryside.

Big Jim's theory was retaliation. He felt the Carny was gathering the troops, calling the franchisees and freelancers in from around Italy, and that he had devised the perfect plan to cripple Byron and his thugs once and for all.

Dostoevsky and Tolstoy thought the Carny was going to order us all away for our own safety until everything blew over. Marco worried the Misfits were being disbanded. Madame Butterfly didn't say anything, but I could tell by her downcast eyes she feared the worst.

I did too.

"Why the 64 Bus?" Shelley said as we all walked up the stairs to exit the Necropolis.

No one had an answer for that.

But I knew. The Carny had a sense of storytelling, after all. All that talk about fate and destiny, he knew how to spin a good yarn. And what better way to end a story than where it began? He picked the 64 Bus because that was where fate had chosen to intersect his life with mine.

Ouroboros.

***

We rode the bus for two complete loops around the city. Even Eleanor had climbed on, though she sat silent in the back and stared out the window. It was funny, in a way, to watch us all try not to steal while on the bus. Hands twitched, fingers drummed, Marco even bumped into someone before catching himself and thinking better of it.

Our third pass of the Coliseum, the Carny climbed on.

He didn't say anything at first, simply took a seat at the front and watched the city drift by. We looked to one another, not sure if we should ask him what was going on. In the end we stayed seated. The Carny would let us know when he was ready.

After another complete loop, he stood and approached us.

"Fidelity," he said.

The Misfits leaned forward, eager to hear.

The tourists around us looked bewildered, a little frightened even. They had every right to be.

I slunk back in my chair and wondered if I could rush past him and out the doors at the next stop before anyone could catch me.

"Fidelity," he repeated. "It's a virtue, innit? More than a virtue, really. It's an inherent gift from the gods. There are few things prized as high as loyalty, as brotherhood, and for a damned good reason. Without it, everything falls apart."

An elderly couple near him listened to every word. For whatever reason, his speech hit home for them.

"This is why history hates the betrayer. Who are the foulest men through the ages? Those who have betrayed their own. There is no lower rung on the Great Ladder of Life than the betrayer. Luckily, I believe in karma. I believe that ye reap what ye sow."

They all nodded agreement, even the elderly couple.

I looked to Madame Butterfly. Her face had gone pale and she rubbed her trembling hands together over and over. The poor woman thought he was talking about her.

The Carny took a deep breath and stood tall. "I am karma's blade, children. I am the gods' fiery retribution."

He slipped his hand into his jacket and removed a pistol. Someone gasped. The old woman screamed.

"Where did you get that?" Was that Sappho? I wasn't sure.

His eyes fell on me. "You betrayed me," he said. "You sent me straight into the hands of our enemies."

Sweat ran down my neck. I could feel everyone's eyes on me.

The bus driver yelled something.

The Carny shouted back. Their Italian was too fast to get a grip on it, but I think the driver threatened to stop the bus and the Carny told him to keep going.

"Carny," Ravenna said as she stood and slowly approached him, "this not right. I know you go through much, but this bad attention you bring on us."

Thank God. A voice of reason. I looked around the bus to see if the others were thinking similarly. I couldn't tell.

The Carny grabbed Ravenna by the hair and yanked her close. "Don't tell me what to fucking do. You'd still be scrounging through garbage cans if it weren't for me."

A man in a shiny jacket came barreling toward him from the front. He was obese, his t-shirt dirty under the jacket, a thin mustache on his face. Was this man going to be our hero? It seemed unlikely but there he was, rushing down the aisle.

The Carny pointed the gun at a window and pulled the trigger. A pop and the glass shattered. The man ducked and dove into a seat. People screamed. We all lurched forward as the bus slammed to a halt. The driver dove out the door, the passengers following like rats after the Piper. I lost my balance and fell, really fell for once, not just faking it to snag a wallet. I found the irony amusing for about half a second before my head cracked against the leg of a seat and a hundred constellations blocked my view.

He fired again. My ears popped and everything muted except for a ringing in my head like one of Dostoevsky's tuning forks.

I was still tracing the line of Orion's belt from the floor when the Carny threw Ravenna into a seat. Some of her multicolored tangle came off in his hand.

"You fucks!" He slammed his fist against a seat. "You goddamned Judas Iscariots, each and every one of you!"

He aimed the gun at us in turn: me, Shelley, Ravenna, Dostoevsky, Tolstoy, Mansa Musa, Marco Antonio, Big Jim, Sappho, Eleanor Rigby, Madame Butterfly, and Miss Fagin.

My family.

A thousand thoughts rushed by. I can't say my entire life passed before my eyes, but I did see a highlight reel in those few dangerous seconds. The look on the others' faces confirmed that they were tuned to the same channel, thoughts of parents and children and homelands flooding through each of them. An odd collection of destinies tied us to Roman Municipal Autobus Number 64 in that moment and none of us could predict what was about to happen.

Whatever occurred, it would be my fault.

"You have to take responsibility for yourself," the Carny had always said.

He was right.

I pulled myself to my feet and sucked a deep breath, ready to yell my confession, to let the Carny know that I had acted alone and no one else had any part of it.

Before I could say anything, he locked eyes with me and grinned.

Then he fired.

***

Shelley and I had made love the night before. It was desperate and intense, our need to be with one another stronger than ever. I couldn't get close enough to her, couldn't get deep enough inside of her. I wanted to wear her as a second skin.

When we finished, we held each other. Her eyes pulled me in and nothing could have forced me to look away.

"I love you," she said.

"I know."

She pinched me. "Don't be an asshole. I'm being serious."

"I love you, too."

"I'm scared, you know?"

"Scared of what?"

"Of this. Of us."

"Why?"

"Because it's so consuming. Can something like that last?"

"I don't know. I hope so."

"Me too." She pulled herself closer. "I want this to be the last great romance of our lives."

***

Shelley took my hand, but the others had stepped away, not wanting to taint themselves with my betrayal.

The Carny's finger depressed and time slowed.

The barrel of the gun sparked, a flare firing in the black hole like the universe being birthed from nothing. A pop as the air cracked. If this were a movie, it would have been a loud bang. But it was only a pop, little louder than a bottle rocket firing. Maybe this was because my ears were still ringing from the first two shots.

The bullet sliced through the air.

Here it comes, I thought. Death. Fate. Karma. Every horrible mistake I'd ever made had been melted down and poured into the mold for that particular bullet. It would hit me in the heart if there were any justice. I'd crumple and that would be it. I closed my eyes and waited for impact.

It never came.

Time sped back up and I opened my eyes.

The Carny's face twisted, a tear slipping down his cheek.

"No," he said.

Then he darted to the door and leaped from the bus.

Ravenna stared down the aisle slack-jawed. Big Jim took a step toward me, his lips quivering.

Shelley crumpled into the aisle before me, a crimson flower blossoming on her dress.

It was impossible. I had just been holding her hand. And the gun, that gun had been aimed at me.

At me.

But she had stepped forward and the bullet, *my* bullet, had found her.

I went to the floor and took her hand.

She looked up, eyes frightened and fighting to focus.

"Shelley?" The tears rolled hot from my jaw and crashed onto her chest.

She fought to suck breath.

"Drive," I yelled at Big Jim, at anybody. "We have to get her to the fucking hospital!"

Someone started the bus and we roared down the street. I was too focused on Shelley to see who.

Horns honked and tires screeched. Crying and murmuring from the front of the bus.

Shelley's face was slick with tears and sweat and snot. She fought for breath, fought so goddamned hard, but the blood staining her shirt was directly over her lungs. Red bubbles formed and popped on her lips and all she could manage was a wet hiss.

"Please," I begged. "Just hold on. Please."

I gripped her hand and kissed her forehead.

She reached her other hand up toward my jaw, eyes struggling to rest on me but only managing to stare past my face.

"I need you," I said. "Please."

Her hand hovered by my cheek and I placed my face into it.

"Please."

She wheezed.

Blood poured from the corners of her mouth.

She squeezed my hand.

And then she died.

***

There should have been more. The moment from when the bullet hit until she passed should have been longer.

But it wasn't.

***

I fell into her blood and held her against my chest. This was how Sappho found me when the bus stopped. I don't know how close Shelley came to making it. All I remember is feeling how warm she was in my arms and how slowly that faded.

"Keats," Big Jim said. "Keats. We must take her in."

I nodded and lifted her into my arms. She weighed nothing.

In the lobby of the hospital, two interns rushed out with a gurney. They placed her on it and wheeled her down the hall, checking her eyes and wrists and whatever else they check when they know someone is dead but have to make sure.

I don't know who spoke to them or what they said. I don't know where the others went. All I know is that Sappho gripped my shoulder and pulled me out into the street.

"Was it true?" she said, her face a sheet of tears. "Did you set him up to be killed?"

I didn't have anything left in me to explain or reason. I could only nod.

She sucked a sharp breath. Then she slapped me. I didn't feel it.

"Run," she said. "Please, Keats. Disappear." She took off down an alley.

I turned back and watched through the glass doors as they pushed Shelley to the end of the hall. That was the last I saw of her, the interns wheeling her body around a corner.

When she was gone, I left.

CHAPTER FIFTY-SIX

MY BLOODY SHIRT WENT into the trash. It hurt to do so (that was *her* blood), but I never would have made it across town otherwise.

I don't know how long I stumbled around before finding my way back to the Via dei Papiri. A cool breeze blew through the city but my skin still echoed Shelley's warmth.

Giacomo wasn't around. I stomped through the butcher shop and down the stairs, not sure where else to go. I went to Shelley's room and collapsed on her bed. It smelled like her, like rare and exotic flowers, like the shampoo she used, like the detergent she washed her clothes in.

I must have fallen asleep because the Roach Boy woke me with a poke to my shoulder.

Miss Fagin stepped into the doorway. "Keats. I was just getting the children."

"Where are you going?"

"I don't know. But I must think of them. They're my responsibility."

"Tough thing, responsibility."

"I'm sorry about Shelley," she said. Her face was pale, and her lips quivered. "She was a rare one."

The tears came again. "I never learned her real name."

Miss Fagin stood in the doorway and watched me cry. When I finished, she kissed the top of my head and grabbed the Roach Boy by the hand.

"Goodbye, Keats," she said. "Take care of yourself."

The Roach Boy broke away from her and threw his arms around my neck.

"Goodbye," he said.

Sometime later I made my way to the bar and upended a bottle of red wine. The karaoke machine was still out on the floor from where we'd all sung earlier in the week.

That first night in the catacombs, Shelley had taken my hand and dragged me onto the stage, forcing me to sing "Life on Mars."

The Carny's gun sat atop the machine.

I walked over and lifted it. I won't lie or sugarcoat things. For a brief moment I considered chewing on the end of it, of feeling the cold steel between my teeth and ripping that trigger back.

Everything was gone. Our Utopia was no more. All the others had scattered to the winds. I had nothing. No life here, no life to go back to in the States.

And I missed Shelley already, missed her so much that even breathing when I knew she no longer could felt like a betrayal.

I even lifted the gun to my lips, but I knew she would have hated that. She would have accused me of making her tragedy all about myself.

The sound of sobbing drifted down the hall.

Eleanor Rigby? Had she returned here?

I followed it through the dark, twisting hallways of the dead until I saw a light dancing on the wall.

The Carny knelt before Dionysus inside the Temple and wept.

"Do it," he said without looking back to me. "Please, Keats."

I marched across the floor and placed the gun against his skull.

"Oh, what an artist dies in me," he said.

There was no hesitation.

His blood filled the bowls laid out before the marble god.

I placed the pistol on the floor next to his body.

Dionysus stared down at me, expectant.

"What?"

No answer.

"What the fuck do you want from me?"

There was only silence. Even the Freak had fled.

"I can't," I said to the cold marble eyes. "I'm sorry."

Back in the Family Room I sprinted to the piggy bank. One sharp kick was all it took to shatter it. I gathered up the cash, put on a shirt, grabbed my things, and left.

The Necropolis sat, empty and quiet, with only the ghosts to keep each other company.

CHAPTER FIFTY-SEVEN

CARABINIERI OFFICERS PULLED ME from the line at the airport. They said I matched the description of someone involved in a shooting two days earlier. Had it been two days already?

They threw me into a back room and questioned me again and again. I pretended my Italian was worse than it was. They said they would be back with a translator and a lawyer. I didn't care. I wasn't going to the States because I wanted to. I was going to the States because I had no home. They could throw me in prison and it would serve the same purpose.

The door opened and my lawyer walked in. I stared at the table and wondered what was left of my life.

"Keats."

It was Madame Butterfly, dressed in the sharpest suit I had yet to see her in.

Him. Unfortunately, him, now. The slick haircut and Dolce & Gabbana glasses were the height of men's fashion. No more Madame Butterfly. Madame Butterfly was dead, just like the rest of us. Meet Charles Kuo.

"This," he said, "is my scam."

"No bigger scam than law, right?"

"None at all." He tried to smile but the past few days had worn on him. "Do you know where everyone else ran off to?"

"No. I was hoping you would."

"I went back to the Necropolis and it was empty." He took a deep breath and pretended to shuffle through his notes. "The Carny. Was that you?"

"Yes."

He removed his glasses and rested his face in his hands. "I hate this. I hate all of this. I feel like it's my fault, like if we had forced him to go to the hospital or..."

I let him trail off. I didn't have the energy to console anyone.

They held me for forty-eight hours while Charles worked his magic. In the end they chalked it up to being in the wrong place at the wrong time and went looking for someone who matched the Carny's description. In the Italian legal system, Charles told me, they care less about the truth and more about a good story.

That sounded familiar.

The story they preferred was one of star-crossed lovers and romance gone wrong. They weren't too far off the mark, I think.

Charles walked me from the interrogation room to my gate. He had arranged for another flight at some point and I didn't even ask where it headed.

"I guess this is goodbye," he said.

"You don't have to do this," I said. "You don't have to be someone you're not."

"Yes. Well. Maybe I don't know know who I am," he said. "Not up here."

He extended a hand and, to my shame, I shook it. The urge was there for us to embrace, but the officers standing nearby would not have understood.

We turned and walked away from one another. But I couldn't get on the plane without knowing.

"Charles?"

He pivoted, his briefcase held at his side like a damaged shield. "Yes?"

"What was her name? Her real name?"

"Shelley," he said. "Her real name was Shelley."

***

On the plane I sat against the window. A large woman who stank of garlic crowded in next to me and rattled on about how much she hated flying. I couldn't even pretend to listen.

As we climbed into the sky, I looked down on Rome with her cobblestone streets and ancient ruins and marveled at how much the sight still moved me. Shelley would have loved it. She would have slipped her arm around mine and pulled herself tight against me, pressing the side of her head into my shoulder while we stared out the window together.

When we lost sight of Italy and the "Check Seatbelt" light dimmed, I stood and went to the bathroom.

Alone in that cramped room, thousands of miles above the Atlantic, I prayed for the first time in years.

EPILOGUE

LOS ANGELES SEEMED LIKE a foreign country after my time abroad. The traffic, the trees, the people. Even hearing the English language on the streets was strange and uncomfortable.

An old friend of mine, one of the few who had forgiven me for how I'd treated them, let me crash in his spare room until I got back on my feet. I managed to land another boring, bland job in a post-production facility, coordinating digital deliveries of slimy reality shows I never would have watched even if I watched reality television.

When I got home from work, I'd open a web browser but always to the news, always with some hope I would hear about the Carny's body being discovered or Marco or Sappho showing up somewhere. There was never anything.

A bus line ran from near my friend's place. I rode it to and from work every day. It was only three days until my fingers took up their old habits and nabbed a wallet.

**

Sleeping was rare. I'd start to nod off when I'd roll over and my arm would fall onto an empty mattress. Rather than toss and turn, I'd get up, have a cup of decaf, and go explore the neighborhood. There was nothing much to see. It was a former industrial area in the beginning stages of gentrification and the buildings were chipped and filthy.

A week into my nocturnal explorations, I stumbled across a small graveyard. It sat behind a church tucked away at the back of a subdivision. The sign out front was in Spanish. The graveyard itself was tiny, the stones sunken in places and lopsided in the ground, the grass growing wild and ragged. The flowers were old and rotted.

I found the grave of a woman named Maria who died in nineteen ninety-three. She had been twenty-four when she passed. The same age as Shelley. I brought flowers to her at night and sat and talked. If I couldn't visit Shelley's grave, then I'd make this her grave, at least for me. I hoped Maria didn't mind.

Months into this, I gave in to my father's constant urging to fly back east and meet my little brother. He was a cute little guy, toddling around in his Spider-Man diaper and breaking everything he could get his hands on.

They were all doing well. My father wanted to show me the deck he had built over the summer and everyone talked about my divorce. My stepmother worked with a woman whose daughter would be perfect for me, she said. I brushed it off.

My third day back, my father took me aside and apologized for the way I was raised. He'd not only been in AA a few years now, but my stepmother had made him go to both therapy and church. Who knows which one did the trick, but he broke down on that deck he'd built and confessed his failures as a father and how he wished every day that he could take it all back.

It was something I'd wanted to hear my entire life. Yet standing there listening to it, I realized it didn't matter to me anymore. I had no real bond with this man. He no longer had any power over me.

And so, I forgave him. I did make him promise, however, to do better for my little brother. He swore he would, and I believed him.

A few days later, I borrowed his car and drove to my mother's grave. The flowers there were not the ratty ones that dotted the cemetery in Los Angeles. They were fresh. My father still took care of her after all these years. I found that comforting in a way, the idea that people were more fragile than the bonds they shared.

***

Chelsea and I had been having lunch every week for months. We were eating sushi at a place down from our old apartment the last time we met. I say "our old apartment," but Chelsea still lived there. Since our split she had thrown herself into personal training and pulled in a sizable second income.

"We used to love this place," she said while fighting with her chopsticks.

"Still do, don't we?"

"Yeah, but it hasn't been 'we' for a while." She smiled. It wasn't a sad smile.

It was easy to come to terms with the fact that we were friends, nothing more, nothing less. That may seem strange but nothing about our divorce had made us stop caring for each other. Even my infidelity wasn't enough to dent almost a decade of friendship.

I'd been surprised when she first reached out to me. She had just needed time, she'd said. And once she'd had it, she wanted to make certain I had been getting the treatment I needed. I was always vague on that part.

The bill came and she pulled out her credit card. "On me."

"Thanks."

"I've been wanting to tell you something," she said.

"Go on."

"I've been seeing someone."

"Oh?"

"We're talking about maybe getting married. I'm not saying we will, we're just—"

"Talking about it."

"Yeah." She tucked her hair behind her ears and stared at her plate. "I've been nervous all day thinking of how to tell you."

I took her hand. "Don't be. You deserve to be happy. Just because I was an awful husband doesn't mean I want you to be miserable."

"It's just, I feel so selfish. You were sick and instead of being there for you, I—"

"Stop it. Seriously. I was not your responsibility. You did what you needed to do. I could never fault you for that."

I think I'd needed to say that as much as she needed to hear it.

"You know," she said, "you've never told me about Rome."

"Nope."

"Ever since you got back, you've seemed so different. What happened over there?"

I sipped my water and watched the cars zoom by on Wilshire Blvd. If you ignored the bland architecture and the English language signs, if you pretended the SUVs were Smart cars, it could be the Via Cavour.

"I was reborn," I said.

After she signed the bill, I walked her to her car.

"You should go see her."

I almost said, "She's dead," but then realized she didn't know about Shelley.

"You're in a good place now and she'll see that." She put her hand on my arm. "Don't call or write. Just go see her."

She kissed my cheek and climbed into the car.

That was the last time we'd ever see one another.

***

What my ex-wife said stuck in my mind. I kept remembering that day with Shelley, dancing around the fountain. "I want you to always be happy," she'd said. She made me promise to do so.

A part of me worried I was betraying Shelley, but it had been her, after all, who told me love isn't a ring only one person can wear. I loved Shelley and I missed her. But now that I was back, and especially since Chelsea advised it, I wondered about Miranda. These things were not mutually exclusive. It was what my namesake called Negative Capability.

I finally understood and another small enlightenment caught me in its tide and pulled me along.

She lived outside the city and no bus lines could take me to her place. At the car rental office, I couldn't help myself and paid extra for a Fiat Panda. I could almost imagine Coleridge riding shotgun, could almost see Shelley and Marco and Diana in the backseat, Ravenna draped across their laps.

Exiting the freeway, I didn't need the GPS to tell me the way. Muscle memory, I suppose. It was frightening and familiar to traverse those streets again, the streets I had taken so many times when we had been perfect together. I drove through the magic hour and wondered if Miranda would be home. The fear she might have moved hit me like a punch from Spartacus.

It was night by the time I pulled into her subdivision. More houses had been completed since I was last here and her home had disguised itself behind a yard now filled with grass. How long had she fought with those seeds and that dry earth before coaxing some kind of growth? Impossible to say. Her tenacity was legendary.

The Fiat eased to a stop across the street. A light was on in her living room and her car sat in the driveway. I gathered my thoughts and tried to come up with the perfect apology, the perfect explanation, when her door opened and the breath froze in my throat.

She stepped out onto her porch in a cotton top and silk pajama pants. Her hair draped over her shoulders and I could tell from how the image matched up to the thousands of her in my memory that she had just taken a shower. She stared my way and I was afraid she had spotted me first, that my grand romantic gesture would be construed as stalking. But she just lit a cigarette and watched the neighborhood at night. I was safe.

I watched her through the car window and all I could think was that she wasn't Shelley.

I put the car in reverse and backed out onto the street.

***

My therapist was confused by who I'd become. I couldn't blame him. I was not the same person as when I left.

"You seem to be dealing with things much better," he said.

"It is what it is."

"It may be premature, but I'd say you're managing."

I didn't respond.

"You don't seem excited about that," he said.

"I don't really care, if you want to know the truth."

"And why is that?"

"This is who I am, faults and all. I am both enlightened and broken. I am Ouroboros. I am a Misfit."

"I wouldn't call you a 'misfit.'"

He didn't understand. The way he said it, I could hear that little "m." There were plenty of things he didn't understand. Things he never would. I only came to this session because I had prepaid for ten and had one left. I only came because it seemed like the last loose end to tie up.

"Do you still think things would be better if you didn't exist?"

"Honestly? I'm not sure. The feeling's still there. I just don't know if I agree with it anymore."

"That's progress in and of itself. Those feelings may never go away, but how you react to them is the important part. Are you still feeling isolated? Loneliness can be a harsh trigger."

"I have a family," I said. "Had. I don't know."

"Why don't you know?"

"They're still out there. I just..." I trailed off. What else could I say? If I told him what had really happened, he'd have me committed.

"It's okay to need people, you know. We're not built to be loners."

I just nodded. It's one thing to realize that. It's another to act on it.

He placed his notepad down and leaned forward. "What might help you is to understand that your family needs you, too."

I thought of Charles Kuo at the airport, mourning the death of who he really was. Who *she* really was.

What was it the Carny had said? The one lesson he wanted me to learn above all others? *Without one another, we would all be the worst versions of ourselves.*

Grabbing my jacket, I headed for the door.

"Wait," my therapist called.

"I'm sorry, Doc, but you're right. I refuse to drown in regret any longer. Real men don't drown. They set themselves on fire."

I'm sure he made arrangements for me to be institutionalized as soon as I was gone. But I left his office that day with something I hadn't had in a long while.

Hope.

***

Do not steal my pain, Shelley had said. She had seen the hole inside me, seen how its gravity pulled all things into its orbit. But beyond even my narcissism, she saw something else.

She saw Keats.

The wallets I've stolen throughout the week are spread out on the desk in front of me. As I catalog their contents, the news runs a story about a rapidly-spreading virus that threatens to stop all international flights. Any decision to travel now would be a rash one.

Yet I can't live this life of work-consume-work-die any longer. I can no longer be ashamed of who I am. I will no longer deny that there are people to whom I matter. And if I need them right now so much it physically aches, then perhaps they need me, too.

My purpose is clear, with every loose end tied and nothing anchoring me here. For the first time in my life, I have absolute clarity.

Plane tickets were not cheap but, then again, I don't have to worry about paying bills when I return. This time, I won't be returning at all.

Rome, my darling, I'm coming home.

ACKNOWLEDGMENTS

THIS BOOK HAS LIVED many different lives over the years. There's a famous saying that a work of art is never complete, it's merely abandoned. Well, with *Life On The 64 Bus* I'm glad I never abandoned it earlier. I was lucky to have readers for each iteration of this book who helped prevent me from letting it loose as it was. Sure, I could have published one of those versions. Almost did, once. But none of those were the book I wanted to write. Not yet. So, I'd like to thank Maggie Gwinn, Meredith Flatt, Ross Graham, Jason York, Denae D'Arcy, JC Mazza, Adam Fox, Mike Underdown, and Sara Castrale for helping me see what I was trying to do, even when I couldn't. I'd also like to thank Paul Eckstein, James Parris, Kate Jonez, Lisa Morton, and Tom Monteleone for pushing me to become a better storyteller. Lastly, I'd be remiss if I didn't thank my agent, Cherry Weiner, for fighting the good fight with such a weird little book. I'll send you a copy with the filthiest inscription I can think of.

ABOUT THE AUTHOR

BRAD C. HODSON is a recipient of the Roselle Lewis Award for Fiction and the author of *Where Carrion Gods Dance* and *Darling*. An accomplished screenwriter, he's worked as a script-doctor on a dozen films. He's co-written the upcoming films *Tingle*, *The Death of Harvey Mason*, and *Temporal*. A fan of storytelling in all its forms, he's also written for video games, comic books, and the stage, in addition to creating an award-winning sketch comedy group. Born in Tennessee, he lives in Los Angeles with family. Visit www.brad-hodson.com or follow the author on Facebook and Twitter.